THE DRAGON LIBERATOR:

ESCAPADE

THE DRAGON LIBERATOR:

ESCAPADE

Kassidy J. Ridenour

The Dragon Liberator: Escapade
By Kassidy J. Ridenour
Copyright 2023

This is a work of fiction. Names, characters, places, and incidents are products of the author's imagination or are used fictitiously and are not to be construed as real.

All rights reserved. Except for use in any review, the reproduction or utilization of this work in whole or in part in any form by any electronic, mechanical, or other means, now known or hereafter invented, including xerography, photocopying and recording, or in any information storage or retrieval system, is forbidden without the express written permission of the author. Author may be contacted at kassidyridenour@gmail.com.

Identifiers:
ISBN 979-8-9915506-0-4 (paperback KDP)
ISBN 979-8-9915506-1-1 (hardcover KDP)
ISBN 979-8-9915506-2-8 (paperback wide distribution)
ISBN 979-8-9915506-3-5 (hardcover wide distribution)

Edited/formatted by Jenny Margotta, editorjennymargotta@gmail.com
Cover art and map design by Marta Dec

Printed in the United States

Dedication

For Mom and Andrea Torres,

you were my first fans

For Beckie,

God gave me you to support and to be supported,

I wouldn't have been brave enough to share if it weren't for you

Acknowledgments

I have way, *way* too many people to thank for this! Over the eight years I spent writing this story, I was encouraged by family, treasured friends—who may as well be family—teachers, my critique group ladies, and God. I know if I did not have these wonderful people pushing me to take the steps toward publication, I never would have made the jump. For all the times I felt discouraged, you lifted me up and reminded me how important this story and my characters are to me.

I also know that no matter how many names I list here, I am going to think of more who helped me along the way after this book has been published. But I will do my best!

Beckie Lindsey, Patty Schell, Rebekah Ackerman, Marilyn Ramirez, Karla Luther, Rachel Feinstein, Mason Dillon, and Jenny Margotta, all helped to edit and revise my story, whether professionally or just to give insight.

Linda Laymon, Jonathan Bernal, Allison deHart, Paula Hunter, David Boberg, and George Mangum, my teachers and counselors throughout my schooling whose words had a larger-than-life impact on me.

For friends and family, I have to thank you for listening to my ramblings and, for some, even previewing my story before it was fully finished. Heather and William Ridenour, Kamdyn Ridenour, Katie and Joe Nava, Charity and Matt Cabe, Andrea Torres, Rachel Feinstein, Mason Dillon, and so many others.

I mentioned you already, Beckie, but you had the biggest impact on me. You encouraged me, welcomed me, mentored me, and loved me. You never got to see how this book ended, but I'm glad I was able to share as much as I could with you before you went Home. I love you, sweet friend.

Finally, I want to give an extra special thank you to the readers. You may not know me, and I may not know you, but you decided my book was special enough to invest time in. Thank you!

This has been a long and wild journey, and I cannot believe I'm finally done . . . with Book One! I can't wait to publish all the other stories I want to share.

CHAPTER 1: FENDREL

JUST KEEP A STEADY PACE. *Don't make eye contact . . . There he is.*

A grin tugged at the corner of Fendrel's mouth. He snaked his way through buyers and sellers as he followed his target, inconspicuous to the bustling crowd. Fendrel thanked his short stature and hooded coat for keeping him hidden from searching eyes as he waded through the populous streets of Sharpdagger. Caribou fur coats were uncommon in this region, but Fendrel would take the discomfort of sweat over being discovered any day. To his delight, the capital of the human kingdom was tightly-packed, each denizen living oblivious to the shady dealings that run rampant around every corner.

Someone slammed into Fendrel's shoulder as he passed. Out of instinct, he placed a protective hand on his bag. The leather was cracked, scratched, torn, and scorched over years of travel, but it had served Fendrel well.

"Be more careful where you step, boy!" the passerby barked, turning around. His anger turned to shock when he saw who he had knocked into. The man stood in silence until a wave of citizens separated the two from each other's view.

Fendrel ducked his head. He had been recognized. It was only a matter of time before every knight in the city knew where he was. Panic pricked through Fendrel when he realized he had lost sight of his target. With a more frantic pace, he pushed onward, only breathing a sigh of relief when the suspicious figure once again caught his eye.

The target, a devil-like man named Sadon, stopped in his tracks. He, too, wore a long coat but cut from the body of a wolf and tailored with finer craftsmanship. Fendrel suspected it hid Sadon's baldric, armed to the teeth with daggers. Sadon's gray-streaked, blonde hair had been cropped short. Even from where Fendrel stood, he could tell the older man's hair was cut professionally.

Has the royal guard become so lax that even Sadon can be preened here without the threat of arrest? Fendrel wondered as a look of disgust crept across his face.

Fendrel hid behind the corner of a building just as Sadon whipped his head around, his stern face scrutinizing everyone behind him. When Sadon grunted and continued on his path, Fendrel followed in his wake. He turned the corner just in time to see the well-dressed man disappear through a long alley. The stretch led to the side door of one of the tallest buildings in the city, second only to the Sharpdagger palace.

This must be some kind of storage house. Is it for weaponry? Or maybe items for trade?

He waited for Sadon to disappear inside, then maneuvered to the same entrance. The weathered door hung from the top hinge. When he pressed his ear against the door, it creaked slightly, but no one came to investigate.

Voices very familiar to Fendrel came from within the building. The first one—that of a middle-aged man named Charles—was a surprising comfort to hear, although Charles' the soft-spoken tone made his words unintelligible.

The second voice was Sadon's, speaking in awe. "Look at this *monster*. Those claws of hers will grant us a fortune." There was a beat of silence, then Sadon spoke again. "Charles, hand me that snapper."

Something inside the building hissed. It burst into an inhuman screech that chilled Fendrel to his bones and made him grit his teeth as if he were the one being tortured.

They must have used the snapper to break its wing.

Fendrel's heart sank. He looked over his shoulder to see if anyone had heard the noise. He may have to forfeit the mission if his position was compromised. But it seemed as if no one had heard—or perhaps no one cared.

There's a dragon in there, Fendrel thought as he turned his eyes back to the door. *I wonder what tribe it's from.*

Two pairs of footsteps retreated deeper into the building. Fendrel listened until he heard a door inside the room slam shut. Perfect. He poked his head around the poor excuse for an entrance door to make sure no one else was there.

Only the dragon remained. Fendrel carefully opened the door a little more and slipped inside the expansive room.

Traps and snappers were stored in open wooden crates. Axes, arrows, spears, and swords lined the cobblestone walls. Amidst it all, in the center of the room, locked in a cramped cage, was one of the daintiest dragons Fendrel had ever seen. While small for a dragon, she was about the size of a horse. Fendrel's eyes widened, and his breath caught in his throat as he noticed the dragon's tribe.

Silver eyes peered at him cautiously, fearfully. The dragon cowered against the back of her cage. Her dark gray feathers curled at the edges like swirls of mist. Her smooth, shiny horns and claws were dangerously sharp. The dragon's ears, long and fluffy like those of a donkey, were pinned flat against her long neck. One of the dragon's wings bent at an unnatural angle, blood trickling from where the shattered bone penetrated her skin.

This was a Vapor dragon, classified by Sadon's hunters as one of the least-dangerous dragons known to mankind. Fendrel was inclined to believe the rumors about them but kept his mind open. After all, this was the first time he had met one.

How long has she been here? Probably not long. Sadon wouldn't let a dragon keep its claws unless he was busy.

When Fendrel shut the door behind him and stepped toward the cage, the dragon hissed and recoiled. Fendrel winced and waved his hands in front of him, shaking his head. He pointed at a set of double doors on the other side of the room, the only way the dragon hunters could have gone.

The dragon looked at the doors and stopped hissing. She must have presumed the hunters to be a worse enemy than Fendrel. After a moment, she returned her glare to the young man.

"I'm going to get you out of here," Fendrel said, in the language of dragons, as he gave her a reassuring look.

With a noise of surprise, the dragon shoved herself farther back in her cage. There was a leather muzzle around her snout. Fendrel frowned and looked around at the weapons to see if there was anything he could use to break it. He doubted he would be able to use a snapper, not after the dragon had experienced the tool's intended purpose. Spying a long metal staff with a hook attached to the end, he grabbed it.

Immediately, the dragon growled, wisps of mist curling from her nostrils and between her restricted jaws.

She won't let me near her without me proving myself, will she?

Fendrel propped the staff up against the cage bars and reached

The Dragon Liberator: Escapade

under his shirt. He fished around for the necklace he showed to every dragon he rescued. Over the years, it had become something most dragons recognized, marking Fendrel as a sort of urban legend. His fingers closed around the smooth leather strap attached to a circular pendant carved from the bones of a caribou. Slowly, he lifted the necklace over his shirt.

Upon seeing the pendant, the dragon's eyes widened. The mist's descent ceased, and her noises subsided.

Fendrel tried to hide his smile. It was normal for him to be recognized by any common dragon, but not one as elusive as from the Vapor tribe. There was a reason most humans did not believe they existed.

He hid the necklace beneath his shirt and lifted the hooked staff. The dragon did not protest this time as Fendrel stuck the tool between the bars and hooked its end onto the muzzle. With one hand he held the staff, and with the other he unbuckled the strap that secured the muzzle around the dragon's head. He began to pull the staff toward himself, and the dragon tugged her head in the opposite direction. Once the muzzle was left hanging around the hook, Fendrel set the staff down. The dragon scratched her snout with her talons, then moved her head to inspect her broken wing.

Fendrel looked at the lock on the cage to see if there was any way to break it. He sighed in annoyance. This metal was too strong to break or melt in any short amount of time. The lock would have to be opened. "Do you know what is past those doors?" Fendrel asked as he pointed to the doors through which the two hunters had left the room.

The dragon looked down at Fendrel with hesitation in her eyes.

"I know you can talk, and I know you can understand me." Fendrel held his open hands out. "I don't know what rumors the Vapor tribe may have about me, but surely you heard I speak Drake-tongue, right?"

"There . . . there are at least six other humans in this building. I can hear them moving boxes, but I do not know what is past the doors." The dragon's voice was soft and trembled with fright.

Fendrel sighed. He had freed dragons from hunters countless times before but never in this building. And to add to what could go wrong, Sadon was here.

He better not be the one holding the keys, or I may never get this dragon out of here, Fendrel thought.

"I'm sorry to leave you, but I have to find the key for this cage. I will be quick." Fendrel placed a hand on the lock.

The dragon's ears lowered in worry. "Please, be careful."

With a nod, Fendrel turned to walk toward the set of double doors.

"What is your name?" The dragon raised her voice a bit. "My name is Fog."

"Fendrel." He gave Fog a polite grin, then continued on. When he reached the doors, he steeled himself with a deep breath.

He pushed one door open a crack and peeked inside. The sight that met him made him wish he had never come to the city.

CHAPTER 2: FENDREL

FENDREL WAS STUCK, ENTRANCED AT the horrific sight he opened the giant door to.

"Is something wrong?" Fog's voice barely registered in Fendrel's mind. Trapped in her cage, she was still close enough that her words freed Fendrel from his terrified silence.

Fendrel rested his hand on the giant door's edge and closed his eyes. "It's . . . it's fine. Don't worry. I'll be back soon." He opened his eyes. A second look at the expansive hallway ahead turned his disgust into anger.

The hall was devoid of hunters, but the aftermath of their actions clung to it like sharks to a fresh kill. Dragon blood painted the cobblestone walls in splatters. In front of the door lay a dead dragon, its maw gaping in a silent scream. The dragon had been torn to shreds with various blades. Fendrel could hardly tell what tribe it belonged to, and the minimal lighting from sparse torches did little to help. From the char marks on the back of its teeth, Fendrel guessed this was a Fire dragon.

"I'm so sorry I wasn't here to stop this," Fendrel mumbled under his breath and stepped into the hallway, closing the door behind him. At the end of the hall was another set of double doors identical to the set he had just come through. He did his best to keep his steps from creaking on the wooden floor while sidestepping blood puddles, loose scales, and horn pieces.

That body doesn't smell yet, so this must have been recent.

Trying to rid himself of the images that were burned in his mind, Fendrel began his search for the keys to Fog's cage. As he neared the doors, he heard someone yelling. He chanced a peek, opening the door an inch. There were a number of hunters farther in, standing rigid in a shoulder-to-shoulder line with their backs turned to Fendrel. Each one wore all-terrain riding boots and waist-fitted baldrics.

The dragon hunters never wore as much armor as the royal guard, but they did not need to. Charcoal gray and made from the skin of the hunters' victims, dragon leather was more flexible, lightweight, and durable than any ordinary leather. On both shoulders every hunter had a string of dragon teeth stitched into the leather.

Fendrel caught himself scowling and forced himself to survey the rest of the room. Each side held row upon row of half-empty weapon racks reaching to the ceiling beams. Fendrel pushed the door open enough to squeeze through. Then he crept to the nearest rack and climbed to the top as carefully as he could manage. He pulled himself onto one of the beams and lay flat on his stomach to watch the hunters below.

All right. Which one of you has the key?

The yells, now recognizable as Sadon's, grew louder as Sadon approached from the other side of the room with Charles, his second-in-command, one step behind him.

Maybe Charles will help me again, Fendrel hoped.

Charles stood around a head shorter than Sadon, and his features were almost in exact opposition to his superior's. His black hair was curly and cut short. Charles' skin was darker, too, than many of the other dragon hunters. There was an ever-present haggardness in his face and the way he carried himself, like he never got enough sleep.

Sadon stopped in front of the lined-up hunters and glowered. "Which one of you was so incapable of killing a dragon cleanly that you had to ruin my hallway?"

One of the hunters stepped forward and mumbled something unintelligible. His head hung low.

"You're new here, aren't you?" Sadon spoke in a chillingly calm voice. "I will let you off easy this time, but it will not happen again, understand? Clean up that mess and check on the new dragon while you're at it. Come see me straight away once you've finished."

As the embarrassed hunter sulked away, Sadon walked back to the other end of the room with Charles in tow.

Now that it was quieter, Fendrel heard the jingle of keys. His gaze fell to a keyring on Charles' belt. Fendrel dragged his eyes to the beam he lay on, then rose to his feet. He followed Sadon and Charles from above and hoped his footsteps did not disrupt any dust. Once at the end, he lay on his stomach again, reached for a bundle of arrows on the top of a nearby rack, and pushed it off the edge. The bundle clattered onto the ground, the binding snapped, and the released arrows scattered across the floor.

Sadon gave a heavy sigh and walked toward the sound. "I thought we were done dealing with these rats. Those vermin better not have damaged the arrowheads we just bought."

Charles' eyes wandered around the room. When his gaze fell on Fendrel, he jolted in surprise.

Fendrel waved at Charles from above. While Sadon collected the fallen arrows and inspected their tips, Fendrel made the motion of a key opening a lock, then jabbed his thumb behind him.

With a short nod, Charles glanced at Sadon, then casually unclipped one of the keys from his belt and placed it on a shelf. He moved a wooden box to conceal the key from view.

"Are you just going to stand there?" Sadon called, looking back over his shoulder.

Charles shifted another item on the shelf, then joined Sadon where the arrows were scattered on the floor. "I thought I heard a squeak. It must be my imagination."

Fendrel waited several agonizing minutes for the two men and their subordinates to head farther into the building before he climbed down, snatched the key, and made a dash for the doors that led to the bloody hallway.

When he opened the door, he froze. The embarrassed hunter was still cleaning up the mess he had made. Fendrel reached inside his bag and pulled out a small leather pouch full of dark blue powder. Knock-out powder—a valuable find he picked up when he raided one of the other dragon hunter bases. Grinning, Fendrel headed toward the hunter. If he had more time, he might have messed with the man to make him pay for the Fire dragon's drawn-out slaughter, but he was in a rush. He took a pinch of the blue dust and returned the pouch to his bag.

The hunter had his back turned, mopping up a puddle of blood. "Are you here to help? I thought I had to clean this up myself—"

As the hunter turned around, Fendrel threw the sleep-inducing substance in his face. He heard the sound of the body hitting the floor as he entered the room where Fog was being kept. He shut the doors behind him.

Fog's ears perked up. "Did you find the key?"

"I believe so." On his way to the cage, Fendrel prayed the key was the right one. He turned it in the lock and heard a liberating click. Smiling, he pulled the cage door open.

The Vapor dragon stumbled out. Now free, she turned her head to inspect her broken wing again, nudging it with her nose. She winced as the punctured bone rubbed against her flesh.

"I know someone who can help you with that, but first we need to get you out of here." Fendrel looked between the small door that led to the alley and the twin doors to the hall. He sighed and turned to face Fog. "Do you think you will be able to fit through that smaller door? It's a safer option. I can lead you through alleys until we reach the edge of the city. Or we can try our luck through those double doors, but you're going to hate what is on the other side."

Fog stared at the wooden door hanging from its top hinge. "It looks pretty narrow. I do not know if my wings will let me through. Is the other way as awful as you say?"

Fendrel gave her a slow nod. "*I don't want to go back there.*"

"If that is the only way . . . then I suppose we will have to prepare ourselves." Fog shivered as her feathers stood on end.

Suddenly, the double doors opened. Fendrel pulled a dagger from his tattered bag, expecting to see a flood of hunters emerge. He froze. The newcomer was just a boy no older than seven years. Fendrel's mouth opened in confusion.

What is a child doing in a place like this?

The boy's chest was heaving, and his thin, black hair shielded his eyes from view. He was skinny and his clothes had a fair bit of tears and dirt stains. The boy ran to the door and pushed it shut with his back.

After a beat of silence, Fendrel put away his dagger and cleared his throat.

With a gasp, the boy's head shot up. He ran to an axe on the wall next to him and tried with all his might to lift it, but the heavy weapon would not budge.

"Are you all right?" Fendrel reached his hand out to the boy but stopped short.

Overcome by his attempts to lift the axe, the boy paused to gather his strength. For a moment, Fendrel thought he had given up, but the child continued his fruitless struggle.

"She's not here to hurt anyone," Fendrel said, gesturing at Fog.

Still trying to lift the axe, the boy managed to get it out of its holder, but it fell with a clang. With an exasperated sigh, he turned and stared wide-eyed at Fendrel. "It was worth . . . a try. I won't l-let you . . . hurt anyone."

"Wait a moment, boy. What's your name?" Fendrel asked, approaching him slowly.

"My name is Oliver, and I'm almost eight, which means I'm almost ten. So I'm not really a young boy anymore!" He still held the axe handle.

"You are right." Fendrel suppressed a smile. "The dragon is not going to hurt anyone," he said, pointing at Fog. He took another step toward Oliver, but the boy cut in again.

"Not her, *you*! You work for Sadon, don't you?" Oliver stomped closer, finally leaving the axe.

Oliver's statement seemed so absurd that Fendrel burst out with a short laugh. "Sadon? The leader of the dragon hunters. The man who views dragons as a plague that need to be captured, looted, and exterminated to pay for their existence. You think I, who just let this dragon *out* of her cage, work for *him*?"

"Oh." Oliver's shoulders dropped. His anger dissipated and was replaced by a look of sheepishness. "Then why are you here?"

"I should be asking you the same thing. This is no place for a child."

"You aren't going to tell him I came here, are you? I would be in so much trouble if he knew." Oliver looked at the ground in shame.

"Hold on a moment," Fendrel said. "Tell who?"

"My uncle," Oliver mumbled as he pointed at the doors.

Fendrel studied the boy's face. He was pale as though he had not been outside in a long time, and on Oliver's skinny arms Fendrel thought he saw hand-shaped bruises. However, it was the boy's eyes that made Fendrel the most uneasy. The shape and light blue color was all too similar to Sadon's eyes.

"Could you take me with you?" Oliver pleaded. "I'll be quiet, I promise!"

In all these years, I have never heard Sadon mention family, Fendrel thought. His lips pressed into a thin line as he pondered. *If Sadon is Oliver's uncle, then where are Oliver's parents?*

"I'll bring you somewhere safe," Fendrel vowed before he could think.

Oliver nodded and scurried away from the door to stand next to Fog. "What are your names?" he asked

Fog smiled down at the boy then she looked at Fendrel. "What is he saying?"

"He's asking our names," Fendrel explained. He turned to Oliver and gestured at the Vapor dragon. "This is Fog. My name is Fendrel."

"You can talk to dragons?" Oliver had wonder in his eyes.

"I can." Fendrel nodded. An idea popped into his head. "How long have you been here, Oliver? I'm trying to help Fog escape, and the only way she'll fit is through those twin doors. Do you know of any other exits?"

Oliver hid behind Fog's foreleg. "I am *not* going back in that hallway!"

Fendrel held his hands out. "It's all right. I don't want to go back either, but we have to. Now, please tell us how we can get out of here, and we'll get *you* out of here, too."

As Oliver opened his mouth, the sound of many footsteps pounded from behind the double doors.

We're too late, Fendrel realized as his blood turned cold.

He pulled a dagger from his bag. "Fog, hide. I'll distract them, and Oliver will guide you out of here."

Fog's pupils turned to thin slits. She dove behind a stack of crates.

"Oliver, when those doors open, wait for the hunters to enter, then sneak out," Fendrel ordered. "Do not run or they'll hear you. I'll find you once it's all over." He pointed to Fog's hiding place, and his adrenaline rose as Oliver dashed out of sight.

Fendrel barely had time to look at the twin doors before they flew open, revealing four dragon hunters armed with crossbows slung over their shoulders. They rushed in and stopped in a disciplined line. Sadon himself and Charles stepped out to the side of the line. The hunters loaded their weapons in unison with bolts and aimed at Fendrel.

Sadon's hateful eyes bore into him. "Where is my dragon?"

"I don't believe you're stupid enough to think I'd tell you." Fendrel began to walk backward, raising his arms in false surrender.

Charles scowled at Fendrel. "I assume you know where my key went as well?"

Fendrel shrugged. "Guilty."

"Charles, give me your crossbow." Sadon held his hand out toward his second-in-command.

There was a hint of reluctance in Charles' eyes as he handed over his weapon.

Sadon sighed, but it sounded more like a growl. He pointed his crossbow at Fendrel as he spoke to his soldiers. "On my count.

Three . . ."

Fog's head poked out from cover. She had snuck just next to the door and stood behind the dragon hunters. Oliver sat on her back with both arms wrapped around her neck.

I can't let them be seen! Fendrel thought as his eyes widened.

Smirking at his terror, Sadon continued. "Two."

Fendrel threw his dagger, aiming at Sadon's heart.

Sadon dodged, but not quickly enough. The weapon embedded in his shoulder where an old wound had never quite healed. He grasped his shoulder and shouted between clenched teeth, "What are you waiting for? Shoot him!"

The shock of Fendrel's attack gave Fog enough time to take a deep breath and hiss out a jet of mist so thick it shrouded everything in its path. She reared up and batted her wings through the mist to keep it from settling. The cloud billowed forward, enveloping Fendrel until all he could see was gray.

Angry shouts sounded from the hunters as they scrambled around. Crossbow bolts zipped haphazardly through the air. Fendrel could hear the heavy thunk of bolts sinking into the wooden beams of the building's supports and pinging off metal weapons and cobblestone. This was his chance. Fendrel charged forward, one arm held in front to block anything in his path. He ran until he was free from the mist, then his foot landed in something wet. As he blinked away his confusion, he found himself in the hallway. The bottoms of his shoes began to stain red with the Fire dragon's blood.

Fog was a bit farther down the hall, frozen in place. Her eyes were glued to the corpse of the other dragon and her feathers began to stand on end. Oliver had his face buried in her nape.

Fendrel grabbed the thumb claw of Fog's good wing and pulled her along. "Come on! We have to get out before they collect themselves."

Oliver opened his eyes once they had left the hall. "Keep going straight," he said. "There's another door ahead."

The three dashed through the rack-filled storage room, what looked to be sleeping quarters, and finally an armory. Heavy footfalls and shouts spurred them onward, out the exit, and into the alleyway.

"We're not safe yet," Fendrel said, still holding Fog's thumb claw. He led Oliver and the dragon through the winding alleys. "These passageways are far enough from the streets that we won't be spotted."

At least, I hope so, Fendrel thought. He had traversed these streets innumerable times before and never been caught, but that was when he was alone. It only took one person to walk their way and see a dragon for panic to spread. Then the full force of the royal guard would be on their heels.

The walk to the city's edge was long and arduous with two escapees tagging along. Fendrel had to backtrack and change course more than a few times to avoid running into anyone. After sneaking for some time, they came to the edge of the city where a formidable flat stone wall stood in their path. Cracks showed themselves throughout the ancient structure which rose higher than any building in the capital city. The wall had been built centuries ago when Sharpdagger was one of several human kingdoms ruling the Freelands, but now the wall was more of a historical landmark than a means of defense. It was ever-present, and its monotony made it so no one looked at it for too long.

It's the only way to get Fog and Oliver out without making a mad dash through the gates, Fendrel thought as a plan took form in his mind.

"Fog, can you take Oliver over the wall? There's a grove of trees just outside the city that you can hide in." Fendrel gave the dragon a relieved look when she nodded at him.

"Wait!" Fog shrank in fear as she seemed to second-guess their agreement. "You are not joining us?"

"I am, I just have to meet up with someone first. You'll be fine. They never station guards up there." Fendrel smiled reassuringly. "Oliver, I'll be back. Hang on tight to her."

The boy began to protest, but Fendrel was already walking away. As he distanced himself, he could hear Fog's claws scratching on the wall as she climbed.

CHAPTER 3: FENDREL

FENDREL CHARGED THROUGH THE ALLEYS of Sharpdagger until he reached a cluster of abandoned houses. He made his way straight to a dark-colored wooden building, on the cusp of collapsing. As he knocked, the front door shook, and splinters freed themselves.

"Raaldin, I told you to leave! I won't ask you again," came a woman's voice from inside. The door flew open, revealing a young woman with her arms crossed and her face etched with a tired glare. She wore a long dress stitched from different scraps of soft, pastel-covered fabrics and whose skirt was layered and flowy. It perfectly complimented her dark skin, as did the tight braids that cascaded down her shoulders.

"It's me, Thea," Fendrel greeted the woman. "Your neighbor is still giving you trouble?"

Thea sighed with relief and nodded. "As always. You should come inside. He could be watching." Thea pulled Fendrel into her home before he could answer and shut the unstable door. Once she threw moth-eaten curtains over the windows, she turned to face Fendrel. "So, what do you need help with this time . . . unless this is an *actual* visit?"

"I rescued another injured dragon." Fendrel drummed his fingers on his bag, feeling its coarse scratch marks.

"So, nothing different?" The woman's interested gaze morphed into being unimpressed. Ever since she had forced herself into one of Fendrel's missions—and thus became a friend—years ago, Thea had become desensitized to situations most humans would find mind-boggling.

Fendrel's finger-drumming picked up speed. "This dragon was actually snuck in here, right under the royal guard's nose. I can tell she was a special find for them. Oh, and she has a broken wing."

"That's strange. The hunters only ever bring eggs and hatchlings to the capital city." Thea's nose crinkled in confusion. "So, you want this dragon healed?" She walked to a desk near the back wall. The surface was covered in so many scratches and stains that one might have thought it was as old as the house. Various bottles and jars were organized on the desk in groups, each one containing a mixture of small items.

Fendrel approached the desk. "What is all this for?" He picked up a jar full of dead leaves and gazed at it with curiosity.

"Those are the herbs you brought me from the Hazy Woods. I dried them so I can use them later for experiments." Thea had a child-like spark in her eyes as she answered, "I'm trying some new spells." She gently took the bottle from him and placed it back on the desk. But then she tilted her head, as if an idea had struck her, and she stuffed the jar into a fold in her dress where Fendrel presumed a pocket was.

That's right, Thea can't craft spells unless she uses items from the Hazy Woods or shed dragon parts, Fendrel remembered. *I need to collect more berries or river stones for her the next time I travel north.*

"Are you trying out different kinds of magic?" Fendrel asked. "I've only ever seen you make illusions or healing spells."

"Oh, no." Thea shook her head. "That's the only kind of magic I can perform. *But* I want to test the limits on what kinds of illusions I can make, or how fast or slow I can heal someone."

Fendrel nodded with intrigue. "Will you sell those experiments, or do you think you'll stockpile them?"

"If you're asking whether I'll give you some of the spells I craft, the answer is yes." Thea rolled her eyes in mock annoyance. "You just have to be patient. Although, I won't be able to give you as much from this new batch. I need to sell more so I can find somewhere a bit more . . . livable." As if on cue, a board creaked under Fendrel's weight.

"You're leaving Sharpdagger?" Fendrel blinked in surprise.

Thea shrugged. "Perhaps. Perhaps not. It depends on where is safer for me."

The mage did not have to elaborate for Fendrel to understand her. Mages were not looked on kindly due to the danger magic could pose if put in the wrong hands. Magic, though Thea had tried explaining it to Fendrel dozens of times, was hard to comprehend, and he knew from personal experience that humans feared, even hated, what they did not understand.

"Enough about the spells. Where are you going after you heal this dragon?" Thea headed toward a cabinet on one side of the room. "Off to free another one or chase the hunters again? Maybe listen to some rumors of corrupt guards floating around an inn? Or maybe you're finally taking a break for once in your life?"

Fendrel scoffed. "I don't need a break. I'm perfectly fine right now. And, I'm not going to think about the hunters just yet. The dragon I just helped is free, but she won't be for long if anyone finds her while you hold me up here with all your questions," he teased.

"That seems like a lot of trouble for the hunters to go through for one dragon." Thea grabbed a few bottles in the cabinet and walked to him. She hid a few more in the folds of her dress but kept one in her hand. "I want to come with you. I have everything I need in my pockets."

"You want to come? Why?" Fendrel gave her a quizzical look.

Thea burst into a cynical laugh. "Have you seen my home? It's about to fall apart. I need to find somewhere else to live, but I don't feel safe roaming the wilderness alone. *Besides*, I have never heard you talk about a situation where a specific dragon was so special to the hunters. Why do they want it so badly? I'll go insane if I don't find out!" Thea led Fendrel out of her house and shut the shaky door behind them.

"I'm not exactly sure yet, but my guess is because she's a Vapor dragon." Fendrel smiled and continued on his way while Thea stopped in her tracks, bewildered.

"Fendrel, get back here!" Thea ran after Fendrel and cut off his path with her arms spread out. "You cannot just say something so *outlandish* and then walk away!"

"Why not?" Fendrel chuckled. "You do it all the time!"

"Exactly! *I* do it all the time. It's *my* thing!" Thea placed her hand on her chest.

"You're acting like a child," Fendrel said, not wanting to let her win.

"And you're the one who comes to me for help," Thea responded in a sing-song voice.

Fendrel said nothing more, only rolling his eyes as Thea strutted beside him to the main gates that led out of the city.

Fendrel and Thea kept their heads down and passed the guards at the mouth of the gate. Posters displaying Fendrel's face with a large bounty underneath were pinned on both sides of the city gates. "Dragon Liberator" was written in place of a name.

His likeness on the posters was close to his real features but not a perfect match. Still, the posters looked newer, and his appearance was more accurate than it had been the last time Fendrel visited the capital city. Despite spending all his time outdoors, Fendrel had pale skin, framed by wavy hair that was a lighter brown in the poster than in reality. Fendrel's freckles, too light to see from afar, were missing from the poster entirely. The artist had gone a little too dark on coloring his eyes, depicting them as a deep chocolate brown. Fendrel had always looked a bit younger than he truly was, and even in this poster he looked just on the cusp of adulthood instead of twenty-two-years-old. The royal guard did not always spend money on paint for wanted posters, but every one of Fendrel's was fully-colored.

I must be doing something right if they are trying to make the posters look as authentic as possible, Fendrel thought as he smirked with pride.

Once they were clear of the gates and had distanced themselves from other people exiting the city, Thea elbowed Fendrel's ribs. "I should turn you in for all that money."

"You would probably be set for life if you did. Speaking of which, what do you do with the money you earn from selling spells?" Fendrel glanced at Thea as they looked for the grove he had told Fog to hide in.

"I trade it." Thea picked under her nails.

"For what?"

"Food, clothing, more glass jars for more spells." Thea patted her pockets. "Anything, really."

Several leagues away, dark clouds shrouded the foothills that led up into the northern mountains of the Freelands. Lightning lashed at the dismal air beneath them and gray dragons with vibrant markings darted from the clouds to catch the powerful whips of electricity.

"Those are storm, er, Spark dragons, right?" Thea pointed to the dragons drawn to the lightning like fish to a baited hook. Humans had their own names for each dragon tribe, but Thea was quick to fix her vocabulary once Fendrel told her what each tribe called themselves. She gave him a smile, seemingly proud that she had remembered something Fendrel taught her.

"Yes." Fendrel only half heard what she said. He walked around the outside of the walled-off city. His eye caught a shadow that freed itself from the crescent-shaped grove of trees surrounding the wall.

Thea froze beside Fendrel, waiting for him to make a move.

Fendrel hurried toward the grove. Once he and Thea reached the

The Dragon Liberator: Escapade

edge of the trees, they could see two silver eyes shining out of the shadows and peering with curiosity at them. Soon Fog's gray head emerged.

"You rescued *her*? She's so beautiful." Thea held her hands to her chest, awestruck.

"You're staring, Thea. Don't be rude." Fendrel gave the mage a teasing smile.

Oliver, who until then was hidden by the leaves, almost fell from Fog's back as he stood up. Too excited for words, he waved at Fendrel and Thea.

"And who is this?" Thea gestured at Oliver. "You didn't tell me you were taking traveling companions now."

"I'm not. That's Oliver. It's a long story. I will tell you later." Fendrel turned and addressed Fog. "We have to fix your wing before anyone realizes you're here. There's a law against dragon trading, but that doesn't necessarily mean the citizens have the same mindset as the king."

Fendrel looked to Thea once again. "You brought the healing spell, right?"

"Uh-huh." Thea's wide-eyed gaze was once again set on Fog. She grabbed a glass vial from her pocket and placed it in Fendrel's hand.

He stepped toward Fog and peered at the bottle's contents—a small branch with berries still attached. He pulled the branch out and uncertainly placed it on Fog's broken wing. The branch lengthened and wrapped around the bone, shifting it into place as if the branch had a mind of its own. The berries popped and their juices traveled to the torn skin to mend it.

Fog jumped at the branch's magic. "What was that?"

Fendrel handed the empty bottle back to Thea. "Ah, sorry. I should have warned you. Thea here is a mage. I have been able to get hundreds of dragons home, thanks to her." He gestured at Thea with both hands.

"Real magic?" Fog's voice was nearly a whisper. "I have only heard stories about it before."

Fendrel said to the mage, "I've never really asked how your magic works."

Thea shrugged. "I put a spell on the branch and told it to heal whatever it touched. The branch figures it out on its own if I don't give clear directions."

Fog opened and closed her wing to test it out.

"Usually, I journey with the dragons I've helped to make sure they get home safely," Fendrel said, drawing Fog's attention away from her wing. "Is that all right with you, or would you rather fly home by yourself? I'm assuming your tribe doesn't like having humans intrude."

The Vapor dragon seemed to remember something. "I actually have a favor to ask of you."

Fendrel nodded, eager to hear her. "What is it?"

"Well . . . the story is long, but I will keep it simple. My sister is missing. I was looking for her when I got captured. She is still out there, and I do not know what I would do if she never came home. The whole tribe is torn up about her absence," Fog explained in a meek voice. "There are others looking for her too. Perhaps we can all exchange information. Please say you will help us find her. I do not know who else to ask."

The entire tribe is worried about her? Either Fog has a way of exaggerating, or this missing sister is an important member of the tribe.

"Of course I'll help," Fendrel replied. "Besides, I haven't been close to any dragon civilization for a while."

Am I really going to the Hazy Woods? To see the home of the Vapor dragons? That place feels too special to have a human's presence.

Fog smiled and she beat her wings once in excitement. "Oh, thank you! Is your friend coming with us?"

Fendrel looked at Thea. "I'm going to help this dragon find her missing sister. She wants to know if you're available to help."

Thea's eyes widened. Her hands clenched with excitement. "Let's see . . . do the same old thing with my week or go on this once-in-a-lifetime opportunity? Which one do you think?"

Fendrel smiled and returned his attention to Fog. "She'll help."

"Oh good." Fog smiled. "You three can ride on my back, but it may take a while to reach my home. You all are too heavy for me to fly any long distance with, so I will have to travel on the ground."

That might be a problem. What if someone spots us on the way?

"Thea, Fog is going to have to run with us rather than fly. I'm afraid that might draw too much attention." Fendrel drummed his fingers on his bag. "Do you have any ideas?"

"I can . . . give her a spell so other humans and animals will think she's a horse." Thea looked through her dress pockets.

Fendrel shook his head. "Can't you make us temporarily invisible?"

"Well, what if we did cross paths with someone on the way.

Wouldn't an invisible dragon trotting along, making all that noise, be even more suspicious?" Thea paused in her search for a moment to glance at him.

Fendrel sighed. "Fog, I'm sorry if this sounds demeaning, but Thea thinks it's the best idea to make other humans think you're a horse by putting a spell on you."

"Will that work?" Fog cocked her head to the side.

Fendrel messed with his bag strap in discomfort before he replied, "Thea seems confident it will."

"That sounds fine to me, as long as it works." Fog's wings lifted as she shrugged.

With a nod, Fendrel looked at Oliver. "As for you, we're going to figure out a safe place for you soon. For now you'll have to stick with us."

Oliver grinned with excitement.

When Fendrel turned to look at Thea again, she had her eyes closed and was whispering into a vial housing a single vine. Thea opened her eyes, removed the vine, and tied it to one of Fog's thumb claws.

Fendrel looked between Fog and Thea. "Did it work?"

"Yes! I can smell it." Thea stuffed the now empty vial back into its pocket.

"You can . . . smell it?" Fendrel approached Fog's side and hoisted himself onto her back, just in front of Oliver.

"Making a new spell is like lighting a scented candle," Thea explained as she climbed on behind Oliver. "It is the only way mages know for sure if a spell has been placed without seeing its effects."

"Interesting—" Fendrel leaned to the side to catch Fog's attention. "Is this all right?"

"I would be lying if I said you three were not heavy, but I will be fine." Fog left the tree cover and started toward the Hazy Woods, an expansive pine forest shrouded in eternal mist.

Fendrel kept his eyes on the humans traveling the main road. A few looks were sent his way and Fendrel's heart stopped for a moment. However, each glance was just that, and the travelers went on as though everything were normal. Soon Fendrel stopped worrying about the other humans seeing through Fog's disguise, and he turned his attention to what lay ahead. Before nightfall they would be in the Hazy Woods, deeper than Fendrel had ever ventured before.

CHAPTER 4: CHARLES

CHARLES LEANED AGAINST THE WALL of the alleyway. Grumbling guards surged through the streets, searching for dragon hunters.

Or pretending to . . . Charles thought.

One of the knights began to stare at him. He gave the dragon hunter a long look from his riding boots to the outline of dragon leather armor veiled beneath Charles' shirt. Charles had left his daggers in the armory, but his baldric was still fixed around his waist. As soon as the knight's eyes landed on Charles' stoic face, he turned and continued his search elsewhere.

Only pretending, Charles confirmed. It had been months since any dragon hunters were arrested, but still the patrols continued. *There must be too many of us for them to waste their efforts with.*

Having spent enough time away from the others, Charles turned to head inside the storage building. But before he could step through the threshold, his eye caught on a series of wanted posters. He could have sworn just a few days before his own likeness had been on one, and Sadon's, too. However, now only Fendrel's remained.

"Hm," Charles hummed quizzically. *Perhaps the knights have stopped worrying about the dragon hunters and want to focus all their attention on Fendrel. Be more careful next time, Fen.*

Charles retreated back into the cool, dim interior of the newest dragon hunter-owned location. "This will be our base of operations," Sadon had told Charles a week prior after securing it from a seller known only to Sadon. Charles hated it when Sadon kept secrets from the rest of the hunters. He was dangerous enough when you knew exactly what he was going to do, but when he made plans without consulting anyone, it was best to keep on his good side. Just in case.

Dust rustled up by the day's earlier commotion now settled on the wood plank floor. Weapons also lay across the ground, some with metal dented beyond repair and others with split wood. After a closer look,

Charles realized there were crossbow bolts on the floor, too, some of them tipped red with blood after being pulled from wounded hunters. No one was killed, but with how thick the mist from that dragon was it would not have been a surprise if someone died in the confusion. Charles sighed in relief, realizing how lucky he was not to have been injured.

Sadon is probably tending to his shoulder wound. Would it be safer to report to him immediately while he's fixing it, or should I wait for him to finish? Charles wondered as he continued deeper into the building, trying to remember his way around. Deciding it would be better for himself if he was farther inside the storage building, Charles made his way to the twin doors and braced himself before opening them.

Nearly a decade of service to the dragon hunters had desensitized him to some gruesome sights, but he was not immune to the dastardlier images. He told himself that the dried blood on the walls and the floor was red paint. The abundance of scales littering the ground were rubies, and the teeth and claws were carved from polished marble and obsidian. Even while trying to drill these lies into his head, he was already too distracted by disappointment to pay close attention to the carnage he saw.

If Sadon hadn't moved an inch, the knife would have sunk into his heart. If he had only stayed still, I would be free right now.

Charles repressed a sigh as he stooped down and began scooping the scales, teeth, and claws into his hands.

"I don't recall asking you to go on clean-up duty." Sadon emerged through the other set of twin doors, quiet as a mouse. He glowered at Charles as he approached, now making his footsteps audible.

Managing not to jump, Charles continued to clean. He was used to Sadon sneaking up when he least expected him. He lifted his head. "I figured it would be unwise to leave this mess here where Oliver can find it again," Charles said in a monotone voice.

Sadon snorted. "Oliver is gone."

Charles' throat constricted. He dropped what was in his hands and stared at Sadon's emotionless face. Oliver had been in Sadon's care for only a couple months, but in that time, Charles grew fond of the boy. He had grown accustomed to the child's onslaught of questions, his desire to explore, and his kindness. "Did he get hurt during the fight?" Charles asked. He tried to keep his hands from shaking as an image of the bloodied bolts appeared in his mind.

"Thankfully not. But, Fendrel took him. Just another reason to end that rodent's incessant meddling. First, he ruins my operations, and now, he's kidnapped my only family." Sadon's eyes flickered with hatred.

You don't care because he's your nephew, Charles thought with animosity. He almost scowled at Sadon. *You only care because your ego was hurt.*

Charles caught himself staring at Sadon's shoulder, then looked away. "Are you going to send someone to bring Oliver back?"

"Charles." Sadon looked at him with irritation. "For years, Fendrel has evaded our attempts at tracking him down. Why now would it be any different? He has a dragon with him, and he can move just as fast as usual, even with a child in his company. We *will* bring Oliver home. I just don't know when."

Charles stood up. "It was just a thought, sir. For now, do you have a new assignment for me?"

Sadon glanced around the room. "That new hunter still hasn't woken from the knock-out powder. You can pick up his duties until he is well enough to finish."

As Charles looked down to continue the clean-up, Sadon drew his attention back. "You didn't see any sign of them after their escape, did you? I know you went outside recently."

Charles shook his head. "The dragon's blood trail dried up while she was still in the building."

Without another word, Sadon turned and left, the doors behind him thudding as they shut.

So Oliver is with Fendrel now.

A smile crossed Charles' face.

Hopefully, a safer home can be found for the boy.

Charles closed the door to his room, exhausted from the effort he exerted to lift the blood stains from the hallway. His room was a cozy space, or it would be if there was ample time to clean. Charles did not have many personal possessions, and he brought with him all he owned. A tiny dresser in one corner held his clothes, armor, and gear, and on the other side of the room was a fireplace. In Charles' eyes there were not many perks to being Sadon's second in command, but having the privilege of extra warmth was a welcome one.

Even though his door left no space for peeking, he felt as if he were

The Dragon Liberator: Escapade

under constant surveillance. Perhaps it was because he was not yet used to the sleeping quarters in this building, which looked like it had been built as a barracks. Or perhaps his anxiety was due to Sadon never being farther than a few rooms away. Charles was unsure of the cause, but there was nothing he could do to ease his mind.

After all, how could he feel secure when he did not have a choice of when to lock his door? Sadon was the only one with a key to this room. It was the same for every single base. Every night, Sadon locked the hunters' doors so that when they went to bed, they could not sneak out. And every morning, Sadon unlocked the doors to start work.

Sadon had never barged into Charles' room, but Charles thought the man would if he were paranoid enough.

He scoffed.

Right, he's the paranoid one.

While listening carefully and keeping his eyes on the doorknob, Charles felt along the bottom of the dusty cobblestone wall behind his bed. He removed a loose stone where he had hidden a journal and a sharpened piece of charcoal. That was his first priority when he was shown his room, to find a hiding place for his most treasured possession. Carving out the stone was not difficult, given how the storage house had been abandoned for years without any upkeep.

Pulling the journal and writing charcoal out, Charles winced when they scraped against the floor. He held his breath and listened. All was quiet. He sighed in relief and sat on his bed. Facing the door, he opened the journal to its first page and began to write.

> *Fendrel was able to save another dragon, but I may have been the reason why this one was captured. When Sadon decided to go to the Hazy Woods, I was made to join him as always. I saw the ghost dragon, and something on my face must have alerted Sadon that I'd seen her. He got a glint to his eye that I would have called child-like if I didn't know his murderous history, and the way he set up a trap while he watched her was disturbing.*
>
> *This was a ghost dragon after all, or vapor dragon as Fendrel calls them. If any normal person was lucky enough to see one, they would freeze in awe. But Sadon . . . he treated her with the same*

cruelty he treats all dragons. To him, every single one of them is a monster, even one as harmless looking as she . . .

There was a shuffling sound outside Charles' room. He threw the journal and charcoal under his pillow and waited, but no one came to the door. The noise did not return. Everything was as dead silent as it had been moments before.

Despite not having written his thoughts out completely, Charles began the routine he used every time he wrote in the journal. He undid the bindings that held the pages together, removed the page he had written on, and with a needle hidden in the spine, he stitched the rest of the journal back up again. He stashed the journal and charcoal in the hollow in the wall and fitted the stone back in place. Then he moved to the fireplace in his room and used the written page as kindling, destroying any bit of evidence that may put his life in danger. Even though he never kept his entries, it always felt better to write out his thoughts than keep them bottled up.

CHAPTER 5: FENDREL

FENDREL LIFTED HIS HEAD AFTER what seemed like an eternity of traveling. The mist surrounding him, and the others, was so thick it made him lose his sense of direction. He felt as if he were leaving all his memories back at the forest's borders and if he ventured too deep, he may lose his sense of self.

"Is my head supposed to feel this blank?" Thea's hesitant voice made Fendrel look over his shoulder at her.

"That's normal. It's something about the Hazy Woods that is meant to keep humans out." Fendrel gave her and Oliver a reassuring smile. "It's why no human goes in too far."

"Does it get worse?" Oliver kept his voice quiet as if he were afraid to disturb the ambiance of the woods.

Fendrel tilted his head, unsure. "I have never been this far before, so I don't know." A few more minutes passed with the only sounds being pine needles crunching under Fog's paws. The empty feeling in Fendrel's head peaked as the mist thickened. He wondered if he was even awake as he could not feel a thing. Not the chill, nor Fog beneath him, nor his bag at his side. But then, his mind began to clear ever so slightly.

Despite their being shrouded in vapor, Fog never faltered in her steps.

"How do you know where you're going?" Fendrel asked.

"I can see through the mist." Fog swerved away from a tree that disappeared from Fendrel's view as quickly as it came. "All Vapor dragons can."

So they can see through it! Fendrel smiled at the revelation. *I've never met a Vapor dragon before Fog. Perhaps she can help me fill the gaps in my knowledge about her tribe.*

"It will not be like this for long." Fog turned her face to look at her passengers. "Once we reach the border, the air will clear."

"The border?" Fendrel took a map of the continent out of his bag. There was nothing noticeable about the interior of the Hazy Woods. No landmarks, just charcoal scratches made to look like trees.

"We do not quite understand how it works, but the inside of the woods is very different from where we are now. The weather is not as heavy there," Fog explained.

Fendrel absorbed every word and realized Fog had just confirmed what he was taught when he was a child. Each dragons' domain had some way of keeping humans out. He knew from experience that the snow bordering Frost Lake was so deep and powdery you would sink if you tried to walk through it, just as the geysers to the southeast would spew water only when humans approached them. Each tribe's home had some way of deterring humans, its inner workings a mystery even to the dragons themselves.

Fog lifted her head and seemed to peer at something. "Here we are," she said. As soon as the words left her mouth, the haze began to dissipate. Fendrel held his breath in preparation for the new sights that would soon grace his eyes.

He did not prepare enough.

The colossal trees and pillar-shaped cliffs of the Hazy Woods towered over him. Broken bridges and towers made from cracked stone connected the cliffs, remnants of a long-passed human city. Vapor dragons looked like silver and gray ghosts as they wove through the trees and walked up stone-carved staircases on the cliffs' sides. Thick streams of mist poured down the rocky structures like waterfalls trapped in slow motion. Fragments of brilliant dusky sky peeked out from the cloud cover and every breath Fendrel took felt like he was walking on air.

"I wasn't expecting this—" Fendrel shook his head in awe. His shoulders relaxed just taking in the sights. From outside, the Hazy Woods looked to be a dark, miserable space where all year long the gloom never ceased. Now that he was inside, Fendrel knew its outward appearance was yet another ruse to protect dragons from human interference.

Fog spread her wings. "Hold on tight," she cautioned.

After shaking himself from his amazement, Fendrel relayed Fog's warning to Oliver and Thea just as Fog lifted off. Thea yelped at the

The Dragon Liberator: Escapade

sudden change in movement, but the rush of air made Fendrel feel more alive in flight than on the ground.

As they climbed higher, Fendrel could see that Fog was heading for the tallest and proudest cliff of the Hazy Woods, almost as wide as the entire city of Sharpdagger. Vines mingled with the pouring mist along the sides of the glorious structure. Stone stairs wound down its cylindrical exterior, with detailed doorways carved wherever the stairs leveled out. A hypaethral palace sat on the cliff edge like a crown, its stained-glass windows sparkling like jewels in the sunshine. A platform stretched out to the sky from the palace's entrance like a runway.

Standing in the doorway of the palace was a massive silver, scaled dragon, three- or four-times larger than Fog. His neck arched like a swan, and he kept his wings held back in a dignified stance.

Fog slowed her flight and landed on a platform. Her claws clacked against the stone, stirring the blanketing mist that clung to the cliff top. When she stopped, Thea slipped down from Fog's back in a desperate attempt to be on solid ground, while Oliver jumped off behind her. Fendrel followed them and crouched next to Thea.

"You might want to bow," Fendrel whispered. "I believe that silver dragon is the king."

"Oh!" Thea dropped to her knees and bowed her head. Oliver copied her movements.

The silver dragon looked young despite his size, which was more in line with the Ice dragons who lived just eastward. Fendrel had never seen dragon royalty before, but given what he had been told, this was undoubtedly a monarch. Before Fendrel could fathom where he was and who he was in the presence of, Fog rushed ahead of the humans.

She performed what Fendrel could only describe as a sloppy curtsey. A torrent of words rushed from her mouth, "Please forgive me, Your Majesty. I know you told me to stay, but I just could not help myself. I needed to find out what happened to Mist before she got too far, and I got captured. But then I met—"

The larger dragon held his paw out in a gesture clearly meant to cease her explanation. He stared down at Fog and the three humans. "Fog, I already know where you went. You left your earring behind, so I figured you must have gone somewhere you knew you might lose it."

Fog's ears drooped in embarrassment. "I am sorry, Your Majesty."

"And in times as strange as these, please treat me as you normally do. Call me Cloud. Mist would not want us to grow impersonable to

28

each other in her absence." The king's tail swept out in front of him. His tail tip was curled around a brown conch shell attached to a metal ring. The earring looked small enough that even a human could wear it.

Standing from her bow, Fog reached out and accepted the seashell earring. She put it on—her paws, while animalistic in appearance, functioned as human hands could. "Thank you, Cloud."

Jewelry . . . Is she nobility? She must be. Commoner dragons don't typically wear jewelry, and she knows the king by name. Fendrel lifted his head just a bit to stare at Fog and Cloud. *Who is this dragon?*

"Now, please tell me why you brought humans here, and do not lose your breath over it." Cloud waved the group in with his wing as he turned and entered the palace.

"Come on." Fendrel kept his voice at a whisper while he looked at Thea and Oliver. They followed the two dragons and crossed through the palace's tall, sculpted threshold which led into a long hall bordered on both sides by painted glass windows.

"I was taken by dragon hunters." Fog did not look at Cloud, even as the larger dragon gave her a concerned glance. "Do you remember those rumors we heard about a human who protects dragons from *other* humans? I met him!"

"Then—" Cloud looked over his shoulder at Fendrel. "The Liberator is real?"

"Yes, I think the child was a captive of the dragon hunters, and the woman is a friend of the Liberator." Fog flicked the end of her tail at Oliver and Thea, respectively. "But . . . I could not find Mist. I still do not know where she went."

The king led the others out of the hallway and into an expansive circular room, also filtering colored light through its many windows. There were holes in the ceiling where time must have claimed the architecture, allowing flowered vines to dangle in. A round stone table was set in the room's center with wolf fur cushions placed all around it. Fendrel figured they must be seats, but he had never seen a seat look so extravagant before.

Cloud sat at the far end, which faced the hallway, while the others spread around the sides of the table. Cloud asked, "Did anyone see you fly in?"

Fog shook her head. "I did not notice anyone watching."

Thea leaned toward Fendrel. "What are they saying?"

Despite knowing Thea for almost five years, Fendrel had never taught her anything in Drake-tongue. He had tried, but the language was hard to pick up by someone who was not exposed to it every day.

"They're talking about us." Fendrel avoided meeting the king's eyes, unsure if staring would seem rude.

Cloud's pupils narrowed as he looked at Fendrel. "You understood us the whole time? Well, I suppose that makes sense. Why did you not speak up earlier?"

I forgot royalty knew both languages, Fendrel thought as embarrassment flushed his cheeks.

Fendrel dipped his head. "I apologize . . . Your Majesty. I didn't want to interrupt."

"Well, I appreciate your honesty." Cloud placed a paw on his chest. "I am Cloud, Monarch of the Freelands. And you are?"

"My name is Fendrel. I suppose you already know my title." Fendrel gestured to the other humans. "This is Thea and Oliver. They don't speak Drake-tongue."

"How do you know our language?" Cloud's head lowered toward Fendrel in interest.

"My mother was close friends with a dragon when she was just a girl, and she went on to teach me." Fendrel rubbed his thumb over the surface of his worn bag. It had been his mother's once, but that was a long time ago.

"I take it she befriended a dragon of the Dusk tribe?" Cloud tilted his head a bit.

Fendrel blinked in surprise. "How did you know?"

"Dusk dragons have a reputation of being quite warm toward humans, and a few of your words have a sort of southward accent to them." Cloud grinned and cleared his throat. "We are straying from the reason of your visit."

"Right, yes. I was asked to come here by Fog. I agreed to help her find someone. Well, Thea and I agreed to." Fendrel wrung his hands under the table, his whole body filled with nerves.

"Ah, about Mist." Cloud shifted his position as if uncomfortable. "There are others we must include in this discussion. I would like to speak of this once they are present. All available nobility have agreed to reconvene here after settling matters in their domains, and they are set to arrive later tonight. Your arrival could not have been more perfectly timed!" Cloud bowed his head in appreciation. "The stars must be guiding our quest."

Fendrel nodded. "I understand."

"Thank you. We should not have to wait long. The sun is already setting." Cloud gave Fendrel a respectful nod and stood. "And welcome to the Hazy Woods, Liberator and friends."

While Cloud left to wait in the palace's threshold, Thea poked Fendrel's arm. "So am I supposed to read your mind or are you going to explain what just happened?"

"We're going to talk more about why we're here once other dragons arrive." Fendrel gave her a quizzical look. "Can't you craft a spell so you can understand what they're saying?"

"I—" Thea pointed at him as if she were about to call it a stupid idea. "Wait, I think I can. I'll get to work on that." She sequestered herself to one of the room's walls and pressed a river stone to her forehead. She began to whisper, shutting her eyes tightly in concentration.

A tug on Fendrel's shirt drew his attention to Oliver. The boy was staring wide-eyed at him. "Do you know a lot of dragons?" Oliver whispered.

"I do." Fendrel looked curiously at Oliver. "You like dragons?"

Oliver nodded. "I think so. Uncle Sadon says they're evil, but I think he's a liar. He says dragons took my parents away and that's why I have to live with him."

Fendrel tried to mask the concern he felt building in his chest. "And you think he's lying about that?"

"I don't know," Oliver said in a more somber voice. He stood up suddenly. "I'm going to see what the magic lady is doing."

". . . Have fun." Fendrel nodded with a forced smile.

How long has Oliver been in Sadon's care? I have never heard of the boy before today, but then again, I have not infiltrated a dragon hunter base Sadon was in for a while now, Fendrel pondered. *I hope he wasn't there long.*

The palace threshold at the end of the long hall drew his gaze. Cloud sat disciplined, like a breathing statue. Beyond him, the horizon grew purple in color. Fendrel returned to his wondering while he waited for the "others" to arrive.

Who are the dragons involved in this case? I hope they're helpful. It will be nice to have some support in a mission for once. But . . . what if that means this case will be too difficult for us all to solve?

CHAPTER 6: FENDREL

THROUGH THE EYE OF THE threshold, Fendrel saw dragons approaching the palace-topped cliff. The sky was darker now with the sun hidden beneath the horizon. Fendrel returned to the meeting room through the hall while they flew nearer. "Thea, did you finish your spell?" he asked.

"I did, but I don't know if it will work yet." Thea came up to him from the stone table. She had two flat river stones cradled in the palm of her hand. "There's a scent to them. I think I got the spell right, but I will need to hear the dragons speak to make sure."

Thea waved Oliver over and gave him one of the stones to keep in his pocket. She stuffed the other stone in one of her pockets.

As the approaching dragons landed on the cliff's outstretched platform, Fendrel stepped away from the table. Thea and Oliver followed suit.

The mage grabbed Fendrel's arm in excitement as the dragons greeted each other with words of warmth and gratitude. "It works. I am a *genius*!"

Fendrel observed the newcomers as Cloud greeted them at the threshold. Each one sported some type of jewelry, marking them as the nobility hailing from the other nine dragon tribes—Dusk, Spark, Air, Water, Ice, Fire, Flora, Earth, and Stone. Not all of them showed. There were only four representatives.

Why? Fendrel wondered as his face contorted in exasperation. *What business could be keeping them when someone important to the king is missing?*

Other than Fog, Fendrel thought it would be best if he referred to the nobles by their elements. It was hard for him to remember a handful of new names all at once.

Dusk was the first to enter, his yellow-eyed gaze so piercing that Fendrel wondered if the dragon could see right through him. He was as tall as Cloud but more muscular and considerably older. Stone maintained an attentive aura and a posture as rigid as the crystal spikes that jutted from her back. Ice's neck seemed to sink into her wooly fur while she smiled cordially at the humans. Air was a lanky male dragon who did not look happy being there, but Fendrel could not discern whether it was from the humans' presence or the emergency that he had been called to help with.

Fog and Cloud joined behind them and, along with the other dragons, took their seats around the table.

"You may sit here." Cloud looked to Fendrel and gestured at a small spot between himself and Fog. He raised his voice. "We shall begin now."

"Yes, I would like to know why these humans are here," Dusk, sat on Cloud's right, said as he stared at Fendrel.

Dusk dragons were known for their black hides splashed with markings in green, gold, or purple. Unlike any dragon from the other tribes, Dusk dragons had fangs capable of delivering a life-ending toxin.

This Dusk noble happened to have a sprinkling of gold scales across his chest which matched the band around the midsection of his tail. He proclaimed, "I do not understand the importance of having humans here if they cannot understand us."

Fendrel returned the dragon's gaze for one very long second before he replied, "I understand you perfectly."

Dusk's eyes traveled to Fendrel's bag. A humming, almost growling, sound emanated from his throat.

"He is no ordinary human, friends." Cloud gestured at Fendrel with one huge paw. "I am sure you all have heard of the man who hunts the dragon hunters."

The assembly of dragons—other than Fog—fixed their astonished expressions on Fendrel.

Fendrel gave a small smile and a nod to the gathered dragons. "It's a pleasure to meet with you all."

Air cleared his throat and looked at Cloud. "While this occurrence is strange and new to all of us, would you please tell us what it is that caused you to hold off on this meeting for so long? I would have thought with the situation at hand you would be more proactive."

"Yes, of course." Cloud exchanged a tired look with Fog. "I . . . sent Fog out on the slim hope that she could find some additional help. It appears our prayers have been answered."

But Fog said she left without permission to find her sister. Did Cloud lie to spare Fog the embarrassment of telling the others she got captured?

"Speaking of, I must explain the situation to our new allies, and refresh the memories of those who may have forgotten," Cloud said as he seemed to ignore the suspicious looks he garnered from the Air dragon. "The dragon we are looking for, Mist, is betrothed to me. She disappeared the day of our wedding leaving no trace of where she left for."

The future queen of the Freelands. Fendrel blinked in surprise. *She truly is as important as Fog claimed her to be.*

Fendrel's brow furrowed. "She left without telling anyone?"

"That we know of." Fog lifted her wings like someone might lift their hand for permission to speak. "She could have been taken by humans or dragons. She would never just leave."

"A dragon abductee is highly unlikely, for the Hazy Woods and surrounding area, at least." The Air noble glanced at the ceiling as if recalling a memory. "We could not find any trace of her or possible captors on the day of her disappearance."

"If she did leave, do you know where she might have gone?" Fendrel visualized a map in his mind in preparation of Cloud's response.

"I have no idea. Mist never left the Hazy Woods all the days of her life. If she left, I fear it means she does not want to be found." Cloud's eyes filled with sorrow. He appeared to take a moment to collect himself, then continued. "Which is why we are asking for your help, Liberator. We know you have taken requests from all kinds of dragons to find those who have gone missing. We believe you can do it again for us. So please, will you help us find Mist?"

Fendrel felt the eyes of all the dragons on him.

This is a much more important mission than I have ever been on before, Fendrel thought as nerves crept into his fingers, causing them to tap his bag. *If I agree to help them, I may not be able to track down the next dragon hunter captures for a while. That could put a lot of dragons in danger, but . . . so could the disappearance of a soon-to-be queen.*

I can't pass this up. If I help them bring the future queen home, I can forgive myself for not being able to do more. The hunters have taken so much already. I won't let them take Mist, too.

Fendrel steeled his gaze as he looked at each of them. "I will help you. Even if it takes a month, or a year, I will not give up."

All of the dragons sighed in relief, with the exception of the Dusk dragon, who studied him unblinking. Fendrel avoided his eyes.

"Your enthusiasm is admirable. However I do not think it would be wise to search indefinitely," Ice said with reluctance. "Mist has already been missing for seven days. In the worst-case scenario that we do not find her, we need to be prepared to drop the search and continue with our duties."

"You are suggesting a time limit?" Dusk asked.

"I am." Ice looked to Cloud. "Our tribes need us, Your Majesty. It would be regretful to abandon the search, but I believe we can only afford to halt our responsibilities for another seven days."

"Seven days?" Fog's wings sank to her sides. "That is not enough time!"

"Do not fret," Dusk consoled. "I am sure even if we cannot find her within a week, we will all keep an eye out for her."

Cloud seemed to ponder Ice's point for a moment. He sighed and his wings dropped like weights. "You are right. We cannot search forever. I do not want it to come to that, but if we must stop, we will."

"If it's any consolation—" Fendrel met Fog's and Cloud's gazes "—I'll keep looking for her if worst comes to worse."

"Thank you," Fog muttered as a discouraged expression overtook her face.

The dragon king cleared his throat, then nodded to Fendrel. "I cannot thank you enough, and when this is all over, you shall be rewarded accordingly."

"That won't be necessary." Fendrel gave a nervous laugh, shaking his head.

All that I do for the dragons is my responsibility. I don't deserve payment for it.

"I insist." Cloud peered down at the human. "I will not take no for an answer."

Fendrel sighed as he gave in and nodded. "Thank you."

Cloud spoke to the assembly. "Good. I know this meeting was short, as its purpose was to get you all caught up to speed before we began our in-depth search. If there is nothing else for us to discuss, you are dismissed."

Something popped into Fendrel's mind. "Wait, there is something I should mention." When Cloud nodded, Fendrel continued. "There's a possibility Mist could have been taken by dragon hunters, so we should be on the lookout for them. And make sure to stay on high alert on the outskirts of each tribe's domain. That's where they like to hunt."

"Understood." Cloud responded.

"There is also a rogue Fire dragon that's been giving me a bit of trouble for a while." Fendrel's eyes shifted between the nobles and the king, unsure of how they would react.

Will they exclude me from the mission for this? Fendrel wondered, feeling dejected. *My presence could be a liability if that rogue decides to make an appearance.*

While most dragons had the same intelligence as humans, rogues were not so fortunate. They acted purely out of animalistic desires and had an unshakeable prey-drive for humans. Some rogues went after any human they crossed paths with, while others targeted a specific victim. They were easy to tell apart from other dragons due to their uncanny black eyes, which harbored no irises, and the thick, dark-purple sludge that drained from their mouths, nostrils, and eyes.

That rogue probably hates me so much because its companion died the first time it attacked me. Perhaps it's seeking revenge, Fendrel pondered. He had tried for years to find a good enough reason for why his rogue was so obsessed with him. However, there was no clear answer, and there never would be one.

The Dusk dragon frowned deeply.

Oh, Fendrel remembered. *Dusk dragons are responsible for taking down any rogues before they can hunt humans. Is he upset one slipped by him?*

"Then we may have more to look out for than just Mist," Cloud said, rising from his seat. "Thank you for this warning. I doubt it will give us much trouble as long as it is alone."

It's more determined than you think.

Fendrel smiled out of politeness. The nobles and Cloud left the meeting room and made their way down the hall. Fendrel did not realize he had lost himself in his thoughts until Thea tapped him on the shoulder. "That black dragon seems odd. He wouldn't stop staring at you." Thea kept her voice at so low a whisper Fendrel could hardly hear her.

"You can speak up. They can't hear us from here." Fendrel stood.

"Oh, no, I'm whispering because Oliver fell asleep." Thea pointed at the boy, who sat slumped against the wall.

"Ah." Fendrel nodded. "I'll go ask Cloud about rooms for the night." As Thea went to sit beside Oliver, Fendrel started down the long hall which was now illuminated by the softer, colder light of the moon.

After Fendrel brought up the subject of rooms to Cloud, the king led Thea and Oliver down a level of stairs to a room they could share. The nobles had already retired to rooms reserved for their visits.

Fendrel knew he would not be able to sleep for a bit, so he stayed on the cliff top. He was too excited to sleep, and too nervous thinking about the scope of this mission. He sat on the outstretched platform with his legs dangling over the edge. From his vantage point he could see where the nobles—save for Fog and the Dusk dragon—had flown.

"It is pretty, yes?" Fog came up to his side and laid down.

"It is . . . it's peaceful." Fendrel took a deep breath, reveling at how crisp the air felt entering his lungs. The night was dark with cloud cover, but there were breaks that allowed ample moonlight to see by.

Fendrel took his eyes off the still forest below to look at Fog. "If you don't mind me asking, how did you assume the title of noble? Your earring just seems so simple compared to the jewelry of the others."

"Oh, well, my mother was the royal advisor to Cloud's parents before she died. Mist and I were always close to Cloud and his family because of our mother's position, so Cloud offered me the title of noble when he assumed the throne," Fog explained. Her head tilted as though she were remembering something. "I was also asked to take the position because of a rare ability I hatched with. I can heal surface wounds by breathing vapor on them. It is a useful skill, but it is a little strange. No one from my tribe knows how this ability was first discovered. Did someone get a scratch and decide a little vapor would help it heal? Perhaps they assumed the vapor would soothe the pain, but . . . Oh, I am sorry, I am rambling!" Fog used her wings to cover her mouth and sighed. She nodded to where the nobles had flown off. "They say that I should focus on not talking as much."

"No, it's fine. You don't have to apologize," Fendrel said in a mirthful tone. "And, you're right. That is a useful skill, especially if we run into trouble during our search."

"Well, since you asked me a question, may I ask you one?" The end of Fog's tail curled and uncurled with excitement.

Fendrel could not decide if he wanted to say anything personal. He suppressed a sigh of relief when the Dusk dragon's voice cut through. "Fog, His Majesty asks that we retire to our individual rooms. We need our rest for tomorrow."

Fog nodded at the older dragon and stood. She hooked her front talons onto the edge of the platform and called over her shoulder,

"Goodnight, Venom."

Venom. That seems like a fitting name.

The Vapor dragon tilted her head to look at Fendrel. "Thank you for helping us. Sleep well!" She pushed herself off the platform, spread her wings, and gently drifted downwards.

"Goodnight." Fendrel's voice was below a mutter as Venom took up the space Fog previously occupied.

The black dragon did not immediately say anything, opting to simply stare at Fendrel. When he finally did speak, his tone was flat. "Are you some kind of thief?"

Fendrel leaned away from the dragon. "Excuse me?"

"That bag you have there." Venom nodded his head toward Fendrel's bag. "Did you steal it?"

"It was a gift." Fendrel subconsciously placed a hand on the beat-up leather.

Why do you care? Fendrel wanted to say, but he kept his mouth shut.

The dragon averted his gaze and sighed, deep and heavy. He then returned his sight to Fendrel. "Who gifted this to you?"

"Why should that matter?" Fendrel's voice came out quieter than he had meant it to.

After a few beats of silence, Venom hung his head. "It was from your mother, yes? You came from the town of Stone Edge, did you not?"

A strange sense of fear latched onto Fendrel's heart, making it stall a moment. No one had brought up his mother in years. He wondered for a moment if the Dusk dragon had been stalking him, then realized how ridiculous of an accusation that would be. Deciding to test the dragon's knowledge, Fendrel said, "If you know of Stone Edge, then you know what happened fifteen years ago."

Venom did not meet his eyes. "I did not see it happen. I only saw the aftermath about a month later. I apologize. There was nothing I could do at that point. The rogue had left, and its scent was already too faint to pick up."

"How did you know this bag was my mother's?" Fendrel rubbed a thumb across it.

"I only wanted to make sure it was you. You do not look the same as her." Venom lifted his head and appeared to study Fendrel's face. "Although you do have a similar scent."

Fendrel wanted to respond but found that his mind had gone blank, starstruck by the Dusk dragon's revelation. Finally, he managed a quiet, "You knew my mother?"

Could this be the dragon she befriended when she was young?

Venom nodded. "Axella. She was the only human I ever truly trusted. Then she disappeared while I was away. I did not know what happened to her until I found Stone Edge in ruins." His voice hitched a little and he cleared his throat to cover it up.

Did she know he was of nobility? Fendrel wondered.

"My apologies for acting harshly towards you earlier." Venom bowed his head in respect. "I suspect Mist's disappearance is due to humans. It was alarming for Cloud to bring you here so suddenly, especially when no human has ever ventured deep enough into the Hazy Woods to see any of what you have."

Fendrel tried to think of a response, but his mind and his mouth appeared to be disconnected.

"I know this hardly seems like an appropriate time, but your mother was an important friend to me, and I would like to get to know you." The black dragon gave Fendrel a small smile.

"Thank you . . ." Fendrel's mind continued to reel. His mother had been dead for fifteen years and only now was he meeting someone close to her. He did not know if he should be glad to meet Venom or spiteful that they had not found each other sooner. "Well, as you said, we need our sleep for tomorrow."

"Yes, of course." Venom's face seemed to show slight disappointment as Fendrel stood. "I will see you in the morning."

The two parted ways with Venom taking off into the air and Fendrel down the stairs to an empty room. Fendrel had to push aside a door made from hanging flowered vines to get inside. It was small, round like the palace's meeting room, and carved completely out of the stone cliff. A woven basket in the back held wolf fur blankets.

Fendrel pulled a few of the furs from where they rested and laid them out. From his bag he retrieved another fur blanket, this one made from caribou just like his cloak. Even amidst the softness and warmth of the blankets, Fendrel doubted he would get much sleep. But as lay there, his eyelids grew heavy. He welcomed sleep and soon found himself in a dream. As with all his dreams, he was watching a memory. It did not take him long to realize which one this was.

The Dragon Liberator: Escapade

Fendrel sat with his legs dangling over a rocky cliff. Waves pounded the rocks below and saltwater rose up to sprinkle his shoes. On any other day he would have welcomed the sea spray. He liked to pretend it was the ocean waving to him. Instead of waving back, he sniffled and wiped his tear-stained cheeks with a fist. Only six-years-old, and he was already learning how cruel humans could be, especially his father.

He had never liked his father, but how that man treated his mother only solidified his feelings. All his mother wanted was to visit, so why was she being screamed at? Screaming was for when someone did something wrong. Fendrel knew that. He was screamed at often. But what could his mother have done to deserve all that yelling?

Gentle footsteps crept over the pebbles of the clifftop toward Fendrel. The one approaching sat down next to him and she gave a tired sigh. "Did he scare you?"

Fendrel did not meet her eyes. Showing fear was another reason to be screamed at, and so was crying. Fendrel did not want to let anyone see him cry, even his mother.

"Hey." She tapped his nose. "I know you're not upset enough to ignore me."

The corners of Fendrel's mouth twitched up.

"I see that smile," she teased as she pulled him into a hug.

Fendrel's muffled laugh betrayed him. He wrapped his arms around his mother.

"Don't ever let him steal your happiness, all right?" She pulled his face away from her neck and looked into his eyes.

Fendrel placed his hands over his mother's. He nodded.

A large wave crashed into the cliff, showering both of them in saltwater.

His mother laughed in surprise. She grabbed his hand. "Come on, love. Let's go somewhere dry, and I'll tell you as many stories as you'd like."

CHAPTER 7: CASSIUS

IN THE EARLY MORNING, THE prince of Sharpdagger hurried down the streets, his head swiveling as he went. After a few moments of no one recognizing him, a carefree smile brightened his features. Anyone watching could only tell by the crinkle of his eyes, since the bottom half of his face was covered by a bland scarf.

Cassius had been itching to get back into the city after hearing the Liberator snuck in again. No criminal was as sought after as him, and neither was any other criminal so vexing the royal guard had to use paints on the wanted posters to portray his visage with more accuracy. That man was keeping the royal guard busy, which meant there were less eyes on Cassius, and he could go wherever he wanted. The prince silently thanked the wanted man for drawing all the attention away.

He had forsaken his royal garb in the stable stall behind his horse, which he seldom rode. He was free to roam the streets of his city until sundown, when his father would send out guards to call him to supper.

The prince shrugged off that thought.

I am an adult. I need to make my own decisions. If I miss dinner, that is no one's problem but my own. But of course I would never say that to Father's stubborn face. Cassius frowned as his thoughts turned sour. Ever since he had turned eighteen-years-old nearly a year prior, his father had been bringing suitor after suitor to him.

There are criminals running rampant in the streets, a surplus of orphans begging for scraps, refugees from dragons attacks overcrowding our smaller villages, and knights neglecting their duties. Father should be teaching me how to deal with those issues first, but instead he wants to play matchmaker, Cassius thought with disdain. He loved his father, but he rarely got along with him. The king's failing to educate Cassius in recent years was only one of his flaws. Another, one Cassius despised above all others, was that, in the king's eyes, the head of the royal guard could do no wrong.

Father must not see any bad in him because he is family. Just because he is

41

mother's nephew does not mean he is perfect. Cassius took a deep breath to calm himself before his thoughts consumed him. *I cannot blame Father for not seeing Zoricus' misdeeds, since Father is not patrolling the city like I am.*

The prince scoffed as more petty thoughts invaded his mind.

Patrolling. That is what Zoricus should be doing every day. Instead, he and his underlings are buying dragon parts off the black market to impress the next maiden they fancy.

Cassius kept on his usual path. He had learned the art of looking at something without letting everyone know he was watching. It helped him notice things that were of interest to him. As his eyes scoured the crowd, his gaze landed on one of the knights Zoricus considered a close friend. The man ducked into a building. His armor was unequipped, and his commoner clothes made him look like an everyday citizen.

Should he be on duty today? Cassius could not resist following the guard. One of the few things his father had taught him, and one he was eternally grateful for, was which high-ranking guards were stationed on a particular day.

As Cassius approached the door, his fingers itched to turn the knob. Despite the sense of anxiety growing within him, he entered the building. It was a small shop dealing in high-quality clothing and jewelry. Much of it looked to be imported.

Cassius eyed the shop owner, who was speaking to the guard. He turned his back to them and fiddled with a rack displaying a variety of necklaces.

"I'll be right with you, sir," the shop owner called, glancing at Cassius.

The prince nodded but kept his eyes on the jewelry. He was hungry for more dirt revolving around the royal guard. More dirt meant more evidence, and more evidence meant a possibility that Zoricus would be defenestrated.

Cassius slipped a piece of paper and writing charcoal out of the coat he wore. It had a list of code words he heard wealthy merchants use and had written their meanings beside them. He strained his ears on the two at the counter.

"Good morning, sir. You're up early." The shop owner placed his hands on the counter that separated him from the guard. "What are you looking for today?"

The guard made a humming noise. "I'm looking for a gemstone."

Cassius looked at his paper. Next to "gemstone" he had written

"Armored dragon."

He is buying one of those dragons with the crystals on their backs. This is a first for him, Cassius thought as he listened. *Usually he only purchases horns or claws.*

The prince made a note of the interaction on the back of the paper. If he could prove this transaction took place, it would be another step toward getting rid of his corrupt cousin.

"Hmm, what type of jewelry?" The shop owner's voice grew softer, as if afraid of attracting Cassius' attention.

"A ring." The guard matched his tone of voice.

Beside "ring" Cassius had written "hatchling."

Really? Cassius scowled. *They usually only buy eggs to hatch at home. Perhaps the smugglers are not selling eggs anymore, or the eggs were not hatching . . . or the guards were accidentally breaking them.*

Cassius fidgeted with the large, clear gemstone of a necklace in front of him, angling it to spy on the men behind him. The image was distorted, but he could see the guard tossing cautious glances over his shoulder.

He saw the shop owner nod.

"Right away, sir. Wait right here." The shop owner opened a door behind the counter and left.

The prince stepped to a table displaying vibrantly colored clothing. A small smile played on his lips.

Sadie might enjoy this.

Cassius pictured his twin sister in his mind. He picked up the garment, a yellow shawl with blue and green thread stitched in to look like peacock feathers.

He pressed his lips into a thin line, suddenly unsure.

No, Zoricus probably bought her something like this already. Besides, her seamstress could just make something for her if she really wanted it. Perhaps I could just mention the pattern to her when I return home—

He was so enthralled with the shawl that he nearly missed the shop owner returning through the back door with a bag the size of a melon. The shop owner set the bag down on the counter and carefully opened it to allow the guard to peer inside.

"It won't . . . make any noise, will it?" The guard poked the bag.

Shaking his head, the shop owner said, "I just finished priming this one. I assume you know how to keep it well-maintained?"

"Yes, yes." The guard reached for the bag impatiently. "I'll pay five hundred gold pieces for it."

Cassius almost dropped the paper and writing charcoal.

That is the most I have seen one go for!

"No, no, no." The shop owner pulled the bag closer to himself. "Six hundred and fifty, at the very least. It nearly cost my supplier his life to obtain this one."

The guard sighed. "Fine." He took a pouch from his pocket and dropped it on the counter with a loud thunk. The coins inside chimed as they settled.

Grinning like an imp, the shop owner emptied the contents and scooped them into a wooden box he pulled from beneath the counter. He gave the guard a smile. "Have a wonderful day, sir."

Grumbling under his breath, the guard grabbed his empty coin pouch, stuffed it in his pocket, and took the "ring" bag in the other hand.

When the guard left the shop, the owner looked at Cassius. "Are you wanting to do business as well?"

Cassius froze.

I could buy a hatchling as proof and bring it to Father, but . . . no. How would buying a hatchling prove that Zoricus and the other knights are doing the same? And what kind of a person would that make me?

"No, I just realized I am running late to . . . an event." Cassius left the shop and took a deep breath as the door shut behind him. He started off down the street but paused when a conversation caught his attention. He pretended to gaze at a stand full of fruit as he listened. Two women were speaking beside a stall, one with a silver band around her arm, marking her as a guard's wife, and a slightly younger woman.

"Zoricus is losing his temper quite frequently." The younger woman wrung a scarf in her clenched fists. "He has begun to berate the other knights for not being able to catch this *one man*. But he should not be so harsh if he cannot even accomplish what he wants them to do."

"My husband tells me Zoricus' pride is hurt." The older woman chuckled. "After all, it's been years, and that criminal has managed to escape him time and time again."

"They call him the Liberator, right? The one on the posters." The younger of the two gestured at a nearby wall.

Cassius' eyes widened. His gaze traveled to where she pointed. "The Liberator," he read. He studied the poster. This one was new, as it included a list of signs to look out for. "A specialist in close combat, always alone. Short stature, brown hair and eyes, carrying a damaged leather bag."

The prince smiled as a plan formulated in his mind. He usually did not return home this soon, but this morning he looked forward to locking himself in his room to brainstorm Zoricus' downfall.

If I can find the Liberator and tell him what Zoricus and his underlings have been doing, perhaps he will help me take Zoricus out of his position of power! Cassius plotted. He fought to keep a smile off his face, lest someone grow suspicious of his overly excited visage. But then, doubts began to drown out his glee. *No, this is a stupid idea. How would I of all people be able to find him when even Zoricus cannot? And why would the Liberator even help me? My father has been neglectful of our royal guard's corruption, and that reflects badly on my reputation. We are complicit. The Liberator probably hates me just as much as he hates dragon hunters.*

Cassius backed himself into an alleyway and shut his eyes. He spent a few minutes clearing his head and resolved he would cling to hope. The prince turned on his heel and sped for the royal stables, remembering he could not show up in the palace dressed as he was. He had not felt this exhilarated for an adventure in years.

CHAPTER 8: FENDREL

FENDREL TOOK HIMSELF BACK TO the platform on the clifftop. The sun was climbing high enough to be seen over the northeastern mountains and the air seemed even fresher than it had the night before. Fendrel had awoken before everyone else, or so he thought.

"Good morning!" Fog whispered behind Fendrel. "Could you come with me? There is something I want to show you."

He whirled around, thinking he was alone.

"I am sorry." Fog smiled in apology. "Come this way." She gestured with her wing for Fendrel to follow her. There was a staircase made of stone winding down the side of the cliff. It looked like it had been carved out of the cliff itself. There was no railing. Fendrel had taken that same staircase to go to bed, but now the morning light was showing just how high up it was.

"Do not worry, I will fly right beside you so I can catch you if you fall." Fog leapt into the sky and beat her wings to hover beside the edge.

Fendrel did not like the thought of dying before he could participate in the strangest mission he had ever signed up for. Still, he headed down the winding staircase that clung to the cylindrical cliff. Just as she had promised, Fog flew by his side, her feathery wingtips almost brushing the steps.

Where the staircase leveled out there was a doorway whose threshold was carved to resemble vines and mist coiling around each other. The room beyond was spacious enough to fit two royal dragons with their wings spread out. Fendrel ventured in, with Fog landing right behind him. There was a stone table in the center of the room, much like the one within the palace. Large disks of wood only half an inch thick were laid out on the tabletop. Fendrel inspected the disks. There was Drake-tongue script carved into them and filled with ink.

"Each noble is meant to be the leader of their tribe, but with Cloud as King, I do not have many responsibilities. I have taken to record-keeping as my main occupation." Fog looked about the room as she spoke. There were stone-carved shelves housing more wooden disks all along the walls.

"What is this place?" Fendrel dragged his fingers across one of the shelves.

"This is where we store all our important documents. Royal decrees on this shelf, maps up there, old legends passed down from each tribe over here, and customs regarding the other domains." Fog smiled with glee. "At this point, I live here."

She sidled up beside Fendrel. "And speaking of the other tribes, we will be traveling to a few different ones on our journey, and I do not want to seem ignorant. Although I have read everything I can about them, I still do not know much. Can you tell me a bit of your experiences with each tribe?" Fog asked. She moved the disks on the table to their respective sections.

"I'll do my best." Fendrel put his hands on the tabletop. "I only really know Fire and Ice customs, but I know bits about the others."

"Why only those two?" Fog reached for a stack on one of the shelves.

Fendrel shrugged. "Well, I grew up with Ice dragons, in one of their clans, and I visit the Fire dragons frequently."

I would visit my clan more often, but . . . no. Now's not the time to think about home. Fendrel shook his thoughts away from the snowy pine forest where he had spent the latter years of his childhood.

"I see." Fog set the new stack on the table and spread them out. Pointing at one of the texts, she said, "It mostly says here that Dusk dragons act as a royal guard for the other tribes."

"That . . . makes a lot more sense to me now." Fendrel nodded. "I've seen them all over the continent, but I thought they were just hunting rogues. So they patrol the Freelands, too?"

"Yes." Fog moved the top disk off the stack. "And Flora dragons. I am distant friends with one but do not know much about his culture."

"Well, Flora dragons grow up to mimic a specific plant, and they gain abilities from that plant by eating it. So some of them look like trees, others like flowers, fruits, cacti, even meat-eating plants." Fendrel peered at the flowered vines that wound their way into the room. "I've noticed the prettier ones tend to act haughtier than the others. I don't usually have normal conversations with the dragons I rescue, but Flora dragons tend to think they don't need help being rescued."

"Interesting." Fog nodded with an amused smile. "And Fire dragons?"

"They'll find an excuse to celebrate anything. Sometimes, their festivals can last for weeks." Fendrel couldn't help the smile that pulled at the corners of his mouth. "Speaking from experience, it's harder to convince them not to have a celebration than it is to leave one prematurely."

"That sounds fun but tiring." Fog leaned down to read the customs on Fire dragons. "Us Vapor dragons celebrate a lot too, but mostly, it is just dancing. Not festivals."

Fendrel leaned his elbows on the table. "They're very friendly."

"It is too bad we will not be able to stay for any festivities. Perhaps I can one once this is all over." Fog moved on to the Earth tribe disk. "This says they are rather tough and have jumped to defend other tribes in the past."

"They're absolutely terrified of humans, so I've never spoken to one. As soon as I get them out of the hunters' reach, they bolt without a word to me." Fendrel moved his eyes down the disk, reading each line with care.

"Water tribe?" Fog tapped the space his gaze ended up on.

"Skeptical of humans, but at least they make an effort to act welcoming."

"Air?" Fog spread her wings out.

Fendrel chuckled at her impression. "Full of interesting stories, and they generally keep to themselves. They believe the wind itself is alive and whatever happens is the will of the wind."

"Hm," Fog hummed in interest. "Stone dragons?"

"They live underground, like the Earth tribe does, so they don't see humans all that often. It's made all the ones I've met curious, but not friendly. After all, the first exposure many of them have to humans are through dragon hunters." Fendrel looked over the Stone tribe's section. "I think they mimic like the Flora tribe, but with gemstones instead of plants."

"And finally, Spark." Fog looked out toward the doorway as though she was trying to find one of the lightning-like dragons. "I know much more about them than the other tribes, but that is only because we have many holidays in common, and they live so close."

"I've only met a handful. Because they typically stay in the Storm Peaks, I haven't met one that wasn't captured by hunters. They seem to like me, but that may just be due to my pendant," Fendrel said as he reached under his shirt for the necklace he showed to Fog when they first met. "They share a lot of traditions with the Ice tribe, too, and they recognized my pendant was from one of the clans."

"Oh, that is interesting! I had no idea the Spark dragons were so close to *both* tribes. I suppose that makes us neighbors." Fog said as her eyes lit up. With a smile still on her face, she collected the disks and set to reordering them. "Could you tell me more about the Ice tribe later? I think everyone else is awake by now, and I do not want to keep them waiting."

"Of course." Fendrel nodded. "We . . . we won't be visiting Frost Lake during our search, would we?"

"Oh, no." Fog shook her head. "Venom and a few other nobles already surveyed Frost Lake the day Mist disappeared, so we will not be looking there again."

"Ah." Fendrel tried to hide his disappointment. It had been too long since he saw his home and his clan. He was due for his annual visit soon.

You wouldn't have time to catch up anyhow. There is a life at stake. Focus on the mission, Fendrel told himself.

If he only had the time to reconnect with his clan, visiting would not be so difficult. As much as he wanted his relationship with his clan to go back to how it used to be, home had not felt like home in years. Every year Fendrel made the journey back to Frost Lake, but it never felt like how it did when he was a child.

"Let us join the others now," Fog said as she led Fendrel back up the stairs to the Meeting Cliff. "And thank you for your insight so far! With your knowledge I am sure we will bring Mist home in no time."

The company of nine were once again gathered around the meeting room's stone table. Cloud and Fog had provided rations but decided they would be for Thea, Oliver, and Fendrel. The dragons could eat whatever the land provided for them.

Fendrel avoided Oliver's pleading gazes when Thea told him he would not be able to stay for the whole mission. Oliver was only a child and needed to be taken somewhere safe, although Fendrel had no idea where that would be.

He would be better off homeless than back with Sadon, but we can't let that happen. Fendrel sighed through his nose. *Where is he going to go?*

Cloud opened his wings partway to attract everyone's attention. "There are eight of us here, excluding the child. We should split up into two teams. The Liberator and his companions can join me."

Venom lifted his wings, a sign of asking permission to speak.

"Yes, Venom?" Cloud nodded at the elder dragon.

"May the Liberator and his companions join me instead?" Venom asked. "If the rogue he mentioned attacks again, the humans will need someone who is experienced in combat."

Fendrel doubted that was the real reason, but it was a well-thought-out excuse.

Fog's eyes brightened. "If you get hurt, you will need a healer. I will go with you!"

Cloud made a thoughtful noise. "I would like to keep the humans together. Now you two want to accompany them. That is four, excluding the child, which leaves four left to be grouped."

"I believe that makes the rest of the decision easy, yes?" Venom gave Cloud an expectant nod.

"In addition, this will be a very strenuous journey, Your Majesty," the Ice noble said. "In the end, the decision is up to you, but I think it wise for you to stay here and take care of your subjects while the rest of us search. What we are experiencing is a time of chaos, and what we need is order."

Cloud opened his mouth and looked as though he wanted to turn down her request, but then he stopped. "You are right. I was being . . . selfish. I must put my subjects first," the king said, though something in his voice told Fendrel that the monarch was far from happy with this proposal. He looked to Venom and Fog next. "Your group will go west. I am not sure how slow your travel will be with humans on your back, so I suggest you head out now while the rest of us determine the second group's route."

Venom nodded in agreement and stood. "You are making the right choice, which is often the hardest choice. Mist will understand. You need not fret."

"Venom is right!" Fog agreed as she gave Cloud a smile. "We'll bring Mist home." She tapped Fendrel on the shoulder with her wing claw as she followed Venom out of the meeting room.

"Thank you for this opportunity." Fendrel bowed his head to Cloud before he departed, then ushered Thea and Oliver along with him.

Once they were moving down the hallway, Thea nudged Fendrel in the shoulder. "We're going with the dragon who stared at you all day yesterday?"

Fendrel shook his head to dismiss her question. "I know it looks strange, but I have a suspicion he's just curious about us."

"Well, he wasn't staring at *us*." Thea gestured between herself and Oliver.

Fendrel shrugged "We'll figure out why sooner or later, all right? There's no need to worry. And besides, if he does have bad intentions, I can hold my own."

Thea gave him an incredulous look. She eyed his thin stature, which was a bit lighter and shorter than her own. "You look like even I could snap you in half."

"Looks can be deceiving," Fendrel said defensively. He sped up his pace before Thea could continue to tease him. When he crossed the palace door's threshold, Venom was bringing together travel bags he had set against the palace's exterior wall.

"We have the food and water bags for them." Venom pointed his wing at the humans as he spoke to Fog. "Do you have any sparrow-catchers?"

Fog tilted her head. "Why would I need those metal claws? Surely there will be enough plant-based food that I will not need to hunt."

"Most likely, but there is always the chance that there will only be live prey." A troubled look crossed Venom's face for a moment. "Besides, you could use them as weapons if we run into trouble."

"Oh." Fog nodded in understanding. "Yes, I have some. Give me a moment." She ran for the edge and flew off.

Fendrel watched her leave as he thought, *I've never heard of dragons using claw attachments before. Perhaps Vapor dragon claws aren't as sharp as other dragons?*

After a few minutes, Fog glided up to the cliff edge. The metal claws she wore on her talons scraped against the stone as she landed. She lifted one of her paws. "I sharpened them earlier this year and I have not used them since, so I am set."

Fendrel knelt down and fit the travel sacks into his bag. "Great, so are we ready?"

Venom lowered himself to a crouch. "I believe we are."

Thea froze. She leaned toward Fendrel to whisper in his ear. "Can I go with the Vapor dragon?"

"Vapor dragons' wings aren't strong enough to bear more than their own weight for very long. You'll just have to ride with Oliver and me. Look, he isn't scared." Fendrel gestured to the boy, who was attempting to clamber onto the black dragon's shoulders.

The mage cautiously approached Venom. After helping Oliver onto Venom, she hauled herself up behind him. Fendrel hoisted himself in front of Oliver right at the base of Venom's neck where the dragon's spines tapered off.

As soon as they were all seated, Venom stood, and the humans readjusted at the sudden movement. "All right, let us head out," Venom said while starting for the cliff.

"Yes!" Fog leapt into the sky.

Venom sighed and launched himself after her. "Do you know where you are going, Fog?"

She slowed in the air until Venom was beside her. "Right, sorry. You should be leading."

"You've never left the Hazy Woods before?" Fendrel asked, astonished. He couldn't imagine what his life would be like if he had never explored the Freelands.

"No, the only time I left was to find Mist, and I did not get very far. I have only seen maps and, sometimes, on *really* clear days, I can see the silhouette of the human palace." Fog stared out at the land.

Venom smiled with endearment. He was fast, even with three humans holding him back, and he had to hinder himself so Fog could keep up. Trees and lakes passed in a blur, and soon, they were approaching the edge of the Hazy Woods.

Before they crossed into the plains, Venom titled his head so he could see Fendrel. "That rogue dragon you mentioned before, what does it look like?"

Without hesitation, Fendrel spoke as if he had recited the line hundreds of times. "He's a Fire dragon. Red scales and white stripes. It's the same one from Stone Edge."

What if he's in the clouds watching us right now?

Fendrel gripped the spines on Venom's neck and shook away the thought.

"He will not lay a claw on you as long as I am here." There was not a shred of doubt in Venom's voice.

Fendrel nodded, not fully trusting the Dusk dragon's judgment.

They soon passed the forest's tree line and began to fly over a large expanse of grassy plains. Fog looked at Fendrel with a smile. "I wish we were going east so we could see Glass Beach."

"Glass Beach, that's a human village." Fendrel smiled at her. "How do you know about that?"

"I uh—" Fog laughed with nervousness. "I study the royal maps with human villages a lot more than the ones with our own cities." Her voice trailed off at the end of her explanation.

"Fog, you know you and I cannot go near any of the human villages, even *if* we were traveling east." A twinge of warning laced Venom's voice.

Fog sighed. "I know."

"Your longing has something to do with your earring, yes?" Venom jutted his chin in her direction. "Will you remind me of how you got it?"

The Vapor dragon's eyes lit up. "It is from my mother, remember? She found it right on the shore of Glass Beach at sunset. Then she sent it home to me and I had it made into an earring. I have always wanted to go there ever since I got her letter about it."

Fendrel felt himself relaxing as Fog continued to talk. He did his best to banish the thoughts of the rogue from his head while he watched the hills roll by. But in the back of his mind, a frightened voice was urging him to keep his head on a swivel.

CHAPTER 9: FENDREL

FENDREL'S EYE CAUGHT ON A cluster of buildings in the distance, nestled between two steep, grassy hills. From his vantage point atop Venom's shoulders, he could tell this was Lightgrass, one of the many human cities scattered across the Freelands. He pointed at the city and raised his voice to be heard over the wind. "I know that city. Thea and I could ask around for information on Mist. There are usually a lot of dragon sightings whenever I pass through."

Venom shook his head. "We need to stay focused. I doubt we would gain anything useful about Mist there."

"It might be a long shot, but I would rather be thorough than skip over something that at first seems trivial." Fendrel viewed the sun's position and noted it would reach the horizon in a few hours. "Even if we stop to take a look, we should still have enough daylight afterward to keep flying. We might as well check."

"Please, Venom." Fog pumped her wings so she could fly beside the black dragon. "He seems to know what he is talking about."

Venom stayed silent.

"Most humans have never seen a Vapor dragon. If Mist was spotted, she'd be the talk of the town." Fendrel gave Venom a look of assurance. "We wouldn't have to be there long."

"Where do you expect Fog and me to hide while you are there?" Venom shot a look at Fendrel over his shoulder.

"The hills surrounding Lightgrass are steep. If we descend now and skim them until we're close enough, the humans will never spot you." Fendrel tried to make his tone as agreeable as possible, but he felt himself getting frustrated.

Before he could say anything more, Fog interrupted him. "Oh, oh! And—pardon me if I am misremembering your name—Thea? You said the spell you put on me disguises me as a horse to humans other than you two, yes?" Fog's feathers stood on end in excitement. "Could I join you?"

"You put a *spell* on her?" Venom growled. He angled his wings into a steady dive.

Fendrel heard Thea and Oliver gasp in surprise. He clung to them as the wind bit into their skin.

When Venom landed, Fendrel took Oliver and Thea down from Venom's back and put himself between them and the dragon. Fendrel scowled in confusion and began to ask, "Why did you—"

"You." Venom pointed a curved, gleaming claw at Thea. His lips curled up into an ugly snarl. "You cast a spell on Fog. That is *extremely* forbidden!"

Fendrel pulled a dagger from his bag before he realized what he was doing. He pointed it at Venom and felt his feet shift into a battle stance.

Venom's nostrils flared as he eyed the dagger. "Put that away, boy."

With a steeled gaze, Fendrel stared at Venom. "I don't know who you think you are, or what you plan to do to her, but your king wanted both of us to help find your future queen. So until we do, we are going to be cordial and respectful to each other. Understand?"

Fog, breathing heavily, landed beside Venom with a thud. "What is going on?"

"In what insane world is placing a spell on a living being acceptable?" Venom's fangs twitched as if getting ready to strike. "I do not know what culture you grew up in, but that is disgusting."

"W-wait!" Thea's trembling body slowly shuffled back from the enraged dragon. "I didn't break any mage laws. She misspoke. I put a spell on that vine around her wing claw, not on her."

Venom glanced at Fog and saw the vine swaying in the slight breeze. "Is this true, Fog?"

Fog looked between him and the dagger in Fendrel's hand. She started to tremble. "Yes, the spell is on the vine. Can you both please calm down? You are scaring me."

Fendrel stayed steady. He had never fought a Dusk dragon before, but he readied himself, nonetheless. He studied Venom's posture and waited for him to make a move.

Venom gazed just past Fendrel and Fendrel turned his head to see what he was looking at. Oliver hid behind Thea, not letting anyone see his face. Thea, trembling just as much as the boy, appeared more terrified than Fendrel had ever seen her before. Fendrel gripped his dagger's hilt tighter and felt his heart pulse with adrenaline. When Venom folded his fangs back and stepped away, Fendrel's brow furrowed in surprise.

"I . . . apologize for the assumption," Venom said softly. He gave Thea a curt nod. "I was concerned for Fog's autonomy."

"This isn't going to happen again," Fendrel warned. He returned the dagger to his bag.

Venom sighed. "All right. I will take you closer to Lightgrass."

Fendrel opened his mouth to refute, then stopped himself.

It's too far of a walk if we want to make it there before sunset.

"Fine," Fendrel said. "But this mission isn't going to go well if you jump at every miscommunication."

"I understand." Venom crouched low enough for the humans to step up.

Fendrel helped Oliver and Thea onto Venom's back and seated himself in front of them. Then, in the humans' tongue, he twisted around and spoke to them. "Are you two all right?"

Thea had her eyes squeezed shut. "Can we talk about this later?"

Moving his attention to Oliver, who sat between them, Fendrel tried to put on a reassuring smile. "And you?"

Oliver looked down. "I had my eyes closed," he said, just above a whisper.

"That's all right." Fendrel nodded his head. "We're going to look around Lightgrass for a bit. I think you'll like it there."

While Fendrel spoke to Oliver, Venom took off as gently as possible with Fog in tow. He stayed low, and when they were close enough to the hills that cradled Lightgrass, he landed just out of the city's view.

"Now, Oliver—" Fendrel slipped down and caught Oliver as he jumped "—you can come with us, but you have to stay with Thea."

"Why?" Oliver shuffled away from Venom.

"Do you know what a wanted poster is, Oliver?" Fendrel helped Thea down.

Thea gave him a look as if to say, "watch your mouth."

"It means that there are some people who don't like me and want to find me," Fendrel explained. "And it would be safer for you to be around Thea instead."

"Aren't wanted posters for bad people?" Oliver asked, taking

Thea's hand once she was down.

Fendrel opened his mouth but found he did not have a good enough explanation for the boy. "Why don't we head over now before it gets too late." Fendrel made his way to the hill before Oliver could ask any more questions. When he reached the hill's apex, he could see the city bathing in the sun's descent. It was small, compared to Sharpdagger, with its tallest buildings being only a few stories high. "It looks like we may have an hour to search around, then we'll come back here." He blinked in surprise when Fog joined them at the hilltop.

Fog gave them a shy smile. "I thought it might look odd if you showed up without transportation, especially since we are a bit far from the nearest human city."

"Venom is all right with you leaving?" Fendrel asked as he cast an annoyed glance at the older dragon below them.

"He is not happy, but he is still letting me go." Fog's ears sank in embarrassment. "I am sorry for how he talked to you all. He is very . . . protective."

"I can see that." Fendrel sighed. "Well, thank you for being a good traveling companion so far."

"I will have a talk with him tonight. He is a little on edge about this whole situation with Mist." Fog moved one of her wings out of the way so the humans could climb on.

"Thank you." Fendrel gestured for Thea and Oliver to board with him, then added, "When we get there, if you see any humans wearing armor approaching me, run."

"Oh my." Fog shook her wings out and started a light run toward Lightgrass. "Does that happen often?"

"Not really, but more often than I'd like." Fendrel shrugged. "We should be fine."

Well, even if I get caught, I'll make sure no one else does, he told himself.

Fendrel found himself holding his breath in anticipation. Thea was sure her spell worked, but they had not tested it so close to other humans yet.

"Just remember, Fog—" Thea kept her voice at a whisper as they neared Lightgrass "—this spell only works as an illusion, so even if your tail and wings are invisible to these people, they could still feel them."

"I understand." Fog nodded. She squeezed her wings closer to her sides and curled her tail like a chameleon. "I will be careful."

Fendrel raised his hood as if it would better aid Thea's illusion.

No barriers protected the city from the surrounding wilds, save for a hip-high cobblestone wall. The city's only borders were marked by a small river and lush farmland with a gravel path cutting through to the entrance. A watchtower stood at one side of the gateway, but the window seemed to be blocked off as if it had not been used in some time. The plaza just ahead was crowded with citizens encircling armored guards on horses.

The royal guard, Fendrel thought to himself. *They couldn't have shown up at a worse time.*

Fendrel suppressed a groan. He kept his eyes away from the wall of the entrance gate, as a wanted poster lurked in his peripheral vision.

A guard at the head of the others held a folded piece of paper. He opened it and began to read from the parchment. "Loyal citizens of Sharpdagger! We bring good news from His Majesty regarding Prince Cassius. Our prince has finally selected a bride. You may know that our king has been under the weather as of late, but as he feels his strength returning, he has decided to host the wedding celebration in seven days' time. Our kingdom can rest easy knowing our future is in the good hands of future rulers."

"Which girl is this, number twelve?" Thea muttered as she smirked at Fendrel.

Fendrel entertained her remark with an eyeroll, but his thoughts were much more cynical than he let on. *Does it matter how picky the prince has been?* Fendrel wondered. *Unless his criteria involves finding someone willing to clean up the muck this kingdom calls its royal guard, then it doesn't matter who his fiancée is.*

"Let's start looking," Fendrel said as he tugged at one of Fog's wings to lead her off the city's main path. He nodded respectfully at the armored horsemen as they entered the plaza of Lightgrass.

One of the guard's horses stretched its neck out to sniff Fog. It stamped away, thrashing its head with a terrified noise.

Before Fendrel could take control of the situation, the guard of the frightened horse urged his steed to move away. He shouted at the animal as if disciplining a child. The other knights followed their comrade, laughing at his unruly transport.

With a sigh of relief, Fendrel slipped down from Fog's back. "Are you all right?"

Fog opened her mouth to speak then shut it. She nodded her head.

"I'm sorry, everyone." Thea had her hand pressed to her chest as if to calm herself. "I thought my spell would trick the eyes and the nose, but the spell must not have been strong enough to do both."

"Good to know. We'll be more careful." Fendrel stepped toward a massive message board full of wanted posters and requests to the knights. "This is our best bet."

Fog joined Fendrel at the message board and stared at the charcoal and ink script etched into the paper. She used her wing claw to flick one of the papers, marveling at its thinness.

"This mess of papers and pins?" Thea crossed her arms.

"New requests every day, it seems. See? They have dates on them." Fendrel stuck his finger on a message at the top of the board. "Thea, can you help me find anything regarding Vapor dragons? Let me know if you see anything even remotely dragon-related, or spirits in the forest, anything."

Thea got down from Fog's back. "What about dragon hunters?"

"Yes, especially them." Fendrel continued to leaf through the requests without finding anything useful.

"Well, there's a bard over there talking about the dragon hunters." Thea pointed at a gathering crowd in the plaza.

Fendrel's head whipped toward the storyteller. There was indeed a bard standing on the ledge of a fountain. After staring at the man's face for a moment, Fendrel realized he had gotten tips from this bard's stories before.

The man's mouth curved into a smile as he collected coins into his hat from the growing crowd. "Thank you, dear listeners, for your kindness and donations. Of course I will tell a tale, too incredible to be believed! I happened upon a group of dragon hunters gallivanting into the wilderness, pulling a horse-drawn wagon. And what luck to see such rare a sight as a dragon strapped down to this wagon!"

If that's true, they could be taking that dragon to the Ravine Base, Fendrel thought as he pictured a map of the Freelands in his mind. His eyes widened. *It isn't far either! This could be Mist, but even if it isn't her, I might find out where she is when we break in.*

The approach of a burly-looking man snapped Fendrel from his planning. "You three must be weary, traveling all this way without a saddle!" The stranger gestured at Fog. He wore a genuine smile framed by a bushy mustache.

"We're all right, actually. Even if we wanted one, we don't have the money for that," Fendrel lied, his head buzzing with excuses.

"No, I insist. I'm moving my family soon and need to get rid of these extra saddles before we leave. I won't charge you anything." The stranger jabbed his thumb at a stable on the far side of the plaza. He approached Fog and reached his hand out as if to rub her nose.

"The um, the horse bites, and she doesn't like saddles." Fendrel fought the itch to pull his hood farther over his face. "We've tried saddling her before, and she just throws a fit."

"Ah." The stranger nodded and put his hands on his hips. "I see . . . Well, you folks have safe travels." Despite the man's words, he did not back away. His gaze moved from Fendrel's bag to his face and lingered there. "Do I know you from somewhere? You look rather familiar."

Before Fendrel could refute, the man's eyes lit up in recognition. In a panic, Fendrel thrust his hand into his bag and pulled out two dragon scales he kept for emergencies. "If you keep quiet about this, I'll give these to you."

"I-I can't take them!" The stable owner stepped back. "I could get arrested for having those."

Fendrel flinched as the man raised his voice. He shoved the scales back where they came from. People were beginning to stare, and the guards resident of the city now had their eyes trained on the exchange. "We need to leave. Now," Fendrel whispered in Drake-tongue.

Fog's eyes widened and her ears flicked back while Fendrel helped Thea and Oliver onto her back.

Ignoring the stable owner's panicked expression, Fendrel rushed himself and his companions out of Lightgrass. He only let out the breath he was holding once they'd passed the surrounding farmland and could no longer hear people behind them.

After a few moments, Fog glanced back at him. "What happened?"

"That man recognized me." Fendrel felt a chill run through him.

That's never happened here before. This village has so few wanted posters that I've always been able to slip in and out undetected. The new posters popped into Fendrel's mind. With a groan, he thought, *I must be more noticeable now because of my painted likeness.*

Fog continued to look at him. "Why do you have dragon scales?"

"And why did you bring them out in the open? You know it's illegal to have them." Thea crossed her arms.

"I panicked. I'm sorry. I thought he might take them as a bribe for leaving us alone." Fendrel looked to Fog. "And I get them from the rivers after they've been shed. I would never take them by force."

"But *why?*" Fog had a concerned look on her face.

"Some humans use them as a second form of currency. They go for a very high price and make good bargaining chips, but it didn't work this time." Fendrel couldn't shake the feeling of dread clouding over him. He felt shame shiver down his spine. "Should I stop taking them? I thought it wasn't wrong since they were shed."

Fog shook her head. "No, if they were shed it is all right. It just seems odd that humans would find value in them. I do not understand why."

"Well, they're pretty and shiny and sometimes look better than gemstones." Thea held up one finger, then a second. "This doesn't go for all humans, but there are some spells mages can't cast unless we use dragon materials as ingredients. If I had used any for your disguise, Fog, that horse would have thought you were a horse, too."

"Really?" Fendrel scrunched his brows, perplexed. "Dragon materials make spells stronger. Why?"

"You act like I know everything there is to know about being a mage, Fendrel." Thea rolled her eyes but smiled in a joking manner. "In all seriousness, I have no idea. That's just the way it is."

Fendrel allowed himself a short laugh, but his smile died as quickly as it showed itself. "I'm sorry I took you all in there with me. You would have been in danger if things had gone south."

"No!" Fog refuted. "No, if we have to go to more human cities, I still want to be involved. It was exciting there. I have never seen writing so small and *foreign*. What was the material it was written on?"

"That would be paper," Fendrel answered. After Fog gave him a prompting look, he continued, "It's made from cloth."

"*Paper.*" Fog tried the word out. There was no Drake-tongue equivalent for it, and somehow her accent made it sound more amazing than it really was. "How do you keep from tearing it with it being so thin?"

Fendrel and Thea took turns answering her questions, with Oliver chiming in every now and then, while they returned to where they had left Venom. When they crested the hill leading to the large black dragon, their conversation died.

Venom stood from where he had been lying. "Did you find anything?"

"Not exactly. We didn't hear new specifically about Mist, but there's a chance she could be nearby in one of the dragon hunter's bases. But just because we couldn't find anything in Lightgrass doesn't mean going there was completely useless." Fendrel steeled himself for Venom's retort.

When Venom simply sighed and said, "You are right," Fendrel blinked in shock.

"This is unfortunate, but we must press on." Venom looked Fendrel in the eye. "I thought about what you said earlier, and I agree. We must leave no stone unturned. Even if it appears insignificant, we must examine every hint to the fullest extent. It seems your experience may be more fruitful than mine."

"What do you mean?" Fendrel approached the Dusk dragon, with the others following close behind.

"I have spent decades hunting rogues, but you have dedicated yourself to finding dragons who still have their sanity. We are not looking for a rogue, so your perspective is more useful to us." Venom bowed his head. "I apologize for my arrogance in thinking my methods would be enough for this investigation."

This is . . . a welcome surprise, Fendrel thought.

"And as for you, mage—" Venom turned to Thea and bowed his head again "—I apologize for my explosive accusation. Though I know my excuse will not suffice, I must give a reason for my behavior. My tribe has had a history of being harmed by the effects of magic, and I sometimes lose my temper when those I care for have been wronged. I promise it will not happen again."

Thea gave him an odd look as if she did not believe him. "Th-thank you. I don't get apologized to often."

Venom turned his attention to Fog and Oliver. "Fog, I apologize for letting you see me in such a state. And, child, I apologize if I frightened you."

After the others stated their forgiveness, Venom stood to his full height. "Now, the only information you could garner was inconclusive?" he asked.

Fendrel nodded. "A bard said hunters had captured a new dragon recently. Usually I would not believe him, since it seemed like he was making it up for money, but I have gotten good tips from that bard before. And he reminded me that there *is* a dragon-hunter base nearby. If Mist isn't there, we might still be able to find information on where she could be."

"I see." Venom paused as if in thought. "Very well. Let us keep flying until sundown. Then, we should all get some rest and leave at daybreak."

Fendrel glanced at the sun's position once more and gathered they still had a few hours of daylight left. He waited for Venom to crouch before climbing on. As he pulled Oliver and Thea up behind him, Fendrel said, "Thank you for listening to me."

"You should not have to thank me. Being on a team implies we should take all ideas into account." Venom tilted his head. "Speaking of which, does anyone else have a suggestion?"

Thea raised her hand. "There's another village nearby where all the residents are mages. They might know something."

"Is that the place with all the strange-looking buildings and unwelcoming faces?" Fendrel squinted at her suspiciously.

"They're *unique* buildings, and yes. They could tell you weren't a mage," Thea said as she waved her hand dismissively. "They're very wary of outsiders."

"Do you want to take the scales with you as incentive for getting information?" Fendrel was already reaching into his bag.

If they won't help me get out of trouble, then I don't need them anymore.

"I will *gladly* take them off your hands." Thea smiled. "But I'll use them for any emergency spells on our travels. I don't need to bargain with my fellow mages. They'll tell me anything." Thea stretched out her hand and accepted the scales once Fendrel retrieved them form his bag. "And I'll take Oliver with me, too. He should stay as far from any danger as possible."

"Good idea." Venom nodded. He spread his wings and lifted off. "You know how to find the village from here?"

"Definitely." Thea pointed to the south.

"Fog, I do not want you being exposed to danger as well. Could you accompany them while Fendrel and I investigate the dragon hunters?" Venom gave the Vapor dragon an expectant look.

Fog was nodding before Venom finished his question. "Yes, I will go with them. But if you two get hurt, you *must* tell me when we reconnect."

"That village won't see through the disguising spell?" Fendrel asked as he eyed the vine woven around Fog's wing claw.

"They may or may not." Thea shrugged. "It won't make much of a difference. As long as Fog stays with me, no one will be afraid of a dragon in their midst."

"We are agreed, then." Venom looked relieved. They flew onward over the plains as the sun sunk lower. When the color of the sky melded from the bright hues of sunset to a dark, dusky purple, the dragons descended. The grass was taller here, far from any man-made roads, and rose to Fendrel's knee.

"I will keep watch," Venom proclaimed as Fendrel pulled a few caribou fur blankets from his bag.

"When do you want me to take over for you?" Fendrel asked. He handed two of the blankets to Oliver and Thea, then spread the third out for himself.

"There will be no need for that." Venom laid in the grass but kept his head held high. "Dusk dragons can remain aware of our surroundings even while asleep."

Fendrel nodded. He laid on the blanket and wrapped himself up the best he could. Stars began to poke through the sky like needles in a pincushion. Their slow yet steady appearances lured Fendrel into a calm slumber.

CHAPTER 10: FENDREL

A DREAM INVADED FENDREL'S SLEEP. Another memory.

He walked down the streets of Sharpdagger. It was as busy as ever, and the glaring sun above made it hard for Fendrel to traverse the roads without bumping into a few strangers. A man rushed toward him with his head on a constant swivel. The sheen of a dragon egg shone under his coat.

The glimmer caught Fendrel's eye. He bumped into the man's shoulder, on purpose for the first time that morning, and reached for the egg, but the smuggler pulled away. The man gritted his teeth and groaned, "Watch where you're going."

"You shouldn't kidnap dragon eggs." Fendrel once again reached to snatch the egg away, but it was moved out of his reach. The surrounding crowd became stagnant as people began to watch.

The man's voice lightened. "Ha! I didn't steal it. It was abandoned."

"You're a liar." Fendrel clenched his fists. "They wouldn't just abandon their eggs. You bought that from someone, didn't you?"

The man gave him an incredulous look. "It was sitting in the sand by itself. Obviously, no one cared about it."

Fendrel had spent enough time walking the eastern coastline to know Water dragons let their eggs warm in the sun to help them hatch faster. The egg was probably only alone for a short time before it had been abducted. Fendrel said, "You don't know anything about them."

"And you do?" The man eyed Fendrel head to toe. "Don't tell me you're some kind of freak who cares more about monsters than your own kind. If you care so little about other humans, then you can get out of our city!"

Horses' hooves clopped on the cobblestone road, getting closer by the second. Approaching from the outer ring of the crowd was an armored guard.

Shooting one last glare at the smuggler, Fendrel pulled his hood over his face and cut through the crowd. He ducked into alleys and followed a flow of merchants exiting through the city gates. Once there, he broke free from the travelers and traced his way along Sharpdagger's stone wall.

Fendrel sighed in frustration. If he had tried a third time to steal the egg away, it could have gotten damaged. He hoped if the knights found the egg, they would be so afraid of its parents' wrath that they would return it to the beach. Fendrel walked toward the crescent-shaped grove surrounding the city wall, where he had tied a horse to a tree. Upon releasing the horse, he heard approaching footsteps.

"Hey!" a young woman called out.

With a tense body, Fendrel turned around.

The woman ran toward him. Something wrapped in cloth was tucked under her arm. As she came near, she slowed to a walk, her breathing labored. "It's a little heavier than I thought." She laughed and unwrapped the bundle. It was the egg. She held it out to him with outstretched arms. "Here!"

Fendrel cautiously accepted the egg. "Why are you doing this?"

"Because I don't like that man. He tried to back out of paying me about a week ago because he thinks 'freaks like you don't deserve payment.'" She gave a nervous laugh. "And because you're like me, sort of. The way he looked at you told me everything I need to know about how people like him treat people like us. We've got to look out for each other, right? I'm a mage. My name's Thea." She smiled and extended her hand.

"I'm Fendrel. I'm a . . . uh, dragon liberator, I suppose." Fendrel shook her hand.

Thea cocked her head to the side. "Liberator, huh? So what are you going to do with that one?" she asked, pointing at the egg. "It can't find its parents when it's in a shell."

Fendrel gave her a confused stare. "I'll find its parents."

"Can I come with you?" There was excitement in her eyes.

"Why? We don't know each other." Fendrel cautiously stepped away from her.

Thea shrugged. "Like I said, we should look out for each other. I'll make sure that whenever you come to the city, you'll have anything you need. Deal?"

What part of this is a deal? Fendrel wondered. What does she get in return?

He searched her face for an answer. There was nothing but genuine curiosity and eagerness in Thea's expression. "I suppose," Fendrel replied.

"Great!" The mage clasped her hands to her chest.

Fendrel stored the melon-sized egg in his bag and mounted the horse, with Thea climbing on behind him. He grabbed the reins and guided the horse onto a trail that would take them to the coast.

Although the eggshell's color was indistinct from eggs of other tribes, Fendrel could tell from the shape it was a Water dragon's egg. Shiny and perfectly round, like a pearl.

After a few hours of riding in uncomfortable silence, they reached a hill that sloped down to a black sand beach ridden with barnacle-covered rocks. The waves were calm, softly tumbling over the sea stones.

Squinting, Fendrel saw a Water dragon, its head submerged, surveying the shallow waters. He dismounted the horse and took careful steps down the slope. His hand fished the egg out of his bag.

As the sand under Fendrel's feet slipped to the bottom of the hill, the Water dragon's ears swiveled as if listening to his every move. When Fendrel reached the bottom, his foot kicked a loose pebble, sending it skittering into the calm waves.

The dragon whipped his head out of the water and eyed Fendrel. When his eyes landed on the egg, he roared and flared his wings.

Fendrel took one short step forward, then another.

Hissing, the dragon flew to the edge of the rocks, throwing a huge spray of seawater into the air. His wings formed menacing arcs above Fendrel, and his claws curled around the rocks with a grating noise.

Avoiding the dragon's gaze, Fendrel held out the egg.

The dragon stared at Fendrel, his growling growing quiet. He scooped the egg into one of his paws and cradled it to his chest. When Fendrel looked up, the dragon uttered a small snort and turned. With two mighty wing strokes, he flew over the rocks and dove into deeper water.

Fendrel smiled as Thea ran up beside him. He glanced at her, cleared his throat, and put on a straight face. "I should go now."

Thea followed him up the sand hill. With a chuckle, she said, "I can help you! If you tell me secrets about dragons that nobody else knows, I'll craft some spells for you."

So that's what she wanted with me, Fendrel thought.

She stuck her hand out again. "I'll tell you what. I'll enchant that bag of yours so you can have as many things in there as you like. Deal? Anything that can fit in the bag as if it were empty will stay in the bag, no matter how much else you stuff inside."

"There has to be more that you want from me than that." Fendrel gave her a confused stare.

"Not really." Thea shrugged. "I don't have any friends in Sharpdagger, but it's the best place for business. I assume you don't have friends there either, so perhaps we could look out for each other?"

Fendrel couldn't help but smile. Her charm was growing on him. "Deal." He shook her hand again, wondering how many deals they were going to end up making.

"Great." Thea smiled. "So, can you take me back to the city? I don't have any way to get back home."

Fendrel nodded, finally letting his smile show freely. "Sure."

Fendrel awoke at the sound of whispering coming from the other side of their miniscule camp. One was deep and had a bit of growl underlining each word while the other was soft and a little frightened. Fendrel lay still on his blanket and kept his eyes shut as he listened to who he now realized was Venom and Fog.

"When have I ever given you a reason to worry about me?" Venom asked gently.

"You have not, but these are *dragon hunters*. They are called that for a reason." Fog's tail thumped the ground as if to add weight to her statement. "What happens if you get hurt?"

"I will be fine."

Venom's footfalls sounded as if they were drawing nearer to Fendrel, so he continued to lie perfectly still.

"We both will," Venom said. "Now, it is daybreak. It is time to leave."

Thank the stars he's as keen on going to this dragon-hunter base as I am.

Fendrel felt the cool of the dragon's shadow fall over him. Before he could pretend to wake up, the Dusk dragon spoke to him.

"You are a terrible actor." Venom's words sounded only inches from him. "I heard your breathing change as soon as you awoke."

Fendrel felt his ears burn in embarrassment. He sat up. "I didn't want to interrupt you. It sounded personal."

"Hmm." Venom raised his head. "It was, but now we must go. How far away is this dragon-hunter base?"

"Not far at all." Fendrel stood and rolled his blanket to pack up. "This fortress has sky-viewing scouts, so we should walk there. It isn't safe to fly anywhere near that place. Even the Air dragons have started avoiding that end of their domain."

"Very well," Venom said as he stepped away.

Fendrel walked to where Thea lay. He stooped down and tapped her on the shoulder. "Time to go."

The mage gave a hefty sigh and pushed herself up. Before she went to sleep, she had gathered her braids into a protective satin scarf, which she still wore. She woke Oliver and took his hand, leading him to Fog.

"Don't get into trouble over there. I'll see you all later tonight,"

Fendrel called after Thea and Oliver. He packed their blankets into his bag.

Thea threw a noncommittal wave his way. "*You* stay out of trouble."

Venom began to walk away from the others, but then he looked over his shoulder at Fendrel and asked, "Would you remind me about this village they are headed towards?"

"I don't know much about it," Fendrel replied, following him. "I just know the people didn't like me being there."

After a pause, Venom gave him a quizzical look. "You're going to walk too?"

Fendrel nodded. "I think better when I walk, and we need a plan for when we get to the hunters' base."

Venom chuckled. "Will you be able to keep up?"

"I used to hunt caribou with a pull-your-own-weight veteran in knee-deep snow." Fendrel gave him a tired smile. "I'll be fine."

"Veteran." Venom made a noise of intrigue. "I did not realize the humans here were involved in a war recently."

Fendrel shook his head. "He was an Ice dragon."

"Interesting," Venom said. "Who was he?"

"His name?" Fendrel's eyes darted to Venom then back to the hilly fields ahead. "Blizzard. His clan, the Inviers, lived at the western end of Frost Lake."

"You said he is a veteran. So he fought in the War Across the Sea?" Venom jutted his chin out in the direction of the Freelands' sister continent, too far for the naked eye to see.

From what Fendrel had been told about the war, it was between the humans and dragons of the Fauna Wilds. The Wilds' dragons were losing ground and asked for aid from the Freelanders, but even with their combined efforts the humans still prevailed. The war ended when Fendrel was but a child, just shy of a year before he met Blizzard.

Fendrel nodded. "Yes. He told me he fought at the battle of Broken Wings. I remember him saying he would have stayed longer if he could, but he was commanded to retreat."

Venom gave a respectful nod. "I was at that battle. He is a brave dragon to have wanted to stay longer than he had to. How did you meet him?"

"He . . ." Fendrel studied the ground sullenly. "He and his wife found my brother and me during a snowstorm after my mother passed."

A moment of silence followed in the wake of his statement. Fendrel knew if he concentrated hard enough, he could almost feel the cold and the hunger from all those years ago. The sleet- and snow-filled air was too blinding white to see through. He remembered how little his clothes did to shield him from the elements and how he believed he was losing his mind when the form of a massive dragon manifested out of the storm. Despite how dire his situation had been, Fendrel was comforted by the memory. It had been the start of a brighter time in his childhood.

"They took you in." Venom's voice softened. The black dragon's voice snapped Fendrel from his reminiscing.

With a nod, Fendrel continued, "After the attack on Stone Edge, my brother and I wanted to get as far away from the rogue as possible. Since the rogue was a Fire dragon, we thought we'd be safer somewhere cold. It took us a *long* time to get to Frost Lake. When we finally did Blizzard and Flurry found us, thankfully, before we froze or starved to death."

"You will have to introduce us some day." Venom kept his gaze on Fendrel. He looked at him as though they had known each other for years. The look in Venom's eyes made Fendrel forlorn, like part of him was missing and he only then realized how incomplete he was.

Fendrel looked away. "I can't introduce you . . . They died."

The two became quiet again. Venom's moth opened and closed a number of times as though he were searching for the right words. Finally, in a much softer voice, Venom said, "I am . . . very sorry, young one."

I said too much, Fendrel thought. *I don't want to talk about this anymore.*

"The dragon hunters' base is just ahead." Fendrel quickened his pace, passing Venom. He pointed forward to where the ground dropped off into a steep ravine. "I doubt the tip I got was old, so the capture must have happened two days ago at most."

When they reached the cliff's lip, Fendrel continued, "They're traveling by horse-drawn wagon, with a dragon tied down. That means they'd have to go all the way around to the ravine's entrance. Huh . . ." Fendrel spied into the ravine. Upon first glance he saw no trace of life. "We might be here early."

"You say it is here—" Venom reached the edge and peered down "—but I do not see a settlement."

"It's in that cave," Fendrel replied, pointing to a gaping opening fixed in the wall of the ravine's opposing side. "They house the wagons there, and the actual base is farther inside. That's the only entrance."

When Fendrel laid on his stomach at the edge of the lip, Venom laid beside him and sniffed the air. Venom said, "I smell other humans somewhere down there."

"Those are the scouts. They're camouflaged behind boulders and bushes. If you want to spot them, look for the gleam of dragon teeth." Fendrel scanned for hunters with his own eyes. There was grass covering the ground they lay on, but the ravine walls and floor were made of harsh, reddish-brown stone. What few plants inside were wiry and dull as if a lack of water made them lose their color. Boulders jutted up near the stone walls, some as tall as a farmer's house. Wind whistled through the rocky passage, disguising any sound that may emanate from below.

"Why are we looking for dragon teeth?" Venom's voice sounded distraught.

"Every hunter has the teeth of the dragon they slayed sewn to their uniform. It's to show rank." Fendrel focused on a prickly bush that moved as if something were taking refuge within. At first, he thought it was the wind, but this bush did not move with the same grace as one filtering a breeze through its branches. "One tooth on each shoulder for lower-ranking members, all the way up to Sadon, who has five teeth on each shoulder."

Venom's deep voice rumbled in a thoughtful hum. "That is informative."

A slice of light, caused by the serrated edge of a dragon's tooth, shone through the prickly bush.

"There." Fendrel pointed at the spot. "I think the safest bet is to say there are three scouts out at any time."

"Why that specific?" Venom inched forward.

"Well, the last time I was here, there were only two scouts, and I lured them away with a signal fire. I doubt they'll fall for that again." Fendrel shrugged. "We need a new distraction for at least one of us to sneak in."

"Is it not an option to dispatch them?" Venom glanced at Fendrel.

"Dispatch as in to kill them?" Fendrel felt his blood run cold. "No, we're not going to kill them."

"If we lead them away then sneak in, there is a chance they could follow us, and we would be caught between hunters on both sides." Venom gave him an incredulous look. "What is the good in letting them live?"

"We don't even know what rank they are yet. They could be one-fanged." Fendrel heard his voice rising in defensiveness. "If they're that low ranked, they've probably never even killed a dragon and were stationed here so they wouldn't be liabilities."

"You just said their ranks come from the dragons they have slain."

"I meant *fought*. Even if you fail to kill the dragon, as long as you were brave enough to fight it, you get initiated." Fendrel refused to meet the dragon's eyes, but he could feel Venom's stare bore into him.

"You are very well-versed in their customs, Fendrel."

"It's all part of the research." Fendrel bit the inside of his cheek. "We need a distraction. But killing them is out of the question."

Venom stared at Fendrel for a few long moments. "Very well. If that is the way you operate, and you have been successful thus far, I will comply with your methods. However, I will not hesitate to defend myself if the situation escalates."

"Thank you." Fendrel took a moment to gather his thoughts. "It could take me a bit to scale down to the ravine floor. Could you lead the scouts away? I doubt you'll be in any danger."

"How so?"

"Well, scouts aren't exactly the most proficient in fighting. If they were good at hunting dragons, they wouldn't be standing watch over dragons that have already been caught." Fendrel nodded back at the moving bush. "And you're a Dusk dragon, so if any of them were to get zealous and pursue you, the rest of the scouts would join him to make sure he didn't get himself killed."

"Who is to say they will follow and not just alert any hunters inside?" Venom's eyes traveled among the passage's hiding spots.

"We can't know for sure, but in my experience, scouts have always had big-enough egos to think they don't need any help." Fendrel gave Venom a smile, trying to look as convincing as possible. "Besides, sitting outside for hours with next to nothing to do makes them itch for excitement."

Venom made an indiscernible noise.

"Do you trust me?" Fendrel looked Venom in the eyes.

The dragon tapped his claw on the ground as he thought. "We will see after this experience. How long do you need this distraction to last?"

"As long as you can manage it. There's a small system of connected caves down the ravine you can lose them in." Fendrel pointed off to

Kassidy J. Ridenour

their right.

Venom nodded. "Do not get caught."

Before Fendrel could respond, the black dragon launched himself into the air. He effortlessly glided to the valley floor, making sure to strike the hunter-hiding bush with his tail. Venom tucked his wings in and landed with a thud, kicking up dust around his paws. As soon as his talons touched down, his nose was to the ground like a bloodhound searching for foxes. He made a show of flaring his nostrils with each sniff and lashed his tail.

Agonizing seconds ticked by.

Are they going to chase him? Or are they too afraid to come out?

Fendrel was about to sigh in resignation when the bush rustled again.

Almost in unison, three scouts poked their heads out of their hiding spots. They crept into the open a good several yards behind Venom and readied slings with fist-sized, cloth pouches.

They're using startlers on a Dusk dragon? Fendrel almost laughed in disbelief. *They expect those little noise pouches are going to scare him?*

The first pouch was flung forward and sloppily hit against the ground. It exploded with a resounding pop and smoked.

Venom looked over his shoulder at the pitiful attack. Fendrel could almost see him roll his eyes before he snarled and pretended to flee.

With shouts of shocked accomplishment, the hunters stalked after Venom. The single fang on each of their shoulders bounced as they picked up their pace to keep up with their target.

Fendrel took one more glance at the base's entrance before he began to climb down the ravine slope. Rough, jagged rocks bit into his fingers. As long as he was careful, Fendrel knew the sunbaked mud would make a good grip for his boots. A few cuts, scrapes, and risky slides later, Fendrel found himself at the bottom. Covered in dust, he scurried to the other side of the ravine and entered the flat-floored cave's mouth.

He strained his ears and tilted his head. There was nothing but silence. Just him and a row of empty wagons. Each wagon was neatly lined against one side of the cave with plenty of room to walk beside them. Even here the wind whistled, but fainter than out in the open. A shiver traveled down Fendrel's spine from the shadow cast by the cave's interior. He rolled his shoulders as if to psych himself up and continued onward.

I need this mission to go off without a hitch if I want Venom to trust me. We won't find Mist if we're constantly at each other's throats. I just hope he doesn't pry any further into my past.

CHAPTER 11: CASSIUS

CASSIUS SEQUESTERED HIMSELF INSIDE A ring of hedges amidst the royal gardens. The only entrance to his hiding spot was a small slit off the gravel path. In the center of the ring was a gazebo, but Cassius sat in the grass with his back pressed against the prickly hedge wall. He felt cold with sweat as he heard footsteps approach.

All morning he had been trying to sneak into the guards' training area. He wanted to learn more about their animosity for the Liberator, and eavesdropping seemed like a good enough way to do so. However, in order to get there, he had to pass through the gardens.

The voice of Cassius' twin sister chimed, "Good morning, soon-to-be sister!"

Cassius paled.

Adila is here. The woman I chose to marry, but did I truly make that decision? Cassius wondered. He shivered at the thought of his fiancée. There was something about her that made the hair on the back of his neck stand on-end.

"Good morning, princess," said another woman's voice, this one solemn. Even from the minimal interactions Cassius had with her, he knew it was his fiancée.

He grabbed fistfuls of grass and continued listening.

"How has your morning been?" There was Sadie's cheery voice again. Silence followed her response.

"My lady, it is rude not to respond to your princess." The stomp of guard boots accompanied this new voice.

Cassius took a deep breath and peeked around the edge of the hedge.

Sadie wore her favorite dress, which she used whenever she wanted to make a good impression. It was a brilliant gown as yellow as her hair.

To Cassius, she had always been like the sun, cheerful and bright with eyes as blue as the sky. Completely opposite to Cassius with his lanky build, dirty blonde locks and hazel eyes, Sadie looked like their late mother.

"Oh, it's all right." The princess waved her hand dismissively at her guard ant, who stood just behind her.

Adila stood facing them with a flower clutched to her chest. She gently stroked the petals with her fingers and kept her misty gaze down. She had gray eyes and wavy, silky black hair that spilled over her shoulders and back. Her skin was pale, almost as white as the moon. Resting against her collarbone was a heart-shaped pendant that hung from a silver necklace. Despite her long-sleeved blue dress and the warm weather, Adila looked cold.

Cassius pulled his eyes away. The first time he looked at her, three days earlier, he felt trapped as if he were a puppet on a string. He had completely lost control of his words and his actions. It felt like what Cassius imagined magic to feel—invasive and startling. All he wanted in that moment was to leave the room, but his legs refused to obey.

How am I supposed to leave when I cannot even control my body? I was stuck speaking to her—no, something was speaking through me to her. It must be a spell, but does it activate on proximity or on eye contact?

His prior encounter with Adila only accounted for half of his worries. The day she showed up, Cassius began to feel ill. It was not the same type of illness that came with the winter and resulted in sniffles and coughs. This sickness made him physically weak, soured his stomach, and only came after he ate something. Cassius had taken to eating less of his meals, yet even the smallest bite worsened his symptoms.

Is Adila poisoning me? Cassius feared. He wished he could sink into the ground. As his eyes slowly raised to witness the scene again, he heard Sadie sigh.

"Lady Adila just isn't comfortable with me *yet*," Sadie said to her guard, leaning forward with an endearing smile. She stepped closer to the other woman. "I see you looking at those flowers a lot. Do you want us to use them in your wedding?"

Adila breathed in sharply and dropped the flower, clutching her hands against her chest as if the plant had burned her. She stepped away and shook her head as tears brimmed in her eyes.

Sadie traced the back of her finger against Adila's cheek just as a tear raced down. She waved her ants off and grasped Adila's shoulders gently. "Everything is all right," Sadie reassured, though her voice was so faint Cassius strained to hear her.

Adila shook her head again as more tears ran down her cheeks. She cupped her face in her hands as sobs made her shudder.

"We're going to be a family soon, so you can speak with me any time you'd like," Sadie said, brushing Adila's hair out of her face. "You can trust me, I promise. But I can't help you if I don't know what's wrong."

Adila ripped away from the princess' grip. "I cannot tell you, even if I wanted to! I just *cannot*. I am sorry, but you must understand. Please, leave me alone."

As Sadie opened her mouth to speak, Adila hurried away, her dress flowing behind her as wispy as a cloud.

Cassius frowned when he saw the despair on his sister's face, and he hid behind the hedges once more. He waited for the princess and her ants to leave. Only once they were gone did Cassius stand and take a quick look at his surroundings. There was no one in sight, so he sped toward the training grounds. As he drew closer, a disturbing thought intruded his mind.

What if Adila put a spell on me to make me want to marry her? But, if that were the case, why is she behaving like she does not want to be here?

Perhaps . . . perhaps it is true that she is poisoning me, so she will not have to be married to me for long. That way she could remain in the palace whilst not having to spend time with me.

The thought made him pause midstride.

Perhaps I should see what she is doing. For all I know, she could be concocting more poison right now.

He changed course, heading in the way Adila had left. Cassius tried to keep his steps light while catching up with her. He passed by rows upon rows of rose bushes in bloom that boxed him in on each side and made a winding path farther into the garden.

She is heading for another of the secluded gazebos. Does she know where she is going? Cassius wondered. He dismissed the thought with a shake of his head. *Most likely not. She has only been on palace grounds for a couple of days.*

After a few minutes of not finding Adila, Cassius began to ponder if she had gone a different way. Then, he rounded a corner in the maze of roses and came face-to-face with the strange woman, nearly slamming into her.

Adila jumped back, startled. At the sight of her, Cassius felt overwhelming dread. The corners of his vision darkened with swirling shapes that changed color and size, leaving him stunned and blinding his periphery. The unmistakable pressure of a headache accompanied the shapes.

Not again! Cassius could feel his heart racing. *The feeling is back again.*

Cassius' mouth quirked up in a smile without his own doing. He reached out his hand to Adila, palm up. His arm was no longer his own, and neither were his words. "I was looking for you! Here, let me lead you out. This garden's layout can be confusing to navigate."

"I . . ." Adila took a nervous step backward. "That is all right. I know my way back." She made a move to sidestep him, but the prince blocked her path.

"I insist." Cassius reached for her hand once more.

Adila pushed past him and rushed through the rose-bordered maze. Once she was out of sight, Cassius' vision cleared of the shapes and his headache vanished. He wiggled his fingers to make sure he could control them again. Once he was certain he was his normal self, Cassius let out a shaky sigh of relief.

It appears she wants nothing to do with me. That is a good sign, I think. But, why do I get those strange headaches whenever I am near her? I have never heard of an illness like this before.

Lost in his thoughts, Cassius did not realize Sadie was behind him until he turned around.

"Oh!" Cassius said in surprise. He forced a smile to his face, but when he saw his sister's, his smile dropped. "Are you all right?" he asked.

Sadie's eyes were downcast. She fiddled with her dress skirt. The princess's ants stood just behind her.

"Sadie? Are you all right?" Cassius repeated.

The princess finally looked up at him. She put on a performative grin, much more convincing that Cassius' own, and said, "I'm fine, I just wish Zoricus were here. He's the one who introduced us to Lady Adila, so I wonder if perhaps he knows what is troubling her. I saw her come from this way. Did you try to cheer her up, too?"

"I—" Cassius rolled his shoulders to disguise a shiver. "She did not want to speak with me . . . Sadie, do you get a strange feeling when you are around her? Like something about her gaze draws you in?" Cassius searched his sister's expression as he spoke, trying to gage her response before it happened.

Sadie let out a close-mouthed laugh. "No, Cas. I'm not the one who fancies her," she teased.

"That is the problem. It is not a nice feeling." Cassius could sense his hope fleeting. "There is something off about her."

"Perhaps you simply need to spend more time with her so the two of you can get used to each other." Sadie clasped her hands in front of her chest. "Which reminds me, Father wants us all to have supper together. I hope then we can ask Adila what has been making her so upset."

"Wait. Father will be there, too?" Cassius asked as his brow scrunched with worry. "I thought he was not feeling well after last night."

"He wants to make an effort for Lady Adila feel welcome," Sadie explained. She rolled her eyes and made a face that conveyed, "I wish he would rest instead."

Cassius nodded in silent agreement. "Well, I will see you all at supper."

Sadie gave him a smile. "I hope you feel better, too, Cas."

"What do you mean?" Cassius held his breath, hoping Sadie would finally see his unease.

"You haven't been eating well recently. I hope you aren't sick like Father," said the princess.

"It is probably just nerves from having Lady Adila here," Cassius' answered, though his excuse did not sound believable even to himself. He started back out of the rose-bordered path. "I will see you tonight."

Fear seized his heart as he left, and his thoughts began to spiral. *Father and I are both feeling ill, and it started the exact same day Adila arrived. However, everyone else is fine. Is this a coincidence, or is Adila poisoning both of us? What is her plan? . . . How can I stop her?*

CHAPTER 12: FENDREL

AFTER A SINGLE STEP INTO the dragon hunters' Ravine Base, wingbeats sounded from outside the cave. The gust brought on by Venom's landing wing strokes sent a breeze Fendrel's way. Fendrel paused in his stride and waited for the black dragon to join him.

Venom hunched down to keep his horns from scraping the cave roof. He crawled forward and gave Fendrel an indiscernible look as he said, "I left the hunters alive in the caves. They are asleep."

"Thank you," Fendrel whispered.

"Tell me, how do you typically go about these infiltrations?" Venom stared ahead where a far-off light danced on the walls.

"I eavesdrop on the hunters to see if they'll say where they're keeping or killing the dragons." Fendrel gestured at the path forward. "Not all the rooms are always occupied, so I listen to make sure I don't waste my time searching an empty room."

Venom cocked his head to the side. "What do you mean 'or killed?' I thought all bases killed the dragons they capture."

"Some hideouts harvest from dragons. Others are designed to train hunters how to kill," Fendrel explained. "This place has always been a harvest base, since they don't have an arena."

Venom's snout wrinkled in disgust. Fendrel thought he could see Venom's fangs twitch as the dragon asked, "Where are these murderers?"

"This way." Fendrel pointed down the passageway. He ventured farther into the cave, keeping his steps light.

Venom followed close behind, crouched like a prowling wild cat. Torches adorned the walls the closer they crept to the farther light. It was well-lit enough for them to avoid tripping on stones and stalagmites, but some crevices remained dark as night.

They peered around a corner to see the torches had been replaced by a large bonfire in the center of a round chamber. Weapons, chains, and snappers hung on one of the walls. There were hunters swarming around the bonfire, teasing and shoving each other despite the roaring flames they encircled. Ten doorways hidden behind curtains of tattered cloth were set in the wall at the back of the chamber. Fendrel remembered each passage led to a room reserved for dragons of a certain tribe. Both Fendrel and Venom quickly hid back around the corner.

"What is the plan?" Venom whispered. He lowered himself to the ground with his legs ready to spring at a moment's notice.

"Hold on." Fendrel held his hand up to stop Venom. He pressed his back against the cave wall and strained his ears to hear the hunters. For a few minutes they did nothing but joke and brag. The conversation did not seem to yield any useful information, and Fendrel found himself sliding down in defeat. But then, one of the hunters with a young, cheerful voice made Fendrel lift his head in interest.

"We're getting a new dragon here soon?" she asked.

Another hunter with an old, gruff voice, answered, "Yes. The wranglers sent someone ahead to alert us. We'll be getting one of those forest dragons."

With a disappointed groan, the younger hunter said, "There are *so many* empty cages and all we have are a taiga dragon and a lousy forest dragon? When are we going to get something more exciting?"

The only dragon they have caged up is an Ice dragon? Fendrel found himself scowling in confusion. *Why only one, and why so far from the northern bases?*

"What is it?" Venom's voice brought Fendrel out of his pondering.

"The hunters have one Ice dragon here already. The dragon being brought on the cart is from the Flora tribe." Fendrel resisted the urge to drum his fingers on his bag, lest he alert the hunters to their presence.

"I see, and no mention of Mist . . . That is disappointing, but we must free these two." Venom glared into the chamber, then recoiled his head. "How?"

Fendrel shifted his stance into a crouch. "We need another distraction. Something big enough so they won't notice me."

"All right. I know what to do." Venom's tail swung in excitement. "That room is large enough for me to move around in easily. I can charge inside and keep their attention on me."

"Are you insane?" Fendrel shot him an incredulous look. He fought

The Dragon Liberator: Escapade

to keep his voice from rising. "You saw all the weapons in there."

"They will be too surprised at first to think about attacking." Venom angled himself toward the chamber's entrance.

Fendrel grabbed Venom's foreleg as if to keep him in place, knowing full well the dragon could push him aside with little effort. Fendrel warned, "There are at least ten hunters in there."

Venom let out a deep sigh. He looked at Fendrel and nudged him with his wing claw. "If I need to, I will lead them outside where I will have more space. Trust in my abilities."

Fendrel stared into Venom's eyes with as much stubbornness as he could muster, but his expression did little to quell the determination in Venom's face. He looked down briefly, then took his hand off the dragon's foreleg. "All right."

The black dragon gave Fendrel a curt nod before he sprang around the corner and burst into the circular room. He roared and smacked the flaming logs of the bonfire against a wall, dislodging most of the mounted weapons. With shocked exclamations, the hunters backed away. Those nearest the logs dropped to the ground and cupped their hands over their necks. Venom flung a hunter against the wall with his tail, and the young man crumpled on the ground, unconscious.

As the fog of confusion lifted, the gathered humans snapped into action. Although few weapons remained undamaged, every hunter got their hands on something to fight with.

"Watch his mouth and claws!" one hunter shouted right before he was swept off his feet by Venom's wing.

Rushing to his aid, another of the fighters was pinned under Venom's massive paws.

Fendrel peered around the corner at the hallways behind the battle. Picking up a bent metal spear from the ground, he stuck close to the walls as he made his way toward the first hallway. The hunters paid him no mind, seeming to ignore his lack of dragon leather or ranking fangs. Still, Fendrel kept his eyes peeled for anyone who might recognize he was not supposed to be there. He finally reached the doorway that would lead him to the Ice dragon's cage. "TAIGA" was marked above the entrance. He pulled the curtain aside and walked down the short, torch-lit hall. He pulled his caribou-bone pendant necklace out from his shirt as he neared the end.

This is an Ice dragon, so they should recognize the pendant's craftsmanship, no matter what clan they're from, Fendrel thought. However, after one look at

82

the captive, he found there was no need to display his necklace.

A massive rogue Ice dragon, just a bit taller and bulkier than Venom, lay in a cage. Her blood-red stripes looked like scars across her white fur. As soon as she saw Fendrel, she lunged at the bars with an awful crashing sound, nearly tossing the cage onto its side. She gnawed and scratched, screeched and snarled. Purple-stained saliva flew from her jaws with every snap. The Ice dragon seemed to have gone insane. Then again, all rogues behaved in the same manner when they encountered humans.

Bile rose in Fendrel's throat. He choked it down and left the Ice dragon's room. With his back pressed against the wall, Fendrel tried to distract his mind before repressed fears could claim him. But he was too late. The memories had already started to creep back in.

This was far from the first rogue Ice dragon he had ever met. He killed one before in a bitter fight for survival. The encounter had terrified him, but what frightened him more than almost losing his life was how similar that rogue looked to dragons from his home in Frost Lake. His clan, the Inviers, believed rogues used to be normal dragons who became mysteriously ill, and with the resemblance that rogue shared with the Inviers Fendrel was inclined to believe the legend. For all he knew, that rogue could have been a cousin he never got to meet before it was driven mad by sickness

However, the Ice dragon who was howling and screeching for him to come back into the room was a stranger. Its roars of fury made Fendrel flinch. He squeezed his eyes shut and willed his mind to block out her cries.

She isn't going to stop until she can't smell me anymore, Fendrel realized. He forced himself out of the hall and checked the other rooms, just to make sure the hunters were telling the truth about their number of captives. No more dragons. Fendrel felt his pounding heart settle back into its normal rhythm and breathed a sigh of relief.

Why are the hunters refraining from capturing dragons? Are they sending more dragons southward to train new recruits?

The commotion in the main chamber continued. Fendrel peeked his head in. Almost all of the hunters lay still and their weapons were strewn across the floor. Venom threw the two remaining hunters against the wall with his forelegs. His chest heaved. There were cuts around his legs and tail, and as Fendrel watched, the dragon's wings sank a little from the exertion.

Fendrel rushed forward and eyed some of the bloodier cuts. Glad to see the injuries were not major, he took a step back.

"So how is the captive?" Venom's words came between gasps.

"Still in the cage. She's a rogue." Fendrel nodded his head at the hallway.

Venom growled. "What are you going to do with it?"

"I usually . . . I—" Fendrel averted his gaze.

"You leave them?" Venom asked.

"N-no—" Fendrel cleared his throat. "I kill them. It's too dangerous to free them, and if I leave them, the hunters will be able to harvest more materials. That's just more tools to weaponize and trade."

"I see. I had hoped there would be lives to save here," Venom said, disappointed. He looked at the unconscious hunters around the room. "And what do you do with them?"

"These are all two-fanged hunters, so they're well-trained. But since they're stationed at a harvesting base it's likely they don't do much killing." Fendrel gestured at them. "For those kinds of hunters, I just tie them up and light a signal fire for any patrolling guards to arrest."

"What happens if these murderers get free?" Venom asked. "They could cause even more harm with their rage than they ever would have if they died."

"Not all of them deserve it." Fendrel's tone grew defensive, and his ears burned in embarrassment. "You seemed upset about killing the rogue. Why is it all right to kill those hunters but not her?"

Venom snorted. "That rogue will keep the dragon hunters busy enough to neglect searching for *sane* dragons. No dragon hunter has done a lick of good for us."

Fendrel shook his head, already regretting his next words before they left his mouth. "You don't know that."

"And you do? Do you hear yourself?" Venom shouted. His snout wrinkled in disgust as the spines on his neck bristled. "What would your mother think?"

The dragon's words made Fendrel jolt. He glared up at Venom. "She would say to have grace. You of all beings should know that. You're the one who got to with her." He grabbed a long chain that lay on the ground, one of the few tools left undamaged by the fight. "I'm tying them up and letting them live, whether you agree with me or not."

Venom stood in silence while Fendrel struggled to drag the hunters, one by one, to the mouth of the cave. He sat them with their backs pressed against each other, but the hunters kept falling forward before Fendrel could tie them all together. He had never handled this many by himself before. After a few more fruitless attempts, he groaned in frustration and dropped the chain.

As Venom emerged from the cave, Fendrel avoided meeting his eyes. After a moment of stifling silence, Venom spoke, "Your mother was an enigma to me in many ways, even while we discovered more of each other's lives." He sat on his haunches and held the hunters together with his front paws. "The dragon hunters were not around while she was alive, so I do not know how she would feel, but I do see her in you. Even if I do not understand your beliefs, I am willing to listen."

Fendrel took the chain back in his hands and wrapped it around the hunters as many times as he could before retrieving a staff from within the cave to stick between the links. The staff was already bent, and with a little more effort he managed to warp it into a makeshift lock. Fendrel sighed and stepped away. After a few seconds of silence, he answered, "I don't think I'm ready to talk about it yet."

The Dusk dragon nodded. "Whenever you are ready, tell me. Now, as for the scouts I led away?"

"I'll show you—" Fendrel glanced into the cave "—after we take care of the rogue here."

After a short flight to and from the cave system down the ravine, Fendrel and Venom combined their efforts to bring the scouts back and tie them up with their comrades. Venom's cuts had stopped bleeding, but his claws were now stained with the Ice dragon's blood. It was an easy slaying, given Fendrel had put the dragon to sleep with his knock-out powder. Even still, he looked away while Venom slit the rogue's throat.

"What was that substance you put on the rogue's face?" Venom asked. He stared at the new additions to the ring of hunters.

"That's knock-out powder." Fendrel sprinkled a pinch on the noses of each hunter. "Dragon hunters buy it from sea traders since the ingredients don't grow here."

"Hm," Venom hummed thoughtfully. He aimed his sights at a bend in the ravine where the incoming hunters should appear. He lifted his snout and sniffed. "I smell a horse, dragon blood, and citrus . . . a pair of

The Dragon Liberator: Escapade

humans, as well."

Fendrel blinked in surprise at how well Venom's nose could distinguish all the scents. His mouth pressed into a thin line as he pondered this new information.

If there are only two hunters, it either means they went out with the intention of obtaining a non-dangerous dragon and thus sent low-level hunters, or those are two high-level hunters who just happened to come across a Flora dragon first.

"We should be careful," Fendrel warned.

Venom angled his ears forward. "I can hear it now, the horse. It sounds agitated."

Fendrel nodded. "The hunters could be rushing it to get here sooner."

"Let us meet them halfway then," Venom said and crouched.

"This isn't what I had in mind when I said we should be careful." Fendrel shook his head but nonetheless climbed on the dragon's shoulders.

Venom lifted off, flying up to the lip of the ravine. He dug his claws into the rocks to keep steady. "There are only two hunters, and they are busy steering a wagon. We will not need to be too careful if they are occupied."

Fendrel found it a bit difficult to hold on while prepping a dagger from his bag but he managed to retrieve one without slipping from Venom's sleek scales. Venom pushed off the ravine edge and once he leveled out his flight, Fendrel also took out his small sack of knock-out powder. As he clenched the dagger's hilt between his teeth, he tied the sack around his wrist, then grabbed his dagger with his other hand.

"Are you all right back there?" Venom called over the wind.

"I'm fine, just getting ready," Fendrel answered as he grabbed Venom's spines with his free hand. "What's the plan?"

"Separate the hunters from the dragon and immobilize them." Venom began to arc his wings, sending them lower. "We are going to surprise them."

Fendrel felt like his stomach was rising into his chest. He could not tell if he was terrified of Venom's diving or excited for the encroaching fight. He felt himself lift from his seat and held on to the dragon tighter than he had ever held anything before. Even as they hurtled toward the ground, Fendrel felt a strange sense of security. He had seen dragons this size dive before and could tell Venom was being cautious in his movements so Fendrel would not fall off.

Still heading for the ravine's bend, Venom angled himself to land.

The sounds of horse's hooves and wagon wheels on uneven earth made it to Fendrel's ears.

Just as the horse and wagon appeared from around the bend, Venom swooped lower. A hunter, reins in hand, yelped in shock when Venom's wing nearly knocked him from his seat.

Even though hunters' horses were desensitized to dragons, it was impossible to train them to keep calm when one flies right in their path. The steed took off in a panic, causing the wagon to jolt and tilt as it reached a breakneck speed. The Flora dragon strapped to the wagon wrestled under his restraints, but he would not be able to free himself without assistance.

Venom circled around and quickly passed by the wagon, whipping the front of it with his tail. Fendrel looked over his shoulder to see the yoke break, freeing the horse. Much to his relief, the wagon did not crash into a wall or tumble over. It did, however, begin to disassemble and make an awful noise of shattering wood. The hunters fell from their now-nonexistent seats as pieces of the wagon narrowly missed their tossed bodies.

The black dragon landed harshly with his paws digging into the earth. Fendrel used the momentum to dismount, tucking into a roll with the dagger clutched to his chest. He sprang to his feet and rushed for the nearest dragon hunter.

An expression of dread filled the target's face. He stumbled away in an attempted escape but fell as Fendrel kicked the back of his knee, where the hunter was not wearing any dragon leather. Fendrel pulled one of the hunter's arms behind him and pressed the flat of his blade against the man's neck. Then, Fendrel brought the man to his feet, and shoved him in Venom's direction.

Venom had cut the ropes tying the kidnapped dragon. He landed a large paw on the second hunter to hold her down.

The rescued dragon stumbled off the wagon's wreckage and cowered beside Venom. Now that Fendrel was not focused on falling, he took in the dragon's appearance.

Well, it makes sense why Venom smelled citrus. This is a lime mimic, Fendrel realized. The dragon had green scales with leaf-laden branches growing from his neck and back. There were markings in the shape of a lime's interior ring on the dragon's wing membranes. A blue substance caked his nose.

The Dragon Liberator: Escapade

"Where is your stash of the knock-out powder?" Fendrel asked the first hunter.

The hunter gave him a frightened look, and he reached into his boot. His hand shot out and whipped toward Fendrel's face, a small gleaming blade clutched in his fist.

Before Fendrel realized it, he had grabbed the hunter's wrist and twisted it, making the man drop his knife.

Venom snapped his teeth mere inches from the hunter's face. "Rat!" he shouted.

Fendrel could not tell if his hands were shaking out of anger or adrenaline. He pointed his dagger at the hunter. "Get rid of your powder."

The hunter nodded rapidly and took a small leather pouch out of a pocket. He tossed it to the ground before Fendrel, then raised his eyes to Fendrel's own supply of the sleeping drug. "Please, don't use it. That'll kill me."

"Don't worry." Fendrel dropped his dagger in his bag and untied the strings on the pouch. "A pinch won't hurt you," he said, flicking the powder onto the hunter's face.

The hunter flinched but soon slumped to the ground, unconscious. His comrade gasped and squirmed under Venom's paws.

Fendrel took another pinch and sprinkled it onto the second. Venom lifted his paws only after she went limp, and her breathing deepened.

The Flora dragon stepped timidly out from behind Venom. He looked between his two rescuers. "You are not going to kill them?"

"These two are young, barely even seventeen." Fendrel stuffed his own pouch as well as the hunter's into his bag. "And that's why we're not going to tie these ones up."

"What?" Venom's voice was dangerously close to a growl.

Fendrel tried to conceal a flinch at the dragon's reaction. "They're low-ranked, inexperienced, and scared. They probably didn't join the dragon hunters by choice."

"What do you mean they did not join by choice?" Venom waved a wing at the sleeping hunters.

Sighing, Fendrel sorted through his jumbling thoughts to produce an explanation. "Some hunters had their families threatened. Others were tricked into thinking the dragon hunters were an elite branch of the royal guard. Some just wanted somewhere they could belong. There's a large portion of them who don't buy into Sadon's beliefs."

"So some of them do not kill dragons for fun?" Venom scowled as if nothing would ever make sense again.

"Yes." Fendrel tried to nod but found his movements freezing. "And I'm sure these hunters will run away and start new lives as soon as they wake up. They'd be idiots if they decided to stay."

"Fendrel, I want to trust you, if not for your sake, then for the sake of the mission. However, this?" Venom snorted. "This is too forgiving. I need them to feel real consequences for their actions."

Fendrel stared deep into the black dragon's intense eyes. "They will. I have a way, but we'll need them to be awake."

"Can you at least explain to me what you are going to *do*?" Impatience oozed from Venom's words.

"I'm going to frighten them. It will only take a few minutes." Fendrel set his bag on the ground and crouched as he began to rifle inside it. At his side, he laid a wooden bowl, a waterskin, and what had once been an ordinary root from the Hazy Woods, now enchanted and blood-red.

"What *is* that?" Venom turned his nose up as he stared at the root.

"An invention of Thea's." Fendrel poured the waterskin's contents into the bowl. He snapped the tip of the root off and pinched it between his thumb and index finger. "When exposed to water, this root will disintegrate and turn the water into faux blood."

Fendrel dropped the piece of root into the water and watched the mixture transform. "It looks, smells, feels, and tastes just like human blood. It even turns brown as it dries."

Venom's ears flattened and his mouth twisted into a grimace. "Yes, I can see that."

The rescued green dragon gagged and shuddered as he caught a whiff of the liquid.

"And how is that supposed to aid us?" Venom took a few steps back and turned his nose away.

"It's a long, complicated story, so I'll explain later. I want to get this over with in case some passerby shows up." Fendrel gave Venom an apologetic look, then averted his eyes so he would not have to see Venom's disapproving expression. "You're going to have to trust me."

Fendrel walked over to the first hunter he had knocked out, bowl in hand, and plugged his nose. After a few seconds, the young man awoke with a jolt. He looked around wildly before setting his eyes on Fendrel.

The Dragon Liberator: Escapade

"Wh-what are you doing?" the hunter asked.

"Be quiet. I'm about to save your life." Fendrel showed him the bowl's contents. "This is fake blood. I'm going to splatter this around to make it look like you and your friend died here. You will abandon the dragon hunters and live a quiet life away from their influence. Do you understand me?"

"What are you saying?" The boy's voice shook.

Fendrel glowered. "I'm saying that if you don't do as I just told you, things are going to end very badly for you. If I find you with the hunters again, I *will* kill you. Do you see that shadow dragon right there?" Fendrel pointed to Venom, using the humans' term for Dusk dragons.

Tears began to brim in the hunter's eyes as he nodded.

"You must know how incredible their sense of smell is." Fendrel swirled the fake blood around. "I can get him to track you down and catch you when you're alone, and no one will be the wiser as to what happened to you."

"I-I, even if I did leave them, where could I go?" The hunter's chest rose and fell in quick succession. "They'll find me and bring me back. They're *everywhere* and—"

Before he could finish, Fendrel pulled a coin purse from his bag and flung it at the hunter's chest. "There's enough money in there to get you and your friend a one-way trip on a boat to Cilrud. Now use those fancy whistles they taught you to call your horse back and leave for good."

The two stayed frozen for a moment, staring at each other. Tears flowed freely down the boy's cheeks. He shakily stood up and called the wagon's horse back.

Fendrel began spreading the enchanted liquid as the first hunter hoisted his sleeping friend over the horse's back. Once the hunter had mounted the saddle, Fendrel threatened, "Remember that I don't want to kill you, but I will if I find you in Sharpdagger."

"Yes, sir!" The terrified hunter steered the horse away from the ravine base to where a far-off road would take them to a port.

"Let them go." Fendrel waved at Venom. "I've done this a few times before and it's always worked. If I find them again, I'll handle them your way. Does that satisfy you?"

Venom clenched his jaw. "We will speak of this later."

CHAPTER 13: THEA

"WHAT ARE WE DOING HERE?" Oliver asked as he looked at Thea's face. "Fendrel and Venom are going on an adventure. Why can't we?"

Thea had positioned the boy in front of her so he could get a good view of her favorite place. Wing's Caress was the smallest village in all of Sharpdagger, but its population was ever growing. During Thea's infrequent visits, there were always new mages, likely having moved in after facing too many glares and jeers from conventional society.

"We *are* going on an adventure, Oliver," Thea said as she squeezed his shoulders. "I don't think you'll like the kind of adventure they're on right now. But this village here is full of mages, like me, and they'll love to meet you." She tried to keep her pounding heart from exploding out of her chest.

It would be amazing if I could find someone here to take Oliver in. These people tend to have a soft spot for outcasts, Thea thought optimistically. *It's safer for him here than with Fendrel and me, and the fact there are no other orphans begging for scraps is a good sign. I just hope he doesn't feel like we're abandoning him.*

"Am I walking like a horse?" Fog whispered out the corner of her mouth. She had been attempting and failing to replicate a horse's gait the entire journey.

"You don't need to pretend here." Thea kept her voice at its normal volume. "Yes, my spell works on these mages just like any human, but even if they find out you're a dragon, they won't be afraid since you're with me."

Just as she finished her sentence, Thea, Fog, and Oliver passed through the stone block pillars that marked the village's gateway. Each building was made unique to its neighbors. Some had small, flourishing vegetable gardens or cats lazing about in the sun. Thea could smell the aroma of hundreds of spells in the air.

"Other people who do magic live here?" Oliver asked while he looked at the villagers who smiled and waved their way as the trio passed through.

"Yes. They taught me everything I know." Thea returned the mages' greetings with warmth. She let herself drop from Fog's back, then guided the dragon and the boy to a small, colorfully-painted clay hut with a round wooden door. "But the main reason we're here is because this is the only place Fendrel can't get any information out of."

"Why not?" Fog asked, though her eyes roamed about their surroundings.

"Well, the people here aren't exactly friendly unless you yourself are a mage or are traveling with a mage. Fendrel has never come here with me, so the residents wouldn't know to trust him," Thea answered before knocking on the door. "And this house used to belong to my mentor. She has since passed, but all the trinkets she enchanted are still inside. I'm hoping one of them might be able to help us find Mist."

"I am surprised I do not see more . . . magic happening," Fog said.

Thea nodded. "Spellcasting saps our energy, and our materials. It's better to save up for an emergency than to spread magic like weeds."

Fog returned her gaze to Thea. "If other mages live here, why do you not?"

"I did, for a while." Thea shrugged. "But I wanted to use my talents for trade. Mages don't need to purchase spells when they already have magic of their own, so I needed to relocate."

The door opened to reveal a tall, slim figure wearing a hooded maroon robe. A black cloth covered the bottom half of his face, making his twinkling magenta eyes his most striking feature. He was covered head-to-toe in fine black leather and well-tailored cotton, so that the only skin he showed was his partially concealed face. "Why, hello there, Thea," the man said in a cheerful voice. He glanced over at Oliver, still seated atop Fog, and added, "And who is this charming young fellow?"

Scrunching her brow, Thea tried to fight off an assailing headache at the mere sight of the much taller mage. At the edges of her vision danced swirling shapes that changed colors and molded into each other. It was almost hypnotic, but unsettling and painful at the same time.

Thea wanted to slam the door shut and lead Oliver and Fog away, but she stayed still. Such a reaction might set the man off. She resolved it was better to play nice for the time being. She smiled, forced with grit teeth, and answered, "Raaldin, I thought you were in Sharpdagger. Why are you in Riva's house?"

He shouldn't be here, Thea thought as a chill ran down her spine. *I assumed the other villagers would be maintaining Riva's house, so why is he here?*

Raaldin waved his hand as if to dismiss her question. "Why have you brought this boy?"

Thea could not help the worried look she gave Oliver. He too seemed off-put by the man as he squirmed backward in his seat. Even Fog appeared disturbed with the feathers on her spine standing rigid.

"Oh!" Raaldin gasped in delight. "I know. You're taking on an apprentice, yes? It's so good to see a new mage here in Wing's Caress."

"Raaldin, what are you doing in Riva's house?" Thea asked again, trying to block his diversions.

"I am here to collect artifacts I allowed her to borrow." Raaldin stepped aside and gestured for Thea to enter the hut. "I would have done so prior to her death but was unable to."

"Was it the same 'business' that kept you from ing her funeral?" Thea crossed her arms. She had no transportation, and no one to escort her for safe travels, but even still she had made the trip to say goodbye to the woman who taught her about magic.

You knew her longer than I did, Thea confronted Raaldin in her head, knowing she was too nervous to say it out loud. *The least you could do was show up.*

Raaldin blinked at her, and for a brief moment his eyebrows furrowed as though he were scowling. "I am swamped with responsibilities, Thea. As I am sure you will soon understand now that you have this boy. By the by—"

Thea was forced to catch a small bundle of folded papers as Raaldin flicked them from his robe.

"Here are the same training papers I used to teach Riva when she was my apprentice, and the same ones she used to train you. Call it a family heirloom, without the blood ties of course." Raaldin's eyes crinkled in what Thea could only assume was a smile.

"Why are you giving these to *me*?"

"Thea, I know you are brighter than this." Raaldin pointed at Oliver. "The boy is a mage, and you've brought him *here* to Riva's house, of all places. Don't lie to me. There is no other reason why you would have done this . . . or am I mistaken?"

I shouldn't let him know why we're really here, Thea thought as her blood raced with nerves. Something in her mind screamed for her to keep her mouth shut, and she complied.

Thea stuffed the papers into a pocket with indignance. The headache and dancing shapes seemed to swell as she grew annoyed. "I'm not so easy to read. We should be going now," she said, curtly.

"Well, take care then," Raaldin said in a voice just barely masking his displeasure. He retreated back into the charming clay hut and closed the door.

Once he disappeared from sight, Thea's headache ceased. She blinked the remaining shapes away and sighed, frustrated that her main goal had been thwarted so quickly. But soon a creeping doubt entered her mind, chasing away all other thoughts.

Was Raaldin toying with me or is Oliver truly a mage? Oliver hasn't performed any spells while he's been with us, Thea reasoned. *He is so young, though. If he is a mage, I doubt he would know it.*

"Are you okay?" Oliver jumped down from Fog and touched Thea's arm. "You're acting strange."

The boy's light touch jolted Thea back to herself. She grabbed his hand and ushered for Fog to follow. "Let's go somewhere we can talk."

She led them to a fountain with a sculpted bird in the center. Thea sat on the edge with Oliver taking a seat beside her. Fog sat as well. Then, her eyes glazed over for a moment, and she lay down, seemingly deciding that sitting was not very horse-like.

"I'm sorry." Thea clasped her hands in her lap. "I got a headache. That's why I was acting strange."

"Oh, so I was not the only one." Fog flicked her tail. "That is a funny coincidence."

"I got a headache too! With spinning shapes and pretty colors!" Oliver swung his feet.

Everyone gets that same headache, mage or not, if they've encountered dark magic after experiencing good magic first, Thea thought as nerves forced her to fidget with the skin around her nails. *Oliver only got the headache because of the Drake-tongue speech stone I gave him . . . But, what if Raaldin was right? I need to make sure.*

Thea gathered her thoughts and looked at the boy. "Oliver, do you often have strange dreams about people you've never met before? But the dream feels so real you believe you are right there with them?"

Oliver looked down for a moment and watched his swinging feet as he pondered. Then, he nodded. "I had a dream about dragons in the Hazy Woods once, but before."

"Before you went to the Hazy Woods?" Thea asked.

"Yes," Oliver said with a smile. "But also, the dream was about *before* we went there. None of the bridges were broken, and the castle looked brand new."

Thea felt like her lungs were being constricted. *Raaldin was right*, she realized. *Oliver is having visions, and he doesn't even realize it. That's how it all starts, and soon after your powers manifest.*

"Do you get those dreams, too?" Oliver asked, oblivious to the shock on Thea's face.

"I do, but mine are of the future," Thea confirmed while placing a hand on her chest. "Oliver, if you ever feel like you can't tell someone about something, just know you can always tell me. *Especially* if it is something odd."

"Odd . . . like how that man with the weird eyes feels scary even though he talks nice?" Oliver looked back at the hut.

"Yes!" Thea let out a short laugh. "Exactly like that."

"I feel as though I am missing something," Fog muttered, scooching closer to the humans.

"That's all right. Let me explain." Thea shifted in her seat, so she was facing both Fog and Oliver. "That headache we all felt is a side effect of coming into contact with a dark-magic practitioner. Such mages have an unsettling feeling around them, and items housing their spells also give you those same headaches. But the only reason you were affected is because you have already been exposed to normal magic. My magic."

"So that human practices dark magic?" Fog inched away from the hut.

"He does, and he's not welcome here, but we're too afraid of what he might do to us if we tell him as much. No one knows what he did for all his spells to give off that horrible feeling, but we do not want to find out by angering him." Thea's voice grew quieter the longer she spoke of Raaldin. When she saw Oliver shiver and tuck his legs against the fountain, she stood up. "Let's, um . . . let's go back to story hunting. Someone here might have an idea of where Mist is." The folded papers in her pocket jabbed her as she took Oliver's hand and, with Fog following, walked away from the fountain.

We can deal with the magic later. Oliver deserves to be a normal child for once. He doesn't need to know that he might be a mage yet . . . but those night visions are a clear sign, Thea thought. She squeezed the boy's hand with affection.

But if he is a mage, it may be safer for him to be around another mage he can trust, someone he's familiar with. I won't leave him here, at least not yet.

Hours passed like minutes and the Wing's Caress search turned out to be as unfruitful as the investigation into Lightgrass. Fog's wings seemed to sink lower as the day flew by. She was the first dragon Thea had ever met in person, and the mage was still trying to learn the dragon's nonverbal cues, but the forlornness in Fog's eyes was unmistakable.

I've never had any siblings. I can't begin to imagine what it must be like to lose one of them, Thea thought as the three made their way back from the village of mages. A piece of her felt compelled to try and comfort the dragon, but all she could think to say was, "How long has she been missing?"

Fog blinked in confusion at Thea's words. She had been silent since they concluded their search and was seemingly lost in her own mind. After a moment, she answered, "Nine days."

Thea, seated on Fog's back with Oliver just in front, mumbled, "I'm sorry. I know it must be hard, but we'll find her. I'm not experienced with any of this, but Fendrel knows what he's doing."

The Vapor dragon nodded and whispered back, "I hope so."

Oliver leaned forward and hugged Fog around the neck.

At first Fog tensed, but when she turned her head to see the boy, she let herself smile. "Do you like your new . . . what are they called?" Fog asked.

Thea smiled. "They're called clothes. I suppose you don't have a similar word in your language."

"I like them!" Oliver sat back and spread his arms to show off his shirt. Thea had gladly accepted the new clothes from another mage who took pity on Oliver's old, ripped, and dirt-stained attire.

Fog smiled again, then turned her face back to what lay ahead. After a brief silence, she asked, "Are dragons included in the spell you placed on the disguising vine?"

Thea shook her head. "No, just humans and animals. Although since we're traveling westward it should be fine to get rid of it. There are no other human villages where we're going, and the spell will most likely fade soon."

With a nod, Fog cut the vine from around her wing claw with one of her talons and let it drop into the grass.

Night was fast-approaching, and it was getting harder to distinguish between shadows and the objects that cast them, but soon the three found themselves spying Fendrel, Venom, and an unfamiliar dragon in the near distance. After traveling close enough, Thea and Oliver slipped down from Fog's back to make the rest of the short walk on foot.

Thea would be lying if she said she was not alarmed by the abundance of slash marks on Venom's body. Before she could say anything, however, Fog was healing him with her vapor breath—an ability Fendrel clued her in on during their flight out of the Hazy Woods.

Their new companion, a rescued green dragon, seemed afraid at first but was slowly turning unlikeable. He held his head in such a way that forced him to look down his nose at anyone speaking to him, including Venom who was much taller. His one-syllable responses only seemed to heighten his self-held superiority, as though the others were not worthy of a full conversation.

"I will be tonight's lookout." The Flora dragon, Sour, sighed as if being forced to keep watch. "My father always said I had the best eyes of all my siblings."

Venom gave Sour a tired glare. "Perhaps by 'best' he meant 'best looking', not 'best functioning.'"

Sour gaped at Venom as if the black dragon had exposed his most vulnerable insecurity.

"That's all right," Fendrel spoke for the first time since saying a quick hello when the two groups had reconvened. "You must still be tired from the knock-out powder the hunters gave you. Sleep it off."

Fendrel and Venom looked at each other with mutual understanding.

Ooh, something interesting happened today, Thea realized with a grin.

The mage took a glass vial full of moss out of a pocket, placed it in the center of the group, and poked it. Where her finger prodded, flames sprang up and soon spread to the rest of the moss. There was little heat, but the magic fire illuminated their small camp.

As everyone gathered around the fire, Thea thought back to the training papers in her pocket once more. The memory of her encounter with Raaldin made her shiver. She took a deep breath, smiled to cover her anxiety, and tried to quiet her worries for a bit.

CHAPTER 14: FENDREL

FENDREL SAT BEFORE THE FIRE and stared into its glow. The others were also crowded around the camp, and if the enchanted flames had not been there, Fendrel doubted he would be able to see any of them clearly. "Thea?" Fendrel asked.

Thea did not respond right away as she fiddled with something in her pockets. She then lifted her head toward Fendrel. "Yes?"

"What exactly can you do as a mage? How did you do . . . this?" Fendrel waved at the fire.

With a gleeful smile, Thea sat up straight, ecstatic to talk about her abilities. "Well, here, I enchanted some moss to ignite fake flames once I touched it. Did you have a specific spell in mind?"

"I don't know." Fendrel shrugged. "You said you could only do illusions or heal people. Do those illusions only trick the eyes?"

"No, I can trick as many senses as I want, given I have the right materials." Thea plucked a vial from her skirt and held it up to the light, allowing everyone to see the tiny scales inside. "If I use shed dragon parts like teeth, hides, or claws, my spells could last for centuries. That's what I used to enchant your bag. This fire, though, I already said I used moss to make it. It won't last long, definitely not through the night."

"It's warm!" Oliver stretched his hands out in front of the blaze.

"This spell works on your eyes and sense of touch. That's why it feels warm, even though it really isn't," Thea explained. "I did something similar with the translation spells. To Oliver and me, it sounds like you're all speaking our language, and the spell affects our eyes so that your mouth movements match what we're hearing."

"Did you choose to have that kind of magic?" Fog asked.

Thea shook her head. "I was born with it, like every other mage. From what we can tell, our type of magic depends on where we were born. But even then, we don't know *why* different locations are associated with different kinds of magic."

"Oh, like how a dragon's tribal element depends on where they hatch!" Fog smiled and looked at Venom. "Perhaps mages get their powers from the same source as us."

Venom nodded in agreement. "Perhaps they do."

Fog sidled closer to Thea. "How did you find out that you were a mage? How does anyone find out?"

"I was fortunate enough to grow up in a village where a mage already lived. She sold magic, like I do, and treated all the children like her own, but she noticed something different in me." A grin of bittersweet fondness took over Thea's face. "I told her about visions I had been having, which are a telltale sign that someone is a mage. But she didn't need me to tell her that, she already knew what I was. Mages feel a strange, almost instinctual trust in each other."

She can trust someone just from a feeling? Fendrel raised an eyebrow in skepticism. *No one can trust or be trusted that easily. That's strange . . . Thea never struck me as naïve.*

"We also have a sense that tells us when we're around mages who have practiced dark magic." Thea tapped her temple. "We get an intense headache, and our vision becomes cloudy with swirling shapes and colors. It's very disorienting. We call it a stain."

"A stain? Why?" Fendrel asked.

"Because any dark mage and their enchantments are tainted by that affect for the rest of their life." Thea gestured at Fog as she said, "I suppose dragons can experience the stain, too. We ran into a dark mage at Wing's Caress and Fog got the same symptoms as Oliver and me."

Venom looked at Fog with concern. "You are not hurt?"

Fog shook her head, but she kept her eyes on Thea, too engrossed in the conversation to look away. "What is dark magic?"

"It could be any spell as long as the components used to cast it are still living, if the spell itself is placed on a living being, or if the dragon parts used for the spell have been . . . forcibly taken." Thea shook the vial between two of her fingers and the scales inside made a soft clinking noise. "That's why I only use shed materials or plants or stones. Besides, using dragon materials that were torn from the dragon don't yield very good spells. They're unreliable, quick to lose effect, and have an awful smell."

Fendrel tilted his head in interest. "It's like the stars themselves, or whatever creates magic, made it so mages would be punished for hurting dragons."

"That makes sense to me, I suppose." Thea put her vial away. "Mages use elemental materials for spells, and dragons are the way they are because of the elements. Well—" Thea chuckled breathily "—that's enough about me. What about you, Fendrel?"

"Me?" Fendrel blinked in surprise. He tensed.

"Yes. What can you do?" Thea smirked as she turned the group's attention to him.

Once everyone's gaze had shifted from Thea to Fendrel, his mind went blank. It was not so much that all his thoughts had vanished, but more so he had too many thoughts to settle on. His head whirled with half-sentences and words just beyond his grasp. After a few stifling moments, he settled on, "I rescue dragons. There isn't much else to know."

"Well, we *all* know that already." Thea rolled her eyes. "But how? It must be difficult doing what you do alone."

"I'm not alone," Fendrel said as he mimicked Thea's eyeroll. "You help me."

"No, no, no." Thea shook her head slowly. "I know that you know what I mean. *I'm* not the one storming into dragon-hunter bases. That is all you."

"It must be difficult," Fog added. "You were gone for so long when you were trying to find the keys to my cage. How did you manage to get them?"

Fendrel's heart stalled a beat. *I was only able to rescue Fog because Charles was there to help me, but I doubt she would be happy to know I got a dragon hunter's aid with some of my missions. I had better keep that to myself. I don't want her to think I associate with the hunters.*

"Did Charles tell you where the keys were?" Oliver asked gleefully as he sat up higher to be seen over the flames. "Uncle usually gives him all the keys."

Fog looked between the boy and Fendrel. "Who is Charles?"

Fendrel did not need a mirror to know all the color had drained from his face. He locked eyes with Thea, who looked equally shocked despite her best attempts to hide her expression by scratching the bridge of her nose.

"Oliver, I think it's time for us to go to sleep." Thea reached her hand out toward Fendrel. "Let's get our blankets."

"But I'm not tired!" Oliver protested.

Fendrel took the mage's cue and dug a couple fur blankets out of his bag for them.

Thea accepted the furs and said, "I am, and I'm not staying up waiting for you. Come on, let's go to sleep." She ushered the boy out of the circle and a short distance away.

Venom kept his eyes on Fendrel. It was only then Fendrel realized the Dusk dragon had been giving him the same skeptical look all evening.

He still wants an answer for what happened at the Ravine Base. Fendrel squirmed under Venom's scrutinous eyes. *How long can I put this off for? I can't tell him about Charles, about any of it. Not until I've done enough to make up for my mistakes. Not until the mission is over.*

"Who is Charles?" Venom repeated Fog's question.

Fendrel's throat dried. Once again, his mind was running too fast for him to think up a worthy answer.

In the silence that followed, Sour rose from his spot and wordlessly shuffled away. Venom and Fog continued to stare.

They aren't going to let up, Fendrel realized with a sinking feeling. He thought he had prepared for this moment. For years he had planned out exactly what he would say when someone asked how he learned to fight, but now those plans were gone. *I need to salvage this. I can't let them think I'm a monster.*

"Charles is . . . an ally of mine." Fendrel froze as the words left his mouth.

"Why was this ally inside a dragon-hunter base?" Venom pressed.

"He's a prisoner, of sorts," Fendrel mumbled.

"A prisoner who is in charge of the keys to cages they lock dragons in." Venom glowered. He looked as angry as he had when Thea was the target of his questioning, but there was a steadiness to his voice that made Fendrel feel like a child being scolded.

Fendrel picked through all he knew about Charles, trying to find attributes he hoped would make a good case. "He was forced to join the hunters, or his family would be killed. Charles has been secretly helping me for as long as I've been invading their bases. He lets me sneak in, free the dragons they have captive, and only sounds the alarm once I've left. He's a friend."

Venom snorted. "A *friendly* dragon hunter. First, you tell me not all of them hate dragons, and now, you claim that some of them want to *help* us?"

"Trust me, he doesn't have ulterior motives." Fendrel traced his fingers along a scratch in his bag in an effort to calm himself. "Siding with me only puts him and his family in danger, so I know he's doing it out of the goodness of his heart. Besides, he's the one who taught me how to fight, both dragons *and* humans. If it weren't for him, I would be dead by now."

"Wait." Fog's eyes widened and her pupils turned to slits. She leaned away, as if being near Fendrel would get her killed. "You fight using dragon hunter techniques?"

"Yes, but only on rogues," Fendrel said hurriedly, feeling his ears burn in embarrassment. He softened his gaze, trying to look as convincing as possible, but Fog only looked more horrified.

Venom stood and gestured with his wing for Fendrel to follow him. "Come with me," he commanded.

Fendrel's breath caught in his throat. He gave one last look to Fog, but her face was turned away. He rose to his feet, mumbled a quick apology, and walked in Venom's wake. They moved a short distance from the others, far enough to be out of earshot.

Facing away from Fendrel, Venom asked, "This friend . . . how did you meet him?"

Dread filled every ounce of Fendrel's body, and he feared his words would fall on deaf ears. Nonetheless, he answered, "After my brother, Frederick, and I were old enough to take care of ourselves, we left Frost Lake to find work among humans. We went to the nearest village and while we were there, we met Charles. He was welcoming and when he found out we didn't have any human currency, he offered to buy us shelter at an inn for the night."

The black dragon did not respond right away. When Fendrel did not elaborate, Venom turned around to face him. "And?" he prompted.

"And . . . Charles' employer offered us work." Fendrel lowered his gaze as shame took hold of his heart. He could feel Venom's stare analyzing every breath he took.

"You know too much about the hunters to just be their enemy. You know where their hideouts are, how they rank their soldiers, how they fight, what materials they use and how they obtain them. You are even personal with one." Venom lowered his head, so he was eye-level with Fendrel. Distanced from the fire, all Fendrel could make out of Venom's form were his piercing eyes, full of contempt. Venom said, in a tone laced with fury, "You used to be one of them."

Some instinctual part of Fendrel urged him to defend himself, but he knew he could not lie. He gave a shaky nod and said, "I'm not proud of it, it that's what you're wondering." He stayed still, afraid that any slight movement would make the situation worse. "I wish I could change it."

Venom shook his head in confusion and anger. "Why would you join humans like them?"

Fendrel opened his mouth to answer, then shut it. He sighed in resignation. "Anything I say will sound like an excuse. You don't trust me, so why would you believe me now?"

"I want to hear the words from your own mouth," Venom said as he continued to glare.

Is this where I'm forced to leave the mission? Fendrel wondered. *Or is he going to kill me in order to protect everyone else?*

Either way, there's no point in hiding anything.

"The hunters lied to my brother and me. They told us they were a secret branch of the royal guard tasked with hunting down dragons that had attacked humans," Fendrel started. "They said they would help us find the rogue that killed my mother. I was uneasy about them, but I pushed that feeling aside and joined regardless."

And now I pay for that mistake every single day, Fendrel thought as he fidgeted his fingers against his bag.

"Is your brother still one of them?" Venom asked. "Is that why you are so soft with the hunters?"

"No. When I left, they killed him to punish me." Fendrel dropped his head just low enough to where he could still see Venom's face at the edge of his vision. His words tumbled out of his mouth, too fast to stop. "And I'm only lenient with the hunters who were forced to join. Like I said earlier in the ravine, some of them had their families threatened if they didn't become dragon hunters. Charles is one of those few."

Venom scoffed. "He knew what they were like, and he still allowed you to join."

"That wasn't his fault," Fendrel retorted.

"You said he offered you and your brother the position."

"No, that was Sadon!" Fendrel raised his voice. He flinched at his own outburst and looked back to see if he had awoken anyone. The others appeared to be deep in sleep, unaware of the conversation taking place not far from them. Fendrel returned his sights to Venom and paused a moment to steady his breathing. Then he said, "Sadon showed up at where Charles was staying, unannounced, and recruited us. We all traveled together and by the time Sadon left our side, we were already at their main base. It was too late by then for Charles to warn us about him."

Fendrel waited for Venom to say something, but the black dragon only stared as if searching for any miniscule sign that Fendrel was being untruthful. When Venom crouched and gave him an expectant nod, Fendrel continued. "The first night we were at the Stronghold, Charles took me aside and told me Sadon was a liar. He must have seen how skeptical I was, because he only told me. Charles was our instructor for the next two years, and every night he would try and craft an escape plan for me and Frederick, but the timing was never right. There were always too many lookouts, or there was a dangerous sandstorm, or one of us would have been assigned a task we couldn't skip out on. At the end of the two years it was time for us to be initiated. Leaving the night of the ceremony was just as dangerous as every other night, but if I didn't get out before my initiation, it would be impossible to escape."

After forcing himself to stop, Fendrel realized how much he was quivering. He pulled his fur coat tighter around his shoulders, but it was not the cold that made him shiver. "I tried to take Frederick with me, but he didn't believe anything I told him. So, I left and vowed I would come back for him. But, when I did, he wasn't there. I went to *every single* dragon-hunter base, until I ended up at one Charles was stationed at. He said he had gotten Frederick out, but neither of us ever heard from him again."

It's my fault he's gone. Fendrel swallowed a lump that began to form in his throat. A devastating emptiness panged in his chest. He tried to push the feeling down, but it still roiled within him. *We never should have trusted Sadon in the first place. Frederick would still be here, and everything would be so much better . . .*

Most of the anger had left Venom's face, but there were still traces bubbling beneath the surface.

"Neither of us had the money to leave by sea, and Frederick was never sneaky enough to stowaway. Sadon must have sent hunters after both of us, but they only caught him," Fendrel finished. The lump in his throat seemed to grow. It was becoming painful, and Fendrel felt tears starting to brim in his eyes. "Listen . . . I know I kept this from you, and I shouldn't have, but can we have this conversation later?"

"No. We have put this off long enough." Venom's voice was as unshakeable as his yellow-eyed stare. "You are involved in a matter of the utmost importance, and I must know for certain that you can be trusted."

"I can," Fendrel proclaimed in a voice threatening to break. "Let me prove it to you. I'll tell you anything you want to know."

"Why did you become this 'Liberator?'" Venom drug out the last word as though it had lost its meaning.

"Because . . . I was the only one who could. No human cared about dragons, at least not enough to protect them. And no dragons had the knowledge on where the hunter's bases were or how they operated." Fendrel's body felt hot with shame and cold with fear all at once. "I couldn't let them get away with everything they had done."

Venom narrowed his eyes. "So this is revenge?"

"It's responsibility," Fendrel corrected. A tear broke free and raced down his cheek. He ducked his head to hide it. "And atonement. No one is safe, dragon or human, until the hunters are gone. I'm the only one who can stop them, but no matter how hard I try it's never enough."

"Has no one been aiding you all this time?" Venom's tone seemed to change. It was still angry, but now the rage seemed to be aimed at someone, or something else. Fendrel thought he must have imagined it, but the dragon also sounded concerned. A cursory glance at Venom confirmed what Fendrel heard. The Dusk noble's ears were still pinned back, but they also drooped as if saddled with a heavy burden, and his head tilted like he was trying to decipher a puzzle.

"I . . . I've had help," Fendrel stuttered. "Charles helps me, when he can. So does Thea, and I have a friend in Twin Oases who gives me leads on dragon captures."

"But, as Thea mentioned, no one to fight them in person alongside you." It was Venom's turn to look away for a moment. When he met Fendrel's eyes again, his expression held a hint of softness. "I have two more inquiries. How easy was it for the hunters to convince you and your brother to join them? And, why did you not tell your brother the truth sooner?"

Fendrel suppressed a sigh of relief, having expected the questions to be more grueling. He drummed his fingers on his bag to help himself calm down further. "The hunters weren't well-known at the time. Nowadays they have wanted posters for high-ranked members, but back then the group was much smaller. They didn't even have the resources to make dragon leather or weapons out of dragon claws. Besides, even if they did have a reputation, Frederick and I had only just left the Inviers, our home clan. It was our first time interacting with humans since we were adopted. We had no idea what the hunters were really like."

Venom nodded in understanding. "Go on."

Once again guilt crept up to seize Fendrel's heart. He tried to answer at a volume that wouldn't let tears loose, but he could not tell if his voice was audible enough. "Frederick was always talkative. Charles asked me if he could keep the secret, but I knew if we let Frederick in on the plan, he would have let it slip somehow. Frederick and I would have been killed, and Charles' family, too. We couldn't afford the risk . . ." Despite his best attempts, Fendrel couldn't keep his face stoic enough. He quickly wiped at a few tears before they could travel far. "I thought he would believe me once it was time to leave, but he accused me of lying because I've always been slow to trust humans. He thought I was trying to get him to abandon all the friends he made because I was jealous. I wanted to drag him with me, but I knew that would only cause a scene, and then neither of us would ever be free."

"You said he did end up leaving." Venom stretched his neck just a bit closer to Fendrel. "What happened there?"

"Charles got him out a few hours after me," Fendrel whispered. "He confirmed my story and made Frederick leave, but neither of us saw him after that."

Fendrel froze when Venom placed a wing claw on his shoulder. It was hefty and sharp, but Venom was careful with how much force he used. "Who else knows of all this?" Venom asked.

"Thea and a Fire dragon friend of mine, the one I get my leads from," Fendrel admitted. He shut his eyes and leaned into the pressure of Venom's claw. His adoptive parents used to do the same gesture, though with more tenderness than the Dusk dragon bestowed upon him. After a long, quiet moment, Fendrel said, "I suppose this isn't what you meant when you said you wanted to get to know me." He let out a curt, cynical laugh, then frowned just as quickly once the noise escaped his lips.

"No, it is not. But at least you are honest with me now." All harshness had dissipated from Venom's voice, leaving behind a gentle tone that ushered Fendrel into a sense of calm.

His steadying heart jumped at the sound of wings whooshing

overhead. It sent Fendrel's gaze upward, but the night was too dark for him to see much more than stars and the moon.

What was that? Is that the rogue? Fendrel wondered. He shuddered at the thought and hoped the beast would not be so bold as to attack when Fendrel was in the presence of a Dusk dragon.

"Did you hear that?" Fendrel asked as he silently prayed his mind was playing tricks on him.

"I did." Venom's ears swiveled, trying to listen. "The noise is gone now, but I can still smell it."

"What is it?" Fendrel asked before he could realize if he wanted to know the answer or not.

"Nothing you need to worry about with me keeping watch," Venom assured. He jutted his chin to where the others were deep in slumber. "Get your rest. We are going to take the Flora dragon home tomorrow, as Everspring Grove is our next destination."

Fendrel found this to be of little comfort, but he complied. When Venom retracted his wing claw and ushered him back to the now dying enchanted flames, Fendrel reached in his bag for a caribou fur blanket. As he wrapped himself and laid down in a patch of sparse grass, Fendrel found he could not keep his gaze off the sky. If it were possible, he would have liked to sleep with his eyes open, but he soon found his eyelids growing heavy.

True to his word, Venom sat with his full attention pointed upward.

"Venom?" Fendrel said just above a whisper. When one of the black dragon's ears twitched in his direction, Fendrel continued, "Did what I tell you frighten you?"

"About the rogue or the hunters?" Venom stayed immobile.

So the rogue is here.

For the first time in his life, the thought of his pursuer being so near did not send Fendrel into a panic. He formulated his thoughts and settled on answering, "About how I used to be one of them. You were right about what you said in the ravine. Mother would have been horrified with me." Even as he awaited Venom's response, his eyes closed. Fendrel fell into a half-sleep. In his drowsiness, he thought he heard the Dusk dragon's answer.

"I am merely frightened for you, but you have no reason to fear."

CHAPTER 15: FENDREL

DEEP IN A MEMORY, ITS *edges blurred in a dream, Fendrel found himself sitting on a snow-blanketed log beside a frozen lake. Dainty snowflakes drifted about him, settling on the iced-over water so that it looked like the rest of the forest floor. It was early in the morning. The sun still had not risen, but pink and gold hazed what little of the horizon Fendrel could see through the pines. If it had been the beginning of the month, the lake's bank would be crowded with the Inviers and all neighboring clans trading goods and sharing stories. But Fendrel was alone.*

It had been three long, stressful years since he was home. The last time he saw his parents was during a farewell ceremony for himself and his brother. They had just reached fifteen years of age, the age when all members of the Invier clan leave their parents' den to start a life on their own. Blizzard and Flurry tried to convince them that they did not need to follow that tradition, but Frederick wanted to see the world and meet other humans.

I would have followed him anywhere, Fendrel thought.

Now, at eighteen years old, Fendrel feared how his clan would react once they found out Frederick would never be coming back home. His search for his brother had been unfruitful. There was no denying that Frederick was gone, and Fendrel was the only one who could tell his family what happened.

Why wouldn't he just listen to me? Fendrel wondered. I know he missed being around humans, but did he really prefer them over me?

Behind him, snow crunched under the paws of a dragon. It jolted Fendrel from his thoughts.

Fendrel wondered if Blizzard was awake this early, and if the dragon could smell him all the way from the den. Fendrel did not turn around. He wanted a few more moments of calm before he would need to confess. He kept his eyes ahead, toward the snow-camouflaged lake and the deep, narrow-mouthed ravine just ahead of it.

The footfalls stopped. A chill traveled up Fendrel's spine at the eeriness of the sudden silence.

If this is Blizzard, why hasn't he said anything yet? Is it someone else from the clan? Fendrel thought.

He turned his head and immediately wished he had not.

Crouched low, wheezing purple sludge from its maw, was a white-striped Fire rogue. The same one that had destroyed Stone Edge and sent his mother to an early grave. The same one that had hunted Fendrel ever since that day, eleven years ago.

The rogue lunged forward with its claws splayed. For a second its roar sounded like the screams coming from that old, burning city.

Out of pure instinct, Fendrel ducked. He crawled under the thick log as the rogue soared over him. Panic surged through his body as a branch caught on his bag. With a grunt, he tugged and freed his most prized possession from the wood, but not without it receiving a few scratches. Another roar caused him to clap his freezing hands over his ears.

It was not long before the rogue had its paws on the log. The fallen trunk creaked under the forceful push of the dragon's forelegs.

The snow was piling around him as Fendrel squeezed backward out from under the log. He pushed his body farther back, between the rogue's hind legs, just as the log split and impaled the ground.

Fendrel's boots slipped while he struggled to his feet. Surprised that he was not knocked down by the rogue's tail as he stood, Fendrel ran toward the lake.

I can trap it in the water! he thought.

Snarling, the rogue turned to face its escaping prey. It drew in a hissing breath.

"No!" Fendrel dove onto his belly, yelping as the wind knocked out of him.

A jet of blue flame raged where he had been standing. The unbearable heat forced Fendrel to shut his eyes. He gritted his teeth. His breath returned to him in tandem with the rogue's gasping.

Fire dragons had to recuperate after breathing fire. This was his chance to run. Without looking back, Fendrel got up and let his feet carry him over the thick ice.

But, in one bounding leap, the rogue cleared half the space between itself and Fendrel. Before it could leap again, it crashed through the lake's frozen surface. Water splashed around its impact, and the squeal of claws scraping through ice traveled to Fendrel's ears.

Cracks spread from the hole in all directions. Like a path of doom leading to Fendrel, the biggest cracks followed where the fire had softened the top of the lake.

Fendrel did not stop running until he was sure the ground under his feet was solid earth. Then, against his better judgment, he let himself stumble to his hands and knees. He looked back at the rogue, still thrashing in the water.

Shards of broken ice tore tiny cuts in the rogue's leathery, bat-like wings. The

Fire dragon's haunting cries pierced the alpine air.

A relieved shudder escaped Fendrel's lips. But the feeling was gone all too soon.

The rogue managed to haul itself out of Fendrel's trap. It pounded across the lake toward Fendrel, the cracks growing larger beneath it, but it did not fall in again.

Get up! Fendrel's mind screamed at him. He did not think his legs would get him very far, but he ran, nonetheless. He knew that if he stopped running, he may never be able to force himself forward again.

But he had to stop. The ravine was mere feet away. Almost casting himself beyond the cliff's lip, Fendrel fell onto his belly and dug his fingers through the snow in an attempt to root himself. With the cold biting his cheek, he stared wide-eyed at the beast coming to kill him.

With a prowling gait, the rogue approached. Its muscles rippled beneath red and white scales. Smoke tumbled from the dragon's jaws, which still leaked purple saliva. The beast stalked closer. Its slowed approach seemed to be taunting, as if to prolong Fendrel's fearful state.

"I hate you." Fendrel clenched fistfuls of snow. His eyes began to well up with tears, but it was too cold for him to tell if they fell down his face. "I hate you, I hate you."

Booming wingbeats and a different dragon's roar trumpeted from behind Fendrel.

Limber as a cat, the rogue jumped away to avoid the new dragon. A spray of powdery snow erupted from the white, furred dragon's paws and into the rogue's eyes.

"Pa!" Fendrel shouted. His heart was overcome with elation at the sight of his adoptive father. He shakily brought himself up to his knees.

The daunting Ice dragon stood thrice as tall as the rogue. Blizzard pummeled the red beast across the face with a huge paw, and with a crack, the rogue's head whipped backwards from the attack. It rose on its hind legs and spread its wings, but it was still shrimp-sized in comparison to the Invier.

Blizzard rammed it in the chest, sending the predator onto its back. He moved to pounce, but as he engaged, the rogue shot a short burst of flame.

The smell of singed fur met Fendrel's nose.

For a moment, Blizzard backed away. That brief pause allowed the rogue to regain its composure. It snarled at them and launched into the sky.

Fendrel's heart sank. Blizzard was not fast enough to catch the rogue now that it had taken flight, but Fendrel knew it would return. It was only a matter of time until he would be by himself again.

As Blizzard made his way back to the ravine, Fendrel reached out and clasped the woolly fur of Blizzard's neck in his shivering hands. Blizzard shielded Fendrel from the ravine's edge with his wings and pulled him against his chest.

Fists finding better purchase in whitish-blue fur, Fendrel felt himself be rocked by the dragon's breaths. He could not help the tears that were freeing themselves from his eyes, and he hoped Blizzard could not feel them through his thick hide.

Blizzard nuzzled the tip of his nose against Fendrel's head. It made Fendrel feel like a child again, helpless and vulnerable. "Are you all right?" Blizzard asked, his voice deep like a thunderstorm. There was a calmness to it that anchored Fendrel's tumultuous emotions.

Fendrel wanted to say that he was fine but that would be a lie. Even if he was able to, the words refused to make it past his throat.

The Ice dragon did not ask again. He just held Fendrel steady.

In a moment of clarity, Fendrel felt himself waking up. He tried to fall back into slumber, but darkness cut off his dream. Fendrel opened his eyes. His cheeks felt sticky, and he wondered if those were tear tracks from his talk with Venom or if they happened while he was asleep.

Venom paced around the group. Grass crunched under his paws, but the sound did nothing to wake the others.

Did he get any rest last night, or did he stay up watching for the rogue? Fendrel wondered as he untangled himself from his blanket. He sat up. *And why is he so worked up?*

"Has something happened?" Fendrel asked.

The black dragon sighed, frustrated. "No. I had hoped we would be traveling by now, but our 'adventures' yesterday seem to have tired everyone out."

Fendrel almost snickered at Venom's eagerness. He clapped his hands, startling the rest of the group awake. "Come on, everyone. The sooner we leave, the sooner we get Sour home, and we can be on our way to the next lead."

Fog, eyes squinty from sleep, arose and stretched her wings. "Where are we going next?"

"Coincidentally, Everspring Grove," Venom responded with a hint of disgust in his voice. "The home of the Flora dragons."

Fendrel had been to the outskirts of Everspring Grove many times. It was not often he stepped inside, but when he did it felt as though every tree, every leaf, and every root was watching him.

A safety measure to keep humans out, Fendrel remembered as he collected his blankets back from Thea and Oliver to shove in his bag.

Like the empty-headedness of the Hazy Woods.

"Oh, we are going to see Fragrance!" Fog lifted her wings jovially. All drowsiness cleared from her visage.

"We are," Venom confirmed in a tone as listless as his expression. He crouched for Fendrel, Thea, and Oliver to clamber on.

"Who's Fragrance?" Fendrel asked once seated.

"He is the noble of the Flora tribe!" Fog grinned wide. She did not seem to pick up on Venom's reaction to her excitement.

"And my father." Sour puffed his chest out proudly. "The finest noble in all the Freelands."

"Right." Venom spread his wings and took flight. Fog and Sour followed close on his tail. When they were higher, Fendrel surveyed the area. There was no sign of the rogue.

Perhaps it saw Venom and got spooked. Or perhaps it's waiting for the right moment to attack. That thing won't leave without a fight. It never does.

Something in the back of Fendrel's mind told him that his assumptions were correct. He vowed to himself that he would keep an eye out, at least until they found cover under the tree canopy of Everspring Grove.

CHAPTER 16: CHARLES

"NO." SADON LOCKED HIS STEELY gaze upon Charles, who blinked in confusion. The two hunters were alone in Sadon's study, a small room in the heart of the Stronghold. It was filled only by a chair, a desk covered in neatly-piled documents, and a floor-to-ceiling map of the Freelands hammered to the back wall. Charles stood before the desk while Sadon sat and tapped the dull end of his writing charcoal against the desktop.

"With Oliver temporarily gone, you've lost one of your duties, and I can't have you lazing about. So, you're going to the Stone Edge ruins in search of more shadow dragons," the blonde man instructed without a drop of emotion in his voice.

Dusk dragons, Charles corrected Sadon in his head. *Fendrel says they're called Dusk dragons.*

"We currently have a shortage." Sadon leaned forward as if to give his next statement more weight. "I am giving you *one chance* to prove your worth and regain your previous position."

Charles nodded. "So we'll be leaving today." He had learned early on to phrase his questions as statements when speaking to Sadon. His leader tended to get short with hunters who lacked absolute certainty in their assignments.

Sadon shook his head. "Not with me. You'll be accompanied by hunters of my choice. I expect you to be back within seven days. That should allow you enough travel and hunting time."

Without supervision? Charles thought. *I've never been more than a few rooms away from him in years. Is this a trap to see if I'm loyal?*

"I see." Charles nodded again. His mouth dried in anticipation. "By my 'previous position,' do you mean—"

"Teaching the new recruits," Sadon finished for him. "You saw how delayed they were at the Sharpdagger storage house. Even after Fendrel attacked, they still waited for my order to fire. You're the one who trained Fendrel, and it seems your teaching really brought out his potential. We could use more soldiers like that."

Charles eyed his leader's shoulder. The fabric bulged with bandages where Fendrel's dagger had landed.

If only he hadn't dodged, Charles thought for the hundredth time that week. He drew his gaze away from the injury and bowed his head. "I understand the task."

"Good. Start packing. You're leaving before sundown." Sadon held a small stack of papers out to Charles. "And take these to my quarters."

As the second-in-command retrieved the handout and departed from Sadon's study, he felt a strange mix of dread and elation. Charles had always loved interacting with the students, especially Fendrel's group. He used to enjoy sabotaging Sadon's operations in miniscule ways. But the one time he went too far, when he helped Fendrel and Frederick escape, he lost his instructor position in its entirety.

But if I want that position back, I'll have to doom a few more dragons to death, Charles told himself. *And they're Dusk dragons! I thought we had enough of their resources. What more could we gain from their scales and claws that we don't already have? We're not short on money, are we?*

Charles walked down the cobblestone halls of the dragon hunters' main base—a formidable castle in the heart of the desert. He flipped through the papers, trying to find a document on finances to answer his question. Perhaps if he found the issue, he could solve it without hurting anyone.

What's this?

His brow furrowed at one of the pages. A letter from one of Sadon's informants in the city of Sharpdagger. After each sentence he read, Charles looked over his shoulder to see if anyone was nearby. He was soon engulfed in the contents of the message, which was printed in a clear hand:

> The family has left their house under the cover of night. We were unable to track them, and we are not sure if they are still within the city. I would advise acting as you normally do around Charles.

What he was reading did not feel real, like a cruel joke was being played on him. Charles expected the messenger to appear around a corner and mock him for believing the letter, or for the paper to disappear from his hands as though it had never existed.

Has Sadon read this yet? Does he really not know where my family have gone?

An army of conflicting emotions swelled within him. Sadon no longer had eyes on his wife and daughter. Now that they were gone, Sadon could not hurt them if Charles disobeyed, but where were they?

Are they safe? Where have they gone, and why at night?

His pace down the hall increased which each new thought.

Did they realize they were being watched this whole time? They must have. Why else would they leave so secretly and so suddenly?

"Charles!" Sadon called from behind him.

Charles hid the page in the center of the stack before turning around. "Yes, sir?"

Sadon approached his underling with a hand outstretched. "I'd meant to give you a different stack, but it appears I've misplaced it. I'll take those back."

Trying to keep a stoic face while his head swam with confusion, Charles returned the stack of papers. "I can help you look for them."

"No, no." Sadon waved his hand in a tired and dismissive manner. He looked as though he had not slept well in weeks, but Charels would never mention that out loud.

Sadon scowled at a hole in one of Charles' dragon leather gloves. With a sigh, he shoved the stack of papers in his armpit and removed his own gloves. "Your equipment is defective. Take mine. You'll need it for your mission."

Charles nodded and accepted Sadon's gloves.

"Now go pack." Sadon jutted his chin in the direction of Charles' room. "Oh, and when you go out there, try to find a few younger dragons. They last longer."

"Of course." Charles bowed his head as Sadon left. The fear of almost being caught made his hands shake. He stood there for a moment before regaining his composure and scurrying off to his room. As soon as he shut the door, Charles was overcome with the irresistible urge to write in his journal. Anxiety pricked the back of his neck as he tossed the gloves on his bed, took his journal and writing charcoal from its hiding spot in the cobblestone wall, and began to write:

I think I can finally leave. I don't remember the last time I felt this free.

He's sending me away for a week under supervision of other hunters, but I fear it may be a

The Dragon Liberator: Escapade

*trap to see if I am truly loyal. So, I have two choices: I
can pretend the letter doesn't exist and carry out this
mission. Or I can run.*

But where would I go?

Charles stared at his floor, unblinking, as he weighed his options. Then a pair of footsteps passing by the other side of his door brought him out of his stupor. He followed his writing routine of removing the page from its binding and burning it in his room's fireplace. As Charles moved his hand under his bed to store the journal back in the spot he carved for it, he froze.

If this is a trick and Sadon planned for me to read that letter, he will find out that I know of his ruse, Charles thought. He pondered for a moment longer and pushed his worries aside. *But why would Sadon lay this trap now after all this time? It doesn't make any sense . . . unless Raquel and Josephine truly have gotten away. They're smart. They would have made sure they weren't followed.*

"There's no point in leaving this then," Charles said aloud as he placed the journal onto his bed and prepared a travel bag. He kept his voice at a mutter as he continued. "I have to believe they're safe. And if Sadon's going to kill me, he'll have to find me first."

Charles' chest swam with worry at this reckless new attitude that carried him, but he was also sick of being afraid. He felt a rebellious smile tug at his lips. As he packed his bag, Charles began to plan how he would make his escape, and where he would flee to.

I can't send a message to Fendrel in case someone else finds it. I suppose he'll have to figure this out on his own.

The second-in-command believed the young man would understand. He just hoped rescuing the dragons would not be too difficult now that he would no longer be there to help.

CHAPTER 17: FENDREL

PARANOIA KEPT FENDREL'S HEAD ON a swivel. It was making him dizzy. He searched his thoughts for anything to keep his mind off the possibility of the rogue making an appearance.

"So, what is this Fragrance like?" Fendrel forced himself to look forward at the sprawling plains below. He knew the forest just a few leagues away was their destination.

Venom snorted. "He is one of the nobles that neglected to show up for Cloud's emergency meeting."

"Perhaps he was preoccupied," Fog offered.

The Dusk dragon lowered his voice. "Perhaps he was fretting over his own precious scales instead of his future queen."

Fog gave Venom a curious sidelong glance but remained silent.

Before anything more could be said, Venom suddenly flared out his wings to hover midair. Fendrel, Thea, and Oliver lurched forward in their seats. Venom's shoulders and back were broad enough that they did not fall off, but nonetheless Fendrel grabbed onto the mage and the boy.

Venom's neck snaked about as he looked at their surroundings. His lips pulled back to bare his teeth, and his snout wrinkled in a snarl.

Fog and Sour also halted to hover just beside Venom. Fog attempted to follow Venom's gaze, but he was moving too quickly for her to keep up. Sour appeared annoyed as he narrowed his eyes at the other two dragons.

The Dusk dragon sniffed the air, deep and drawn out. A low growl emanated from his chest. He commanded, "Everyone land. Now."

There was no hesitation as the dragons descended. Once they touched down in the grass, Fog asked, "Venom, what is it?"

"Keep your voices low." Venom sniffed once more. "I smell a rogue."

"Is it a Fire dragon?" Fendrel found he could not move. His heart

The Dragon Liberator: Escapade

began to pound loudly in his ears. From his seat on Venom's shoulders Fendrel saw Fog and Sour flatten themselves against the ground.

"Yes," Venom confirmed. He crouched so his human passengers could slide off. "Go to the Grove, I will catch up later. Do not *dare* fly unless it starts chasing you."

It took every bit of willpower Fendrel had to dismount and leave Venom's side. "Do you see it yet?" he asked.

Venom turned around to face where they had flown from. He held his breath for a moment as his eyes glued to a single spot.

Fendrel looked to see what Venom was staring at. Dread made his rushing blood feel like it was freezing and burning all at once. There, as unmissable as a speck of color on a white cloth, was the Fire rogue.

The beast was sitting on its haunches as it peered at their group. It seemed to notice it had drawn Fendrel's attention, and the maddened dragon flicked its tail like a cat who had discovered a mouse.

"You need to leave now," Venom said in a hushed tone.

After a series of deep breaths, Fendrel was able to move his body again. As he backed away, his eyes still on the rogue, Thea and Oliver entered his peripheral. He stuck an arm out to keep them behind himself.

I'm not the only human here, he remembered. *They're in danger, too.*

"Thea, Oliver, back up slowly. Don't take your eyes off it." Fendrel wished his voice was not quivering. He wished he could reassure them.

"Here." Fog crept toward the humans and crouched.

Fendrel helped Oliver onto Fog's back while Thea climbed up unaided. Fog stumbled and spread her wings to regain her balance. Her sudden movement made the rogue advance a few steps, before it stopped again.

"Go. I will get rid of it." Venom flared his wings and lashed his tail, trying to draw the rogue's attention. He roared loud enough for his voice to carry on for miles.

With a shrill roar to match, the rogue surged forward to meet Venom's challenge. He leapt into the sky on enraged wings.

Venom lifted off and raced toward the rogue.

Go! Fendrel screamed inwardly at himself. He reached out for Sour but then retracted his hand. *Flora dragons hate humans touching them, and Fog won't be able to run very fast with all three of us weighing her down.*

"Come on!" Fendrel sprinted off toward the expanse of trees the Flora tribe called home. Fog and Sour were quick to join him, and the green dragon was even quicker to surpass them. Fog kept her pace slow enough to not leave Fendrel behind, despite his head shaking in protest. Against his better judgement, Fendrel looked over his shoulder.

High above, Venom and the rogue latched on to each other, snapping at one another's throats. The rogue was smaller than Venom, but its neck was also shorter and made for a difficult target. It tried to slash at the softer scales of Venom's belly, but the Dusk dragon kicked it away.

Before the rogue could regain his bearings, Venom hooked his claws into one of the Fire dragon's wings and the back of its neck. In one moment, they were airborne, and the next Venom had tucked in his wings and was forcing them both into a plummet. The rogue roared in pain and fury as it writhed within Venom's grip. They fell faster, and just before they hit the ground, Venom flung open his wings and dropped the rogue.

There should have been enough time for the red dragon to recover, but one of his wings refused to work. It flailed at his side until the beast crashed.

"Fendrel!" Fog shouted.

Fendrel snapped his head back to what lay ahead and realized he had slowed his pace while he was watching the battle. He ignored the combating bellows of the dragons behind him and pushed onward. His temples pulsed with blood flow as fast as his feet pounded the ground. Fendrel's legs began to burn, but he barely noticed it over the adrenaline that surged through his veins. He watched as Sour's lime green form retreated into the threshold of the Flora dragons' domain.

Just a few more seconds, Fendrel encouraged himself. *You'll disappear into the forest, and you'll be safe.*

He kept running and soon passed the first line of trees. The exposed roots forced him to slow down, and Fendrel caught himself with both hands against a trunk before he could trip. Fendrel leaned against the tree until his heart quieted enough for him to hear his own breaths. Fog stumbled in just next to him, her chest heaving from exertion.

Thea and Oliver dropped down from Fog's back and scurried just a few steps farther into the forest. Both looked frightened and Oliver trembled as though he was on the verge of crying.

Looking at Oliver's tiny frame, Fendrel was reminded of just how young he was. In the hunter's warehouse the boy had proclaimed himself to be seven years old.

That's too young to go through something like this. He's far too young . . . Fendrel's heart sank. The first time he had encountered the rogue was when he was Oliver's age, and it had hunted him ever since. *I can't let Oliver be fearful his whole life, not like I've been.*

Fendrel collected his thoughts and went to crouch before Oliver, so he was at eye-level with the boy. "Hey, you're all right," he said in the most reassuring voice he could muster. "Venom is going to scare it away. We're safe in here."

His words did not seem to affect the boy. Oliver's face scrunched up as tears welled in his eyes.

Fog approached them. She plucked a feather from one of her wings and held it between two claws. The Vapor dragon had a shy smile as she said, "Oliver, I have something to show you." She released the feather and used her breath to blow it upward.

Oliver watched the feather flutter down, only to be lifted again by the gray dragon.

"Now you try," Fog said, stepping back. "Don't let it touch the ground."

Distracted by the new game, Oliver sniffled and took Fog's place in keeping the feather afloat. After a few puffs, his face broke out into a competitive smile.

I hope this doesn't affect him too badly, Fendrel thought. *We need to find somewhere safe for him before we run into more trouble.*

His calm was interrupted by a chill traveling down his spine. Fendrel looked deeper into the forest. Peeking out from behind trees and bushes were Flora dragons in a myriad of colors, shapes, and sizes. Some were skinny with blossoms and fruits growing out of their hides. Others were tall, broad-shouldered, and covered in tree bark. Wherever Fendrel looked, Flora dragons retreated into the greenery. Snapping twigs and rustling leaves were the only signal that the dragons had been there. The sounds of fleeing made Thea and Fog turn their heads.

Though he was just on the edge of the forest, Fendrel could already feel the domain's attempts to keep him out. The Flora dragons were gone, but the feeling of being watched, of being hunted, persisted. He stopped himself from reaching into his bag for a weapon.

It isn't real, Fendrel told himself. *The forest is safe.*

His own thoughts did nothing to calm his nerves. Fendrel leaned against a trunk in an effort to appear more relaxed and said, "We should wait for Venom before we continue."

"We should," Fog agreed with a nod. "I have never been here, so I cannot lead us through."

"Good idea," Thea mumbled. She had her arms crossed in a nervous manner and goosebumps pricked across her skin. She too was staring into Everspring Grove. From the look on her face, Fendrel could not tell if she had seen something or if she was keeping an eye out for some voracious predator.

Venom did not return for a few minutes, and each second that ticked by made Fendrel want to leave the forest and check on the Dusk dragon. The last Fendrel had seen of Venom, it appeared he was winning against the rogue, but anything could have happened once Fendrel looked away.

Is Venom hurt? Why hasn't he shown up yet? Fendrel kept his head swiveling from the tree line to the depths of the forest as time continued to pass. Finally, just as Fendrel became antsy enough to pace, Venom landed just outside the tree cover.

Fendrel smiled as a sigh of relief escaped him. He left the others to meet Venom halfway. "You're all right."

Venom had an array of superficial cuts, and his breathing was labored, but otherwise he looked normal. Once Fendrel was before him, Venom too sighed. "I am. You are all right?"

"Yes, we all are," Fendrel said as he gestured to Fog, Thea, and Oliver. "Is the rogue dead?"

"It will bother you no longer," Venom assured.

Fendrel nodded, but a piece of him was unconvinced. *I can't believe it's gone until I see its body. Did Venom truly kill it? . . . If he is here, it means he won. I shouldn't let my fears interfere with the search for Mist.*

"The Flora dragons know we're here," said Fendrel.

"Of course they do." Venom's snout wrinkled in what Fendrel assumed was contempt.

"What do you have against the Flora tribe?" Fendrel asked.

"They are not fond of humans." Venom started off to join the rest of the group. "And I have personal reasons."

Fendrel followed just behind with the inclination he would get a real answer soon enough. When he regrouped, Fog was already tending to Venom's wounds with her breath. Every cut her vapor touched knit together, leaving behind no trace of his injuries.

Dusk dragons must have thicker skin than other dragons if that's all the rogue managed to do to him.

Venom gave Oliver an amused grin as the boy continued to keep the feather in the air. He jutted his chin forward and said, "Let us continue. We have much ground to cover, and we cannot afford to spend more time here than we must."

Fendrel stuck close to Venom's side as they pushed through the forest. He felt the presence of more lingering gazes but saw no Flora dragons to accompany them. The air felt burdened with stares. Every rustling bush sounded closer than the last and each step Fendrel took was more difficult as his sense of danger spiked.

"They are not real," Venom reminded. He was looking down at Fendrel with that same concerned face he had exhibited the previous night.

"I know," Fendrel said, though some part of him was screaming that he needed to run out of the forest as quick as his legs could move. Beside him, Thea still had one of her arms crossed while she held Oliver's hand with the other. The boy maintained the challenge of keeping the feather off the ground, but every now and then he looked off into the greenery as though something moved in his peripheral.

Fog, unaffected by the domain's defense, marveled at the plants surrounding them. "These trees are shaped so strangely from the ones at home," she said as she stumbled over an exposed root. "And they are so short."

There was no clear path to follow. Flowers, fruits, small woodland creatures, and leaves of varying shapes shielded Fendrel's view of what lay ahead. The plants pressed in on him. He was starting to feel trapped. Just as his heart was becoming too loud to focus on anything else, a melodic greeting rang out ahead.

"Fog, is that you?" asked a male voice.

"Fragrance!" Fog's face lit up and her wings lifted in excitement. She hurried in front of the others to follow the sound.

All at once, the oppressive feeling of being stalked vanished. Fendrel felt his heart settle into its normal rhythm. He pushed aside a particularly large fern and found himself in a clearing where the sun dappled the earth.

A short, fat oak tree sat at the back of the clearing, encircled by a stream. Laying in leisure among the roots was a dragon with lemon-yellow scales and a haughty grin. All along his spine grew branches abundant in bright green leaves. His horns were similarly shaped, but longer, thicker, and barren. Fendrel found himself staring at the Flora dragon's ears, adorned with jade earrings that matched the bangles around his wrists. Other Flora dragons were crowded around him, picking specks of dirt from his scales.

Another dragon, alike in every way save for her bright orange scales and lack of jewelry, lay by his side. To Fendrel's surprise, Sour rested on the yellow dragon's other side.

"Thank the stars you are safe, dear," said the yellow dragon. "We were all so worried when my son—" he flicked his tail in Sour's direction "—reported you were being chased by a rogue!"

So, this is Fragrance, Fendrel realized.

"We are safe now, thanks to Venom," Fog replied cheerily.

Fragrance gave her a smile devoid of happiness. "Well, seeing as how you have already met my son, let me introduce my daughter, Divine." He gestured to the orange dragon beside him. Only then did Fragrance's eyes land on the humans. His smile dropped and he rose from his seat to approach the group. Twigs cracked under his splayed talons. "Why have you brought humans with you? They are not welcome in our domains."

Divine and Sour turned up their snouts as they moved to stand by their father. The surrounding Flora dragons shared worried glances between each other before melting into the forest's coverage. Within seconds, Fragrance and his children were the only members of the Flora tribe still in the clearing.

Fog blinked in surprise. "Oh . . . this is Fendrel and his friends. They are helping us look for Mist."

The branches on Fragrance's back bristled. "Why would humans, of all creatures, be *helping* you? Fog, dear, you are so naïve."

"I know you have not been fond of humans in the past, but they truly are here to help," Fog defended. Even as she kept smiling, her ears and wings began to sink.

"How do you know?" Fragrance smirked. "Did they tell you these things?"

"Yes, actually, they did," Venom cut in. Fragrance rolled his eyes as Venom spoke, but the Dusk dragon ignored him. "Fendrel here learned Drake-tongue as a child, and these two—" Venom pointed at Thea and Oliver with one of his paws "—are in possession of enchanted items to aid them in understanding us."

From the size of Fragrance's horns, Fendrel guessed he was as old as Venom, although he was nowhere near as tall. Still Fragrance lifted his head in such a way so he would have to look down his nose to address Venom.

Fendrel nearly scoffed at the gesture. He had run into a number of ungrateful, arrogant Flora dragons during his missions.

If this is their leader, it makes sense why they have all been so rude to me thus far. Sour never even thanked me or Venom after we rescued him.

Despite his better judgement, Fendrel wanted to annoy the Flora noble. He smiled as courteously as he could manage, and said, "So, you're the noble who was too preoccupied to the king's emergency meeting."

Fragrance pried his eyes away from Venom to scowl at Fendrel.

"Forgive me if my expectations are too high, but I thought after spending all this time away from the trouble you'd be *shinier*?" Fendrel said with an exaggerated wince.

"Hmm. Quite the personality your little friend has." Fragrance grinned toothily before answering, "Ah! That reminds me, I received an update from His Majesty. You see, though I was unbale to the meeting, I am still very much involved in this matter."

A dragon whose fur was short and fuzzy like moss approached with her head down. She held a thin tablet of bark in her wing claw, which she promptly handed to Venom before scurrying to Fragrance's side.

Venom took a moment to read the short report. He nodded. "The other search party has found no trace of Mist either."

"That is unfortunate," Fragrance said.

The moss mimic retrieved the message and ran back to her cover.

"Speaking of Mist, why are you all here? Shouldn't you be looking for her among the dragon hunters?" Fragrance asked.

"We are leaving no stone unturned. Thus we are investigating humans as well as our own kind," Venom explained. "This was our next stop. Do you have any information that may be useful in our investigation?"

Fragrance shook his head. "I do not, so you and your little companions should be set to move on."

"We would, but as I said, we are checking every possibility," Venom said as Fragrance's smile faltered. "We will be looking around, asking a few questions, and—" Venom placed a wing claw on Fendrel's shoulder "—His Majesty endorsed Fendrel specifically to help."

"Right. Of course. But you will not find anything here. You are wasting precious time while Mist's whereabouts still remain unknown." Fragrance gave Fog a curt wave before returning to his seat between the thick oak's roots.

Venom ushered Fog and the humans away from the clearing with his wings. Once they were out of earshot, he released a groan.

"I am sorry," Fog mumbled as she looked between Fendrel, Oliver, and Thea. "I knew he did not like humans, but I thought if he knew why you were here, he would have been welcoming."

"It's not your fault. We had to come here, regardless. Besides, in my experience, it's rare to meet a human-friendly Flora dragon," Fendrel reassured her. "So, where are we going first?"

"Not far at all. Some of the dragons here are a bit more curious than they would like to admit." Venom glanced up at the branches. "They are hiding around here now."

An acorn and a few twigs plummeted to the ground. Fendrel followed Venom's gaze and saw a cluster of dragons hiding in the trees, freezing when they realized they had been spotted.

Venom sat in the grass and called to them, "Come down now if you would like to speak. We do not want to take more time than we must."

One by one the dragons slinked down from the trees. Fendrel marveled at how different each one looked from its neighbors. They all appeared nervous as they looked over their shoulders at one another and ducked their heads. Fendrel wondered if their apprehension came from being around a dragon as large and intimidating as Venom, or if they feared whatever consequence they may face from Fragrance.

Is Fragrance hiding something and they all know it? Fendrel wondered. *I suppose there is only one way to find out.*

Fendrel grinned at the gathered dragons, this time attempting to look approachable. He tried to shake the creeping feeling that Fragrance was dangerous and joined Venom in questioning the gathered dragons.

CHAPTER 18: CASSIUS

SOMEONE DEFINITELY WANTS ME DEAD.

The prince held a note in his shaking hands. It had been sticking out from under his pillow just enough to be noticed. He whispered it to himself again, drinking in every word, "You shouldn't stick your nose where it doesn't belong. I know you've been following me. Stay out of my business and I'll keep my blade from your neck."

No name.

The only people I have been following are Zoricus and his allies in the royal guard, but Zoricus is not here. He is on his annual patrol across the kingdom. Cassius clenched the threat in his fists. *Did one of the other knights do this?*

He felt his mouth go dry. The words in the note sounded like how his cousin spoke to him when no one else was around. Zoricus was the perfect man in public, but would turn cold, insulting, and disdainful if Cassius was his only witness. For as long as Cassius could remember, Zoricus had been sending harsh words and looks his way. But there were never threats like this before.

Did Zoricus hear about me eavesdropping and ordered someone to leave me this letter? I will have to get some of his own writing and compare to really make sure—

He stopped his thoughts short. "Poking around is what got me into trouble in the first place." Cassius tossed the paper on his bed.

I cannot tell the guard about this, in case they are compliant with the sender, Cassius thought. He paced before his bed, casting uneasy looks at the letter each time he passed it. *I cannot tell Father or Sadie either. Zoricus has always been good to me when they are around. They would never believe he would write something like this. I need help, but who can I trust?*

Cassius' chest felt like it was full of stone. He moved to one of his windows and threw it open for some fresh air. The palace grounds and royal gardens sprawled out before him and he could see the streets even farther out were teeming with his people. The citizens were too far for him to pick out any recognizable faces, even among the armored guards who surveyed the streets. As outside air filled his lungs, Cassius continued to linger by the window.

The streets are so crowded that if I was down there, the guards would be none the wiser to my presence. I would be able to slip in and out like the Liberator. A wistful smile played on his lips. He had not snuck into the city that morning, and every bit of him was itching to return. *The Liberator can come and go as he pleases, regardless of how hated he is by the royal guard.*

Cassius' eyes shone with reverence. "I bet he hates them just as much," he mumbled. "He *must* know about Zoricus buying dragon eggs. Surely, he wants to stop him."

An idea began to take shape in Cassius' mind. He shut his window, tucked the threat into his pocket, and resumed his pacing.

If I can convince the Liberator to help me find proof that Zoricus sent me that letter, I will have undeniable evidence of his mistreatment toward me, Cassius plotted. *Father and Sadie will finally believe me, and I can have Zoricus banished. But I have no idea where the Liberator is. Perhaps . . . perhaps the High Mage will be able to help me with that.*

Without a second thought, he hurried out of his room and started down the hall to find the royal family's High Mage. Mages were not commonly employed within the palace due to the potential danger of a wayward spell. However, a High Mage was one who had been vetted and approved by all members of the king's council. Cassius had only ever seen his family's mage during trials when magic would be used to draw the truth out of someone. He hoped that was not the only kind of spell the High Mage could cast.

Dread pricked the back of his neck.

Should I be doing this? Cassius wondered. *If I leave to find the Liberator, Sadie and Father will be upset.*

Yes! Of course you have to leave, Cassius told himself. *With every meal you become more ill, and you just received a death threat! It is no longer safe for you here. Whoever threatened you and whoever is poisoning you will not be able to do anything if you leave. With Zoricus and some of the guards out of the city, now is the perfect time to act.*

As Cassius passed through the halls toward the High Mage's living quarters, he glanced out the floor-to-ceiling windows that overlooked the gardens. Adila was there, somewhere, though he dared not search for her. He instead averted his eyes.

I am making the best decision for myself, Cassius thought with more assurance. *Sadie and Father may be upset by my leaving, but it will all be better in the end.*

The prince continued down a corridor he had never ventured before and ended up in front of an ornate door that was not too different from any other door in the palace. He wondered if this was the right place. His suspicions were alleviated when he raised his fist to knock, and the door opened before he could make contact with the polished wood. As it gently swung inward, out stepped the High Mage.

In all the years the mage spent working for the royal family, Cassius had never seen the man's face. He was covered head-to-toe in a hooded maroon robe. His identity was further concealed by gloves, high boots, and a black mask that covered the bottom half of his face. Cassius once knew the man's name, but due to the mage's services being seldom used he had long since forgotten it.

Did he hear me coming and wanted to greet me before I could knock, or did he somehow know I was going to visit him today? Cassius wondered uneasily.

The mage nodded his head in greeting. His magenta eyes had all the mischief of a fox, even when his voice was full of sincerity. "Hello, young prince."

Odd-colored eyes were strange enough, but Cassius never understood why the mage's skin—what little of it he could see—was gray.

Perhaps he has a disease and that is why he wears so much clothing?

As Cassius looked at the man, his vision was suddenly assaulted by a throbbing headache and puzzling shapes and colors, the very same ones he experienced whenever he spoke with Adila. Cassius stabbed his thumb nail into his palm to make sure he still had control of his body.

Why is this happening? The High Mage has worked for us for years and never once has this happened to me when he is around! Cassius fought through the headache to collect his thoughts. *All this started with Adila. What did she do to me and my father's staff?*

Cassius returned the nod and forced a smile to his lips. "Good afternoon. I have a task for you. I hope you are not busy."

"Not at all." The mage pushed the door open wider and motioned for Cassius to enter his chambers. "How may my services be of use to you?"

The prince held his breath and stepped through the threshold. The room was darkened by thick curtains. When the mage shut the door,

Cassius could only see by the light of a few candles on a desk. Cassius approached the candles, wondering how the mage could navigate the room with so little to see by. He almost jumped when the high mage stepped to the other side of the desk, his eyes shining in the darkness as if they were floating in void.

"I—" Cassius struggled to keep eye contact with the man as his headache intensified. It was more painful now that all he could see was the man's piercing gaze. "I was wondering if you would be able to find someone for me."

"Find someone?" The mage drummed his gloved fingers on the desk. "As in tracking someone down?"

"Yes, a wanted man," Cassius blurted. "The Liberator."

"Much brighter than your cousin, you are." The mage chuckled. "You seek to find the Liberator so you can apprehend him before he causes more upset? How virtuous."

Cassius forced out a short laugh. "How did you know?" he asked playfully.

"Give me a moment," said the mage as he shut his eyes.

For a few seconds, all Cassius could make out was his silhouette in the dim light. Then, the mage's eyes opened.

"He is in the western forest, heading southward." The mage made a contemplative, almost humming sound before he said, "I would advise caution. He is accompanied by a dragon. A shadow dragon."

Cassius swallowed. "Thank you for your time," he said before he turned around and stumbled toward the door. He placed his hand on the knob, then looked back at the older man. "Do you have a way of testing a person's body for poison?"

"Poison. How morbid." The mage seemed to ponder briefly. "I do not. My magic does not work that way. Do you have a concern about someone, my prince?"

I should not have asked him that. If he has been corrupted by Adila, I do not want her to find out that I am suspicious of her.

"No," Cassius said too quickly. He cleared his throat. "I was just curious." It was only after Cassius left the High Mage's quarters that his vision returned to normal, and his headache ebbed away.

I knew this would be difficult, but now there is a shadow dragon involved, too? Cassius shuddered with worry. *Those things are strong enough to kill other dragons. And those fangs of theirs are as long as daggers!*

The prince kept a brisk pace as he began the trek back to his room.

I am not brave enough for this, but my life is in danger here! Cassius shoved a hand in his pocket to feel the note, to remind himself of what he needed to do. He hardened his gaze as though trying to convince himself that his plan would work. *I am being poisoned by my fiancée and my own guards want me dead for trying to expose their corruption. I cannot stay here.*

I need to leave. Tonight.

CHAPTER 19: FENDREL

VENOM HAD GONE TO SEARCH Everspring Grove for any sign of Mist, but he returned without luck. Not a scent was picked up for miles. Looking defeated, Venom resumed control of interviewing the Flora dragons from Fendrel, who had similar success getting information out of the plant-like dragons. Most of them appeared innocent enough, but Venom was steadfast in speaking to each one regardless.

I suppose I don't blame him. Fragrance wasn't at Cloud's meeting, so he may have something to hide.

The last dragon they spoke with had scales that curled like the petals of a pink rose and whose paws were green and covered in thorns. She scowled at Fendrel as she left, but her words were directed toward Venom and Fog, "I don't know why you're getting yourself into trouble with these humans. It's more likely they'll hurt Mist once you find her than help her return home." The Flora dragon disappeared into the foliage without a trace.

Fog's feathers bristled at the statement. She trudged off into the forest. "Come with me."

"To where?" Fendrel sped up to walk alongside her.

"I am going to have Fragrance apologize to you, Thea, and Oliver," she announced.

Venom sighed. "Come back, Fog. He will not apologize. That is just the way he is."

Fog halted in her tracks, then turned back around. Her expression was that of resignation. "I have just never seen him act like that before," she said as her wings sank. "He is always so kind during his visits to the Hazy Woods."

Venom ushered her and Fendrel back over. His claws sank into the earth as he explained, "It is a political ploy. He tries to make a good impression on you, so if he ever got into trouble, you would vouch for him. If you refuse to vouch for him, he slanders your name using secrets you told him in confidence."

Fendrel raised his eyebrows at Venom. "You sound like you're speaking from experience."

"I nearly lost my title years ago due to his sly games. Unfortunately, young Cloud is as naïve as his father was. He believes Fragrance truly cares for him and Mist." Venom shook off a leaf that his claws had punctured. "We should get back to finding the poor girl. The sooner we finish here, the sooner we can leave this place."

"We already checked what we could and asked who we could," Thea said. "You said you couldn't smell her, either. Where else is there to look?"

"There is only one spot I avoided. I did not want to stoop to this level, but we have not yet searched the area around Fragrance's den." Venom sighed through his nose. "I would feel better about leaving if we looked around the perimeter of his home, but if we cannot find anything we must move on."

"Should we let him know first?" Fog asked. "I think it is only fair, seeing as this is his domain."

"Well, we won't be going *inside* his home." Fendrel shrugged. "Besides, do you ever think Fragrance would give his permission?"

Fog shook her head sullenly. "No, I do not."

"Now is as good a time as any, since he is still busy being preened." Venom shot a disdainful glare in the clearing's direction. "We only have about an hour of daylight left. Let us finish so we may travel a little longer. I do not want to spend the night here."

"I don't blame you," Fendrel mumbled.

Venom crouched low. "Climb on, if you would like. It is not far from here, but the roots are more unruly where we are headed."

Thea and Oliver lifted themselves onto the black dragon's shoulders.

"And you would like to walk, yes? To help you plan?" Venom asked Fendrel as he stood.

"I would." Fendrel nodded, appreciative that Venom had remembered their conversation from the day prior.

Fendrel, Fog, and Venom slunk through the forest toward Fragrance's living quarters. Leaves littered the ground, softening their footsteps as they advanced. Just as Venom said, the trees farther in had roots that wound over the ground and braided together to form a bumpy wooden floor.

"What does Fragrance's den look like?" Fendrel asked. From between the trees he could see nothing but more forest. Everything appeared the same to him, but Venom led as though he had walked this route a million times.

Venom snorted. "You will know it when you see it."

As they traveled deeper, Fendrel understood what Venom meant.

In a small clearing, a cluster of citrus trees stood together with their branches twisting and tangling to form a spherical den. Two small, gurgling waterfalls framed the trees and converged in front of it before winding off into the forest. Beside the above-ground den was one of a similar design but shorter and wider.

That lower one must be for his children, Fendrel assumed.

Everything about the scenery before him looked like the essence of spring itself, and it would stay that way. As the name claimed, it was always spring in Everspring Grove just as it was always summer in the Fire tribe's Twin Oases, always winter at Frost Lake, and always autumn at the Dusk tribe's Black Brick Ruins. Seasons never changed for the dragons, and neither would Fragrance's den as long as he remained the noble of the Flora tribe.

"How selfish," Venom muttered, snapping Fendrel from his thoughts.

"What is?" Fendrel followed the Dusk dragon as they walked around the perimeter of the clearing. Venom momentarily stopped to let Thea and Oliver down before resuming his stride.

"Here in the Grove, all dragons that mimic the same type of plant are supposed share a space." Venom gestured at the only present citrus trees—the ones making up the dens. "All the Flora dragons whose bodies mimic those of citrus fruits are supposed to live in this area, but it seems Fragrance has kicked them out in favor of claiming the plants for himself and his family."

"That is awful," Fog said barely above a whisper.

"I gather that's important, but I was never clear on why their bodies mimic plants in the first place," Fendrel said while he looked for anything out of the ordinary.

"When a Flora dragon is in its egg, it is the parents' duty to bathe the eggshell in the juice of whatever plant they wish their child to hatch as. If there is no juice, they will grind up the plant matter and mix it with water," Venom explained as he lifted a few leaves off the ground. "Even these can be used. Fragrance's egg was likely covered in lemon juice, and he in turn covered his children's eggs in the juices of a lime, blood orange, and grapefruit."

Fendrel paused. "Grapefruit? I only saw two of his children."

"Yes." Venom gave Fendrel a look of concern. "His second daughter was not with him. I have no idea where she may be."

Is that why Fragrance wasn't at the meeting? Because something is wrong with his daughter? Fendrel wondered. He started to feel sorry for the lemon mimic, but then something caught his eye.

"You see that, as well?" Venom asked. He pointed to a spot in the ground, closer to the cluster of trees, where the dirt was darker than anywhere else.

The group approached the oddity and Fendrel stooped down. "Here," Fendrel said as he placed his palm on the ground. "The dirt is churned up."

Venom lowered his nose to the dirt and sniffed about the area. A troubled look overcame his face, and he paused.

"What is it?" Fog lowered her head to be in Venom's line of sight.

"Fendrel, could you back up a little?" Venom asked. "There is something strange buried here, and your scent is confusing my senses."

Fendrel felt his ears burn in embarrassment, but he complied, taking a few steps back. "Just mine?"

Venom ignored Fendrel's words and began to scoop loose, cool dirt away with his paws. Fog joined in, although her efforts were vastly outshined by Venom's.

Suddenly, the black dragon stopped with one paw still submerged in dirt. There was something in his eyes that made the hair on Fendrel's arms stand on end. Venom said, "Fendrel, come look at this."

The Dusk dragon unearthed a head-sized rock. He cradled the stone and held it out toward Fendrel, who peered down quizzically.

There was a word carved into it with messy lettering: Axella. Fendrel balled his fists, understanding now why his scent was troubling Venom. "Why does Fragrance have that?"

"What is it?" Fog's face was etched with worry. "Who is that?"

All feelings of disdain Fendrel had for Fragrance were replaced with rage. He stared at the rock, too shocked to move. "That's my mother's headstone. I carved her name on that the day she died."

CHAPTER 20: FENDREL

VENOM AND FENDREL STORMED IN tandem to the clearing where Fragrance rested. Tucked under Fendrel's arm was the headstone. His other hand was balled into a fist. He could scarcely hear the others behind him as his pounding heart overwhelmed his hearing.

Fragrance lay in his same spot, still being preened by a host of Flora dragons. Sour and Divine sat on either side of him. Almost in sync, the siblings whispered to Fragrance, and the lemon mimic's head lifted toward the approaching group.

Fendrel clutched the stone tighter to his side. It was cool with dirt, and Fendrel could not help but wonder how long it had been buried. He put his thoughts aside and stopped mere feet away from the citrus dragons.

"Fragrance," Venom said in a voice on the verge of becoming a growl. "You have some explaining to do."

"Mist is not here. Must I prove you wrong?" Fragrance's eyes rolled, then settled on the stone. He batted his ants away with his wings. "Where did you get that?"

It took every ounce of willpower Fendrel had to keep his composure. He held out the dirt-stained stone. "I should be asking you the same thing," he said.

Fragrance snorted. "A rock? What are you trying to get out of me?"

"A rock," Fendrel repeated, failing to restrain himself. He could not help how his voice rose in volume. "This is my mother's headstone. Why did you take it and hide it by your den?"

"What were you doing poking around my personal quarters?" Fragrance's voice matched Fendrel's in intensity. He stood and flexed one of his paws, making the claws lit up with an eerie brightness.

"Answer the question," Venom commanded.

The Dragon Liberator: Escapade

Fragrance's head snapped up to glare at Venom. The branches on his back bristled in agitation. "You came here looking for Mist and you found nothing. Now you must leave."

"We are not going anywhere until you explain yourself." Venom flared his wings to corner Fragrance against the tree. "Why did you take Axella's headstone?"

"I sent my scouts to collect items of interest. I never told them to steal from the dead," Fragrance spat as his ears flattened against his head.

Fendrel clenched his teeth. "Everything there belongs to the dead."

"Listen well." Fragrance turned his attention back to Fendrel, his snout wrinkling in disgust. "You have been nothing but a nuisance to me since you arrived. If you do not leave now, I will make you regret coming here."

Venom hissed, deep and menacing. "Do *not* threaten him!" He bared his fangs.

Fragrance stretched his neck, so he was almost nose-to-nose with the Dusk dragon. "Why not? He is a human. He is *vermin*."

"I will not allow you to disrespect him. I promised his mother I would protect him, even from my own peers—"

"Oh, please, Venom. You act as though this creature is your own son." Fragrance laughed in incredulousness. When Venom did not back away, his eyes flickered between Fendrel and the Dusk dragon. "Oh, you do . . . Have all these years of protecting his kind from rogues made you lose your mind?"

Venom barely knows me. He wouldn't see me in such a way from just a few days of traveling together, Fendrel thought. He shook his head in disbelief, but the black dragon made no move to deny Fragrance's claim. Fendrel narrowed his eyes on Venom and tried to glean some hidden meaning from his face, but there was nothing but animosity for the Flora noble.

"The next time you speak to him that way, it is you who will be in danger," Venom threatened.

Fragrance waved his children off with a single flick of his tail. He sidestepped Venom and circled around them, so the clearing was at his back.

Fendrel kept his glare on Fragrance. He was about to ask why Fragrance wanted his mother's headstone, but the lemon mimic was already speaking.

"Venom, if you harm me, Cloud will strip you of your position as a noble and as the commander of the royal army. You cannot do anything to me." Fragrance kneaded his claws into the dirt and the strange light in his claws grew more intense. "Therefore, if I have probable cause to harm your *son* such as for trespassing, then I am obligated to take matters into my own paws." Without warning, he slashed Fendrel's face.

Fendrel gasped in pain, dropping the stone so he could clutch the wound.

Venom rushed past Fendrel and dug his claws into Fragrance's shoulders, forcing the smaller yellow dragon onto his back.

Something grabbed Fendrel and pulled him away from the nobles. He felt cold, sharp steel against his skin, but whatever dragged him did so gently. Fendrel kept one eye closed so his blood would not trickle into it. When he looked up, he realized it was Fog who had grabbed him. The Vapor dragon stopped at the edge of the clearing where Thea was blocking Oliver's view of the fight.

"Shields!" Fragrance shouted while he batted at Venom with his wings and talons.

At Fragrance's command, three large Flora dragons—whose bodies were covered in bark like that of oak trees—slammed into Venom, driving him off their leader.

Venom growled. He got back to his feet to charge the newcomers. He grappled with the larger of the three. The second went to Fragrance's side and helped him stumble out of the clearing.

"Hold still." Fog took Fendrel's hand away from his face.

It was only then that Fendrel's wound started the burn. The sensation sunk into his veins and started to spread through his body.

"Oh, *stars!*" Fendrel grit his teeth. He tried to bring his hand back to his face, but Fog held it still.

"I need to clean it first, or you will not fully heal." Fog wiped Fendrel's blood with the back of her paw, making sure to keep her metal-tipped claws away from his skin. As she cleared away Fendrel's blood, she said, "Fragrance must have some sort of citric-like acid in his claws that make cuts hurt more than they should."

Fendrel worried that if he tried to respond his words would be unintelligible through the pain. He simply nodded in agreement. After closing both eyes, a cool mist greeted his face. His wounds itched as the skin knitted back together. The burning persisted, but its effect began to dissipate while it spread. Fendrel opened his eyes.

Venom roared in victory at the largest oak mimic. The Flora dragon backed away, dragging his wings in shame, or perhaps because they were broken.

The second oak mimic strode to the headstone Fendrel dropped. She reached for it.

"Get away!" Fendrel shouted. He rummaged through his bag, pulling out a restrictor he had nabbed from a dragon-hunter base during a previous mission. The tool was a short chain with a large cuff on each end. Fendrel pushed his bag to the side and, carrying the tool, ran at the oak dragon.

"Fendrel—" Fog tried to grab him again, but she was too late. "Do not be rash!"

As Fendrel neared, the oak mimic turned toward him. She braced her talons against the ground with a roar.

Fendrel kept on, faster. Adrenaline soon overtook any residual burning left over from Fragrance's attack.

The oak dragon tried to thrust her wings out to stop Fendrel, but he ducked under them. He cuffed one end of the restrictor to one of the dragon's horns and the other end around the nearest thumb claw of her wing. While the dragon lifted her wings, she pulled her head along with them. A surprised, frightened yelp escaped her as she fought with herself. Even as the dragon tripped, she continued to thrash and holler, but the restrictor stayed fastened.

There was a snarl behind Fendrel. He looked over his shoulder to see the last oak mimic, the one who had ushered Fragrance away. He barreled toward Fendrel, but before he made it far a raging jet of blue flame burned the side of the charging dragon. The flames ate up the bark on his hide and covered him as he writhed in agony.

From where the attack was sent, a Fire dragon limped into the clearing, dragging one of his broken wings behind him.

No—

Any Flora dragon watching the scene, and the ones who had aided Fragrance, retreated into the depths of Everspring Grove. The Fire dragon's roar urged them on, a haunting cry that often-plagued Fendrel's dreams.

Venom put himself between the newcomer and Fendrel.

It's still alive. Venom lied to me! Fendrel's heart thundered in his ears. Something wet ran down his face. He wiped his cheeks, expecting to see blood on his palms but was instead met with tears. *Why would Venom lie?*

Fendrel backed away from the Fire dragon, but his legs were

Kassidy J. Ridenour

shaking so terribly he fell to his back. The beast made no move to pounce. It stayed still and watched him. There was something different about the rogue.

What happened to the purple sludge that leaks from its mouth? What happened to its eyes? Fendrel wondered. The red beast's eyes were no longer black and abyssal. Instead it had silvery, almost white pupils like the stripes across its body. *And why isn't it trying to kill me?*

There were sections of the Fire dragon's hide where Venom's claws raked away scales, leaving behind exposed gray skin and gashes. Its chest heaved as though it had been running for hours. The beast locked eyes with Venom, then broke contact to meet Fendrel's gaze. To Fendrel's horror, it spoke. "I understand that a simple apology won't make up for what I have done. I also do not expect you to forgive me any time soon, or at all, but please understand that I will do the best I can to be redeemed. As my first step, I would like to introduce myself. My name is Sear."

Fendrel stayed frozen. His mouth had gone dry. Some part of him wondered if Fragrance's acid had a hallucinogenic component. Fendrel kept his eyes on the rogue as he said, "Venom, you told me you killed him."

Venom moved to stand before Fendrel and lowered his head, so they were at eye-level. "I apologize. I said he would no longer be an issue, and I believe that. Sometime during our battle, he collapsed, and the darkness in his eyes disappeared. He started speaking and behaving as though he had been freed from something. I could not leave him out in the field, so I told him to stick close enough that I could still smell him but to stay out of your sight."

"You told him to follow us?" Fendrel backed farther away from Venom.

"I will be taking him to Black Brick so my tribe can assess and study him," Venom answered. "He will travel behind us, but as far from you, Thea, and Oliver as possible. He will not speak to you. If I am able, I will prevent him from even looking at you. I promise you that."

"How can I trust you?" The words fell from Fendrel's mouth before he could fully realize them.

Venom brought his head even lower. "I . . . I will need to regain your trust. Let me do so by proving my word is true. The rogue will not bring harm to you. If he tries, he will die."

Fendrel wanted to look away, but he kept his gaze on Venom.

He trusted you when he had no reason to. He believed you were a dragon hunter, but he still let you say your piece, Fendrel told himself. *Return the favor. It's the least you can do to thank him.*

"Fine," Fendrel muttered as he broke his stare. "But I'm only going along with this because I never quit on my missions. You better stick to your word."

"I am sorry, Fendrel," Venom whispered.

Fendrel got to his feet and moved away from the Dusk dragon. He hurried to the others, glancing over his shoulder over and over to make sure the rogue was not advancing on him. Each look at the Fire dragon made his heart quicken. His head became fuzzy. He spoke but did not register what he was saying, only understanding that he was attempting to relay what Venom said.

Venom pointed into the forest and spoke loud enough for them all to hear, "Go on and head for Black Brick Ruins. That is our next destination. I will stay behind you all to keep an eye out."

In a daze, Fendrel found his mother's headstone, rolled it into his bag, and slung the bag over his shoulder. There was no sign of any of the Flora dragons, even the ones who had gotten injured in the fight. His stomach dropped at the realization of what they had just done to Fragrance and his guards.

Venom is going to face heavy repercussions for this. I hope Fog doesn't suffer as well, Fendrel thought.

He trudged straight through the Grove with the others following. The forest had grown dark from the setting sun and Fendrel found himself squinting to make out any obstacles from their shadows.

Thea knocked Fendrel's elbow with her knuckles. "What is Black Brick Ruins?"

Fendrel gave her a tired look. "It's the Dusk dragons' domain. We'll be safer there."

"Are you all right?" the mage asked.

"I don't think so," Fendrel mumbled.

If Black Brick is next, that means we're almost done searching our assigned direction. We still haven't found any sign of Mist, Fendrel thought. *The mission is what's important. Not any rogues. Not any feuds between the nobles. I have to stay focused and bring her home. Then, I can let myself rest.*

"But that doesn't matter," Fendrel finished. "Finding Mist is our priority."

"At least we are a step closer," Fog said with a sad smile.

"What do you mean?" Fendrel glanced over at her. "We didn't learn anything about her disappearance here."

Fog sighed. "No, we did not, but we did check one more hiding place off our list."

Her words did not sound like she believed them. Fendrel returned the smile to hide his skepticism.

The group continued onward through the darkening forest. As they left the Flora tribe's home, Fendrel felt stares at his back. He wondered if it was the domain's defense against humans, if it was the plant-like dragons, or if it was the rogue. Fearing the worst, he dared not look behind him.

CHAPTER 21: FENDREL

FENDREL STEPPED OUT FROM THE tree line of Everspring Grove into the stretch of moonlit plains. He let Fog, Oliver, and Thea walk ahead of him. After a few minutes of waiting, Venom caught up.

"I'm going to put this back in Stone Edge, since it's on the way," Fendrel said as he pulled Axella's headstone out of his bag.

"Are you sure you do not want to rest it in Black Brick Ruins? Your mother did live there, after all." Venom gave Fendrel a look as if to encourage him to change his mind. "She was only visiting Stone Edge."

"No." Fendrel shook his head. He rolled the stone back in his bag. "It's bad luck to place one's headstone where they didn't die."

"Who taught you that?" Venom sounded unconvinced.

"The Inviers. I had the stone with me when my brother and I first met our adoptive parents, but they took us to return it once they found out what it was." Fendrel glared past Venom into Everspring Grove. "Fragrance already did enough damage by removing it."

"All right," Venom said with a sigh. "But we should stop for the night. It is a full day's travel from here."

"I'll keep the first watch. I know you said you could stay alert while you sleep, but I think you should rest after all the fighting," Fendrel said. Before the black dragon could respond, Fendrel walked away to join the rest of the group. He once again handed Thea and Oliver his fur blankets while he retrieved one for himself. Fendrel laid it flat and sat down, facing Venom and the rogue. In his peripheral he could see Thea, Oliver, and Fog settle around him, but his eyes never left the dragons farther away.

The bloody rogue laid down on tender legs, his broken wing splayed out next to him. It was not long before the beast shut his eyes to sleep.

Fendrel crossed his arms to hide his shaking hands.

Grass crunched to his left. He momentarily glanced to see the cause of the noise. Fog was laying beside him with her neck arched like a swan. "Are you all right?" she whispered. "I mean—I saw you trembling."

Wishing he could sink into his fur coat and hide, Fendrel sighed through his nose. "That's the rogue that killed my mother."

"Oh stars . . . I am so sorry." Fog shifted in the grass.

Fendrel did not look over to see what face she was making. After a few beats of silence, he said, "It's like he's a completely different dragon."

"How do you mean?"

"He isn't attacking any of us. He's *speaking*." Fendrel shook his head in disbelief.

"Do you think he is faking it somehow?" Fog asked.

"I-I don't know." Fendrel brought one knee to his chest and wrapped his arms around his leg. "I know how rogues behave. I can usually predict what they'll do next, but he isn't acting how he should. I don't want to think about the possibility that he's a rogue trying to pass as a normal dragon."

If they can blend in, then I'll never be able to tell who I should feel safe around, Fendrel thought as fear swam in his chest, making his blood hot and cold all at once. *I'll never know if I'm about to kill a rogue or a normal dragon.*

Fog shuffled an inch away despite how far she and Fendrel were from the rogue. "If he is so dangerous, why did Venom let him live?" Her tone was undoubtedly confused, but there was also a hint of mistrust.

"Venom wants to study him so we can learn why he changed so suddenly." Fendrel shrugged. "If they find the reason why, and if he's still dangerous, I suppose that will be useful. I just hope the rogue isn't smart enough to fool the Dusk dragons into believing he's reformed so he can go on the hunt again."

A chill seemed to make the feathers on Fog's spine stand on-end. "I am sorry this is something you have to deal with."

"I don't want to dwell on it, or I won't be able to focus on the mission." Fendrel let his leg back down. He turned just enough to face Fog while keeping the rogue at the edge of his vision. "Fog, be honest with me. Do you believe Mist would run away, like Cloud does?"

"No." Fog shook her head adamantly. "She would never have left without telling anyone . . . without telling *me*."

"Of course." Fendrel traced a scratch in his bag with his fingertip. "She's your sister."

Fog nodded. "Us Vapor dragons are always close with our siblings. Mist is not my blood sister, but she was raised with me as though we shared parents. Mother never treated us differently from each other, and when she died it only made Mist and I closer."

"What happened to your mother, if you don't mind me asking?" Fendrel held his breath in preparation of Fog's answer.

"I was young when it happened. She had gone across the sea so she could find a way to stop the war between the humans and dragons of the Fauna Wilds. From what I was told, she was attempting to rescue a human from a wildcat, but the other humans killed her because they thought she was attacking their friend." Fog curled her tail around her front paws.

Fendrel looked away, scowling.

Even when dragons are trying to save humans, they still get killed, he thought.

"She sounded very brave," Fendrel muttered.

"That is what everyone tells me." Fog gave him a smile burdened by sadness. "What was your mother like?"

"She was kind. She always had grace on others, even when they didn't deserve it," Fendrel started.

Would she still have grace on me if she knew that I would end up joining the hunters? Fendrel wondered. He tried to picture what his mother's face would have looked like if she knew, but it seemed impossible. Fendrel could not remember a time his mother was truly angry with him, but there were plenty of times she was happy just to see him. The memory made him smile, if just a little.

"She would tell my brother and me stories about dragons she'd met. She would say there were good and bad dragons, just like there were good and bad humans." Fendrel jutted his chin at the rogue as he said, "He was the first dragon I ever encountered, but I trusted my mother's words. I wanted to believe she was right, and that there were good dragons in the world . . . If I'm being honest, I think there are more good dragons than there are good humans."

"She sounded lovely." Fog's voice warmed. She went quiet for a while, and when she spoke again her tone was quieter than it had been before. "I must confess something."

Fendrel sat up straighter. He glanced at Thea and Oliver, then

Venom, and finally the rogue. All were asleep, although Venom's ears were perked. "What is it?" Fendrel asked.

Is she going to say something about Mist? Perhaps I can find a lead in what she's about to say.

"I just wanted to be honest with you . . ." Fog averted her gaze. "I heard that conversation you had with Venom about the hunters."

Fendrel froze. "So, you know."

"Yes." Fog tucked her wings tighter against her body.

"What do you think?" Fendrel asked, not knowing what else to say.

"I think—" Fog shifted her weight in discomfort "—I would not have been brave enough to leave like you did. I am glad you left."

"I am, too," Fendrel said with a nod.

"I just wanted to let you know that I knew." Fog stood. "And, I am surprised about this, but I am not afraid of you."

Fendrel's chest felt like it was constricting. "Then, you forgive me for even joining them in the first place?"

"Well, like you said, you were tricked into thinking they were something different." Fog's wings lifted in a shrug. "You said you wanted revenge for losing your mother . . . I would be a hypocrite if I claimed to be any different. I may have fallen into the same trap you did, but you managed to escape."

Even still, I let it happen. I felt off about them, and I still joined, Fendrel thought. *That isn't worthy of forgiveness. But if I'm able to rescue Mist, then perhaps I can truly be forgiven.*

Fendrel pulled his bag onto his lap and began to drum his fingers on the aged leather, attempting to distract himself. "That's comforting to hear," he lied.

Fog gave him one last smile before she turned and found somewhere else to settle in for the night. The grass beside him stayed trodden where she had been laying. After a few minutes, Fog's soft, rhythmic breathing alerted Fendrel to her sleeping state.

Up ahead, Venom was rising from his place. Fendrel scowled in confusion as the Dusk dragon crept toward Fendrel's other side and rested next to him. He made no move to greet Venom nor look at him. However, his curiosity began to fester, and Fendrel allowed himself to glance at the black dragon.

"What exactly happened when you fought?" Fendrel asked Venom, nodding to the sleeping rogue.

At least, it looks asleep. I don't trust that it really is.

Venom made a thoughtful noise. "I have no idea. I forced him to crash into the ground and tackled him. Then he yelled in pain, but it did not sound like the feral roars all rogues make. It sounded like he was intelligent. That was when he began to speak, and he stopped salivating that purple sickness."

"Why do you call that sludge a sickness?" Fendrel stared at the Fire rogue's mouth and eyes, which were still stained purple.

"We do not know what turns dragons into rogues, but we believe it may be a genetic disease. Thus, we Dusk dragons call it 'the sickness.'" Venom too stared at the Fire dragon.

That's similar to what the Inviers taught me, but they believe all rogues used to be normal dragons once, Fendrel thought.

"Do you think his change could have been caused by something you did?" Fendrel asked. He did not realize until then that he had stopped shaking.

"Possibly, but I have never heard of a rogue losing its 'sick' or becoming . . . whatever he is now." Venom glanced down at Fendrel. "Did the dragon hunters ever teach you about rogues? Perhaps they have some insight we are lacking."

Fendrel cocked his head as he searched through his memories. "They didn't use the term 'rogue,' but they told us those dragons tended to be more aggressive—and more willing to eat humans. The hunters used to paint purple under the eyes and noses of some of the dragons that had gone mad to teach us how to deal with rogues, but they lied and claimed those dragons weren't normal to begin with."

Venom shuddered, the spines on his back bristling.

With a sigh, Fendrel tilted his head back. He felt his eyelids growing heavy. "So what do we do?"

"I suggest we watch him for now until we get to Black Brick Ruins, where we can contain him. But I assure you that if he acts up, he will be dead before he knows it." Venom's claws extended then retracted. "The only reason I have not rid us of him yet is because he is an enigma. Perhaps he is like your dragon-hunter friend, and we do not understand rogues as much as we think we do."

Perhaps, Fendrel allowed himself to believe.

They both watched the Fire dragon's chest rise and fall.

Fendrel remembered the stone resting in his bag. "How did you meet her, my mother?"

"Axella." Forlornness entered Venom's voice. "She was exploring the outskirts of Black Brick. I went to investigate, and possibly scare her off if her intentions were impure. When she spotted me, she walked right up to me." Suddenly, the black dragon chuckled. "As you know, humans are not typically willing to approach a dragon, so I was surprised. I assumed she would leave, but instead she followed me to the heart of Black Brick."

"She did?" Fendrel looked up toward the Dusk dragon. Despite his earlier reluctance to engage with Venom, Fendrel found himself letting go of his animosity.

"Yes. When I tried to scare her off, she got this look on her face like I had called her a flea. She crossed her arms and sat down right on the floor, just staring at me. I did not know what to do with her, and she was not hurting anyone, so I left her there." Venom smiled down at Fendrel. "I had left her side for merely an hour and by the time I returned, your mother was studying a sheet with our alphabet next to the hatchlings. She had the most amazed expression, as if she had discovered all the secrets to the world."

The last of Fendrel's upset melted away listening to Venom's story. He closed his eyes, remembering the first time his mother had brought him something written in Drake-tongue. He imagined his face must have looked like hers in that moment.

"She came back every day until she could hold a conversation with me." Venom nudged Fendrel's shoulder with a wing claw as he said, "We were just a few years younger than you are now when we became friends. I was not yet a noble back then."

Fendrel looked down at his bag, the last gift his mother had ever given him. He asked, "Was this while she was pregnant with me?"

"No, this was about a year before that." Venom paused. "You actually spent the first year of your life in Black Brick, although I do not expect you to remember that."

"I did?" Fendrel blinked in surprise.

I thought Mother had me in Stone Edge and kept me there my whole childhood, he thought.

Venom did not appear to notice the confusion on Fendrel's face. He had a faraway look in his eyes. "I am sorry we could not keep you with us, but there are not many places in Black Brick that were safe for you, especially once you were able to walk. The only places we could guarantee you would not fall or get lost were outside, but then you ran the risk of getting sunburnt or sick from bad weather. Your father's village was the only place that would take you."

"What do you mean?" Fendrel focused on tracing the cracks in his leather bag while he listened.

Venom sighed heavily. "Us Dusk dragons live in a massive cave system full of steep drops, and most everything is too dark for humans to see. Your mother could not bear the thought of you hurting yourself in the ruins. She went to every human village and begged for someone to take the both of you in, but no one wanted the burden of having to house a young mother or her infant. I am unsure of the state of the human villages today, but back then it seemed every city was overrun with humans who had lost their homes to rogue attacks."

Fendrel felt his heart sink at the realization. Not much had changed from what he had seen. There were still orphans sitting around every corner in Sharpdagger, each one likely displaced after a rogue killed their parents.

It's no wonder so many humans turn to joining the hunters. There they can meet people who went through the same hardships. They can build community with each other, but all at the expense of innocent dragons. Fendrel shuddered. *Would Oliver have ended up the same way if I left without him?*

"Axella's absolute last resort was Stone Edge, but she had been banished from there before you were born. So if they were to take you in, she would not be allowed to join you. That is why she lived with my tribe instead," Venom explained. "For years she wept every time you were brought up."

If things had been different, if where the Dusk tribe lives was safer, I could have grown up with her . . .

Venom continued, "She had a plan to take you and your brother out of your father's care, even if it meant by force. Of course, she would only do so once you two were old enough to understand her warnings about which caves were too dangerous to explore." Venom's voice quieted, as if he was afraid to say what had come to his mind. "She heard that one of the humans' monarchs was visiting Stone Edge, and she hoped if she could get an audience with them, the royal family would hand you and your brother over to her. On her own she never would have been able to take you, especially with all the slander your father spread about her to the other villagers. That is why . . ."

"That's why she decided to visit us out of the blue," Fendrel finished for the Dusk dragon. 'The day the rogue attacked."

"Yes," Venom whispered.

The Fire dragon kicked at something in his sleep. For a brief moment Fendrel thought they might have awoken the beast, but it settled back into stillness.

"We should quiet down now. I do not want to disturb the others." Venom stretched out but kept his eyes on the Fire dragon. "And Fendrel, let me take the first watch. You can take the second. You need more rest than I do, and you know it."

Fendrel wanted to protest, but his eyelids kept drooping. He leaned back on his caribou fur blanket. He dreamed.

CHAPTER 22: FENDREL

SOFT BREEZES BLEW OVER THE *grassy fields surrounding Stone Edge. Fendrel sat among the green blades with Frederick beside him, watching the road as his mother crested a hill not too far away. The boys, though only sharing a father in blood, were as close as any bonded siblings, perhaps because they were born merely a month apart.*

Fendrel had a feeling this was going to be a good day. Not just because the gloom of their sea-bordering city had cleared enough for the sun to break through, but because each day he got to see his mother was automatically good. It was a rare joy, but a welcome one.

A chorus of laughter drew Fendrel's eyes to the great cobblestone wall separating him from the city of Stone Edge.

The queen of Sharpdagger was making her annual visit to the towns spread throughout her kingdom, and she would be spending the day in Stone Edge. Her unabashed laughter carried louder than all the others. Fendrel liked hearing it. He had missed it the previous two years when the queen was still recovering from giving birth to her twins.

Is that why everyone is so happy today? Because she is finally back? Fendrel wondered.

Not only was she returning to her annual visits, but the queen had reclaimed her title as the head of the royal guard. She had arrived with a few other knights. From the whispers Fendrel heard in the days leading up to her visit, the queen could hold her own in a fight, but she kept her knights around to give them a sense of purpose.

Fendrel had never formally met the queen, but she seemed nice. Although, most adults seemed nice in public. His father seemed nice in public.

Something touched Fendrel's shoulder. With a jump, he hugged the leather bag that had been gifted to him the previous year. He whipped his head around. It was his mother.

Frederick clapped his hands over his mouth as he laughed. "She got you!"

Axella pulled the boys into a hug. "Did I scare you, love?" she asked.

"No." Fendrel grinned, hiding his face in her neck so she could not tell that he was lying.

"All right, sure." His mother held both boys out at arms' length. She smiled with more warmth than Fendrel had ever received from the citizens of Stone Edge. "It's so good to see you two again. I'm going to come right back out, but I need to take care of something first. All right?"

"Mm-hmm." Fendrel sat back in the grass, feeling the rough edges tickle his skin. He was content to stay outside Stone Edge's walls where he could stare at the sky and imagine dragons racing through the clouds.

"Can I come?" Frederick stood up.

"It's boring adult talk, dear," said Axella. She made her way toward the city's gate. "I'll be back soon."

When she was out of sight, Frederick nudged Fendrel with the back of his hand. "Come on."

Fendrel followed his brother as Frederick bent down and started scooping loose dirt out from under the massive wall. The hole was large enough for the two to spy through if they smushed their faces side by side. Given how easily Frederick pulled the dirt away, Fendrel guessed his brother did this quite often.

The view was not anything spectacular, just a glimpse of gathered adults in the plaza, but Fendrel could make out the captain of the royal guard's infectiously charming laugh.

"Oh, hello! I know I've seen you here before, but it's been a long time." A hush fell from within the city after the queen's greeting.

"Axella, you shouldn't be here right now." The voice of Fendrel's father made Fendrel want to hide but he continued to watch and listen. His father gripped Axella's arm as he apologized to the queen. "We're sorry to disturb you, Your Majesty. She's just passing through."

"No, I'm not leaving yet." Axella ripped her arm away. The tone his mother used was unlike anything Fendrel had heard before. She sounded . . . scared.

But Mother is never scared, Fendrel thought.

"What is your name?" The captain's boots scuffed on the rocky streets.

"I am Axella, Your Grace. May I have a word with you privately?"

Fendrel felt uneasiness creep up inside him.

"What is Mother going to talk to her about? Is she in trouble?" Fendrel whispered.

"I don't know," Frederick whispered back.

Before the conversation could continue, a shrill cry like lightning striking metal rang out from the sky. As if by instinct, Fendrel raised his head. A gray Spark dragon with black eyes and purple tear tracks dove from the clouds toward the city.

Fendrel felt himself shaking and melting closer with the ground.

As the rogue roared again, a quintet of arrows soared up to meet the dragon's flesh. A few arrows tore through the softer scales of its neck, cutting off the dragon's cry. The beast crashed into the city with the sounds of tumbling stone and splitting wood amplifying its impact. Screams, murmurs, and gasps emanated from within the wall.

"That's strange." The queen stepped forward a few paces. "I've never seen a dragon attack people outright before. What is this strange substance coming from its eyes?"

"It must be sick, poor thing." Axella's voice was hushed. "I apologize . . . may I ask you for a favor, Your Majesty?"

"Hold that thought." The queen whistled.

The sound of stomping boots and arrows being nocked reached Fendrel's ears. Then all was silent.

A sliver of red freed itself from the clouds and disappeared in the blink of an eye. A different dragon's roar followed.

"Get down!" The queen's frantic voice made Fendrel freeze.

With red scales marked by white stripes, a rogue Fire dragon spiraled down from the sky, opening his purple-stained jaws to incinerate a new batch of arrows.

The dragon disappeared from Fendrel's view inside the city. Screams and crunching bones followed close behind. Metal clashed against scales. Fire torched everything it fell on. The blue flames climbed higher until Fendrel could see their tongues above the wall. Cobblestone blackened from the fire went flying over the boys, sent from the rogue dragon's tail.

Fendrel heard his mother's voice among the chaos but could not tell what she was saying. It took Frederick pulling on his arm to get him to move.

Heat spread across Fendrel's back. Some of the flung stones still had fire raging on them, and it was spreading to the grass they hid in.

As the boys raced toward Stone Edge's gates, a growl caused Fendrel to turn around. The dragon was crawling through a hole it had made in the wall. Its eyes, although pitch black, seemed to stare straight into Fendrel's soul. Arrows stuck out of its body. Torn clothes hung from its teeth. It was hard to tell what red came from its scales and what was human blood. Another arrow pinged off the side of the dragon's face. Snarling, it lunged at its attacker.

Without thinking, Fendrel dove back into the grass and tried to cover himself in mud and the foul-smelling plants that grew in the field. Frederick followed his lead, and they lay down, arms covering their heads.

Fendrel clenched fistfuls of his hair. He did not realize until then that his hiccup-filled breathing was caused by tears of fear and confusion.

The crackling fire and dragon's bellows continued for what felt like an eternity. Thunder soon joined the orchestra of destruction. Rain began to douse Fendrel and Frederick. Fendrel trembled as he imagined the rain to be the dragon salivating above him, staining his clothes, skin, and hair purple.

Harder, the raindrops fell and pelted the boys. It was only then that Fendrel became aware of his surroundings. Hesitantly, he raised his head. The fire in the fields was being smothered by the sky showers, but the flames in the city remained resilient. Fendrel stared at the broken city, collapsing more with each minute, until all that was left was rubble, smoke, and the smell of burning flesh.

The dragon had gone.

"Mother?" Fendrel was afraid to raise his voice but did so anyway. "Mother!"

There was no reply.

Fendrel sat staring at the rogue, far enough away that he could not hear its snoring. Everyone else was still asleep. The eastern sky held a hint of brightness, barely visible above the horizon.

My watch is over now. I could leave for Stone Edge to get a head start. But I need to let Venom know first, he told himself.

Fendrel nudged Venom's wing.

Venom opened his eyes. "Hmm?"

"It's morning now, and I want to reach Stone Edge soon. I'll meet you all at Black Brick Ruins," Fendrel whispered.

"Take Fog with you in case you run into trouble and need healing, but do not let her get hurt. She cannot heal herself." Venom yawned and sat up. He trained his eyes on the rogue.

Fendrel packed up his blanket, resolved he would get the other two from Thea and Oliver later, and walked to where Fog was resting. He leaned toward her. "Fog?"

The Vapor dragon huffed and rolled over, tossing her wings over her head.

Sighing, Fendrel tapped on her wings. "Fog, wake up."

"What? What happened?" Fog grumbled. "It is still dark out."

Fendrel lifted her wings off her face.

With a groan, Fog sat up. "It is too early for thinking."

"I'm going to Stone Edge." Fendrel looked off to the south, then back to Fog. "Would you come with me?"

Fog set her wings at her sides. "You want me to come with you? I thought you would try to avoid me after last night."

Fendrel shook his head. "It's all right. Besides, Venom suggested you go with me."

"Oh!" Fog groggily rose to her feet. "That was nice of him."

"Let's be quiet for now," Fendrel said as he began to walk away. "We can walk faster once we're far enough."

"All right." Fog crept after him.

Hopefully by the time we finish at Stone Edge, the rogue will have been apprehended at Black Brick. If our timing is perfect, I may never have to see that beast again, Fendrel thought. He kept a hand on his bag as he walked, thankful for the opportunity of returning his mother's headstone to where it belonged.

CHAPTER 23: FENDREL

IF IT WERE NOT FOR the cloud cover, the morning would have been much brighter. Gloom hung low in the sky, so much so that the sun had completely hidden itself away as it climbed higher.

The western coast of the Freelands was known for having harsh cliffs in lieu of sandy beaches, chilly air no matter the time of day, and the sounds of waves hitting rock. Fendrel did not need to see the ruins of Stone Edge to know they were near, as the air already smelled of sea salt. He walked beside Fog, having steered them along the continent's border to where Stone Edge sat less than a league away.

Fog smelled the air, made a strange face, then sniffed in again.

Has she ever smelled the sea before? Fendrel wondered. *The northern side of the Hazy Woods is on a coast, but I'm not sure if she's gone to see it.*

"Is something wrong?" Fendrel asked.

The Vapor dragon's feathers stood on end, but her bewildered expression told Fendrel it was not from a sudden breeze. She sat on her haunches and stretched her neck to see as far ahead of them as she could.

Just when Fendrel was about to speak, Fog asked in a shaky voice, "You do not see that?"

"See what?" Fendrel squinted and tried to make out what Fog had spotted.

Fog broke into a hesitant run, too fast to be merely interested yet slow enough that Fendrel wondered if she was scared of what she would find. When Fendrel caught up to her, Fog was standing still as a statue with her gaze trained on something in the waving grass.

Plopped on the ground was a clump of blue-gray fur. It was matted with dried blood. The stands of fur were silky, fine, and almost shimmered like pine needles covered in dew. The only Vapor dragons Fendrel had ever met were Fog and Cloud, whose bodies were covered respectively in feathers and scales. If he had to guess, Fendrel would say this mass that lay before him was what Vapor dragon fur must look like.

"She is gone." Fog whimpered, tears already pooling in her eyes. Her breaths turned to gasps as she gathered the stringy clump into her paws. "She is *gone.*"

Are we too late? Fendrel started to shake his head in defiance. *Is Mist already dead? Have I failed?*

Fog collapsed into sobs as she held the fur to her chest.

Fendrel flinched. It was the most heartbreaking sound he had ever heard.

This can't be it, he thought. *This can't—*

Something flashed in the corner of Fendrel's vision. He turned his head just in time to see it again. As the grass waved in the wind, it revealed another mass of fur, then another farther ahead, and another. The trail led to Stone Edge.

"Fog, look." Fendrel went to crouch by her side. He placed one hand on her shoulder and pointed with the other. "Fog, listen to me. There's a path. She went this way."

Whimpering, Fog raised her head just high enough to see over the grass. Her eyes were so watery she had to blink in order to see what Fendrel was drawing her attention to. As she tried to stifle her sobs, she said in a breaking voice, "She did?"

Fendrel stared at the fur that was clutched in Fog's paws.

This blood is days old, he realized. *Could Mist still be here, hiding somewhere in Stone Edge?*

"We can still save her." Fendrel stood. He grabbed her wing claw and pulled, as if trying to help someone to their feet. "Come on."

Fog sniffled and dragged herself forward, her whole body moving as if she was burdened by the weight of steel.

The closer to Stone Edge they ventured, the fainter the trail became until there was no sign of blood or fur amidst the grass. "See?" Fendrel gestured at the diminished remains. "She must have found something to stop her bleeding."

With a shaky nod, Fog made a noise of acknowledgement. Her tears continued to fall, but not as quickly as before. She picked up her pace little by little as the two drew nearer to the place Fendrel once lived.

"Keep your voice down," Fendrel said. He stepped over a gathering of charred stone. "Whatever attacked Mist might still be here."

Fog's ears pressed flat against her head. She stepped over rubble and between half-collapsed buildings, whispering, "Mist? Are you there? Mist?"

The dead city appeared to only be occupied by Fendrel and Fog. Even so, Fendrel felt they weren't alone. He heard waves crashing on the rocks beside the city's western side. On the eastern end, farmland that had once fed hundreds of villagers sat desolate and burned or choked with tall grass. Most every building was toppled and blackened from dragon fire. What was left standing only did so precariously with holes and cracks threatening to cause the buildings' collapse.

"Mist?" Fog raised her voice a bit.

Fendrel stepped in front of her and put his finger to his lips. His eyes widened in warning.

Fog shut her mouth.

"You're sure that fur belonged to Mist?" Fendrel asked.

"Yes. It was her scent, and the right color, too." Fog lifted her wings as if to emphasize her statement.

"All right." Fendrel glanced on either side of their surroundings, then back at her. "She was injured, which means her attackers could have followed her. Don't leave my side. There's a good chance her wounds came from dragon hunters. Only the formidable ones hunt here."

"All right," Fog whispered with a shudder.

"Stay behind me." Fendrel pulled a dagger from his bag.

Fog eyed the blade and cowered behind Fendrel as they advanced. She sniffed the air.

"What is it?" Fendrel's eyes wandered around the rubble.

"Mist's scent is stronger here."

Fendrel gave her a subtle nod. "Do you think it's her?"

Fog paused for a moment, sniffing again. "No, it would be a lot stronger if she were here. But someone who has been around her is close."

Two voices arose from nearby, muffled by the fallen structures. One of them was immediately recognizable to Fendrel.

Charles!

Fendrel snuck toward a stone column that leaned against a scorched cobblestone building. A few of the stones had fallen out of the wall, forming a spyhole to the other side where Fendrel could see Charles and an unfamiliar hunter. Crossbows were strapped to both men's backs with bolts loaded in their belts. Each one wore full dragon leather armor. Charles also had a hefty-looking traveling pack slung over one shoulder.

Fog sidled up next to Fendrel and peered through the hole.

"There are no shadow dragons here," Charles said in a bored tone. He gestured at his surroundings in an exasperated manner. "We've searched the whole place. We're just wasting our time."

"Well, we need to find one soon for Stronghold—and *not* a hatchling." The second hunter paced back and forth. He appeared to be the same age as Fendrel but with facial scars that made him look significantly older. "The new recruits can't learn how to fight if they aren't exposed to dragon combat."

"We should be searching somewhere else, perhaps farther north," Charles argued.

The second hunter sighed. "We're already here, and Sadon gave us plenty of time to search. There have to be tracks around here somewhere."

Charles grunted in annoyance. "Why don't you go looking for them, then? I'll focus on this area."

"You don't have to tell me twice. Sadon will probably get me some new gear once *I* bring in a brand-new dragon!" The younger hunter trudged off into the ruins, keeping his eyes on the ground.

Charles shook his head as his companion's footsteps grew faint. He set his bag on the ground and began rummaging through it.

Scanning the wall, Fendrel saw a hole below him big enough to squeeze through. He gestured for Fog to jump over the wall. She shook her head with adamance and backed off.

Fendrel gave her a look of understanding as he put his dagger away. He crawled through the hole to the other side of the wall, stood up, and dusted himself off.

Recognition lit up Charles' face. "What are you doing here?"

Just as Charles began to approach Fendrel, Fog leapt onto the uneven top of the wall. She glared at Charles and hissed. Vapor curled out of her mouth while her claws dug into the stones. Charles tensed as if the younger hunter would suddenly materialize.

Fendrel shook his head at Fog and pointed in the direction of the other hunter. Fog closed her mouth, but her eyes narrowed in suspicion.

"I see you two made it out of Sharpdagger safely." Charles kept his voice at a whisper. Eyeing a still-angry Fog, he held his hands up in surrender.

"Fog, this is my friend who helps me with my missions from time to time," Fendrel said.

"*Him?*" Fog nearly lost her balance as her tail swished in agitation.

"Yes." Fendrel nodded. "You heard me and Venom talking about him, right?"

Fog dropped down from the wall. She snaked her head over Fendrel's shoulder so she could continue to glare at Charles. "I did not realize *this* was the dragon hunter you were speaking of. He was there when I was captured. He was there when their leader broke my wing. He was there when you were almost killed! He did *nothing* to help you."

Charles chuckled nervously. "I'm guessing she's not speaking kindly of me?"

Fendrel opened his mouth to answer, but then—

"Charles!" The other hunter rounded a corner, reappearing from his search. "Did you find something? I thought I heard a dragon over here—" His eyes widened, and his hand reached for the crossbow strapped to his back.

Charles grabbed a throwing knife from his belt whose blade had been fashioned from a dragon's claw. He threw it at the other hunter. Slicing through the air, the knife grazed the target's arm, deep enough to cut through the dragon leather.

With a gasp, the young hunter clasped his injury just as it started to bleed. His eyelids drooped, and he stomped forward, catching himself from falling. "What did you just do to me?" The hunter collapsed sideways.

Fog jumped to Fendrel's side and flung one of her wings in front of him, like a shield. Fendrel heard metal scrape against stone, reminding him that Fog wore the attachable claws Venom had insisted she bring.

I hope she doesn't try to hurt Charles with those, Fendrel thought. *I have to calm her down before this escalates further.*

"Isn't that handy?" Charles approached the fallen hunter and retrieved his knife. "I laced my weapons with a liquid version of the knock-out powder. Didn't know if it would really work until now."

"Was it just you two here?" Fendrel pulled Fog's wing down just enough so he could see over it.

"Yes, just us two." Charles turned around. He froze, and from his expression Fendrel guessed he was trying not to laugh. "Does she normally do that?"

Fog growled at Charles, causing mist to seep from her jaws once more.

Fendrel waved the vapor out of his eyes and stepped away from her. "I don't know. I only just met her a few days ago, remember?"

Charles chuckled. "How could I forget? She's a long way from home, though, isn't she? What are the two of you doing all the way out here?"

"We're looking for her sister, Mist." Fendrel glanced at the direction they had entered Stone Edge. "We followed her blood trail here, but it looks like it disappeared. You haven't happened to see another Vapor dragon nearby, have you?"

"Right, they're called Vapor dragons," Charles muttered to himself. He shook his head and said louder, "No, your friend here is the only Vapor dragon I've ever seen." He looked back at the sleeping hunter. "Oh, we should take care of that."

"I'll help you," Fendrel offered. He made his way over to the collapsed dragon hunter.

Fog's wings dropped in exasperation. "How are you not afraid he might hurt you?" she almost shouted.

Fendrel looked over his shoulder at her. "He was protecting us."

"He was *so quick*." Fog pointed at Charles with one her of armored claws. "And he is a dragon hunter, not a *human* hunter. How was it so easy for him to attack?"

"They teach their members to fight humans, too. Just in case." Fendrel shrugged. "But they did focus more on that part after I started infiltrating."

"Not trying to interrupt you two, but do you want any of these?" Charles pulled knives out of the unconscious hunter's belt. The blades had been carved from dragon's claws.

Fendrel scowled and shook his head. "Not those ones."

"Do you want one of my knock-out-laced knives?" Charles pulled one from his belt and held it up. Much to Fendrel's liking, the blade was made of steel.

"I'll take it." Fendrel accepted Charles' handout.

Fog walked up beside Fendrel. She bent her head down and sniffed Charles' hand as he transferred the weapon. With a hiss, she jumped back. "He has been around Mist. Her scent is coming from *his gloves!*"

Fendrel felt uncertainty well up inside him. He gave Charles a quizzical look. "Charles, do you know anything about a captured Vapor dragon?"

"Like I said, other than this one here—" Charles nodded at Fog "—we haven't had another one. Why?"

"Fog says she can smell her sister's scent on your gloves," Fendrel said as he gestured at Fog.

"That's odd . . ." Charles furrowed his brow. He stared down at his gloves, twisting his hands palm-up. "These aren't my normal gloves. They were Sadon's. Mine got a hole in them and, well you know how particular he is with all our gear being fully functional." Charles looked back up at Fendrel and said with a voice full of sincerity, "Perhaps Sadon has her locked up somewhere and doesn't want anyone to know about her. I'm sorry, I haven't heard anything."

Fendrel turned to Fog. "He says the hunters might have her, but he doesn't know for sure. These gloves used to belong to someone else before he got them."

Fog glared. "And you believe him."

"It's not that I don't believe you or your senses, but I trust Charles." Fendrel felt himself growing defensive. "He's wearing Sadon's old gloves right now because his were defective. I know it's hard to believe me right now, but Charles wouldn't lie to me."

Vapor puffed from Fog's nostrils. She peered at the fangs tied to Charles' shoulder guards. "Why are there so many dragon teeth on him?"

Fendrel sighed. "It's how the hunters show rank. He has four on each shoulder because he's the second-in-command."

"So he is trusted by the leader." Fog shifted backward. "Does the leader know that some of his followers are being attacked by your . . . *friend?*"

Fendrel shook his head. "Sadon doesn't really trust anyone. If you find yourself in a high position, it means he wants to keep an eye on you."

Speaking of, why is Charles here without Sadon's supervision?

"I should have taken up your offer to learn Drake-tongue when I had the chance." Charles gave a short laugh. "I never thought I'd actually use it, but here I am wishing I knew what you two were saying. What *have* you been talking about this whole time?"

Fendrel stuffed the gifted knives in his bag. "We were wondering why you're here without Sadon looking over your shoulder."

"Ah." Charles nodded. He had a gleeful look in his eye. "I got some really good news. Sadon's been a little more tired than usual, and he

The Dragon Liberator: Escapade

accidentally allowed me to see a note from one of his spies."

"What was it about?" Fendrel watched his friend with curiosity.

Could the note have something to do with Mist? Fendrel hoped. *But if it did, why would Charles be so excited about it?*

"Raquel and Josephine, er, my family must have caught on at some point that they were being watched. So they left during the night, and now Sadon has no idea where they are." Charles could not keep the smile off his face as he spoke. "When I got sent out here, it was originally in a group of four. The other two were hunters I'm sure I could trust. They'd been blackmailed into joining our ranks just like I was. So, I asked them to feign being ill and return to tell Sadon I'd been killed by a dragon during our search."

"But what happens when *this* hunter tells Sadon the truth?" Fendrel pointed at the younger sleeping man.

Charles shrugged. "It's his word against two others. He just joined us, doesn't really have any notable rapport. Besides, I haven't been in a real fight in a while, so it wouldn't be unbelievable if I'd been caught off guard by a particularly dangerous dragon."

Fendrel started to smile. "So you're free."

"My family and I are free!" Charles exclaimed. His eyebrows raised as an idea seemed to pop into his head. "Hey! Do you want to stop by the Cliff Base really quick?"

"I thought that base was closed down?" Fendrel gave Charles a confused look.

The older man stood up. "There are still dragons there."

"How many?" Fendrel asked, feeling his stomach drop.

And how long have they been there?

"At least fifteen," Charles said. "After Sadon decided not to hold the final trials there anymore, he left them to die. And of course, with me being stuck to him, I couldn't do anything about it. He said it would take too many resources to transport them all."

"Fog, we're stopping at a base close by here. It's an emergency." Fendrel hoped his face looked as apologetic as he felt.

Fog scowled. "Are you serious?"

It's my fault those dragons are still there. I knew the base was closed down, but I should have scoured it. I have to make this right, Fendrel vowed. He steeled his gaze. *How can I rescue the future queen of the Freelands if I cannot even save dragons from a base devoid of hunters? Those are her subjects locked up in those cages. She would never forgive me if I failed them.*

162

Kassidy J. Ridenour

He nodded. "I have to do this. If you don't want to come with us, just follow the coast until you get to Black Brick Ruins."

"No, no!" Fog looked between Fendrel and Charles. "I am coming with you. You never know, you might need my help."

Fendrel sighed in relief. He gave Fog a smile of pure gratitude. "Thank you, Fog."

As Charles began to walk away, Fendrel and Fog followed.

"Why did Sadon abandon the base?" Fendrel asked.

Charles shook his head in dismay. "I'm not entirely sure. Sadon is planning something. He's holding back on dragon abductions, and our numbers seem to be shrinking, but we have no clue where the disappearing hunters have gone."

"But there have been no rumors of mass desertions," Fendrel countered. "Is Sadon getting rid of his own troops?"

"I believe so." Charles tilted his head back as he spoke, as though he was recalling something. "My guess is he's dispersing them to a new location, one even I don't know about. He's probably gotten so sick of you breaking into his bases that he's building new ones in secret."

Like the warehouse in Sharpdagger where I found Fog. Fendrel's brows furrowed with worry. *Are there other abandoned buildings Sadon is filling with more captives and supplies?*

"Sadon is increasing combat training, too, even of already graduated hunters, but it's all human versus human," Charles said.

"Strange—" Fendrel moved his gaze ahead. "Fog, when exactly did Mist go missing?"

"Eleven days ago," Fog said. Her response was so swift it was likely she had been preparing to answer that very question.

I don't blame her for obsessing over how long it's been. I was the same way when Frederick . . . Stop. Focus on the mission, Fendrel told himself.

"Charles, when was the Cliff Base abandoned?" Fendrel saw the end of the ruined city not too far ahead.

Charles blew out a puff of air and appeared to be pondering once more. "Five days ago, I believe. I'm sorry I wasn't able to tell you sooner. If we'd had a moment in Sharpdagger to catch up, I would have told you then."

With Mist's fur being so close to this base, it's possible the hunters who captured her locked her up here shortly before it was abandoned.

Fendrel nodded but said nothing more. The three were quiet for the rest of their walk to the edge of the dead city and beyond.

163

CHAPTER 24: FENDREL

SUSPENDED OVER THE SEA-BATTERED CLIFF, and attached by metal chains on each end was a small wooden boat. When Fendrel had trained under the hunters, this vessel was the only way of getting into the Cliff Base. He could not help but wonder what it had been used for before the hunters took it over.

Fog hooked her claws on the cliff lip and peered down toward the base's entrance. She looked at Fendrel. "Do you need help down?"

"I won't be too heavy?" Fendrel asked.

The Vapor dragon shook her head. "No, I can fly short distances with you. It just is not something I can do continuously like Venom."

Fendrel peered at the boat. It thumped against the cliffside from the wind and its rusted chains squeaked. "Yes, please." He climbed onto Fog's back.

"What are you doing?" Charles looked between the two.

"Going down." Fendrel placed his hand between Fog's shoulders to steady himself. "I'll convince her to come back up for you, unless you want to use that old boat."

Fog jumped and spread her wings. She let herself drift down to the cave embedded in the cliffside. Seafoam splashed up to dowse the entrance of the cave. Once she landed, Fendrel got back on his feet and looked down at the long tunnel leading into the cliff. There were evenly-spaced notches in the rock walls stained with ash and charcoal, but no fires.

Fendrel looked at Fog. "Can you get Charles? I'll wait for you."

Fog blew a puff of vapor from her nostrils, agitated. "This feels like a trap."

With a sigh, Fendrel shook his head. "Fog, there have been countless times when Charles and I have been alone. He could have killed me if he wanted to. And there's no benefit for him to keep me alive. Sadon just wants to get rid of me, so Charles is risking his life by helping me."

Fog tapped her metal-adorned claws on the floor. "All right—" She walked to the edge of the cave and flew up. Moments later, she was back with Charles, landing clumsily as the dragon hunter had his arms wrapped around her neck in a grip for dear life. Charles ungracefully fell onto his side with a groan.

Fendrel opened his bag and took out a small glass jar with the fragment of a Vapor dragon's claw at the bottom. He walked over to one of the notches in the wall and scooped the ashes into the jar. As soon as they hit the piece of claw, they ignited into flames. Though warmth seeped through the glass, it was still safe to hold.

With a noise of amazement, Charles stood and brushed himself off. "How did you do that?"

"Magic. It's from a friend." Fendrel grinned, remembering when Thea had given him the jar for his birthday. He led the way down the hall, the sounds of boots and metal on stone echoing around him. Soon, they came to a door large enough for a dragon of Venom's size to walk through with ease. Fendrel opened it and stepped through. He mumbled, "It feels weird just walking in without having to unlock it."

Fog had a nervous look in her eyes as she shook loose feathers from her wings. When the door shut behind them on its own, she stuck closer to Fendrel's side.

Fendrel carried the jar in one hand and felt along the rough stone wall with his other. He found the next notch and tipped the jar. A tongue of fire licked the ashes in the notch, and it roared to life. Fendrel repeated this with all the spaces in the walls until the hall was full of light.

A short walk later, Fendrel entered the main chamber of the Cliff Base for the first time in a while. He stood on the top level of a large circular room. Below, accessible only by ladders, was a slightly smaller round space with a massive metal cage—big enough to hold six adult dragons—in the center. Curtains lined the walls of the lower level. Fendrel remembered there were holding cells behind each curtain where the dragons would be kept. Notches for more fire were also between each curtain.

A flood of memories invaded his mind. He remembered stepping into that center cage to face down a rogue Ice dragon with nothing but a dagger to defend himself with. As Fendrel stared at its iron bars, he could almost hear the sound of his peers locking him inside. He remembered being jostled by fellow dragon hunter students after successfully killing the Ice dragon—his first kill. He remembered her face and the sickening way her blood had mingled with the purple sludge that seeped from her mouth. Fendrel remembered how similar her likeness was to some of his Invier cousins. The nauseating horseback ride to the Stronghold where his head spun with fears of being trapped like Charles. If he had not escaped that night before the initiation ceremony, he truly would be stuck.

In hindsight, I can't tell if my luck is good or bad.

Fendrel took a deep breath to ground himself. "I'm going to light those notches down there, then we'll look around the halls on the top level," Fendrel said as he gestured to nearby doorways that led off into darkness. He handed the fire jar to Charles and climbed down the ladder. When his feet hit the ground, Charles dropped the jar into Fendrel's hands.

Fog jumped down to join Fendrel as he lit the lower notches.

"Shouldn't we be hearing dragons if there are so many of them here?" Fendrel gazed at the fifteen curtains.

"Perhaps they're just scared," Charles whispered. "It was humans who trapped them here, so I can imagine they wouldn't be too keen on drawing attention to themselves if they can hear us talking."

"And where are the keys for the cages?" Fendrel looked toward his friend.

"I don't know if the hunters took them when they left." Charles jabbed a thumb over his shoulder. "There might be a keyring in one of the outer rooms."

Fendrel pulled back the curtain nearest him. Just as he thought, there was a metal cage with a dragon in it. A Flora dragon. Her scales were pale yellow with pink wing membranes, identical in shape to Sour and Fragrance. She hissed and pushed herself against the back of the cage. Both of her wings flopped helplessly to her sides, broken. Dried blood crusted where a snapper had been used on her.

"It's all right." Fendrel held out his free hand. "We're here to help you."

She hissed. "I can get out of here myself. I don't need help, especially from puny humans."

Fog came up to stand before the Flora dragon. "You have been here for so long. Do you not want to leave?"

The captive squinted at Fog. "Who are *you*?"

"I am a friend of his." Fog pointed at Fendrel with her wing claw.

"Then you're just as pathetic as he is." She jutted her chin at Fendrel. "Leave me alone!"

"What's going on?" Charles called as he clambered down the ladder.

The Flora dragon eyed the fangs on Charles' shoulders. "You see? Your 'friend' is here with the enemy. How can you trust him?"

Across the room, a new voice came from behind a curtain. "Citrus, someone has finally come to help us, and you're insulting them. Stop it! Just because you're too stubborn to be rescued does not mean the rest of us want to die with you."

"I'd rather die here than lose my dignity by letting a human solve my problems for me." Citrus stuck her chin up.

"Put a deer in your yapping jaws."

Citrus lunged and grasped the metal bars with her front talons, curling her claws as if she were imagining digging them into flesh. "If only we *had* deer. But no. Thanks to *humans,* we're starving here!"

"Then be quiet and let them free us so we can eat!"

With a snarl, Citrus turned her back on the humans and Fog.

Charles winced at the foreign-tongued yelling. He went to climb back up the ladder with the fire jar in one hand. He said, "I'll go look for the keyring."

Fendrel walked around the room, opening every curtain. Most of the cages were taken up by dragons of all ages and elements—except Dusk and Vapor dragons. The captives were emaciated, and some had near-fatal injuries.

The dragon who had yelled at Citrus, a Spark dragon, looked as though he had spent all his remaining energy telling off the Flora dragon. He lay on the floor of his cage with his eyes barely open.

Fendrel crouched so his face was closer to the Spark dragon's.

Fog joined him, looking around at his injuries. "I want to help them, but all I can heal are surface wounds. Why do they all look so awful?"

"The hunters used to use this base when they taught their students how to fight dragons." Fendrel frowned. "And sometimes, they would make the dragons fight each other so they would be too tired to do serious harm to the students."

Fog shuddered. She looked behind her at the central cage, much larger than all the rest. Blood stained the floor and the inside of the bars. Whimpering, Fog rushed to a dragon who looked strong enough to talk. "Have you seen a Vapor dragon here? Blue-gray fur? Taller than me?" She went around the ring, asking every dragon until she came to another trapped Spark dragon. "Have you seen her? Her name is Mist. She went miss—"

The much-older dragon cut her off. "Young one, I haven't been near the Hazy Woods in over a year. And I don't know any dragon by that name."

Fog's ears pinned back. "You have been here for over a year?"

The older dragon shifted his weight. "Not in this same base, though I have been here a lot. They're always moving me, putting me in rooms by myself far away from any exit."

"Why you?"

"I suppose I'm one of their only Spark dragons." He sighed. "That is beside the point. I doubt your friend was taken by the hunters. Or perhaps they lost her soon after they caught her."

Fog backed away from the captive. She looked confused, hopeful, and concerned all at once.

Charles returned to the main chamber, but his back was facing them. He gripped something metallic and shiny in his fist. He continued to back up until his heels were at the edge of the upper level. Then, he descended the ladder, not making a single noise.

"Did you find the keyring?" Fendrel asked, eyeing the metal object in Charles' hand.

The older man turned his head and mouthed, "Quiet." He pointed up toward the upper level as a hiss sounded from the hall Charles had just come from. From an open door came an Earth dragon, pulling itself forward on its muscular wings. It raised its head like a snake and stared blankly at the lower level. Trails of purple stained the scales under its black eyes like dyed tears.

A rogue, Fendrel thought as his legs froze.

Charles waved his hand to gain Fendrel's attention. He mouthed again, "It's blind."

Fendrel studied the Earth dragon. He moved his arms about slowly, but the rogue had no reaction to him. It only stared down at empty space, sniffing and making the occasional hiss.

Earth dragons only had wings for limbs. If Fendrel did not know any better he would have claimed that to be a weakness, but he understood this only made them more dangerous. It was harder to anticipate their next move when they lacked the typical body language of other dragons.

Charles backed toward an empty cage and tried to unlock it without taking his eyes off the rogue. After a few tries, the door made a clicking sound.

The rogue swung its head in Charles' direction and widened its stance. Charles took his travel pack off and tossed it as far as he could across the arena, drawing the rogue's attention to the sound.

"Fendrel, when I throw the keys, get in a cage as fast as you can," Charles ordered between clenched teeth. He stepped into the cage, but kept the door open so he could hold his arm out.

Fendrel looked around the room. Fog was frozen with fear on one side of the ring, her feathers fluffing as if that were all she was made of. "Fog," Fendrel called to her. "Fly out of here. Find Venom and tell him where we are."

The rogue whipped its head toward Fendrel and dragged itself halfway into the lowered room.

"I am not leaving you here." Fog began to tremble.

"Then, as soon as I unlock a cage, run in with me before the rogue gets to you." Fendrel maintained his gaze on the Earth dragon.

Above Fendrel came a roar. From his limited view of the top level, Fendrel saw a lanky Air dragon enter the main chamber. It stepped down into the lower circle, frothy purple saliva dripping from his maw.

Another rogue!?

"Charles, quickly!" Fendrel stretched his hand out farther.

Charles tossed the keyring at Fendrel's order.

His hand closed over the keyring, and he unlocked the cage behind him, the one with the half-asleep Spark dragon. Fendrel dashed inside, keeping the door open for Fog.

With a growl, the Air dragon turned toward Fendrel. Its tail whipped against the cage door, flinging him onto his back. The door's click made Fendrel's heart sink as he remembered that the cages were made to lock upon closing.

Before the tall dragon could attack Fendrel's cage, the Earth rogue hissed again.

Fendrel got to his feet with a groan, just in time to see the two beasts circling each other. Snarling in a low, rumbling tone was the Air dragon, whose wings arced menacingly at its sides. The Earth rogue slugged itself along on its more muscular, but also smaller, wings.

Morphing its hiss into a roar, the Earth dragon used its wings to sloppily fling itself at its adversary. Its jaw split open and latched onto the taller dragon's soft neck. In a flurry of writhing tails and batting wings, the two rogues tumbled about the arena.

Fog jumped out of their way and smushed herself against the wall.

Somehow, the Air dragon managed to pull the biting rogue off of its throat and tossed it into the central cage. The Earth dragon's head hit against the bars, and it fell still. The snake-like dragon's chest continued to rise and fall. Now free from the attack, the Air dragon stalked toward Fog.

Fendrel gripped the cage bars. "Fog, fly *out of here*!" he shouted.

Frozen in place, Fog shielded her face with her wings.

As the Air rogue neared, Charles pulled a knife from his belt and charged the rogue. The blade found purchase in the dragon's temple, causing it to shriek and pull away.

That didn't go deep enough to really hurt it. Will the knock-out elixir put it to sleep? Fendrel wondered.

Fendrel felt his breath and heart rate quickening as he watched, helpless. His eyes fell on the keyring, which lay outside the cage, too far from him to reach.

Fog leapt on the rogue's neck wound and hooked her claws in. Being half the rogue's size, she wound her tail around its chest. The Air rogue yelped and tried to scratch her off.

Quick as a whip, Charles pulled a larger knife from his belt and stabbed the thrashing rogue, avoiding its forelegs and wings. The lanky dragon let out a cut-off, gurgling cry, the Air dragon toppled on its side. Its massive wings cascading around it. Fog unwound her tail and jumped away from the corpse.

With theatrics worthy of a professional actor, the Earth dragon howled as it lay belly-up in the central cage.

Fog cringed. "Should we put it out of its misery?"

"Fog, don't!" Fendrel reached his arms through the bars. "Stop!"

Charles jumped in front of Fog just as the rogue broke its act and attacked. The Earth dragon clamped its jaws around Charles' arm. A sickening, wet snapping sounded as the rogue jerked its head and coiled around Charles, who screamed in pain. Dragon leather was tough to cut with ordinary weapons, but dragon teeth were sharper than any forged steel.

Fendrel did not stop to think. He retrieved a knife from his bag and pressed it into his palm. He dragged it across his skin, creating a bleeding, dark line. Then he kicked against the bars. "Over here! I'm over here!"

Fog clawed at the rogue's body with her metal talons, trying to find the head, which was buried in the layer of coils. "Fendrel, what are you doing?"

Loosening from around its prey, the rogue angled its head toward Fendrel, nostrils flaring. It dropped Charles' arm and left him limp on the ground.

He's just playing dead, like he taught us to, Fendrel thought. *He's faking it. He has to be faking it. I need to make myself a more interesting target so Charles can escape.*

Fendrel stuck his bleeding hand outside the bars. Just as the rogue slithered toward him with saliva slopping on the ground, a roar trumpeted from outside the base, echoing down the tunnel and into the circular room. Fendrel's breath caught in his throat.

Please don't be another rogue.

CHAPTER 25: FENDREL

FENDREL WATCHED IN APPREHENSION AS a roaring dragon burst into the circular room. It was Sear, landing on top of the central cage. He opened his jaws and set loose a raging jet of blue flame on the Earth dragon. The Earth beast exploded into fits of shrieking as its scales melted together. Its gurgling cries continued for a few more seconds before the fire put an end to its struggle.

Fendrel's heart seized with terror. He fell backward and crawled away from the cage door. *It's given up its act!* he thought. *It's come to finish me off.*

Venom barreled inside. He skidded to a stop at the edge of the upper floor. "What are you *doing* acting so recklessly?" he shouted.

The Fire dragon shot a short burst of flame at the bottom of Fendrel's door. It left a sizzling, bubbling gap. Sear answered, "Saving your *son.*"

Fendrel gaped at the destroyed door. He slowly got to his feet, wincing when he used his sliced hand to push himself up.

Was I wrong? Did it truly come to save me? Fendrel wondered. He clutched his injured hand to his chest, afraid to let Sear know he was bleeding lest the smell reawaken the Fire dragon's rogue instincts. He tore his eyes from the dragon to look at Charles.

The older man was still limp on the floor.

A growl lured Fendrel's attention from his friend back to Sear. The dragon stared down at Charles from his perch. He opened his mouth, and the back of his throat lit up blue with a charging flame.

"Stop!" Fendrel dove for the gap in the cage door and pulled himself out from under it. He threw himself over Charles' body and shouted, "Don't hurt him!"

Sear snapped his jaws shut. A hissing sound came from within the dragon's mouth and from the look on his face, Fendrel guessed its source was the fire extinguishing rather than a sound of disapproval. He coughed up a few billowing puffs of smoke. "But, he's a dragon hunter," Sear said between coughs of more smoke.

"He's my friend." Fendrel looked to Venom. "He's the one we talked about. He brought Fog and me here thinking it would be an easy mission, but it wasn't. That is not his fault."

Venom slunk down to the lower level and eyed Charles. His nostrils flared, causing his eyes to flicker toward Fendrel. "Are you bleeding?" Venom asked as he grasped Fendrel's injured hand and held it palm-up. "Who did this to you? Was it one of the rogues?"

"I did it," Fendrel said.

The Dusk dragon looked between Fendrel and Fog, who was cowering in a distressed ball of feathers near the inner circle's wall. Venom growled. "What happened here?"

Breaking from their stunned silence, the other dragons still trapped in their cages spoke up at once. They pointed around the scene and grabbed the bars of their prison.

"Calm yourselves, one at a time!" Venom flapped his wings noisily, letting his wing claws scrape the ground with a horribly displeasing sound. He pointed at Citrus, the Flora dragon who had refused help earlier. "You, tell me what happened."

Citrus snorted. "A rogue attacked these humans and that Vapor dragon. Well, a pair of rogues," she finished, pointing at the Air dragon's corpse.

"How did the rogues get in? The door was shut when I arrived." Venom stepped toward the grapefruit mimic.

The Earth rogue was already here, but where did the Air rogue come from? Fendrel wondered. *Did it break through the door?*

"They were always here," Citrus answered Fendrel's silent question.

Venom's snout wrinkled in anger. "And you did not *warn* them?"

"It wasn't my concern." Citrus turned up her snout the same way Fragrance and his other two children had. "They got themselves into this mess."

So, this is where Fragrance's second daughter was. Does Fragrance even care she's been locked up here for upwards of five days? Fendrel scowled at the pale-yellow dragon, feeling a confusing mix of pity and vitriol for her.

"You ungrateful worm," Venom spat as he lashed his tail. He began ripping off the cage doors, muttering under his breath all the while.

Beneath Fendrel, Charles groaned in pain. Fendrel sat beside him and looked at his injuries now that he was closer. Most of Charles' arm was still covered by his sleeve, but from the perforations in the leather and fabric Fendrel could see blood and pieces of bone. Fendrel felt himself go pale, wondering if Charles' arm even resembled an arm in its current state.

I had better keep him awake and distracted until we can heal him, Fendrel thought. *Oh stars, how are we going to heal him?*

"Charles, look at me." Fendrel snapped his fingers in front of Charles' face.

The older man's eyes fluttered open, but there was little recognition in his expression.

"You lit up the halls, right?" Fendrel pointed at the upper floor. "All over the base?"

"I did. Why?" Charles mumbled.

"You didn't see any rogues?" Fendrel asked.

Charles blinked. He lifted his head a little, becoming more alert. "There were a lot of sheets covering old equipment. Some of them were strung up between cages. The Earth rogue was in plain sight, but the Air rogue must have been hiding . . . I'm sorry, I didn't see them before."

"That's all right," Fendrel said. "They're dead now."

"Oh, good." Charles smiled tiredly. "I'm not doing too well, am I?"

If I tell him how bad it is, he might panic and hurt himself further. If I lie, he'll be smart enough to see through it, even in this state, Fendrel thought.

"Not right now, but you'll be fine soon," Fendrel answered in a tone that even he was not convinced by. "Just stay awake until we can treat you."

Charles gave a small nod, moving his head just enough for Fendrel to recognize the gesture. He laid his head back and stared at the ceiling, muttering to himself.

All around the arena, the freed dragons dragged themselves or limped out of their cages. Some had to be helped by the stronger captives.

Fog waited for them to pass before she crept toward Fendrel and Charles. Her eyes scanned over the hunter's arm. "Is he going to be all right?"

Fendrel let out a shaky breath. "I don't know. He isn't reacting to any pain, and he's having a hard time staying awake."

"He is losing a lot of blood," Fog whispered as though Charles would be able to understand her.

"I know," Fendrel mouthed, not intending for his words to be silent. He breathed in deeply through his nose, trying to steady himself. "Your healing only works on surface wounds, right?"

"I am afraid so." Fog sat down across from Fendrel. Her eyes wandered toward the hunter who lay between them. "What is he saying?" she asked.

"The hunters are taught a way to keep themselves awake until they receive medical attention," Fendrel answered, averting his eyes. He feared mentioning anything about the hunters may cause Fog's mood to worsen.

Contrary to Fendrel's worries, Fog tilted her head in interest. "What does it mean?"

"You're supposed to recite everything you did that day leading up to the present moment and keep repeating it." Fendrel waved his hand in front of Charles' face as the older man's eyes started to close. "Right now he's talking about your reaction to seeing him again."

Fog's ears drooped as she frowned. "He could have run away. He could have saved himself."

Fendrel shook his head. "If it was in his nature to protect himself at all costs, he never would have urged me to leave the hunters."

"I just . . . I thought he would not care if the rogue attacked me, but he jumped in its way." Fog tucked her wings in closer to her sides and coiled her tail around her paws. "And I did nothing to help."

"You did plenty," Fendrel reassured her. "You kept that Air rogue busy so Charles could finish it off."

Fog blew a puff of mist out of her nose in agitation. "And then I got him hurt by falling into the Earth rogue's trap."

"I doubt he cares about that," Fendrel said with a shrug. "He's gotten hurt defending others before. Sometimes I wish he wouldn't, but I'm glad he was here to help us."

Venom walked up to Fendrel, Charles, and Fog with a concerned look on his face. "Has Fog healed your hand?" he asked Fendrel.

Fendrel blinked in confusion before he remembered the cut he had given himself. "No, I'm not worried about that right now."

The Dusk dragon looked down at Charles, still muttering as he sleepily gazed upward.

"I'm guessing you helped the captive dragons back to the surface?" Fendrel pointed at the passage leading out of the main chamber.

"I did. We are going to guide them to Black Brick where they will recuperate before returning home," Venom said.

"Does your tribe have any healers? You must, if your duty is to fight and kill rogues." Fendrel placed a hand on Charles' good arm. "I want to stay here and look after Charles until someone can treat him."

"He will bleed out before I am able to return." Venom looked over Charles' form in silence, seemingly deep in thought. "You are sure we can trust him?"

"Yes," Fendrel and Fog said in unison. Fendrel gave the Vapor dragon a surprised look, before repeating, "Yes. We can. He's free from Sadon now. The hunters lost track of his family, so Charles took his chance and defected."

"He got hurt protecting me from both of the rogues," Fog backed him up.

Venom made a noise of acceptance. "Move aside."

Fendrel tensed. "What are you going to do?"

Before Fendrel could react, Venom snaked his head past. He parted his jaws and stuck the tips of his fangs straight through the damaged, bloody dragon leather on Charles' arm.

"What are you doing?" Fendrel shouted. He tried to push Venom's head away, but the Dusk dragon held like a rock. In the next moment, Venom retracted his fangs and stepped back.

Charles' eyes shot open with a gasp. He grasped at his arm helplessly as the sound of bones popping and shifting came from beneath the armor. Fendrel pulled a dagger from his bag and tried to cut the leather away, but it was tough and difficult for steel to saw through.

"Move your hands," Fog warned before she tore at the dragon leather with her metal-adorned claws.

To Fendrel's surprise, the armor fell away with ease. A part of him marveled at the sight, but his need to help Charles overshadowed any amazement before it could show on his face.

When Charles' arm was revealed, Fendrel paused in shock. A golden, glossy film stitched together the teeth marks and jagged cuts from the Earth rogue's attack. Left behind were raised scars that had a golden sheen.

"What was that?" Charles sat up and stared at his arm. He twisted it back and forth, wincing a bit as he did so.

"I—" Fendrel shook his head in confusion. "Venom, you can heal, too?"

Kassidy J. Ridenour

"Only Dusk dragons with gold markings are able to," Venom said, nodding down at the speckles on his chest. "Fog's healing can aid wounds on the surface, but a Dusk dragon's elixir runs deeper."

"Did you know they could do this?" Charles asked, seeing Fendrel's stunned expression.

"I didn't." Fendrel shook his head. "The hunters don't know about this, right?"

Charles tested his ability to curl his fingers. "If they did, they would exploit it for all its worth."

Fog's wings lifted as though a burden had been taken from her. She reached one of her paws out toward Fendrel. "May I?"

Fendrel let her heal his palm, still staring at Charles.

"Venom?" Fog turned her eyes to the Dusk dragon. "Are we ready to leave?"

"Are you able to heal them, too?" Fendrel pointed up to where the released dragons had been taken.

"Only a few of them, and only to certain extent. Your friend's injury was severe, so I depleted a great portion of my elixir on him. It would make little difference if I attempted to aid the captives, but there are other gold-marked dragons at Black Brick." Venom crouched and moved his wing aside for Fendrel and Charles to climb on. "We will stop at a nearby river before we reach my home. We could all use the refreshment."

Fendrel sighed as a smile escaped him. He took his usual spot on Venom's shoulders. Charles recovered his travel pack, which was a bit trampled, before joining Fendrel.

In the corner of his eye, Fendrel saw Thea's gift to him shattered on the floor. Its glass was spread out and the claw fragment it once housed was similarly smashed to pieces.

The spell won't work now that the components are broken, Fendrel thought. *It must have gotten destroyed during the fight.*

He turned his face away and held on to the spines of Venom's neck. As the black dragon and Fog hoisted themselves to the top layer and through the passage of the Cliff Base, Fendrel realized Sear was gone from the main chamber.

He must have left for the surface with the other dragons, Fendrel realized. A frown came over his face. *I could have sworn his wing looked fixed just now . . . Did Venom do that for him?*

Far to their left sat Stone Edge and ever farther, blurred by distance, were the Black Brick Ruins to their right. As they neared Black Brick, a line of trees, thick and tightly-packed, rose up to block their view of the cliff edge. Their leaves were crimson and fiery orange, and their bark was white mottled with black.

The injured dragons rushed for a winding river just paces away, invigorated by the mere sight of water.

Fendrel slipped down from Venom's shoulders and Charles dismounted when the black dragon crouched.

Venom lowered his head, so he was eye-level with Fendrel. "Your friend is joining us?"

"I assume so. I don't think he has anywhere else to go." Fendrel's gaze drifted to Sear. "And why is *he* here? Thea and Oliver didn't come with you, so you must have made it to Black Brick before finding us. Why isn't he being supervised?"

The Dusk dragon did not look surprised by Fendrel's question. When he spoke, there was anger in his voice, "I told him to stay at the ruins, but he refused when I announced I was going out to look for you. I did heal his wing shortly after you and Fog departed, only so we could reach Black Brick quicker. When I left to search for you, he flew ahead of me, and it took me the entire flight to catch up with him." Venom glared at Sear, who had made his way to the river with the others. "He claims he wants to redeem himself, but he disobeys my orders. Be cautious around him."

"Of course."

I'm always wary around him, Fendrel thought. *That will never change.*

Fendrel walked with Charles to the riverbank. "So you're coming with us?" he asked the ex-hunter.

"Absolutely. I think it will be fun seeing how you operate from the other side." Charles grinned. "So, where are we going?"

"The home of the Dusk dragons." Fendrel gestured to their right.

"Ah." Charles pointed at his armor and the dragon teeth on his shoulders, some of them chipped from years of adornment. "We should get rid of these."

Fendrel nodded. "We can burn them." He looked at the gathered dragons. The only Fire dragon other than Sear was shaking as it stood, snacking on a fish from the river.

While Fendrel searched, Charles removed his dragon leather armor, revealing the simple traveling clothes he wore beneath. He folded the various pieces and handed them to Fendrel.

With an annoyed sigh, Fendrel realized Sear would be his only option. He approached the white-striped, red dragon as he drank from the river. Sear lifted his head to look at Fendrel.

"We need these burned." Fendrel held out the armor and teeth.

Sear's eyes flicked between the gear and Fendrel. He said, "Set them on the ground." When Fendrel did so, the dragon opened his mouth and lit the pieces in blue flames. The teeth blackened, cracked, and turned to ash. The leather burned even faster. Fendrel could feel the intense heat even as he stepped back several paces. With the job done, the Fire dragon went back to drinking, his mouth steaming as the river cooled it.

Fendrel stayed still, watching the red dragon. His wing was indeed back to normal, with a scar down the membrane that shone gold when it caught sunlight. His cuts, however, remained, though they did not look as bad as before. Sear dunked one of his paws in the river and scrubbed the purple-stained scales under his eyes and around his mouth.

After a moment, Sear lifted his head again with a perplexed expression on his face. "You are still here?"

"Why . . . me?" Fendrel struggled to get the words out. After a short pause, he continued, "Why did you keep hunting me? Was it because I managed to get away? Was it revenge because the other rogue you were with died when you first attacked me?"

Sear lowered his head in shame. "I do not believe I have an acceptable answer."

"Well, try to give me one." Fendrel glared. "Don't I have a right to know?"

Sear went quiet and turned his gaze back to the river. "It was not my intention to follow you. After . . . the attack and the years following, I did not think of you until I caught your scent. I remembered smelling it when I destroyed your city. I realized then that you had been alive all this time, and I could not stop thinking about what I had done to you. I think, perhaps—" Sear glanced at Fendrel through the corner of his eye, seemingly afraid to look at him straight on "—because I thought of how I hurt you so often, the sickness drove me to seek you out."

Fendrel froze on the spot. He opened his mouth to speak, but the words did not emerge.

Venom came up beside Fendrel, putting himself between Fendrel and the Fire dragon. "The injured have had their fill. Let us move on," he said. The distance Venom put between Sear and Fendrel helped the young man calm himself.

As they moved away, Charles gave Fendrel a grin. "Fen, I think it's time I took up your offer to learn the dragons' language."

"It's not that easy." Fendrel chuckled. "But I know someone who can give you a shortcut."

Well on their way to Black Brick Ruins, Fendrel and Charles walked beside each other. The herd of dragons hobbled around them. Fendrel squinted ahead at a broken-down castle made of black stone standing against the pale blue sky.

Venom, traversing on Fendrel's other side, paused while his ears perked up. He glanced behind at the grove of read-leaved trees. "Everyone go on ahead," Venom commanded. "I must check on something."

"What is it?" Fendrel looked up at Venom.

"I think someone is following us." The Dusk dragon opened his wings, ready to take flight.

"Let me come with you." Fendrel pulled himself onto Venom's shoulders before the dragon could crouch.

Venom flew to the edge of the forest and landed just outside. Fendrel slid off his shoulders and peered between the trees. At first, nothing looked out of place. Then, a white shape moved between the pale trees.

Fendrel kept his steps light as he approached the object. When he was close enough he realized it was a horse, adorned with a silver-rimmed saddle. It had been tied to a tree by its reins.

Who is the rider? Fendrel wondered. He tensed. *Where is the rider?*

The forest went still when a twig snapped. Fendrel's head whipped toward the noise. Someone was hiding behind a tree trunk, but one of their hands was in plain view, gripping the side of the tree. "I can see your hand," Fendrel announced.

The hand disappeared from view. A brief moment later, the figure stepped out from his cover. Fendrel sucked in a quick breath. He scowled, trying to conceal his surprise.

CHAPTER 26: CASSIUS

THE PRINCE HELD HIS HAND over his mouth in an attempt to stifle any sound he may utter. His back was pressed against a tree. Cassius had donned commoner's clothes during his departure from the city of Sharpdagger, but he had forgotten to bring anything that would conceal his face.

A voice behind him, just on the outskirts of the tree line, said, "I can see your hand."

Cassius looked down to see his other hand was around the side of the trunk. Now more than ever he wished he had learned how to defend himself in a combat setting.

He brought his hand to his chest as if that would keep him hidden. Then he sighed and stepped from behind his cover, turning to face the man who spotted him. A chill went down his spine. It was him. The Liberator. He was shorter than Cassius thought he would be, just a few inches shy of Cassius' lankier height, and his youthful face was a far cry from the battle-hardened expression all the wanted posters depicted. Just behind him towered an *actual* dragon.

That must be the shadow dragon the High Mage mentioned, Cassius thought. One glance at the black dragon's glare made him regret leaving the city. *But I cannot go back. I came all this way for his help.*

"Have you been following us?" the Liberator asked.

Do not lie, Cassius told himself as his gaze flicked between the man and the dragon. *The worst thing you can do right now is lie.*

"Yes," Cassius mumbled. "Just a little! I heard a rumor that you were heading in this direction. And then, by chance, I happened to see you with that group of dragons—"

"*Why* are you following us?" The Liberator took a threatening step toward him.

"I need your help," Cassius blurted. "Let me explain."

The Liberator shook his head. "I'm in the middle of something very important right now." He began to back away.

"What could be more important than helping your people?" Cassius took a few hesitant steps toward the man. "I want to fix the problems with the royal guard, and I want you to help me."

Stopping suddenly, the man scowled at Cassius. "The humans are *not* my people."

Cassius blinked in bewilderment. *I suspected he might hate authority figures from Sharpdagger, even me, but all humans? Why?*

"Why do you think I'd help you? Your cousin has been harming dragons for years with no repercussions." The Liberator jabbed a thumb at himself as he said, "I'm the only one who's been trying to right his wrongs."

"That is exactly why I need your help," Cassius' voice rose as he began to panic. "I am trying to get rid of Zoricus."

The Liberator's scowl morphed into suspicion. He shook his head as a cynical laugh escaped his lips. "Are you?" he asked in a mocking tone. He reached the dragon's side and pulled himself up to sit on its shoulders. "The person sworn in to protect you and your family, a *member* of your family. You want to get rid of him? You'll have to come up with a better lie than that to get me on your side."

"You have to believe me." Cassius clasped his hands together pleadingly.

"As I said, I don't have time for you."

"Please!" Cassius felt his heart sink. "Zoricus is trying to kill me. He sent me a death threat because I have been trying to expose him for being involved in the dragon trade."

The dragon craned its neck, so it faced the man on its shoulders. To Cassius' surprise it spoke, though in a language Cassius had never heard. The dragon sounded annoyed.

Responding in the same language, the Liberator cast a glance at Cassius, then nodded his head at the direction they had come from.

Cassius felt his breath catch in his throat as the dragon spread its wings, about to take flight. He held his shaky hands out to them. "Sir, please! My own sister would never believe me if I told her the truth. I am terrified that if I do not find a way to stop Zoricus, I will lose her!"

A flash of recognition crossed the Liberator's face. He said something to the dragon, making it pause. Then, to Cassius he asked, "You're truly desperate for my help?"

"I would give anything. I would do anything to get you to help me. Just hear me out." Cassius stared the man, waiting for a response. He felt tears start to sting his eyes.

The Liberator spoke to the dragon once more. Their voices were hushed even though Cassius had no means of understanding them. After the two seemed to reach an agreement, the Liberator looked back at Cassius. "If you mean it—" he pointed at Cassius' stallion, still tied to a tree "—get your horse and follow behind us. We're on a time crunch, so I can't speak with you until we get to Black Brick Ruins."

"What is that?" Cassius blinked his tears away before they could fall.

"It's where the Dusk dragons live." The Liberator glanced at the massive black dragon before giving Cassius a taunting smile.

He is testing me to see if I truly would do anything for his help, Cassius realized. *Or perhaps this is a trap. If it is an ambush, I am in danger whether I follow him or go back home . . . I have come this far. I must see it through.*

"All right." Cassius tried to quell the fear racing through his heart. "I will follow you."

With a nod, the Liberator said something to the dragon, and the black beast lifted off.

Cassius raced for his horse, untying it from the tree and hoisting himself into the saddle. He urged his horse into a gallop, trailing the dragon, and praying his steed was fast enough to keep up with it.

CHAPTER 27: FENDREL

VENOM SWOOPED DOWN AND, ONCE he landed, tilted his head to see Fendrel sitting on his shoulders. "That human is still following us."

Fendrel looked and saw the prince on his white horse a good distance away, traveling at full speed.

He meant it, Fendrel thought with surprise.

The survivors of the Cliff Base continued on while Fog and Charles paused for Fendrel and Venom to catch up.

Fog's ears perked toward the Sharpdagger prince. "We have another tag-along?"

"Perhaps, I'm not sure yet." Fendrel gestured at the survivors. "We have to get them help first and plan our next steps."

"Who is he?" Charles squinted at Cassius.

"The prince of Sharpdagger," Fendrel said.

"Ha! Good one." Charles smiled at what he assumed to be a joke. When Fendrel did not share in his laughter, Charles' eyes widened. "Is he really?"

Fendrel nodded. "And he wants me to help him get rid of Zoricus. Or so he says. He seemed desperate."

"He must be if he sought out a known criminal instead of anyone else." Charles let out an astonished breath.

Fendrel relayed the message to Fog and Venom, whose faces showed they shared in Charles' shock.

"Well—" Fog broke their communal silence "—we should join everyone else. Today has been *eventful* to say the least."

"Agreed. In addition, it would be wise to rest at Black Brick Ruins until tomorrow. So, Fendrel, if you need to speak with the younger human, you have time," said Venom.

Fendrel glanced at the sun's position. "But we have so much

daylight left to keep traveling."

"We need to be as rested as possible if we want to continue at the pace we have been." Venom looked between Fog and Fendrel. "Besides, we are not wasting time here. Prior to His Majesty's meeting, I sent out scouts of my own to conduct a search for Mist. They should be back by now, and I want to compare notes with them."

Fog smiled brightly. "Thank you, Venom."

"Of course." Venom gave her a somber smile as he nodded. "Now, we must be on our way."

The four continued forward, swiftly mingling with the group of injured dragons whose strides were slowed by fatigue and pain. However, the freed dragons seemed more hopeful with each step. Not far ahead were the Black Brick Ruins. Fendrel guessed by the speed of Cassius' horse that the prince would catch up to them just as they reached their destination.

The closer they came to Black Brick, the more imposing it seemed. A portcullis with broken bars hung like a row of jagged teeth above the entrance. The space behind the portcullis was like a never-ending abyss. Fendrel waited for a sense of foreboding, but like every time he came to Black Brick's entrance there was no such feeling.

That human deterrent must activate only once I step through the gate, Fendrel assumed.

Two Dusk dragons lay on top of the small, black stone castle. Their eyes were the only visible sign of them, as their scales blended in with the walls. One of them leapt from his perch as the party of humans and dragons approached. He turned and bounded through the building's opening, disappearing into darkness. The second dragon dropped down and nodded at Venom.

Fendrel cast a glance over his shoulder to check on the prince's progress. When he saw the younger man was closer than he thought, Fendrel moved through the group of survivors to meet him halfway.

The prince dismounted and before he could speak a word, Fendrel said, "You truly would do anything to get me to listen to you?"

"Yes," Cassius affirmed with an eager nod. "No matter how much you ask, my answer will always be 'yes.'"

"There's something I have to take care of inside. Wait here."

The Dragon Liberator: Escapade

Fendrel ignored the disheartened look on the prince's face as he weaved through wings and tails on his way back to Venom, Fog, and Charles.

Fog lowered her head so she and Fendrel were at eye level. She asked, "Have you ever been inside before?"

Venom said I lived here for the first year of my life, but I have no memory of that, Fendrel thought as excitement coursed through him. *It will be like I am experiencing it for the first time.*

"I did when I was little, but I don't remember anything," Fendrel answered. He followed Venom into complete darkness with the others trailing behind wearily. Fendrel's breath caught. He could not see anything. Tentatively, he whispered, "When is the deterrent going to start?"

"Deterrent?" Venom chuckled. "There is no deterrent for the Black Brick Ruins. Our tribe welcomes humans, as long as they have good intentions. How else would your mother have made it through the first time without me encouraging her?"

The darkness was oppressive and Fendrel feared he may misstep and never find his bearings again. But just when he was about to ask where they were going, a soft golden light illuminated the path ahead. The light moved as they did. Curious at this, Fendrel sped forward a few paces and saw the light was coming from the speckles of golden scales on Venom's chest.

I didn't know they could do that, he marveled.

Venom grinned at Fendrel's amazement.

The deeper they went, the more lights appeared. Purples, greens, and golds from the markings of other Dusk dragons lit up the darkness. Matching eyes peered at the approaching group.

"Take down the curtain." Venom's voice boomed.

The sound of two dragons taking off filled the chamber. A large cloth above them rippled and dropped on one side, allowing sunlight to invade the area. It illuminated a fair amount of the expansive room they were in but did little to pierce the darkness of the off-shooting tunnels.

Fendrel shielded his face with a hand. When his eyes adjusted, he could see a pit in the center of the room. There were ornate railings built around its edge and bordering a downward-winding staircase. The pit appeared to have been carved out of the ground, extending level by level like an inverted tower so deep Fendrel could not see the bottom. There were dragons staring up at him from each level.

There are so many of them. I thought the Fire tribe had the largest population.

Venom spread his wings to call the gathered dragons' attention. "The Liberator and the rest of his companions have arrived, as well as some guests." He walked to the edge of the pit. "We need immediate medical attention for these new dragons. Understood?"

"Yes, sir!" the dragons called back.

"Good. Guide the injured and the weak to the Sanctuaries. Carry them if need be." Venom waved over two burly-looking dragons that were standing on the side of the chamber. "Keep your eyes on this Fire dragon," Venom said as he nodded his head toward Sear.

The two Dusk dragons corralled Sear—who snorted but said nothing—between them.

"I believe now would be the best time to speak with your visitor." Venom gestured toward the passage they came through with his wing. "Would you like me to accompany you?"

"If you want to, but he doesn't seem dangerous. If I do help him, chances are he'll want to stick close by, so I think he should meet you." Fendrel looked at Fog and said, "You can come too." He repeated his answer for Charles to understand.

That is, if the prince is still there. He might have gotten intimidated by now and given up.

Fendrel made his way back up the hall toward the sunlight. He could hear Venom, Fog, and Charles following behind him. When Fendrel emerged from the passage, he was slightly surprised to see the prince waiting for him, holding tight onto his horse's reigns to keep the stallion from fleeing at the sight of the dragons.

Dirt sullied the prince's boots and the cuffs of his pants. He wore riding gear less fancy than anything else he likely owned, but still put to shame any ordinary travel clothes. If the prince had combed his straight brown hair that morning, Fendrel could not tell as it was tousled from the wind.

The prince gave a curious look to Venom, Fog, and Charles.

"Don't worry about them." Fendrel approached the younger man, leaving his friends at the portcullis. "So, you said you wanted to get rid of Zoricus. Why?"

"I have been spying on him lately, trying to find out just how involved he is with the illegal dragon trade," Cassius said in a rush, his tone full of excitement. "Through eavesdropping I have been able to find out that he has bought a few dragon hatchlings, and even some eggs. I guess he caught me at some point, or one of his friends did, because—" his voice slowed, and he lowered his gaze before continuing "—I found a death threat on my pillow yesterday. It said to stay out of his business, or he will kill me. So, in short, I want him gone because I am not safe until he is gone."

"And by 'gone,' you mean . . ." Fendrel gestured for the prince to continue.

"Imprisoned, preferably," the prince said. The dejection on his face was plain to see. "I do not care for him, but my sister loves him like a brother. It would break her heart if he were exiled or hurt or . . . worse."

"He's the head of the royal guard and all his allies are involved with buying dragons, too." Fendrel crossed his arms. "*Who* is going to arrest him and throw him in the dungeon?"

The prince sighed. "My father is the only one with the authority to do so, but he sees Zoricus like one of his own children. It is going to take a lot of convincing. That is why I cannot do it alone."

If Cassius received that death threat yesterday and he's already here, that means he left Sharpdagger that same day and traveled through the night to find me, Fendrel realized. He studied the prince's face. Dark rings hung under Cassius' eyes. He was thin, almost to an unhealthy point.

When was the last time he slept or ate? Fendrel wondered as he felt a tug of sympathy. *Is all this because Zoricus has been putting stress on him? What did Cassius do to make his cousin hate him this much?*

"Why does Zoricus want you dead?" Fendrel asked, trying not to sound accusatory. "This can't all be because you found out he bought a few dragons. There must be something more."

"I am sure it is because he does not think I am worthy of the crown." The prince flicked his fingers at his sides in what Fendrel assumed was a nervous habit. "He thinks my sister should rule instead, but because I was born just before her, I became my father's heir."

Fendrel's brow furrowed in confusion. "That's two reasons, but neither of them warrant sending your cousin death threats."

The prince stared at Fendrel sorrowfully. He said, "I wish I had a better answer for you. I have been trying for years to find out why he despises me. The only other assumption I have is that he is bitter he had to rise through the ranks of the royal guard while I am handed everything just because of who I was born to. He has never said it aloud, but I *know* that is how he feels."

"And he's only like this to you?" Fendrel tilted his head as he asked.

"Yes." The prince swallowed. A look of realization came over his

Kassidy J. Ridenour

face as he seemed to remember something. "I remember as a child, when I first started noticing his treatment toward me, I confided in my sister about it. But, Zoricus has always been so kind to her that she did not believe me. She told me I must have just misinterpreted Zoricus' actions. I told my father, as well, but he too dismissed me."

Fendrel suppressed a pitying sigh. "You don't have anyone else to help, do you?"

"No," the prince answered quietly, lowering his gaze. "Things were different when my mother was alive, but that was only because Zoricus came to live with us after she passed. She was the head of the royal guard when she died, and Zoricus took her place." Anger flashed in the prince's eyes. "He does not deserve to carry on her legacy."

A strange feeling of familiarity twisted Fendrel's gut. He searched his memories for the source, and when he found it, his eyes widened.

Cassius' mother was at Stone Edge the day Sear attacked.

"Your mother died in Stone Edge?" Fendrel asked, his gaze softening.

Cassius blinked in surprise. "Yes."

Fendrel opened his mouth to speak, but his throat dried. He swallowed and tried again. "Mine, too."

"How—" the prince's voice broke. His eyes started to mist over, and he tried to blink the tears away. "How did she die? Was she brave?"

"She . . ." Fendrel sighed, trying to recall the memory from his childhood. "She died fighting. It was a couple of dragons driven mad by sickness."

A silence fell between them. Then, the prince gave Fendrel a wavering smile. "Thank you, for the closure. We never found out what happened to her. She was making her annual visit to all the villages." The prince smiled again, but this one was genuine. "She always insisted she be the one to lead those visits. She wanted our people to know she cared about them, that she was here to protect them. When she and her guards did not come back, we sent out a search party to follow the route she always took, and that was when we found out about Stone Edge. I thought, er, everyone thought there were no survivors."

Fendrel shook his head. "My brother and I made it out, but no one else did."

Once again, the two fell silent. This time, it was Fendrel who broke it. "So, what's your plan to get rid of Zoricus? You said yourself that no one believes you."

189

"We would need evidence, and thankfully I already have a lead." The prince looped an arm through his horse's reigns so he could wring his hands. "I am sure some of Zoricus' friends are working closely with dragon hunters, and that is how they are able to obtain so many eggs. It also explains how the dragon hunters keep evading capture. If we can prove that, then my father will be more open to listening to me."

"And what is your plan in regard to those knights?" Fendrel asked. "Will they be imprisoned, too? Every single knight who has ever been involved in this mess. Are they all going to be punished? Because if so, your family will lose a massive part of your security. Will your father be willing to cut them out even if it means his safety will be at greater risk?"

"I . . ." Cassius dipped his head. "I have not had much time to think about the aftermath. It has been stressful, to say the least. *But* I will do everything in my power to make sure those knights receive punishment. They are Zoricus' friends, so my life will still be in danger as long as they are free. I hope you understand that I will do absolutely anything to get you to help me. I will pardon you for your crimes. Afterall, you would have a clean record if it were not for these corrupt guards."

That would definitely make rescue missions inside villages easier for me, Fendrel thought.

"I believe it should be simple enough to gain evidence of their corruption. These days, dragon hides are worth more than gold in Sharpdagger." Cassius fidgeted with his hands as he spoke. "So, even if we cannot catch certain people in the act, we can make a list of suspects based on which merchants have inexplicably gained a surge of wealth. They should spill who their clients are if we apply enough pressure."

"And how do you expect me to get inside the city?" Fendrel asked. "There are more wanted posters of me hung up whenever I visit. By the time I make my way there next, I wouldn't be surprised if every door had my face on it."

Cassius grimaced. "They already do. I can . . ." The prince looked to be deciding whether he should keep his next idea quiet. With a sigh of resignation, he continued, "I am not supposed to say this, but there are tunnels beneath the city that allow you access without using any of the gates. It is meant to be an escape route in case of an invasion, so no one uses them at the moment. Once you are in, it will be difficult for anyone to know you have gotten inside."

Fendrel nodded. "All right, but how will your father know we're telling him the truth? Why would he trust the word of a fugitive and his son who you already admit he doesn't take seriously?"

The prince made a noise of frustration. "I am not supposed to tell you this, *either*, but we have a mage who works for the royal family. He has assisted in trials before by drawing the truth out of people. So with all that laid out, will you help me?"

"Give me a moment," Fendrel said. He turned and walked to the others under the portcullis. "Would you be fine with another passenger for the time being?"

"It would not slow down my flight," Venom answered.

Fog shook her head. "As long as he is not a hindrance to finding Mist, I do not mind."

"All right." Fendrel nodded. He returned to Cassius. "I can help you, but you'll have to wait a few days. We're in the middle of a search-and-rescue mission for the future queen of the dragons, but we're set to dismiss the mission if we don't find her in time. You can join us if you want, since you don't feel safe at home."

The prince's face was a mix of elation and disbelief as he broke out in a smile. He released a relieved breath and nodded his head in excitement. "Yes! Yes, that is just fine. Thank you, sir. Oh, may I know your name? I am sure you already know mine."

Fendrel gave the younger man a curious look-over. "You want me to call you by your name? Not your title?"

"Well, you have made it clear I am not *your* prince." Cassius smiled.

"All right, then . . . Cassius." Fendrel nodded his head in respect. "My name is Fendrel."

Fendrel was about to lead Cassius to the others, but he stopped himself. "What are you going to do with your horse?"

Cassius' smile faltered. "Oh, right. You ride on dragon-back, so I do not need my horse anymore."

"Are you feeling all right?" Fendrel watched the prince's complexion grow paler.

"I just—" Cassius' hands fumbled with a travel bag he had buckled to the saddle "—I have never ridden a dragon before. Obviously." He tried to cover his nerves with a laugh. Once he pried the travel bag from the saddle and slid his arms through the straps, he whistled and pointed north. The white stallion galloped away. Cassius turned back to Fendrel. "They are trained to return home on command. He will be fine."

Fendrel nodded. He extended his hand to gesture at his companions. "This is Venom, the leader of the Dusk dragons. Fog, our healer and the missing dragon's sister. And this is Charles, a long-time friend and former dragon hunter."

Cassius grinned at each companion but hesitated slightly before nodding at Charles. "Quite the group you have here."

"We also have a mage with us deeper inside Black Brick who can craft you a spell to help you communicate with us all," Fendrel said.

The prince gave him a worried look. "A mage?"

"Yes, another friend of mine." Fendrel gave Cassius a reassuring look. "She doesn't bite. And there is also a child with us, but he isn't a part of the search party."

"A child?" Cassius' eyes widened in shock.

Fendrel nodded. "Long story short I found him during a rescue mission. He's Sadon's nephew, and terrified of that man, so we took him in."

"I see," Cassius said.

"We should be going now. Keep close," Fendrel whispered to Cassius and Charles as they headed into the dark tunnel. Venom's golden chest scales illuminated their path. They ventured down the hall and into the sunlit chamber with the pit at its center. Even with the sky hole, the far corners of the chamber remained pitch black. Venom led the group to a cavernous abyss on the other side where the wall should have met the floor.

Venom crouched to allow the humans onto his back. Fendrel climbed aboard first, followed by Charles. The two helped Cassius up by grabbing each of his hands.

"You need not worry about flying blind. Just follow my glow," Venom said to Fog.

Fog unfurled her wings. "I will."

The Dusk dragon dove through the opening and began to soar, casting a rush of wind that shocked Fendrel into high alert. Fendrel held the spines of Venom's neck tight. His eyes were wide open, and the lack of visibility gave Fendrel the strange sensation that he had gone blind. Only when the sound of Venom's claws scraping the rock floor did Fendrel understand they were low to the ground.

Venom landed and tucked in his wings. The light from his chest bounced off the cave floor and ceiling, showing itself to be quite narrow. They continued forward as Venom asked, "Fendrel, you are sure you will be able to help him?"

Fendrel leaned forward and kept his voice quiet, "It seems I'm the only one who *can* help him."

"Do his concerns revolve around dragons?" Venom asked.

Fendrel nodded. "Yes. His cousin, who has threatened to kill him is involved in the illegal dragon trade. I assume by pinning what the king would see as a lesser crime on Zoricus will allow us to more easily expose his threats of violence."

Venom sighed. "That sounds . . ."

"Difficult," Fog finished for him.

"I'm sure it will be, but if it will make a difference, I'm willing to try." Fendrel rolled his shoulders as a chill crept through him. "It's definitely different from anything I've done before."

"Do you think he might have information on Mist?" Fog asked. She glanced at Cassius, then returned her gaze to Fendrel. "If his cousin is taking dragons like the hunters are, perhaps he knows something."

Fendrel shook his head. "I doubt he does. The knights only take hatchlings and eggs because they can smuggle them easier than a full-grown dragon. Besides, it costs less money to feed a hatchling."

"Oh, I see." Fog's ears drooped in response to Fendrel's answer. "I thought I smelled Mist's scent on this newer human, but perhaps I am tricking myself into thinking every newcomer smells like her." Her wings lifted as an idea seemed to come to her. "What about Charles? I know earlier you said he has not heard anything about Mist, but he may have information that could *lead* to finding her!"

"Perhaps he could help us." Venom tilted his head to see the humans on his back. There was a look of acceptance and gratitude in his eyes as he glanced at Charles.

Charles stiffened when he noticed Venom's gaze on him. He gave Fendrel a nervous laugh. "What did you tell them?"

"They were just wondering if you had information that could lead to Mist," Fendrel answered.

"Ah, nothing is coming to mind right now, but if I think of something I'll tell you," Charles vowed. "I trust Fog's nose, especially since Sadon has been extra secretive lately. It's more than likely he knows exactly where Mist is, but she could be in any of the hunters' bases."

Fendrel relayed Charles' message to Fog and Venom, who made noises of pondering. It was only then Fendrel realized the ceiling was getting lower while a light ahead of them brightened.

"Duck your heads," Venom warned.

Following the Dusk dragon's instructions, Fendrel called the command back to Cassius and Charles.

A breeze floated by them, tickling Fendrel's skin. Once it had gone, the air grew warmer. He squinted as they approached the light, as bright as the sky hole from the chamber above. The chirping of birds and a small gurgling stream greeted Fendrel's ears. To his surprise, he could smell salt in the air, and the faint pounding of waves sounded from outside the rock walls.

Venom stepped out of the cramped tunnel and stretched his wings, but he stayed in a crouch. "We are here."

Fendrel dropped to the ground with Charles and Cassius stumbling just behind, using Venom's wing as a handhold during their descent.

Fog emerged from the tunnel behind them as Fendrel took in the scenery. They stood within a giant rocky bowl with walls too steep and high to climb. Streams, willow trees, flowers, and butterflies livened the space. On the far end, too distant to hear, sat in the shade of a willow were Thea and Oliver. The two humans noticed the group and started to make their way over.

"What is this place?" Fendrel asked, hearing the crunch of grass under his boots.

"We call them Sanctuaries." Venom stood. "We use them as a place for guests to stay, to house the injured like the dragons we recovered today, or as nurseries for hatchlings. You and your mother stayed in one before you went to live with your father."

Fendrel's mouth became a thin line. "Please don't refer to him as my father."

Venom's eyes closed as he nodded. "Agreed."

Once Thea and Oliver were in ear-shot, Fendrel waved at them. "We're back!"

Thea looked at Charles and Cassius. "They're a part of 'we' now? Who are they?"

"This is my friend—" Fendrel gestured at Charles. Before he could continue the introduction, Oliver ran past him and latched his arms around Charles' waist.

"You're here!" Oliver exclaimed.

"Hey! There you are." Charles ruffled Oliver's hair. The former hunter bent down on one knee. "I knew you would find someone to take you in."

"I did." Oliver pointed with excitement at Thea.

"That's good." Charles mouthed to Thea, "Thank you."

Thea smiled at the two, then said to Fendrel, "I'm glad Oliver had at least one person to look after him before we met him."

Fendrel scoffed. "Yes, stars know his uncle wasn't going to take care of him."

"Who's his uncle?"

"Sadon." Fendrel gave Thea a sidelong glance.

Thea elbowed Fendrel in the rubs. "That's not a funny joke."

"I was being serious." Fendrel looked at her straight-on.

"Wh—" Thea sputtered. "Why didn't you say that sooner?"

Fendrel shrugged and gave her a teasing smile. "What? Don't blame me. You never asked."

Thea threw her head back in exasperation with a heavy sigh. "Anyway—" she stuck her hand out toward Cassius, who was inching closer to the two "—what's your name? You look familiar."

Cassius gave her a flimsy handshake. "My name is Cassius . . ."

"That's the prince, Thea." Fendrel grinned at her puzzled face.

"The prince!" Thea forced her smile wider. "And I'm shaking your hand, and you're here. What are you doing all the way out here and without guards or anything?"

"Well, I, er we—" Cassius pulled his hand away to gesture at Fendrel "—are discussing a plan."

"He wants me to help him take Zoricus out of power," Fendrel explained.

"Ooh, you should!" Thea nodded with exuberance. "You definitely should. He gives me weird looks every time he patrols near my house, which, yes, my house is falling apart, but I can just *tell* he's being condescending."

"So, do you want to make a couple more of those Drake-tongue communication spells for them?" Fendrel pointed between Cassius and Charles, who was listening to Oliver recount their entire journey thus far.

"I'm on it." Thea clapped her hands together. "Oh, and Fendrel, do you remember what I said about springing surprising information on me and pretending like it's nothing?"

"Yes, yes, it's your thing." Fendrel rolled his eyes in mock annoyance.

"You better," Thea said. She waved Charles over. Her question-filled voice faded away as she led Charles, Oliver, and Cassius to the other end of the Sanctuary.

My mother and I used to live in one of these? Fendrel thought as he looked about the structure. He closed his eyes and tried to see if he felt any familiarity. *This is where Mother spent her time when she wasn't visiting me. Did she like it? Was she happy?*

Venom's voice broke Fendrel from his thoughts. The Dusk dragon had perched on a flat boulder. He cleared his throat. "Can everyone understand me now?"

"Yes, sir." Charles' face was full of wonder.

Cassius nodded, his mouth struggling to stay closed.

"Good. For those of you who do not know yet, we will be staying here for the rest of the day. We all need time to rest before we resume our journey, and I need to to certain matters. I will be back shortly." Venom spread his wings and flew out of the Sanctuary.

Fendrel watched him soar over the rim of the rocky bowl and disappear from sight.

I hope Venom's scouts were able to find something about Mist. But, even if they haven't had any luck, I will not give up, Fendrel told himself. *I will bring her home if no one else can. I will prove my worth.*

"All right, everyone," Fendrel called to the group. "Now that we can all understand each other, I think we should compare notes. Anything that might be useful, let's say it for everyone to hear."

CHAPTER 28: FENDREL

THE GROUP COMMUNED IN THE shade of a willow on the far side of the Sanctuary. Thea stayed within earshot, distracting Oliver with a vial full of colorful beads that chimed as the boy tilted it end over end.

"I don't want him hearing anything he shouldn't," Thea had explained just moments ago.

"Let's start with what we know. We can go into speculation later." Fendrel scratched a burned spot on his bag to help him focus. "We know Mist went missing eleven days ago. We know she isn't being held captive in the dragon hunters' Ravine or Cliff Bases. And we know Mist traveled all the way to Stone Edge after she disappeared."

"We found her blood trail . . ." Fog hung her head and spoke in a somber tone.

Fendrel nodded in confirmation. "But the trail stopped in Stone Edge as if she vanished into thin air. We also know Sadon must have touched her at some point, because her scent is on his gloves."

"Sadon gave me his gloves just before he sent me out on my last mission," Charles said. "I know that doesn't narrow down *when* he got his hands on her, but it lets us know Mist has been his captive for two days at the very least."

"The blood trail Fog and I found was several days old, but I couldn't exactly tell how long it had been there. Capturing a Vapor dragon is unheard of for the dragon hunters, so I'm sure whoever abducted Mist brought her to Sadon immediately." Fendrel scratched the blackened leather with more fervor. "With that in mind, I think it's safe to say Mist is being held in one of the bases Sadon has visited within the past several days."

Fog locked eyes with Charles. "Fendrel told me that Sadon has kept you close to him for years now. Is this true?"

Charles nodded. "Yes, I've been forced to stay near him, if not directly beside him."

"That means, any base you have visited in the past several days is where my sister is." Fog leaned toward him. Her feathers stood on end, anticipating his response. "What bases are those and where are they?"

"Within the last eleven days, let me think." Charles tilted his head in thought. He started, "Well, back then we were at the Stronghold. Three days later we headed toward Sharpdagger to finish setting up the Warehouse Base. On the sixth day was when we—" Charles gave Fog an apologetic look.

"That was when Sadon captured *me*," Fog finished his statement.

"Right, and from there we took you back with us to the Sharpdagger warehouse. The next day we spent trying to clean up from your—" Charles pointed between Fendrel and Fog "—escape. The morning after we started traveling *back* to the Stronghold, and finally reached it within two days. Immediately after we were settled, Sadon sent me to Stone Edge. That's when I joined you."

"So, the only place Mist could be is at the Stronghold or somewhere in that same building I was kept in?" Fog asked. She desperately searched Charles' face, looking for a hopeful answer.

Charles nodded. "Yes, unless Sadon has moved her since I left."

"How far is the Stronghold?" Fog stood. "It is like you said, Fendrel, we have some daylight left! We can go there now."

"I—" Fendrel winced as he anticipated the heartbroken expression he knew was about to cross Fog's face. "I don't think that's a good idea yet. The Stronghold is the most well-guarded base the dragon hunters have, and it's in the middle of a desert. It would be impossible to sneak up on them during the day."

Just as Fendrel feared, Fog's hopes were dashed like the waves that pounded against the rocky walls of the Sanctuary. Fog sank into the grass, letting it swallow as much of her as it could. Her eyes started to glisten with tears as she asked, "How are we going to get inside?"

"Well, *you* definitely aren't going inside." Fendrel steeled his gaze. "The only way you'd reach the interior of that castle is if they captured you, and it is nearly impossible trying to free dragons that have been brought to the Stronghold."

"It would have to be at night, and I hate sounding like I'm volunteering you for the job, Fen—" Charles gave Fendrel an apologetic look "—but they'd recognize me immediately if I tried breaking in. The new recruits haven't seen your face, and the instructors and guards probably won't recognize you if you go in with a disguise."

Fendrel nodded. "I was already going to volunteer myself. No one else will be able to."

"But how are you going to get her out?" Fog was still partially submerged in the grass. "You said it was impossible freeing dragons from there."

"*Nearly* impossible . . ." Fendrel bit his lip, wondering if his next words would make the situation more worrisome. He spoke anyway. "In all honesty, I haven't rescued any dragons from the Stronghold before. But I believe it can be done. It will just be more difficult. Especially since I don't know where Sadon might be keeping her."

Charles' brow furrowed in concentration. "I might."

Fog and Fendrel stared at him intensely. Cassius, too, seemed invested in the conversation though he had not yet said a word. Thea tilted her head a bit to listen in, even with her eyes on Oliver as the boy played.

"It's only happened a handful of times. I can think of three, perhaps four cases of it happening in all the years I've been stuck with the hunters." Charles looked between each of the others to make sure they were listening. "Sometimes Sadon finds a dragon so rare he forbids any other hunters from touching it, and he locks that dragon away in a vault behind his study. No hunter, at least not one ranked high enough to be taken seriously, had seen a Vapor dragon before. Sadon would do anything to keep its existence a secret from the others, at least until he studied it enough to be confident in his ability to trap another.

"That's why you were placed in a storage room," Charles continued as he held Fog's gaze. "Sadon didn't want the other hunters knowing you existed, so he isolated you rather than having you imprisoned where we planned to keep other dragons. He only brought hunters into that room once we got the suspicion Fendrel was inside."

Fog nodded in understanding. "And that is why it was only you and Sadon who trapped me that day."

"Exactly," Charles confirmed. "Sadon meant to transport you to the Stronghold in secret, but Fendrel showed up before he got the chance to smuggle you out of the city."

Fendrel felt a chill run down his spine while dread twisted his gut. *If I had been just a day late, perhaps even just hours late, Fog and Mist would both be missing, and I'd be none the wiser that they ever existed. I might never have even been asked to help.*

"But if Sadon did not want other hunters to know about Mist, why was it not him who captured her?" Fog's face filled with confusion.

"Sadon was in the Stronghold at that time. If I remember right, the hunters who were around the Hazy Woods at the time of Mist's disappearance were all pretty high rank, just a step below me." Charles had a far-off look in his eyes that told Fendrel the older man was searching through his memory. "They would know Sadon would want to keep a Vapor dragon's capture quiet. They probably corralled Mist away from the Hazy Woods, all the way to Stone Edge, and finally caught up to her there."

"And from there they somehow brought her to Sadon, completely concealed?" Fendrel asked.

"In a covered wagon, most likely. That's probably why they couldn't catch up to her until she'd reached Stone Edge." Charles switched his gaze to Fendrel. "They must have had a capture wagon they were dragging behind their horses and were only able to subdue Mist once her exhaustion slowed her down."

Fog huffed a frustrated sigh. "Why could she not just fly out of their reach, hide in the clouds, and circle back home?"

Fendrel opened his mouth to speak but pushed down his words when Charles offered an answer instead.

"High-rank hunters are granted a special weapon we call anchors. They're sort of a small cannon, small enough to be fitted on the side of a saddle. Instead of shooting cannon balls, they shoot bolts thrice the size a crossbow can fire, and they're deadly precise. The bolts themselves are made out of . . . well," Charles ceased his rambling. "I suppose it doesn't matter what they're made of, but their purpose is to herd dragons toward the ground."

With a grim nod, Fendrel knew why Charles had cut his explanation short. Dragon bones were often the primary material used to carve the anchor bolts due to their strength and lightweight composition. Fog did not need to hear that. Her face showed she did not want to hear it, but her ears were still perked forward for her sister's sake.

Fendrel cleared his throat, wanting to change the subject. "Charles, you said Sadon keeps these rare dragons in a vault behind his study, but I thought the only door to his study was the entrance from the hall?"

"That's what I thought, too, but every time Sadon finds a rare dragon, he disappears into his study with buckets of water and raw meat. Every time he emerges, the buckets are empty." Charles crossed his arms and leaned back. "He and I both knew what he was doing, but when I brought it up to him, he said to keep my mouth shut."

Fendrel's eyes widened in horror. "Are those dragons still there?"

"No." Charles shook his head. "Once Sadon is done studying them he harvests them."

"Our time limit might be shorter than three days, then." Fendrel felt his heart rate speeding up. He cast a glance at Fog, who looked as deathly as the specters most humans assumed Vapor dragons to be.

"All right." Fendrel brought his bag to his lap and began to drum his fingers on it. "What's the plan on getting me in and out of the Stronghold?"

"We'll need to steal one of their uniforms. Mine won't work since we destroyed my armor and shoulder rank," Charles said.

"We could lure a few hunters out at night, take them by surprise behind the dunes where no scouts can see what's happened to them." Fendrel sat up straighter. "Since it'll be night, my identity will be hidden better, so I think it will be relatively easy sneaking in."

"Especially since the stable workers that greet returning hunters are all newer." Charles nodded in agreement. "From there you'll have to find the vault behind Sadon's study. I'm sure he hides the entrance behind that giant map that hangs on the wall."

"There has to be another door in that vault, too, one I can escape through without going through the halls again." Fendrel's drumming sped up as his mind worked. "The only way to keep a secret dragon a secret is to make sure no one saw it being brought into the vault."

The rush of Venom's wings sounded from just outside the willow's shade. The black dragon joined them behind the tree's green curtains and lay beside Fog. "What is this about a secret dragon?"

Fendrel and Charles took a few minutes to explain Venom what they had been discussing.

Venom tented a wing over Fog to comfort her. "Then we have our destination for tomorrow set?"

"And a plan for how to get inside," Charles added. "Which reminds me, Fendrel. If you're able to, could you check any reports Sadon made recently? Whenever he imprisons these rare dragons, he makes a report stating they died soon after being captured. If you can find one for Mist, that proves without a doubt that she's being kept in the vault."

Fendrel cocked his head to the side. "Why would he write a report like that?"

"He does it with all the rare dragons that were brought in by someone other than himself. Sadon doesn't want anyone messing with those dragons, so he says they died to keep the hunters from questioning why the dragon they captured seems to have vanished into thin air."

"And since it wasn't Sadon who captured Mist—" Fendrel started with a slow nod.

"—the hunters who *did* capture her would no doubt wonder what happened to her," Charles finished.

"Might I suggest we speak with someone before we venture to the Stronghold?" Venom asked as he looked to Fog for approval. "She might have useful information as she lives not far from where we are going. Perhaps an hour away at the most."

"Who is she?" Fog spoke for the first time since Charles mentioned the anchors.

"She is the noble of the Fire tribe," Venom explained. "She often witnesses the dragon hunters' activity near her domain. Perhaps she can give us insight to make Fendrel's infiltration safer."

Fendrel sighed. "I'll be fine."

"I would rather not risk it," Venom said firmly.

Fog stared at the grass for a few moments, unblinking and looking as though she was barely breathing. Then, she said, "If it will help us find the most successful way of saving Mist, I suppose we can stop by to speak with her."

"We should leave at daybreak to allot ourselves the most amount of time," Fendrel advised. The others nodded, quietly.

"I have a question," Cassius spoke up in a meek voice. "I know you said it is more likely that this missing dragon, er Mist, is in the Stronghold, but you said it is also possible she could be in Sharpdagger."

"I doubt it, but it *is* possible." Charles shrugged. "The warehouse might have secret rooms that I'm not privy to."

"I was wondering if . . . well, it sounds stupid now that I think about it." Cassius ducked his head as he said, "There is something I remember my cousin talking about not long ago. He was boasting to his friends that he was in possession of an adult dragon, one with blue-gray fur. None of his friends believed him and I did not either because he was drunk. But I have this nagging feeling that it is connected here."

That is the same color fur that Mist has, but there are several tribes whose dragons have blue-gray fur. Fendrel dismissed the idea with a wave of his hand. "I don't think that's possible. Zoricus of all people isn't capable of capturing a grown dragon."

Cassius pressed his lips into a thin line. "Then, do you think he could have purchased her from the hunters?"

"Ha!" Charles shook his head. "Sadon wouldn't sell Mist even if he was paid double her weight in gold."

"I see." Cassius nodded. He grew quiet.

A long, tense moment passed between them all before Fog rose from the grass.

"It is still bright out, but I think I am going to lie down now." Fog nudged Venom's wing with her own. "Could you show me where we are to sleep?"

"Yes." Venom stood. "I will take you to the cave dens. The darkness will help you fall asleep quicker."

When the two dragons had made it to the other end of the Sanctuary, ducking into the cave, Fendrel heaved a deep sigh. He squeezed his eyes shut and pinched the bridge of his nose.

"Worried?" Charles asked.

Fendrel nodded, holding his position. "What if we're too late? We haven't even seen if Mist is dead or not and Fog is already destroyed. She nearly gave up when we found Mist's bloody fur outside Stone Edge. I don't want to see that happen to her again."

"It won't," Charles said, though he sounded unsure. "Sadon wouldn't kill Mist with her being the only Vapor dragon in his possession."

"What if we find her and Sadon has done something worse than killing her?" Fendrel opened his eyes and took his hand away from his face.

Charles slouched as if burdened by the same weight Fendrel felt in his heart.

What if I fail this mission? Am I supposed to just continue with my life like nothing happened? How could I ever forgive myself?

"We'll deal with it, if it comes to that." Charles leaned toward Fendrel. "Do you hear me? *If.*"

"If," Fendrel repeated. "I hear you."

"I'm sure Sadon assumes Vapor dragons are dainty, so he probably hasn't tried to hurt her." Charles reached out and gripped Fendrel's shoulder. "He's probably just studying her behavior. He usually keeps rare dragons around for months. Mist will be all right."

"Charles, if you knew about these dragons hidden from everyone else, why didn't you tell me?" Fendrel asked.

"The last time this happened was before you completed your training. There was no reason to bring it up. Besides, you said it best. It's nearly impossible trying to rescue a dragon from the Stronghold." Charles' eyes became downcast. "I wouldn't want you getting caught, not after you fought so hard to leave in the first place."

Fendrel cast a sidelong glance at Cassius. The prince read his expression, his cheeks reddened, and he moved to stand. Cassius said, "I will . . . give you two some space."

When Cassius had walked a good distance away, Fendrel sighed. "Mist is the future queen of the Freelands. I can't even imagine how devastating it will be for the whole kingdom to lose her."

Charles whistled in astonishment. He took his hand back from Fendrel's shoulder. "No wonder you're so worked up over this. But Fen, just remember that you're not doing this mission alone. And if you do happen to get trapped in the Stronghold, I'll storm in and get you out."

Fendrel gave a cynical laugh. "Promise me you won't. You were their prisoner for the better part of my lifetime."

"You're not convincing me otherwise." Charles offered up a sad smile. "What would my life be for if I didn't try to save the only friend I've got left?"

Sharing the grin, Fendrel dropped his head. "I'm going to kill Sadon one of these days. Perhaps tomorrow if I can aim right."

Charles snickered. "He was *really* pissed off about that shoulder stab you pulled at the warehouse."

"Well, that's his problem because if he hadn't moved, he wouldn't be here anymore. Then he wouldn't be able to complain." Fendrel failed to suppress a chuckle.

A moment of silence passed between them. Charles glanced about the Sanctuary, then back at Fendrel with a mischievous smile. He said, "You're going to hate me for saying this."

"Hm?" The corner of Fendrel's lip quirked up in anticipation.

"That prince over there." Charles tilted his head toward Cassius, who had taken to absently walking along the Sanctuary's perimeter. "He reminds me of you when you were around his age."

Fendrel's smile dropped, and he punched Charles on his good shoulder. "He does not."

"Sure he does," Charles said, dragging out the words in a teasing manner. "I heard that conversation you had with him outside. Every word. He's scared, confused, doesn't have anyone he can trust."

Fendrel rolled his eyes, but he knew what Charles meant. *Scared of being killed, unable to tell his sibling about his plight because he won't be believed . . . We both lost our mothers the same way, too.*

"I should go talk to him, get my mind off the hunters for a bit," Fendrel said. He rose from the grass and made his way toward the prince, his quicker stride allowing him to catch up to Cassius before he had gotten too far.

Cassius gave Fendrel a cautious glance. "Did you want to sit and talk to me about something?"

Fendrel shook his head. "No, let's walk. I plan better when I walk. Tell me more about your situation."

Thinking too much about Mist's disappearance is only going to wear me out. It's not like I can do anything to help her for the rest of the day. Still, I might as well be productive. I'll lose my mind if I try to relax.

"I am sure I covered the basics with you," Cassius said.

"Then, tell me about your life." Fendrel shrugged. "If I'm going to be working with you, I'd like to know you a bit better."

"Well, I . . ." Cassius laughed nervously. "I like getting out of the palace as often as I can. Not just because of Zoricus, though. I like walking around without anyone knowing who I am. I dress in commoner's garb. That is how I have been able to eavesdrop on unscrupulous merchants."

Fendrel quirked an eyebrow, intrigued. "Has that changed since you got engaged?"

Cassius stumbled at Fendrel's words. The prince caught himself and continued walking as if nothing had occurred. "No. It has made me sneak out more often."

But he chose to marry her after he's denied every previous suitor. I barely spend time around humans and even I know that, Fendrel thought. *Doesn't that mean he likes her?*

Fendrel tried to make his next words sound casual, but decided to ask outright, "Did your family pressure you into saying yes?"

"No," Cassius mumbled. "You are going to think I am insane, but I think she is poisoning my father and I."

"That's a serious accusation." Fendrel felt his eyes widen in surprise. "So you suspect your cousin *and* your fiancée of trying to kill you. Do you think they're working together?"

Cassius shook his head. "No. Zoricus has always hated me, and like

I said earlier, he does not think I deserve the crown. Adila, though, I do not know why she is doing what she is doing. I suspect she wants to make my father and I progressively sick so she can rule after we are gone."

"But wouldn't your sister be next in line?" Fendrel squinted at Cassius.

"Not if my father dies before I am coronated. Otherwise, yes, Sadie would be queen."

Fendrel felt himself becoming more invested in the conversation. "And you're sure it's your fiancée doing this? Doesn't it make more sense for it to be Zoricus?"

"My father and I both got the same illness the exact day Adila showed up. We only got sick after we had dinner, and we had the same symptoms." Cassius shuddered. "I started eating less and less until I would just pick at my food because I would feel so awful if I swallowed anything."

Fendrel eyed the prince's skinny frame. *So, that's why he looks so thin,* he thought.

Cassius huffed. "Now that I think about it, Zoricus is the one who introduced her to us. He said she was the daughter of a wealthy family but did not give us any further details. My father and sister were so happy I said yes that they never followed up with Zoricus."

Before Fendrel could ask why Cassius had said yes in the first place, Cassius was already talking again.

"In all honesty, I think she might have placed a curse on me. I am not myself when I am around her. It is like a wholly different person is controlling my words and my actions." Cassius started waving his hands as he talked. He didn't seem to notice that he and Fendrel were nearing the willow where Thea and Oliver still played. "I get this sickening, dizzying feeling whenever I look at her and I can just tell that something is wrong with her. I do not think it is an effect of the poison, either. I have never heard of a poison that makes your vision swim with morphing shapes and colors."

Thea whipped her head toward them. She stormed over with a fierce look in her eyes. "What did you just say?"

Cassius froze. "About what?"

"What you were saying about the shapes. Does it come with a headache, too?" Thea inched closer to Cassius until they were less than a foot apart.

The prince stepped back. "Yes?"

Thea nodded her head slowly. "You're in trouble. You definitely had a spell cast on you. Tell me *every single time* you remember getting that feeling."

Fendrel watched the two engage in amusement. His mirth quickly faded as Thea's face showed genuine concern.

"So, for the most part it only happens when you look at your fiancée." Thea crossed her arms, tapping a finger against her bicep. "But you also experienced it when you spoke to the mage who serves your family."

"That is exactly right!" A mix of elation and fear filled Cassius' voice.

Thea pursed her lips. "What's this mage's name?"

"For the life of me I cannot remember," Cassius said. "He never shows his face to anyone. The only thing you can see are his strange, magenta eyes."

"Raaldin!" Thea cried with an excited clap.

Cassius blinked. "I-I think you are right. That name sounds familiar."

Horror replaced Thea's shock.

"Isn't Raaldin your neighbor?" Fendrel asked Thea. "What's he doing on the outskirts of Sharpdagger's slums if he lives in the palace?"

"Who cares? He's a creep. He's going to do what creeps do. He was there in Wing's Caress when I took Oliver and Fog with me, too." Thea crossed her arms again. "Good thing you left when you did, Cassius. Raaldin can't be trusted, but he's good at convincing non-mages that they need his services."

"But Raaldin is the only reason why I was able to find you," Cassius protested as he glanced at Fendrel. "Is it possible Adila corrupted him?"

"Not a chance. Your eyes have the stain when you talked to Raaldin, so *he* must have done something to Adila." Thea shrugged as if her logic was obvious to the prince. "Not the other way around."

"What is a stain?" Cassius asked, almost too quiet to hear.

"It's a symptom of coming into contact with dark magic," Fendrel answered.

"You remembered!" Thea's eyes brightened. "And yes, you're right. Raaldin did something to Adila, and in turn must have done something to you."

Cassius paled. "Are my father and sister in danger?"

Thea shook her head in disbelief. "If you're the only one with the stain, that means your family is probably outside of Raaldin's plan, whatever that is."

Fendrel retreated into his thoughts while Thea and Cassius deliberated. *This could be a problem when the time comes to take down Zoricus. I hope that mage doesn't interfere.*

He was snapped from his thoughts at Venom's return to the Sanctuary. The Dusk dragon crawled out of the far tunnel and made his way over. "The sun is lowering," Venom said. "We should get an early rest."

"We'll talk more later," Fendrel said to Cassius, to which the prince smiled in gratitude.

When Venom crouched, the humans pulled themselves onto his back, with Charles lifting Oliver on before he joined them. Venom walked back to the tunnel, warned the humans to watch their heads, and ducked into the darkness. He lit the golden scales on his chest, but it did little to clear the enveloping black that surrounded them. As they traveled deeper into Black Brick, Fendrel was surprised to see that Venom's earlier statement to Fog had been right.

The darkness of the caves is already making me tired, Fendrel thought. *Then again, I did not sleep well last night, and we have been traveling nonstop for a few days. I must have been exhausted for a while and only now realized it.*

In silence they continued until Venom spread his wings and flew toward a sliver of light above. It was the main chamber, and the curtain was being tied back in its place to cover the sky hole. With the light gone once again, Fendrel lost his bearings as Venom seemed to be walking down a slope. Fendrel's eyes adjusted, and he saw Venom was using the spiraling stairs that wound into the pit. A railing of ornately carved stone separated them from the inky, seemingly bottomless drop.

After a few minutes of Venom's stride lulling Fendrel into a state of calm, the Dusk dragon veered into a hall. Venom's voice, almost disembodied in the void, said in a hushed tone, "Fog is in one of these rooms. The rest are empty. You may each choose whichever one you would like for the night."

It took Fendrel a moment to make out there were rooms on either side of the hall, each one's entrance blocked off by a thick curtain.

Fendrel was about to slip down, just as the others were, when Venom nudged Fendrel's shoulder with his nose.

"Can I have a moment with you?" Venom asked.

Resettling himself, Fendrel nodded, knowing Venom could see his gesture even in the dark. He held on to Venom's spines as the Dusk dragon turned and made his way back to the staircase.

"I would fly to make this quicker, but it is a steep drop, and I do not want you to fall," Venom called over his shoulder.

Fendrel smiled. "You can take your time."

Down they went, level by level, around and around until they reached the bottom of the pit. From Venom's light, shining brighter now than when the others were around, Fendrel could see there was a single corridor to enter. The trail was high-ceilinged and adorned with carvings Fendrel could not quite comprehend in the dimness. Venom picked up his pace through the tunnel and when something to Fendrel's left glimmered as it caught the light, Venom stopped. He angled his wing down to let Fendrel use it as a handhold while he dismounted.

Venom stretched his neck and pushed out his chest, which made his markings glow to the intensity of a collection of torches. It was enough to see the object to Fendrel's left in full view. A mural made from colored pieces of glazed clay that had been embedded into the wall.

Fendrel's footsteps echoed through the tunnel as he approached the mural. He reached out his hand and felt the cold, smooth, tiles grace his fingertips, sending a chill through his arm. The scene, using glossy blues, greens, and blacks, showed the Sunken Grotto, the home of the Water tribe. A dead, concaved volcano rested on a beach of black sand and lapping waves. Below the depths rest a system of caves formed from the igneous rock of the volcano's final eruption.

"These murals are how my tribe keeps record of the Freelands' history. Every branch of these caves details a different century, and this branch depicts the one we are currently in." Venom stayed back so his scales lit the whole mural.

"So there are levels below here?" Fendrel asked as he cast a look over his shoulder.

Venom nodded. "Many of them. All the tribes used to work together to record our history in a cave system that spans the underground of our entire continent. Unfortunately, all the chambers and tunnels my ancestors used to access our complete history have been blocked off by cave-ins." The Dusk dragon sighed in a disappointed manner. "Far before I hatched, I presume when our tribes became distanced from each other, the Dusk tribe became the only one to keep

The Dragon Liberator: Escapade

up the tradition. However, even some of the murals we created only centuries ago have also been lost to cave-ins, simply due to being constructed deeper underground."

Fendrel released a breath of astonishment as he drank in the sight again. "Why does this mural show the home of the Water tribe?"

"Every branch begins with the tribe that possessed the monarchy at the start of that century. Before the monarchy was given to Cloud's family, it belonged to the Water dragons." Venom walked along the tunnel, shifting Fendrel's view of the mural over to new ones.

As Fendrel's eyes passed over each new scene, he did his best to decipher what they were made to depict. There were etchings below, above, and around each mural that looked like Drake-tongue lettering, but the marks were too small for his eyes to pick up in the dim lighting, and he wondered if he would even be able to make out what they said had the cave been fully lit. After all, dragons had much better eyesight and could pick out more minute details than humans could. Still, Fendrel worked his mind into sorting out the history of the current century. His breath caught at the mural Venom stopped in front of.

Venom had been quiet during their walk, and now an air of despair and reminiscence hung around him. It made the cave air stifling. Fendrel felt the change in his bones. A sense of longing and anger washed over him.

This was not the first mural to showcase a human as the centerpiece, but it was the first to display Fendrel's mother. It took every ounce of his willpower to keep himself from tearing up, but even still Fendrel found himself failing to do so. "I—" Fendrel swallowed "—I'd almost forgotten what she looked like. She looks so young here."

"When your mother came into our lives, our muralists made this as a reminder to our tribe of our purpose. Not just protectors of the royal family, but also of humankind," Venom said. Fendrel could tell without looking at Venom that the Dusk dragon was smiling.

While the history lesson beforehand had been engaging, Fendrel knew this was the reason why Venom brought him so far beneath the ground.

Behind his mother, with wings outstretched and fangs bared in a display of protection, sat Venom immortalized in black and gold tiles. Their surroundings were that of what Fendrel assumed to be one of the Sanctuaries with its willows, butterflies, and streams, but it was not the Sanctuary he had just been in with the others. This one had a small cove

210

carved into the rock wall in the back. Even with the beauty of the Sanctuary, Fendrel could not take his eyes from the visage of his mother. Her dark brown hair, almost black, hung in thin strands about her face and pooled over her shoulders. Her freckles, which dotted the bridge of her thin nose, were fainter than Fendrel's and almost invisible against her tanned skin. Her eyes, a mix of green and blue, seemed to peer at Fendrel with kindness.

The first time I spoke to Venom, he said I looked nothing like my mother. Fendrel's heart ached. *He was right. I look like the man who betrayed her, the man who got her banished from Stone Edge.*

The young woman's expression was that of pure joy, even as she sat a solitary human in the home of Dusk dragons.

Feeling his tears spill over his cheeks, Fendrel looked away. In all his dreams and memories of his mother, her smile had the unsettling appearance of being forced, but not here in this mural.

I've never seen her truly happy before now, Fendrel realized.

He forced his eyes back to the mural and studied every feature of his mother's face, committing it to his memory. *I'll never forget what you look like. I promise.*

"Venom?" Fendrel asked.

"Yes, young one?"

"Was what Fragrance said true, that you view me like a son?" Fendrel's heart was beating faster in anticipation.

"I am not the best with sentimental words, young one. But—" Venom guided Fendrel onward with his wing "—I can show my answer to you."

The next mural was the largest Fendrel had seen thus far. It stretched from the top of the high ceiling to the bottom of the wall and was far wider than it was tall. Displayed through its tiles were a series of repeating pictures. In them, Venom appeared to be meeting with the nobility of the other tribes. His ears were always pinned backward, and his forepaws upturned with claws curling in dismay and distraught. Across the stretch at the very top, Venom almost seemed hopeful. In the stretch of tiles below where the images were repeated, his wings and head sunk a little. With each repeating section Venom's body language grew more agonized all the while the nobles he spoke to remained unchanged.

However, the final section at the bottom of the mural was different. Venom no longer met with the nobles. He instead looked like he was visiting Stone Edge, over and over again.

"What is this?" Fendrel tried to see if there were words surrounding this mural like all the others but found none. This piece, it seemed, was self-explanatory to the Dusk dragons.

"I, like many others, was across the sea in the Fauna Wilds when your mother died. Dusk dragons made up a large portion of our army. That meant, with us away from home and unable to neutralize the rogues that plagued the Freelands, we were unable to stop Sear from making it to Stone Edge." Venom took a moment before he continued. Fendrel waited patiently for him.

"When I returned, I was alerted to the fact that Axella had not returned to us like she planned to. I would not let myself rest until I found out what happened . . . By the time I reached Stone Edge, everything was destroyed, and your scent was long gone. That meant one of two things." Venom moved closer to stand directly behind Fendrel. "Either the rogue had killed you, or you somehow survived and moved along. I chose to believe the latter."

Fendrel's eyes scanned over the mural once more as Venom spoke.

"Every year since that day, I met with the other nobles to see if they or any of their subjects had seen you. Year after year, they all denied it." Venom paused to sigh heavily. "At some point I had to stop. Not out of choice, but out of obligation. I needed to serve my tribe like my predecessors had, and that meant I had to devote more time at home than I could to my search."

When Venom stopped talking, Fendrel looked back at the dragon to see he too was battling tears.

"I never gave up hope that you had survived, Fendrel. Even with this tragedy brought on by Mist's disappearance, I am eternally thankful the stars have found a way to reunite us."

Fendrel let Venom drag him against his chest. He felt himself rocking with Venom's breaths. That motion, combined with the embracing darkness and the dimming of Venom's markings, lulled Fendrel to a tranquil state of body and mind.

"There is another Sanctuary I want to show you before we rest tonight," Venom said in an almost inaudible voice.

"All right." Fendrel stayed leaning against Venom's chest for a few minutes. Once his tears dried, he left the Dusk dragon's embrace and pulled himself up to the dragon's shoulders, using Venom's wing claw as leverage.

The trek back through the tunnel and up the winding stairs seemed longer than when they had made it downward. Fendrel felt his eyes growing heavy with each passing minute, but the cold of the Black Brick Ruins kept him alert enough to hang on, even as Venom flew through passages too dark for his markings to brighten. When they broke out of a tunnel into the cold night air, Fendrel welcomed the scent of the sea. He closed his eyes and relished the wind that blew his hair while Venom banked toward a Sanctuary.

Venom's paws sank into the ground and Fendrel opened his eyes to see the same Sanctuary laid out in the mural his mother was in. The cove in the back was big enough for a dragon twice Venom's size to fit in comfortably.

Fendrel slipped down Venom's side, his feet landing a bit awkwardly with drowsiness. He approached the center of the chamber and looked around its walls which formed a perfect shelter from any seaborne storm.

"This is where you two were most days, when you wanted to get some sunlight." Venom joined Fendrel's side.

"Why couldn't I come back?" The words left Fendrel's mouth before he had time to process the thought. "I know why I couldn't stay here when I was an infant, but why couldn't I have been brought here when I was old enough to follow instructions?"

"We wanted to bring you back. Your mother, for a few years, tried to sneak you out of Stone Edge, but your fath—" Venom cleared his throat. "The man who got her pregnant never allowed her to take you, even though it never seemed he wanted you there in the first place. I think he held on to you just to hurt Axella."

Fendrel fought through his fatigue-driven brain fog. *Venom said she tried to finally get me out the same day Sear attacked. If Sear hadn't shown up, would I have grown up here?*

"I am sorry we failed you, Fendrel," Venom said, remorsefully.

Leaning back against Venom, Fendrel said, "You did what you could. I don't blame you." Before he could jolt himself awake, Fendrel slipped off into a dream.

Fendrel sat, hands clasped, to keep them from shaking, on the desk in front of him. His feet, however, bounced with nerves. It was dark out, Fendrel knew from the

emptiness in the halls as everyone was settling down to bed. Fendrel would be, too, if it were any other night, but tonight was different. Tomorrow would be the ceremony that would induct him as an official member of the dragon hunters. He hoped to be gone before morning, with Charles' help. But now he was stuck sitting across from Sadon in the man's too neat and tidy office.

"Have I done something to cause trouble, sir?" Fendrel asked.

"Not at all." Sadon was relaxed in his chair. The torches that lined the walls cast a soft glow across his face and blonde-turning-gray hair. "I wanted to talk about your future with us, Fendrel."

This is it, Fendrel thought. This is where he tells me I've been found out!

"You do know what I'm talking about, don't you?" Sadon leaned forward in his chair, his brows arching in anticipation of Fendrel's answer.

Fendrel held his breath. "I'm afraid I don't, sir."

"No need to be so humble." Sadon wore a genuine smile. "You've put a lot of work in these past two years. I can see you doing a lot of good here, hopefully while serving in a high-ranking position."

"I don't follow," Fendrel said in a voice hushed by fear.

"Fendrel, listen to me." The older man held Fendrel's gaze captive as he said, "You did remarkably in your final test today. I'm giving you my proposal tonight, so you have time to think about it before you become one of us. I want you to be my second-in-command."

Fendrel's hands trembled even as he clasped them tighter. He forced a half-hearted smile that faltered as soon as he made it. "I don't understand."

"You have a gift, boy. I don't know what goes on in that head of yours when you're hunting, but I can tell you like being around the beasts. You like taking them down. I understand that's why you joined us in the first place." Sadon carried on as though he were catching up with a childhood friend. "You wanted to track down a certain desert dragon, right?"

"How did you—" Fendrel tensed as the words left his mouth.

"Your brother let me know. He told me about the attack that made you two orphans." Sadon's mouth pressed into a thin line and his eyes fell solemnly. "Those attacks were happening a lot around that time, as I'm sure you know from speaking with the other recruits. I'm sorry about what happened to your family, boy. I lost mine to dragons, too."

Fendrel kept his mouth shut and waited for Sadon to continue.

"I had a wife and son. About—" Sadon paused and sighed, as if he was delivering bad news "—sixteen years come autumn a dragon attacked my home. My son would have turned eighteen this year, just like you." He blinked away his misty-eyed stare and conviction took over his face and voice. "That's why I started this *organization, Fendrel, to make sure no one else goes through the same thing I did. I'm sorry for what happened to you and your brother. I couldn't save my family. I couldn't save yours. But, after the ceremony tomorrow you'll be part of a new family. We're going to take care of you."*

Sadon had been able to avoid a few tears, but Fendrel felt one slip down his own cheek.

I already have a family, Fendrel thought. I'm an Invier. I already have parents, cousins, aunties, and uncles. But . . . how can I return to them after I killed an Ice dragon for my final test? It was a rogue, sure, but it was still an Ice dragon. Would they ever forgive me for this?

In one swift motion, Sadon stood from his seat and reached across the desk to grasp Fendrel's shoulder. "Think about my offer, would you?"

Fendrel gave a subtle nod without meeting Sadon's piercing blue eyes.

"Good." Sadon patted his shoulder. "Now, go get some sleep. We all have a big day tomorrow."

Without a moment's hesitation, Fendrel rose from his seat and left Sadon's study. His heart pounded wildly against his ribs as he hurried to the room he shared with his brother. Fendrel wasted no time in turning the knob, pushing the door open, and slamming it once he was inside. Frederick was there, resting on his bed which sat opposite Fendrel's. Frederick's lips moved in greeting, but his words were drowned out by the roar of blood rushing through Fendrel's ears. Fendrel sulked over to his bed and plopped onto it. He spoke only once his hearing returned.

"We need to leave." Fendrel slouched with his elbows resting on his knees.

Frederick sat up just across from him. He laughed in what sounded like a mix of confusion and amusement. "What do you mean?"

"It's not safe here. We need to go back home." Fendrel steeled his gaze. "Tonight."

"What's gotten into you?" Frederick rose from his own bed and moved to sit next to Fendrel. "You just had a talk with Sadon, right? What did he say?"

"He wants me to hunt alongside him." Fendrel choked down the bile that rose in his throat.

"Congratulations!" Frederick smiled. "That's a big accomplishment."

Fendrel shook his head. "It's all a lie, Frederick. All of it."

"You're not making any sense." Frederick leaned forward to try and meet Fendrel's eyes. "Are you all right?"

"It's not just rogues that are being hunted here, it's all dragons," Fendrel said.

Frederick gave another short, breathy laugh, this one brought on by disbelief. "Fen, when have we ever killed a normal dragon? You've seen them all! They have that purple froth flying out of their mouths."

Fendrel shook his head with more fervor. "It's been faked. Charles showed me. Sadon has this liquid in the basement that he paints normal dragons with."

The two were silent for a few moments. Fendrel felt the mattress shift as Frederick got up.

"Why are you sabotaging yourself?" Frederick asked.

"What?" Fendrel raised his head, dropping his hands between his knees.

"We finally found somewhere we both fit in, and now you want to throw it away." Frederick paced to the other side of the small room. "I was treated well in Stone Edge, but it wasn't good for you there. And Frost Lake . . . I know you felt right at home, but, it didn't feel like home to me."

Fendrel scowled. "What are you talking about? Flurry and Blizzard took us in when we would have frozen to death. They raised us. That is home."

"It may be for you but come on, Fendrel." Frederick swatted the air in incredulity. "Here, I finally feel like I fit in. I like being with people who look like me and act like me. I like being around humans."

"We don't have time for this." Fendrel fought to keep his voice from breaking. "We need to leave now so we can go home before it's too late."

Frederick made a frustrated noise halfway between a sigh and a groan. "I don't want to live the rest of my life pretending to be a dragon. If you do, that's great for you, but I want to stay here. They love us here, both of us."

"They don't know the real us!" Fendrel stood up suddenly. He pointed at the door and inwardly thanked the stars that the walls were soundproof. "They think we were orphaned at Stone Edge and stayed orphans. They think we grew up in human villages stealing food to survive. You want them to keep believing that so you can fit in and act like I'm the one living a lie?"

"You're not a dragon, Fendrel! You never will be one, no matter what rites of passage you complete or who adopted you, you'll always be human.," Frederick spat. "No amount of hating humans is going to make you feel accepted, all right? Just because other humans always treated you like filth doesn't mean they treated me the same way. I don't have to go back with you, and I don't want to. This is my home now." When Frederick finished his rant, his eyes softened with regret.

Fendrel, stunned, sat back on his bed as tears formed in his eyes. Through uneven breaths, he struggled to speak. "Blizzard and Flurry love you, Frederick, just as much as they love me. They did everything they could to nurse you back to health when they first found us. If you won't come back home for me, please come back for them."

"Fen," Frederick said, tired. "I already told you. I'm staying. If you're going to leave, don't make up ridiculous excuses about Sadon lying to all of us. He gave us this opportunity to make a difference. You should be thanking him."

Before Fendrel could find the words to speak, Frederick was leaving the room. The door shut behind him and Fendrel sat in the silence left in the wake of their argument. There was no point in stopping the tears now. Fendrel only hoped his thoughts would not be clouded as he packed his things in preparation to meet Charles. He was escaping, and for the first time in his life, he would be doing it alone.

CHAPTER 29: FENDREL

CHARLES HAD ADVISED AGAINST STOPPING for the night, at least until Fendrel found somewhere safe to sleep, far from Sadon's reach. But Fendrel was exhausted from the stress of the day, from his final trial earlier in the morning, from his fight with his brother, and from saying goodbye to Charles. He needed someone to lean on, and the only friend he had nearby besides his instructor was a dragon in Twin Oases.

Fendrel sped on a horse stolen from the hunters toward the Fire dragons' city. It was as lively at night as it was during the day, perhaps even livelier. Fendrel might have wondered how they managed to stay up all night and never grow tried, were it not for his emotional state or the heat. Even in the darkest hour of night, the temperature was unbearable around Twin Oases.

"It'll pass. It'll pass," Fendrel muttered to himself through the sweltering air.

As his horse crested the dunes, Fendrel saw the city getting closer. The buildings, as well as the walls that encircled the city, were made of sandstone, painted in pastels to the community's liking. Every rooftop hosted a healthy bonfire. As with most times Fendrel visited, a festival was taking place.

Fendrel knew the city well enough. He and Frederick had visited it during rest days in between training at the Stronghold. It was a bustling, crowded place, but Fendrel trusted his friend would catch wind of his appearance and greet him. He was right. While Fendrel was still a bit far from the city, a Fire dragon with strawberry-red feathers and cheerful amber eyes waited for him under the entrance's archway.

The horse would be fine if Fendrel left it tied to one of the spiny tree-like cacti that dotted the desert. It had been well fed before he departed, and it would eat its fill of grass the following day. Fendrel dismounted, fastened the horse's reins to the cactus, and lumbered toward the dragon.

"Welcome back!" the Fire dragon, Ember, greeted. She waved Fendrel over with one wing and used her other to push aside the beaded strings that served as a doorway. "You're here pretty late in the evening. Where's your brother?"

Fendrel froze in his tracks just feet in front of her. "Frederick isn't coming," he mumbled.

Ember's face switched from joy to concern in seconds. "Do you need someone to talk to?"

All Fendrel could manage was a nod.

"Let's get away from the crowd." Ember leapt up to the top of the wall, which was shorter than most of the buildings. She reached down with one paw.

Fendrel backed up a bit, then made a running start. He used the wall as leverage to gain some air and latched his hands around Ember's wrist. She pulled him to the top and the two sat on its flat surface.

"Are you all right?" Ember laid down so she was closer to Fendrel's eye-level.

It took a few moments for Fendrel to gather his words, but soon enough he found himself explaining all that had happened that day. Fendrel wondered if he should keep secret that the reason he and Frederick were in the desert to begin with was because they were training with dragon hunters, but the words tumbled from his lips before he could stop himself.

If she hates me for this, then that's fair. I deserve it, Fendrel thought.

When Fendrel concluded his story, he went silent and waited for Ember to shout at him, tell him he was a monster, or even attack him.

"Where are you going to go now?" Ember asked.

Fendrel blinked in surprise at her response. "You don't hate me?"

"No." Ember shook her head. "I don't like that you joined them, but I don't hate you. I'm certainly worried about you."

Realizing he had not answered her question, Fendrel pondered for a moment. "I think I'm going back home to Frost Lake."

"That's pretty far away." Ember forced a short, breathy laugh. "Do you think we'll ever see you again?"

"I don't know." Fendrel let his head drop. "I'm sorry, Ember. I'll let you get back to the festival."

As Fendrel moved to stand, Ember reached out toward him. She stopped short and retracted her paw.

"Why don't you rest here for the night? You can leave in the morning before the sun gets too hot," Ember offered. She rose and ushered Fendrel to follow her across the wall.

"I'm not tired," Fendrel lied.

"Then let me try and cheer you up." Ember turned and lowered her wing out of the way of her back. "Climb on."

Fendrel had never flown before. He had ridden on his adoptive parents' shoulders, but Ice dragons, with their strong legs that could trek the deepest snow, hardly ever flew. He had always wanted to know what it was like and now he had the perfect opportunity.

Climbing onto Ember's back was much easier than clambering up the towering frames of the Ice dragons. Fire dragons were smaller, lower to the ground, with shorter necks and longer tails. However, there was more room to relax on the shoulders of an Ice dragon and Fendrel found himself studying the spines on Ember's back to see where would be best to hold on. He hoisted himself up and grabbed on tight.

Frederick took his first flight with her a few weeks ago, and he never fell. I'll be just fine, Fendrel reassured himself.

"Are you ready?" Ember tilted her head so she could see Fendrel.

Fendrel nodded, though he was sure his face looked uncertain. He held his breath as Ember spread her wings lifted into the air. They climbed through the night sky. Fendrel felt his heartrate quicken the higher they flew and when Ember leveled out her flight to circle above Twin Oases, Fendrel could not help but smile. The city was beautiful from a ground level, but even more so from on high.

They continued riding the wind, passing other Fire dragons as they went. Fendrel loosened his grip a little. He wanted to feel every gust of wind from the wings of those they shared the sky with. Fendrel did not know how long they flew for, but when Ember started winding down toward the wall, Fendrel wished it could have gone on forever.

When Ember landed on the spot where they had just spoken, Fendrel leaned forward and hugged her around her shoulders. "Thank you, Ember."

Ember squeezed Fendrel between her wings. "You don't need to thank me. It's only fair I show you what flying is like since I showed your brother."

Fendrel released the hug and reluctantly slipped down from her back. His balance was unsteady from drowsiness, and he had to place a hand on Ember's side for balance.

"You are tired," she argued. "Please get some sleep."

Fendrel thought back to his horse. He wondered if Frederick let it slip to anyone that he left, and whether there were hunters out right now looking for him. He worried that if he stayed any longer, they would find the horse and lie in wait for him to retrieve it.

"I can't." Fendrel avoided Ember's gaze, knowing he might change his mind if he saw the look on her face. "I have to keep moving. I'll see you again soon, I hope."

Ember sighed in annoyance. "Fine but stay out of trouble from now on. Promise me you will."

"I promise," Fendrel said as he looked into her eyes for a split second. Then, he let Ember lower him down the wall with her tail. The walk to his tied-up steed seemed to take forever. When he mounted the horse and continued his journey northward, Fendrel wondered if he would ever be brave enough to venture back to the desert.

Although he had awoken just minutes earlier, Fendrel was invigorated at the thought of seeing Twin Oases again.

Fendrel rode on Venom's shoulders and stared ahead at the terrain which was transitioning from barren earth to sandy dunes.

The heat became more intense the farther they traveled. Before they had even taken flight, Fendrel rolled up his coat and stowed it in his bag. He hated removing it. The coat was a reminder of home, and though the temperature made it uncomfortable to wear at times, Fendrel still liked to keep it on. It made him feel safe, but the desert was not sympathetic to his wants. The dunes themselves radiated warmth, and the deterrent of the Fire tribe's domain would soon make even thin, breathable clothes feel unbearable. No amount of water would be able to quench their thirst, and no shade would do enough to keep their skin from burning. Not until they reached the city.

Beside Venom flew Fog, gleefully performing aerial flips.

Like Fog, Fendrel also felt lighter knowing Sear was under surveillance at Black Brick Ruins. Venom reassured him the beast was being held in a cave rather than in one of the Sanctuaries where Oliver and Charles were staying. At first Thea protested to going on with the group while Charles stayed behind with the boy, but her decision swayed at seeing how happy Oliver was now that Charles was there.

"He's known Oliver longer," Fendrel had said to her. "And besides, where we're going, we'll need all the help we can get. Especially if that help comes from magic."

Thea sat just behind Fendrel, like she had for the majority of their journey. Even though she still clung tight to Venom's spines, her face showed she was having more fun flying than before.

"Am I hallucinating, or is that a city?" Thea asked as she shot her arm past Fendrel and pointed ahead.

Fendrel looked back with a smile he could not contain. "That's it, Twin Oases," he confirmed. From behind Thea, he could see Cassius, white as a sheet and trying not to stare at the ground. Despite Fendrel's warning on the danger of the Stronghold, Cassius insisted he go wherever Fendrel went.

If he's sticking around for a while, then he'll get used to flying, Fendrel thought.

The hours flew by like minutes and the group found themselves just a few wing strokes away from Twin Oases. Fendrel had asked Venom to fly lower than he had been. The human-deterring heatwave often made Fendrel lightheaded and, on a few occasions, Fendrel had almost lost his balance and fallen from a horse's saddle trying to trek the desert. He did not want that same experience whilst high up in the air.

Twin Oases looked to be thriving as much as ever. While most other tribes lived in places where structures of past human civilization were crumbling, the buildings of the Oases were well-maintained. Of course, the original houses were too small for dragons to live in, so the Fire tribe had rebuilt the structures on a larger scale. The palace, however, stayed the same size, save for its doors, which were replaced with silk and beaded curtains.

A small channel with a bridge leading over it linked the two oases the city was named for. Painted, box-shaped buildings made of sandstone surrounded the bodies of water, and every inch of the city was teeming with Fire dragons. They did not seem to mind that they were rubbing against each other's wings and tails as they walked. In fact, they hardly seemed to notice how crowded the streets were as they talked with friends and haggled with vendors.

Venom dipped his wings and banked toward a large sandstone circle set in the plaza just before the palace. The Fire tribe did not usually place much significance in formality, but they held steadfast to the belief the plaza should remain clear for any dragons landing for a visit. Venom landed in the center. Fog followed suit.

Fendrel slid off Venom's shoulders and immediately felt as if the whole city was watching him. All the nearby Fire dragons—a sea of brown, red, orange, and tan—stopped what they were doing in favor of murmuring excitedly. Fendrel dropped his head and tried to ignore the crowd, though he knew word would get around fast that he had arrived. Fendrel always came alone, and he suspected rumors would begin to spread on why he was traveling with two members of nobility.

Of all the tribes Fendrel visited, besides the Ice tribe, he was most familiar with the Fire dragons. More often than not whenever he returned a captured dragon to Twin Oases, he would be invited inside for whichever festival, or hatching celebration happened to be taking place. Unlike most dragons who had to see Fendrel's necklace to know he was the Liberator, the Fire dragons recognized him in a heartbeat.

Ember is going to have the time of her life interrogating me when I see her next,

Fendrel thought.

The other humans dismounted and followed the dragons toward the palace, with Venom in the lead. Two Fire dragons with metal helmets and armored plates running down their backs pulled the beaded curtains apart to let them pass. The guards nodded at Venom and Fog as they entered but eyed the unfamiliar humans with curiosity.

"Venom? I didn't know you were coming. Has Mist been found yet?" The voice of a female dragon came from within the palace.

Fendrel cocked an eyebrow as he recognized the speaker. He peered out from behind Venom. "Ember?"

Does she work for the Fire noble? Fendrel wondered. *She's never mentioned that before.*

Ember stiffened. Her wings drew closer to her body and her eyes widened. She stood just on the other side of the room. "Fendrel. What are you doing here?" Ember asked as she made her way toward him. A pair of small amber earrings caught Fendrel's eye.

Only nobility are allowed to wear jewelry.

"You're a noble?" Fendrel scowled in confusion.

Ember chuckled. "It took you long enough to find out. I had the tribe stay quiet about it years ago as a joke, and after the first couple months we decided to see how long we could get away with it."

"This whole time?" Fendrel stared, stupefied. "I suppose that explains why I've never seen your home. You always dodged the question of where you lived."

"You two know each other?" Venom gestured between Fendrel and Ember with a claw.

Ember closed the distance between her and Fendrel and threw her wing over his shoulders. "I knew him before he even thought of becoming the Liberator," she stated proudly. The Fire noble scanned the others with her eyes. "What did you get yourself into this time?"

"He got himself into the dilemma concerning Mist." Venom spread his wings out toward the rest of the group. "We all did."

"His Majesty's first mission, and he let all of you in on it?" Ember tilted her head to the side.

Fendrel nodded. "It's a long story."

Ember sighed and took her wing off Fendrel's shoulders. "I would have come for His Majesty's meeting, but I've got my talons full here. I heard from my scouts that there was an increase in activity at the Stronghold, so I sent them to check it out. They didn't come back. They were trained fighters, so whatever happened to them was too dangerous to investigate without more resources. I have been trying to problem solve ever since."

"This 'Stronghold' is the training center for incoming dragon hunters, yes?" Venom asked.

Fendrel's mouth became a thin line. "Yes, that's right."

Smoke curled out of Ember's nostrils. Her eyes seemed to burn with discontent. "I haven't sent more scouts out that way, but I have doubled the security around the city at night." She shook her head. "Well, you all came here looking for Mist. I'm sorry to say, for once I don't think any of the news I've gathered could help. It's like she has disappeared off the face of the world."

Venom sighed. "Thank you, Ember. We are sorry to bother you."

"It's no trouble. You traveled all the way out here, let me at least be a good hostess before you go." Ember smiled. "I assume you all want something to drink?"

"Yes, please." Thea nodded exuberantly.

Fendrel gave the Fire noble a suspicious glare. "You aren't going to trick me into drinking that cactus juice-scorpion stuff again, are you?"

"Perhaps." Ember winked.

"Ember, I'm serious." Fendrel pointed at her. "I am *not* drinking anything you give me unless it's water."

"Oh, you don't mean that." She threw her wing over his shoulders again and guided him toward a side passage of the palace. She waved at the rest of the travelers with her other wing. "There are refreshments this way."

Ember led them to a room with heightened slabs of sandstone, like counters, housing bowls full of a strange-looking liquid. She sat beside the end of the counter. "These are for the festival, but there's always extra after each night. Go ahead and take what you want. By the way, are you planning on staying for a few of the festivities?"

"Thank you for the offering, but we must leave now. Any minute we waste could be a minute Mist is in danger," Venom replied courteously as he took one of the bowls.

Ember nodded in understanding. "It lasts for a month, so don't hesitate to stop by. While you finish those, I'd love to get to meet you all. Any friend of Fendrel's is a friend of mine." She scooped up one of the bowls and sipped from it. Her eyes landed on Thea first. "You must be Thea. Fendrel mentioned you a few times. Oh, how did I not notice before—" she looked at Fendrel "—she can understand us now, yes?"

Fendrel nodded. "She enchanted something for herself and the others so we can all communicate." He gestured at Thea, who was happily quenching her thirst with the mystery juice.

The Fire dragon flicked her tail at Cassius. "And I don't think Fendrel's ever mentioned you. How do you know him?"

"I have not known him for long." Cassius shrugged. "He is going to help me with our issues with the royal guard. They are buying dragon eggs and hatchlings off the black market, and I have a theory that dragon hunters are the ones supplying them."

A flash of recognition crossed Ember's eyes. Her pupils danced between Cassius and Fendrel, before settling on the prince once more. "Would it be safe to assume these deals being struck are taking place somewhere no one can hear them?"

Fendrel grinned at her interest. *There she goes trying to get as much information out of something as she can.*

"Most likely." Cassius took a sip from his drink. "I have eavesdropped on the knights in the palace, the guardhouse, the middle of the city . . . I never see them talking directly to any dragon hunters, but they *must* be. I do not know how else they are smuggling so many dragons inside."

"Do human knights always wear their armor?" Ember asked. From the look on her face, Fendrel could tell ideas were popping into her head.

"Well, they are not required to if they are off duty. However—" Cassius rolled his eyes "—the head of the guard *always* has his armor on and rides his black horse everywhere just to show off his status."

Ember's grin widened. "Does he have black hair and blue eyes?"

The Fire noble's question made Cassius choke as he fought not to spit out his drink.

"How did you know?" Fendrel asked. "Did you see something?"

"Perhaps, *but* you have a mission to get to and I have to help set up for tonight's festivities. If you want to leave, you'd better do it now before the skies are taken up by celebrating dragons." Ember smiled down at Fendrel and Cassius. "I'd be happy to show you what I discovered once you've found Mist. Whenever you're able, come back to Twin Oases. I'd love a longer visit."

Venom nodded. "Thank you for your help, Ember." He started out of the room and the others followed.

Fendrel waved at the Fire dragon as he left. "Yes, thank you for your offer." He tilted his head as he asked, "Did Frederick know you were a noble?"

Ember chuckled. "Go finish your mission, Liberator. And you better come back to visit as soon as you can!"

CHAPTER 30: FENDREL

FENDREL SURVEYED THE SHIFTING DUNES as Twin Oases disappeared into the waves of heat that marked the horizon. The sun was high in the sky, and Fendrel had faith they would reach somewhere to camp before nightfall. "If Ember said there's more activity at Stronghold, that could mean the dragon hunters have recruited new members," Fendrel said.

However, that doesn't make much sense to me, Fendrel thought.

"Wait, no! Charles told me Sadon has been abandoning the farther bases. The increased activity at the Stronghold must be from the hunters who used to occupy those bases now being forced to live in the main base," Fendrel corrected himself.

Venom glowered. "That means there is more potential for danger."

Fendrel nodded as he agreed, "True, but it also means more potential for disorder." The heat was oppressive and appeared to force Thea and Cassius into silence, but Fendrel's mind would not stop spinning. "If I'm right, there are more dragon hunters in the Stronghold now than there ever have been. I'm sure Sadon has his hands full trying to keep them from causing trouble out of boredom."

"I am worried about our odds." Fog beat her wings at a faster rate than Venom's in order to keep up with the Dusk dragon. Her breathing was labored, but even still she pushed her words out. "Ember's scouts were capable of defending themselves but got taken by these dragon hunters. What does that mean for us?"

Fendrel's brows drew together in concern. "Fog, do you want to land and rest for a few minutes?"

"No!" Fog shouted. She gave an apologetic look, then repeated in a softer voice, "No. My sister is in there, Fendrel. I know it. I am not resting until we get to the Stronghold."

"Let's at least find somewhere to drink, then." Fendrel strengthened his words with a stern look. "We've been flying for a few hours now.

You must be thirsty."

"I wouldn't mind a drink either," Thea said hoarsely as she moved her hair to expose her neck to the breeze. "Do those cacti hold any water?"

Fendrel looked at the cacti that dotted the dunes, bringing a hint of life to the sandy wasteland. He shook his head. "I don't know if that juice is safe to drink. I've only ever seen it used to paint dragons' faces purple, so they look like rogues."

Venom's gaze targeted on a cactus. Without a word, he swooped to the ground and landed. A spray of baking hot sand kicked up around his paws.

Fog followed and dropped into the sand with a huff. The next second, she was in the air again, hovering just a few feet away with her tail curled up. She gasped and said, "It is so hot!"

While Fog kept away from the ground, Venom seemed unfazed by the desert's heat. His scales protected the vulnerable skin underneath from burning, but for how long Fendrel had no idea.

The Dusk dragon had landed just beside a cactus flushed with color. He ripped a chunk of its arm off. The spines pressed harmlessly against his scales, bending and splintering from the pressure of his grip. Deep purple juice oozed from the cactus flesh.

"What is it?" Fendrel leaned over so he could catch Venom's gaze.

"I assume you have a plan on getting inside this Stronghold?" Venom tilted his head just enough to see Fendrel while still keeping the cactus in his line of sight.

"It would be suicide not to."

"What is the plan?"

Fendrel's mouth dried, more from nerves than the aridity. "I thought it would be best to lure a few hunters from the base and deal with them somewhere their scouts can't see."

"Hmm." Venom held the cactus to keep its juice from dripping over his paw. "Lure them how?"

Charles was sent to Stone Edge to hunt Dusk dragons, Fendrel remembered. *That must mean the hunters have a shortage of them.*

Fendrel felt disgusted at himself for what he was about to suggest. "The hunters want more Dusk dragons. If they see you, even from leagues off, they'll stalk you to the point of exhaustion. And because you're a Dusk dragon, they'll send more hunters after you than necessary."

Kassidy J. Ridenour

"So it is possible they will follow me far enough away that their comrades in the Stronghold cannot intervene to help," Venom said. He hummed in contemplation.

"Y-you don't have to." Fendrel felt cold dread seep through his skin, into his bones and straight to the marrow. "We can find another way to lure them."

Venom stayed quiet for a moment. Then, he raised the cactus to his mouth and smeared its viscous, purple juice around his maw.

"What are you doing?" Fog reached for the fruit to pry it from Venom, but the Dusk dragon crushed it in his paw with a squelch.

"I will be our bait. We can find an oasis to camp at until sundown. I will fly to the Stronghold, get the hunters' attention, and lead them to our camp where we will ambush them." Venom used the remaining juice on his claws to paint tear-tracks down his face.

"It will not work!" Fog landed in front of the Dusk dragon, wincing at the scorching sand. Tears sprung into her eyes, but she remained still. "Rogues go after any humans near enough, right? So, if you were really a rogue you would not fly *away* from the hunters. They will know it is a trick, Venom!"

"Actually, there are cases of rogues getting tunnel vision where they obsess over a single target," Fendrel cut in.

That's what Sear was. That's why he never gave up the chase.

Fog scowled at Fendrel. "You are not helping!"

"It is the best plan we have." Venom rubbed his paws with sand to try and get the cactus residue off. "One of us has to go, and it cannot be one of the humans. They will not be fast enough. I will not allow *you* to go. If you deem it too dangerous for me, then that same logic applies to you."

"I just do not want you to get hurt." Fog's tears began to spill over her cheeks, repelled by her waterproof feathers.

"They will not get close enough to harm me," Venom said with a voice of steel.

"He's right." Fendrel nodded. He looked between the two dragons. "Venom can't let the hunters get too close, not just because of their weapons, but also because of his eyes. All rogues' eyes are pitch-black without any irises or whites. Venom's eyes are a dead giveaway if the hunters pay too much attention to his face."

"The last time you went near a dragon hunter base, you came back covered in wounds." Fog's voice lowered. "What if something worse happens this time?"

"Last time I stormed into a tight room full of hunters. This time, we are out in the open," Venom retorted. "The more time we waste arguing, the less time we will have to find an oasis and make camp. I appreciate your concern, Fog, but I have been through much worse than this. You need not worry."

A look of understanding Fendrel could not pin down passed between the two dragons.

Fog sighed. "All right . . . all right. Let us go." She leapt into the air and waited for Venom to join her in the sky.

"Which oasis is nearest the Stronghold?" Venom asked Fendrel.

"There's one that will suit our needs near here. Maybe a few more hours' flight," Fendrel said.

Venom nodded and led their group deeper into the desert. Fendrel's calculations were spot on. The group reached a flourishing oasis by midday, just as the sun was beating down with more ferocity than before. Fendrel felt dizzy and wanted nothing more than to land so he could replenish his water skin, which he had shared the contents of with Thea and Cassius during their flight.

As soon as the dragons' paws touched sand, everyone rushed for the bank of the oasis. Fendrel kept an eye out as he drank. Succulents, palms, and date trees grew over each other, making it hard to see their surroundings. It would be all too easy for someone to surprise them here.

Fendrel smiled as he thought, *That's why it makes the perfect cover for us while we lure the hunters.*

The high palms cast more than enough shade for the group. Fendrel sank back against one of the palm's rigid trucks. He could not tell if his shirt was more wet from sweat or the water he had splashed on himself to cool down. Either way, Thea and Cassius looked equally drenched. The oasis' cool waters refreshed Fendrel almost immediately. He got up and walked around their surroundings, taking note of every hiding place high and low. When he made it to the edge of the oasis, he squinted ahead at the desert.

The Stronghold lay before him, leagues off and wavy from the heat. Its black stone silhouette jutted out from the pale, almost blinding-white sand. Fendrel pointed ahead. "There it is."

Venom's paws crushed through the lower foliage as he joined Fendrel. "If I leave at dusk, then I should return when it will be too dark for the hunters to see you hiding, yes?"

"That's right." Fendrel nodded. The sun had shifted well into its afternoon arc toward the western horizon. "We have plenty of time to plan."

Dusk came all too soon for Fendrel's liking. They had prepared their ambush as best they could, but that did nothing to ease Fendrel's nerves about sending Venom to the most fortified base the hunters had at their disposal. Fendrel wanted to have a more heartfelt sendoff than the quick, "I will see you in a few hours" Venom proclaimed, but he feared that by speaking his concerns he would only be manifesting them.

That's ridiculous. My words have no bearing on our outcome, Fendrel thought. Even still, all he said to Venom as the black dragon winged away was, "See you soon." That was two hours prior.

Fendrel stood, leaning a shoulder against the same palm he had surveyed the Stronghold under earlier that day. The others were gathered by the bank of the oasis with only a small fire, conjured by Thea's illusory magic. It was the same kind of spell she had used for their campfire before they ventured to Everspring Grove. It produced no smoke and no heat.

Thank the stars, Fendrel thought. *Even at night this desert is too warm for comfort.*

The chatter between Cassius, Thea, and Fog had died considerably from when Fendrel first heard it during Venom's farewell. Fendrel pushed through the date trees and palms to rejoin the others. When he found his way back to the fire, Fendrel crouched before its light.

A moment of silence passed between them. Then, Fog raised her head. She asked, "How far did he get?"

Fendrel shook his head. "I don't know. He's flying high so he'll blend in with the sky. I lost track of him once it got too dark. He should be on his way back by now."

"And once he returns, we are supposed to go into hiding." Cassius phrased his question like a statement, but the confusion was still clear on his face.

"We'll all hide, but you—" Fendrel pointed from Cassius, to Thea, and then to Fog "—will stay hidden while I help Venom with the ambush."

"And if you two need help?" Thea quirked an eyebrow in question.

Fendrel swallowed. He lowered his eyes to avoid their collective gaze. ". . . You'll run."

"No," Fog protested. She brandished her metal-adorned claws. "I brought these for a reason."

With a sigh, Fendrel said, "You brought those for defense, not to join the fight."

Fog let out a huff and stomped away into the foliage, disappearing in the dark.

Fendrel looked at Thea. "You already placed your spell?"

"Yes." Thea nodded. "It's set around the perimeter."

"Good. Once Venom gets here, both of you hide on the northern side. Venom and I agreed to keep the fight as far from you as possible." Fendrel rocked back on his feet and used the momentum to stand. "Sound good?"

Cassius nodded. A strain of worry was in his eyes.

Thea agreed with a half-hearted shrug. "I'm no good with fighting anyhow. I don't want to get trampled."

"All right." Fendrel braced himself with a deep breath. "I'm going to go see if Fog's all right."

He trudged through the oasis in the wake Fog's paws left behind. He found her on the edge of the oasis, looking out at where the Stronghold would have been perfectly visible if it were day.

Fog glared at Fendrel as he approached. "Why will you not let me help you?" she asked.

"Because it's dangerous," Fendrel deadpanned. He joined Fog's side. "It's too dangerous even for me, or Venom."

"So, it is too dangerous for any of us, but you are still going to do it." Fog's ears were flicked farther back than Fendrel had ever seen them. "If I help you, we will have a greater chance of this plan succeeding."

She has a point, but . . .

Fendrel shook his head. "No."

Fog slammed the end of her tail on the ground in annoyance. "If you need help, then I will help you, and you cannot stop—"

"No!" Fendrel shouted. "Fog, if you get captured, or if Venom gets captured, I'm going to have to choose between saving you, saving Venom, or saving your sister. Don't make me choose."

Fog flinched at his outburst.

"I'm sorry." Fendrel sighed and stepped away. "I shouldn't have yelled at you."

After a brief pause, Fog spoke. "Saving Mist is your mission. That is why you are out here in the first place. Why do you see Venom and I as equally important?"

"I don't have many friends, Fog. I have Charles, Ember, and Thea. That's it." Fendrel let his gaze fix on hers. "The hunters have already taken too much. I don't want you and Venom added to that list."

Fog's demeanor softened. "I am not just *your* friend. You are my friend, too. And if I can do something to prevent you and Venom from getting hurt, then I am going to."

Fendrel stared at her for a moment. He felt an odd mix of gratitude and uncertainty. *She would feel just as guilty if I got hurt as I would feel if the hunters got her*, he realized as his thankfulness won over.

"I understand," Fendrel relented. "I won't stop you, but please be careful. Venom would be pissed if something happened to us."

A surprised chuckle escaped the Vapor dragon. "You do not have to tell me. I know exactly how he will feel. He has always been so protective. Sometimes I think he still sees me as a hatchling."

"You've known him that long?" Fendrel should not have been surprised, but he was. He assumed that Fog and Venom knew each other well enough since both of them were nobles, but he never considered they had been in each other's lives before that.

Fog nodded, her head lulling as if swayed by the memory of a far off, peaceful dream. "He was close friends with my mother. I never knew my father, but Venom did his best to show Mist and I what it was like having one."

"So he's the closest thing you had to a father while you were growing up," Fendrel concluded.

"Yes." Fog nodded again. "Growing up and ever since then. When my mother died, he tried to get Mist and I to live with him in Black Brick."

Fendrel gave Fog a pondering look. "Why didn't you go?"

Fog shrugged. "Living in the dark, in those caves, that is no life for a Vapor dragon. I think Venom knew that, and that is probably why he only asked us once. Still, he checked in on us when he could."

A silence filled with the dread of their situation smothered the air. Fendrel broke it. "He's going to be all right, and we're going to get your sister tonight. Come morning, everything will be back to normal."

The Dragon Liberator: Escapade

Fog's feathers fluffed out with nerves. She shivered and her feathers settled. "I cannot wait for you to meet her. When I was small, I used to imagine what it would be like having a human friend." Her giggle further penetrated the tension. "Mist is going to tease me for this."

"What are you going to do once you're back home?" Fendrel leaned his back against a palm, sensing the conversation may go on longer than he had initially planned.

"I do not know. With Mist and Cloud married the Vapor tribe will not have a need for a noble anymore. Cloud will handle inter-tribe issues and Mist will handle those concerning just our tribe." Fog's tail curled and uncurled as she spoke. "She will be busy. We will not spend as much time together as we used to. I do not know what I will do with myself once I am back home."

Fendrel gave her a silent nod. His eyes drifted upward to meet Fog's again when she asked, "What will you do?"

"What I've always done." Fendrel shrugged. "I might visit family for a few days, then try to figure out why the hunters are downsizing." He felt a strange pang of loneliness in his chest he thought he had forgotten how to feel. "You know, when I took up this mission, I thought I would have to adjust to traveling with others, but it was a lot easier than I thought. Now, I'm dreading being by myself again."

"I do not want to intrude, but if you ever need a traveling partner, I wouldn't mind coming along." Fog gave a sheepish grin. "It will make travel time for you a bit faster, and I would get to actually explore the Freelands."

Fendrel's mouth quirked up in a smile. It dropped from his face at the call of a Dusk dragon. Venom was signaling his return. They needed to be ready.

He pushed off the palm and stared at the sky. It was impossible to make out how close Venom was, but his roar did not sound too far off. Fendrel said, "If you're serious, consider this your test for how well you can deal with dragon hunters."

"Will do!" Fog hurried back to their camp.

Fendrel followed close behind.

Thea was cleaning up the remains of their fake fire. When Fendrel and Fog emerged from the coverage, she stood.

"You said you already laid your enchantment, right?" Fendrel asked.

"There's just one more step, but I can't perform it until the hunters are here," the mage replied. "Oh, and stay away from the edges of the oasis. You might trample over the spell."

Fendrel nodded wordlessly, then called out, "Cassius stay hidden. Don't come out until we say it's all clear."

"I do not plan on it," came the muffled, fearful voice of the prince somewhere in the foliage.

"It'll be any minute now," Fendrel mumbled to himself. He fished out the knock-out-laced dagger given to him by Charles and sank to a crouch amid the greenery. His grip on the hilt tightened as the sounds of wingbeats and hooves pounding on sand drew nearer. Then, a rush of wind blew past, the moon was blocked out for a mere moment, and Fendrel knew Venom had just flown overhead.

Horses crushed plants beneath their hooves. Then, they stopped.

"Where did it go?" cried a man's voice.

"Keep your eyes peeled," warned another. "It's hiding."

"Smart beast, that one."

There's at least three of them. Fendrel studied the overgrown oasis ahead for any moving shapes. He wouldn't be able to tell how high ranked these hunters were unless he was close, but that would not matter. Darkness did not discriminate between the low and high ranked. They were even, for now.

A shadow freed itself from the surrounding silhouetted foliage. Another joined it, moving in a different direction. The longer Fendrel stared, the more shapes he could make out, and the closer the hunters crept.

There's six of them, Fendrel realized. He steadied his breathing and trained his eyes on the nearest hunter, fifteen feet away and closing in.

The hunter had a dagger of his own which he twirled in one hand. His head jerked toward a slight noise, but the only ones moving were the hunters.

Fendrel's throat dried. He could take care of himself if he was spotted, but Cassius and Thea would not be so lucky. It would be safer to compromise his own position than let one of them be found.

Just a few more paces, Fendrel thought to himself as he watched the nearing hunter. The older man's eyes swept over Fendrel's head. If he had noticed Fendrel, he was doing a great job at hiding it.

As the hunter continued on his self-imposed path, he brushed past the leaves that disguised Fendrel. When he made it another step farther, Fendrel sprang from his cover and clamped a hand over the hunter's mouth. His dagger drew a thin line across the hunter's cheek, just deep enough to draw blood. Deep enough, Fendrel hoped, for the anesthetic to do its work.

Fendrel held onto the hunter for a few heart-pounding seconds. Only once the hunter slumped against Fendrel did he let go, settling the man in the sand.

Five more, Fendrel counted to himself. He sank down and narrowed his eyes to the remaining hunters. They appeared unaware that one of their own had gone missing. Fendrel crept toward them with his dagger still in hand.

The oasis had grown so quiet, Fendrel felt for a moment that only he and the hunters remained within. They were spreading out from each other. Fendrel picked his next target.

Sooner or later, one of the hunters would find Cassius or Thea. He needed to act fast, but he could not rush. Rushing led to mistakes, and mistakes could turn into disasters.

Fendrel stayed low while he advanced on an unsuspecting hunter. As he spied the man for weak spots, a yelp called his attention.

"I found someone!" cried one of the hunters.

"What does that have to do with the shadow dragon?" the hunter in front of Fendrel asked.

" . . . Nothing."

"Exactly. Get rid of the witness and keep looking," grumbled Fendrel's target.

"No, wait! Please!" came Cassius' voice. Fendrel's stomach dropped.

The song of metal sliding from a sheath stole Fendrel's attention from the hunter in front of him. Fendrel could just make out Cassius stumbling away from the sword-wielding hunter. He knew that even if he tried to save Cassius, he was too far away to do anything.

A shadow flung itself from the top of a palm and carried the hunter out of sight. The man yelped, but whatever grabbed him made not a sound.

Fendrel ran to the site, trying to stay low. When he made it to Cassius, the prince was pale with fear. Unharmed, as far as Fendrel could tell, but terrified.

All at once, the other hunters froze and brandished their weapons. They called out to each other, their voices becoming a cacophony of undecipherable noise. As Fendrel looked around for a new hiding spot for Cassius, the perimeter of the oasis lit up in flames.

CHAPTER 31: FENDREL

FENDREL DID NOT REALIZE HOW close he and Cassius were to the oasis' border until the flames erupted. He jumped back, pulling the prince with him. He expected to feel a surge of heat against his skin, but there was no pain, no crackling sound, and no smell. It was like the campfire Thea had constructed earlier, but much larger and wilder.

The flames lashed just a few paces away, reaching ten feet high and stretching around the greenery. Fendrel swung his head around and saw the orange tongues of light waving on the outside of the oasis' other side. It cast everything in shifting silhouettes. Moving even more frantic than the shadows of the palms were the hunters as they continued to call for each other. One of them screamed as something dragged him away from his companions.

"Stay down," Fendrel ordered Cassius. He tried to make sense of his surroundings. The fire did more to confuse his vision than it illuminated what lay before him. As he trudged toward the center where the water sat, his ears picked out another sound. Horse's shrieks and stamping hooves. Fendrel dove out of the way just in time to avoid one of the horses as it attempted to escape the illusory flames. He picked himself back up and hurried onward.

Only three hunters remained, and one of them had spotted Fendrel.

"Who are you?" cried the hunter. He waved his arms at the border of fire. "Did you do this? *Why* would you do this? We'll all die!"

Fendrel tightened his grip on the dagger's hilt and shifted his footing in preparation for a fight. He hoped the anesthetic on the blade had not been accidentally wiped off since he first used it. Just as the accusatory hunter started toward Fendrel, the silent-flying shadow swooped down again. It snatched the hunter up in its gleaming claws and carried him off. The sound of something heavy impacting water told

237

The Dragon Liberator: Escapade

Fendrel what had happened to the man.

The shadow was too small to be Venom, and Dusk dragons were not silent flyers.

Is that Fog? Fendrel wondered in astonishment. He had never paid attention to whether her wingbeats made any noise before, but as he stared ahead Fendrel realized he could not remember what they sounded like. He shook his head and refocused on the task at hand.

Two more—

Not a trace was left of the two other hunters who had been scouring the oasis for an exit just moments ago. Fendrel strained his ears to make sure they had all been incapacitated. Only the horses' whinnies of terror pursued.

"Is it over?" Fendrel called out. Cassius stumbled to his side with his hair full of sand.

Thea burst from her cover and laughed with glee. She raised her fists in victory as she approached Fendrel and Cassius. "How'd you like my little trick?"

"You mean the *wall of fire?*" Cassius asked. His clothes had small rips where the hunter had dragged him out in the open. Combined with his ruffled hair and frightened eyes, he looked truly haggard.

Well, I warned him it would be dangerous, Fendrel thought. *It looks like the reality of his situation is catching up with him.*

Venom's silhouette formed out of the dark. He lit up the scales on his chest so Fendrel could see his face. The black dragon looked tired, but unharmed. A scowl of disapproval came over his visage when Fog made herself visible from the oasis' cover. "You were supposed to stay hidden," Venom said to her.

"The hunters did not know it was me attacking them until I had already gotten to them," Fog retorted with a smug grin.

"You could have gotten hurt."

"But, she's fine," Fendrel interjected. He shrugged when Venom's gaze met his own. "She wanted to help. I think she did a good job." Before Venom could respond, Fendrel made his way toward where the hunters had disappeared. He tracked down each one, sprinkling just a pinch of knock-out powder over each hunter's face to keep them asleep. Illuminated by the fake fire, Fendrel could see each one had the bottom half of their faces hidden with a cloth. The desert-based dragon hunters needed them for protection against sandstorms. On each of their shoulders hung their strings of dragon teeth. There were three fangs on

238

each shoulder.

"Are we going to handle them like the hunters from the Ravine Base?" Venom asked.

Fendrel shook his head. "When a hunter receives his rank, he can only add teeth from dragons he's slain. Every one of these men have teeth from Dusk and Ice dragons. No one goes after those tribes unless they have a death wish, or unless they find joy in the killing." Fendrel wrenched the cloth mask and chest armor from one of the hunters. "These men are nothing like the ones from the ravine."

"Understood." Venom grabbed one of the men. His talons nearly wrapped around the man's entire torso. The black dragon grabbed another with his tail and started out of the oasis. "I will make this quick, then."

Ignoring the sound of claws sinking into flesh, Fendrel donned the cloth mask. He hesitated before lifting the chest armor over his head. He had never worn dragon leather or ranking fangs before. Even if he was only pretending to be one of the hunters, it still felt like he was betraying the dragons. With a defeated sigh, he slid the armor piece over his head. When Fendrel made sure the mask would not slip down his face and give his identity away, he made his way back to Fog. Fendrel set his bag on the ground. He asked, "Could you watch this for me?"

"Of course." Fog cradled the bag with her tail. She may have been smiling, but Fendrel could not tell. He did not want to look her in the eye in his current attire.

"Why are they not fully covered in armor?" Fog asked.

Fendrel gave a curt shrug. "It's late at night and Venom caught them off guard. They probably only had time to gear up with chest armor before riding out."

He took inventory of his daggers and knock-out powder. Then, he set off toward the horses. The steeds were all running past each other, narrowly avoiding palm trees and stamping away if they came too close to the enflamed barrier. Fendrel mimed a whistle he thought he remembered from his training years ago, one that was meant to call a horse to him. Either the animals were too frightened to obey, or he had used the wrong whistle. After a few more tries that bolstered his frustration, one of the horses seemed to respond.

The horse shook his head as he distanced himself from the others and stopped before Fendrel. His nostrils still flared, and he rocked side-to-side as if staying still would be a death sentence.

The Dragon Liberator: Escapade

With careful movements, Fendrel made his way to the horse's side and pulled himself into the saddle. Once he was settled, he called for Thea. "It's not a good idea to release the horses in case they make their way back to the Stronghold, but is there a way to open the fire so the horse won't be scared going through?"

"Absolutely! Just wait one second." Thea led the way to the fire wall and kicked the ground where it sprang up. Amid the displaced sand were small flower petals. Fendrel squinted harder and realized every tongue of flame was tethered to a petal, but once the petal left the line, the flame died.

"Do not stay in there too long," Venom warned. Fendrel gave the Dusk dragon a knowing nod, realizing their roles from earlier had reversed and it was now Venom who would wait anxiously for Fendrel's return.

Once the gap was large enough, Fendrel urged the horse onward. It did not take much convincing. Thea had to stagger away before the horse made a beeline to escape, nearly trampling her. Free from the shadowed oasis, Fendrel urged the horse into a gallop, over the dunes and toward the Stronghold.

The ride to the Stronghold was quicker than Fendrel would have liked. If it were up to him, he would have had more time to settle his nerves. He glanced at the three fangs that hung from his shoulders.

The only hunters who wear these are instructors, advanced hunters, and wranglers, Fendrel thought as though he were coaching someone. *I hope if I'm spotted, I won't have to make up a story as to which I am.*

Jutting out from the Stronghold's side was a modest-sized sandstone structure. Fendrel recognized it to be the stables. A young woman with sleepy eyes sat on a stool just outside. As Fendrel approached, her face broke out in a cheery smile. "What happened to the shadow dragon? Did you catch it?"

Fendrel nodded and did his best to avoid her eyes. "They sent me back to report that they have everything under control."

"That's good!" The stable worker took the reins from Fendrel after he dismounted and led the horse inside the structure. Its base and roofing were solid sandstone and wooden shutters made up the windows, currently ajar to keep good airflow.

Through the shutters Fendrel could see horses of all colors and patterns, but one stood out—a solid black stallion. Other horses had black fur, but no horse owned by the hunters had a coat unblemished by

240

markings. They were a symbol of status in Sharpdagger.

One of the hunters must have been a wealthy man before he joined their ranks, Fendrel reasoned.

Fendrel entered the Stronghold through a door behind the stables. The halls were silent and empty. Not a footstep nor scuffle met his ears. The only movement came from flickering shadows cast by lit sconces on the cobblestone walls. Fendrel made his way through the maze-like passages he was frustratingly still familiar with. If all went according to plan, everyone should be in their rooms for the night, locked up as Charles had been every evening. Fendrel should not run into anyone except, perhaps, for Sadon.

Creeping through the halls was harder than Fendrel wanted to admit, especially as the smallest missteps shot out echoes. He was better at covering his tracks in natural environments, but harsh stone walls were always more difficult to move through silently. Still, Fendrel continued on. He turned a corner, and his heart leapt at the sight of the wooden door leading to Sadon's study. The last time he had been inside was the same night as his desertion. Fendrel steadied his breath, gripped the handle, and pushed the door open.

I'm surprised he didn't lock this door, too. Fendrel stepped inside and shut the door behind him. *Perhaps he left it unsecured for now because he's the only one who can enter.*

The sconces cast dim light from their dying flames. The same old desk sat square in the middle of the room with a single chair on either side. Papers were stacked neatly on one end of the desk beside a fountain pen and a bottle of ink. At the back of the room hung a massive floor-to-ceiling map of the Freelands with marks showing the locations of every dragon hunter base, both ones that were abandoned and others still in use. The bottom of the map rolled up as it was not secured like the top.

Fendrel crept to the map and lifted the bottom. Charles was right. A door was hidden behind the map. He tried the knob and breathed a sigh of relief when he found it unlocked, despite the keyhole. Fendrel's breath caught when he saw what lay ahead. A set of downward stairs led into total darkness. Fendrel did not have a light to bring with him and he almost cursed under his breath, but then his ears picked up on murmurs that traveled up from the depths of the secret passage. Someone was down there, and they were trying to be quiet.

Is that Mist? Is she sitting alone in the dark right now? Every question

The Dragon Liberator: Escapade

Fendrel asked himself made him angry at what Sadon had done to the missing Vapor dragon, and by extension what Sadon had done to everyone who loved and cared about her.

I'm saving her tonight, Fendrel told himself. *By tomorrow Mist will be well on her way home, and the hunters will never get their hands on her again. Tonight, Fog will have her sister back.*

Staring into the darkness, Fendrel braced his hand against the wall and made his way down. The murmurs became clearer as he approached, and he realized they belonged to a man, not a dragon. Anger and fear swelled in Fendrel's chest as he recognized Sadon's voice.

Fendrel prepared himself for what he was about to walk into. Sadon could be armed and ready for a fight. Fendrel had fought the older man before a few times. Most of it was during training when there were no real stakes. But the two most recent times Fendrel had barely escaped when he had stabbed Sadon in the shoulder himself, and later when he had thrown a knife at the very same shoulder while rescuing Fog.

This time . . . Fendrel vowed, *This time I have to kill him.*

His hopes of finally putting a stop to Sadon's life faltered as he heard the sound of a second voice, also from a man. This voice was familiar, too, but Fendrel had a hard time placing it until the second man raised his tone to a shout.

"I don't agree with this!" exclaimed Zoricus. Cassius' cousin, the captain of the royal guard.

The owner of the black stallion in the stables, Fendrel realized. His curiosity spurred him closer until an orange light emanated ahead, lighting up the bottom of the stairs. He risked one pace forward, then another, and soon saw Sadon and Zoricus facing each other. He wanted to be closer so he could get a clearer view of the two men conversing, but instead Fendrel stayed in the shadows and prayed their eyes would not be able to separate the silhouette of his boots from the stairsteps.

"Well, you need to make up your mind here and now before I begin the next phase," Sadon said in a tone as harsh as stone. "No more pushing back the deadline."

"No! I still need to be a part of this." Zoricus began to pace out of sight. "I just don't understand what any of this has to do with manipulating Sadie."

"Are you an idiot? Do you think the princess would forgive you for poisoning her brother and father?" Sadon asked with a glare. "She needs to be dealt with."

Zoricus stormed back to Sadon. "If you hurt her because the poison is taking longer than I expected—"

"I never said I would hurt her," Sadon said slowly, methodically. His glare made Zoricus back off. "I was implying you figure out how to keep her from discovering your treason. If you cannot think of anything, then I will take the king's life in your stead. I do not want to hurt people, Zoricus, but killing a few to save many is a burden I must shoulder."

The captain of the guard furrowed his brow in thought. "I can . . . Once the deed is done, I can have the High Mage cast a spell on Sadie to make her forget Cassius ever existed."

Sadon snorted. "Not a very well though-out plan but keep thinking on it. We need this to be flawless. Now, there is something else we must discuss."

Zoricus looked at Sadon with undivided attention.

"I've recently been informed that my second in command has perished during a mission." Sadon huffed in annoyance. "I'd like for you to take his place once this is all over."

"But I'm the head of the royal guard—"

Sadon waved his hand. "Soon enough, with you as the second head of the dragon hunters, you'll be so much more than just the commander of the royal guard. You will be able to have anything you want."

Zoricus exhaled, a noticeable shake in his breath. "What I want is Sadie spared."

"And you will have that, *if* you accept my offer." Sadon's gaze bore into the black-haired man. "My organization has no room for those who are not devoted to the cause."

Sadon doesn't trust Zoricus one bit, Fendrel thought. *He's giving him this offer so he can keep an eye on him, just like how he kept tabs on Charles.*

"I understand, sir." Zoricus bowed his head. "I accept."

"One more thing." Sadon raised his hand. "If you come across Fendrel—"

The knight tilted his head, confusion marking his face.

"The Liberator." Sadon sneered. "If he shows up, kill him."

"You don't want to kill him yourself?"

Sadon scoffed. "Believe me, I've tried, but at this point I just want him gone so he can't interfere. I don't care how quickly or slowly you kill him, just make sure he doesn't ruin anything." He scratched his injured shoulder with a single finger. "He has quite the reputation for

The Dragon Liberator: Escapade

ruining my plans."

"What if he doesn't appear for some time?" Zoricus asked.

"Then I trust you'll take care of him as soon as you can. Is that clear?" Sadon held Zoricus' gaze, unblinking.

Zoricus nodded and turned toward the stairs but stopped short. "Sir, I have a question."

Sadon raised an eyebrow. "Yes?"

"What should we do with that ghost dragon?"

Fendrel's body stiffened. He fought the urge to lean forward to see farther into the room.

"*You* will not do anything with her. She is mine to kill, but only once I am done with her." Sadon's voice carried about as much emotion as a rock.

"But you've hidden her somewhere no one would ever think to look." Zoricus sounded as though he were choosing his words carefully. "You've hidden her where no one would ever think to look. Is she really that much of a threat that you need to kill her?"

"I am done underestimating my enemies, Zoricus. Everyone and everything is dangerous when given the opportunity to be so." Sadon gestured toward the stairs. "Now, allow me to escort you back to the stables."

Fendrel hoped his footfalls would be light enough to go unheard as he crept back up the stairs. He needed to be quick, lest the torchlight give him away. Fendrel climbed the steps as fast as he could without making a sound, and the pounding in his heart did not cease even as his hand brushed the wood of the door. He tried to squeeze past without letting in too much light. Thanks to the dimness of Sadon's study, any light that may have flowed into the tunnel was not bright enough to alert the older men.

Where do I hide? Fendrel looked about the room, seeing the wooden desk as his only cover. *Should I go around the corner and wait for them to leave?*

Sadon and Zoricus were fast approaching, their steps echoing louder.

What if Sadon locks the vault door after he leaves? I'd be stuck outside. Fendrel slid behind the other side of the desk and pressed his back against it. *Then I'd have to fight him. I don't know if I can take that risk with Zoricus here as well.*

Staring straight ahead, Fendrel heard the door open and close. A desk drawer opened, a lock clicked, and the drawer was shut.

"Why do you have a locked door if no one else knows this room exists?" Zoricus asked.

Fendrel took the opportunity to sidle toward one end of the desk with the knight's voice as cover.

"As I said before—" Sadon started, and Fendrel inched farther away with his body still pressed against the furniture. "I am done underestimating people."

Sadon and Zoricus moved around the opposite side of the desk Fendrel was positioned. When he was sure they would not catch him in their peripheral, Fendrel backed up toward the rear of the wooden desk and hid behind it. The study door opened, closed, clicked with a lock, and Sadon led Zoricus down the hall. Only then did Fendrel stand up.

He placed a hand over his heart and felt its thunder beneath his skin. Sweat had built on his brow. He wiped it with his sleeve and retrieved the secret door's key from the desk drawer. Once he had pulled the map back and opened the vault, Fendrel stuffed the key in a pocket and made his way down. It was darker now and more difficult to navigate how far each step was from the last.

Sadon must have taken one of the torches to lead his way up. Fendrel braced his hand against the rough cold wall and continued onward. *That's all right. I only need enough light to see the whole room, and I can just carry the torch with me if I need to.*

The adrenaline of the situation forced a smile on his lips. He was finally finishing his mission. *Sadon, you were right to not underestimate me. But I bet you didn't count on me finding out this is where you've hidden her. I'm freeing her tonight.*

Fendrel reached the end of the stairs and took a moment to look about the room. It was spacious, dark, and had no windows. The only light came from a sconce on one side of the threshold, mirrored by another sconce barren of a torch. The fire was bright enough to illuminate everything. A desk, less well-made than the one in Sadon's study but housing more drawers, sat against the left wall. A door large enough for a dragon to pass through was set in the rightmost wall. Directly across from Fendrel were shackles. Shackles that held no dragon.

There was no one here. Mist was gone, and the only trace of her were a few strands of blue-gray fur that lay beneath the chains.

CHAPTER 32: FENDREL

"NO," FENDREL MURMURED IN DISBELIEF. "No!" he said again, defiantly. Fendrel ran to the traces of Mist's fur on the ground. He knelt down and picked one piece up, twisting it between his fingers. He shoved as much as he could gather in one of his pockets, hoping Thea would be able to perform some miracle for him on his return.

His stomach dropped. *I told Fog I'd bring her sister back tonight. I promised her . . . I can't leave here empty handed. There must be some clue as to where Mist is.*

Fendrel raced to the desk and hastily pulled open every drawer, shutting the empty ones or the ones that held only writing supplies and blank paper. He flicked through the pages, skimming the words with his eyes. "Records of eggs taken in . . . records of students initiated . . . records of weapons crafted from dragon parts . . . records of bases being shut down. There *has* to be more," Fendrel grumbled, feeling panic rise inside him.

You said her whereabouts would remain a secret forever, Zoricus' words echoed in Fendrel's mind. *You've hidden her where no one would ever think to look.*

"Behind the empty pages?" Fendrel asked himself. He went back to the drawer full of yet-to-be-used paper and rifled through it. At the bottom of the stack was a page that had been written on. Fendrel calmed himself with a slow, steady breath, and began to read aloud. "Subject: female ghost dragon. Site of capture: Stone Edge. Status: deceased." Fendrel shook his head in disbelief and continued reading. "Other notes: Died of unknown causes soon after capture. Body has been disposed of in case a disease was the cause of death."

I . . . I can't believe that, Fendrel told himself, though he was starting to wonder if he was too late.

He filed the paper at the bottom of the stack and returned the pages to their drawer. He shut his eyes and tried to think. "Sadon falsifies the deaths of rare dragons so he can study them without interference from other hunters, and Sadon just admitted she was still alive."

Disheartened, Fendrel went through every drawer once again for more clues, but none turned up. All he had was a pocket of fur and a falsified report of death.

"What are you doing here, boy?" Sadon's voice carried over from the bottom of the stairs. Fendrel whirled to see the older man leaning casually against the wall. One dangling arm held a crossbow with a bolt ready to fire. More bolts sat in a small quiver around Sadon's hip.

Fendrel swallowed. "How did you know I was here?"

"I didn't." Sadon shrugged. "Not until I did one final checkup of my study and found the vault door unlocked and my key missing. So, now that you've invaded my personal business, are you satisfied with what you've found?"

"Where is she?" Fendrel asked as his eyes flicked toward the shackles, then back to Sadon.

"Dead."

Fendrel shook his head. "I know you're lying. Where is she?"

Sadon heaved a deep, disgruntled sigh. He looked exhausted, more so from stress than from lack of sleep. "I'll be honest with you, Fendrel. I have no idea how long you've been sneaking around tonight. I don't know what you've heard or what you've seen, but I *do* know that I can't let you leave with that information." He took his crossbow in both hands and aimed at Fendrel.

Before Fendrel could register what was happening, his body moved toward the dragon-sized door across the room. A crossbow bolt grazed his arm, ripping the skin with its barbed tip. Fendrel yelped and kept running. Luckily, this door had no lock, but it was heavy and slow to open. As Fendrel pulled on the handle with all his might, Sadon loaded another bolt and took aim.

Fendrel opened the door with just enough room to squeeze through. He heard the bolt thud in the door behind him. He was outside the Stronghold, exposed to the warm desert night with nowhere to hide. He needed to get to a horse before Sadon came for him.

Sadon reached the door a moment later and pushed it farther to accommodate his larger frame. The crossbow was slung over his shoulder while he pushed.

With no time to waste, Fendrel sprinted faster than he ever had before. Adrenaline spurred him on, burning his legs and bringing sweat

The Dragon Liberator: Escapade

to his brow. The sand beneath his feet felt shifting and hard all at once, and Fendrel prayed Sadon was having just as much trouble moving across it as he was. Another bolt whizzed just past Fendrel, pelting into the sand a few feet ahead of him.

"There's nowhere to run, boy!" Sadon called out.

I'll be all right, Fendrel tried to reassure himself. *If he wants to aim well, he has to move slow, but he also can't let me out of his sight. I just need to get to the stables, then I'll be safe.*

A trio of bolts rained down just beside him. Fendrel almost fell flat on his belly when one of the bolts stuck in the heel of his boot. He pushed himself up and tried to keep running, wincing and limping as the bolt head pierced his heel with every step.

"Keep firing!" shouted someone above.

Fendrel stuck closer to the Stronghold's wall, so the hunters had a difficult time aiming at him. But he was slowing down, and Sadon was gaining.

The stables were in sight, just around the bend.

Another bolt whistled through the air. Fendrel felt the impact before he noticed the pain. The bolt tore through the back of his thigh, deep enough the tip was completely embedded. Fendrel cried out and crashed into the sand. With both legs stricken by bolts, Fendrel dragged himself forward.

Every slight move of his legs brough tears to his eyes and made Fendrel whimper in pain. His adrenaline was wearing off. He felt hot blood seep through his pantleg as the bolt head shifted in his thigh. He heard Sadon stalking closer.

"Ceasefire!" Sadon commanded.

I can't fail them. I got so close! Fendrel could barely see ahead of him through his tears. *I haven't made up for everything I've done yet.*

Sadon was just a step behind now. "Turn around, boy."

Fendrel knew if he did, he would see a bolt aimed straight at his heart. He would see the man who drove his brother from him, who ruined his life and stole his youth. Fendrel did not want Sadon to be the last thing he saw.

I'm . . . I'm not ready to die.

"You look at me when I'm talking to you." Sadon kicked Fendrel in the ribs. "I said turn around!"

Pain radiated from Fendrel's legs, his feet, and his side. He tried to block another kick from Sadon, but he was not quick enough. One more strike sent Fendrel, groaning and clutching his stomach, to his back. Sadon was above him.

The older man shook his head, slow and disappointed. "All of this could have been avoided. If you hadn't chosen those monsters over your own kind, you would have had a good life. Now look at you." Sadon placed his finger on the trigger. "No matter. It will be over soon."

Fendrel turned his face away. He would not give Sadon the satisfaction of seeing the light leave his eyes.

The sky was starting to brighten on the horizon.

I took too long. They'll know soon enough that I won't be making it back to camp, Fendrel realized as fresh tears further muddled his vision. *I just don't want them to come looking for me.*

Fendrel found it hard to comprehend the next few seconds. He thought perhaps that his mind was playing tricks on him to protect him from what was about to happen. All he saw was in one moment, Sadon's feet were firmly planted on either side of Fendrel, and the next Sadon was gone in a black blur.

Chaos erupted around Fendrel. Sand flew, people screamed, bolts whistled through the air, and a dragon roared. Fendrel winced through the pain in his side and propped himself on his elbows.

Venom had Sadon pinned beneath his paws, ready to crush the man under his weight. Instead, Venom hissed in pain as the bolt Sadon had loaded shot through Venom's palm where his scales were easier to penetrate. The Dusk dragon shook the bolt out and clenched his paw into a fist. Venom released Sadon for only a brief second, but that was long enough for Sadon to roll out of the way as Venom slammed his other paw down.

The archers from above resumed their assault. Crossbow bolts pelted into Venom. Some bounced off as they made contact with his scales. Others tore through the membranes of his wings. One punched into Venom's ear, leaving a bleeding hole.

"Venom, go!" Fendrel cried. "You're not supposed to be here."

At the sound of Fendrel's voice, Venom abandoned his target and leapt to shield Fendrel from the bolts. He grabbed Fendrel with his uninjured paw and held him to his chest. "Be still, young one."

As the bolts rained down, Venom launched himself into the sky and took flight. The holes in his wings stretched with each wing stroke, but Venom flew regardless. Soon they were too far for the bolts to reach, and too far to hear Sadon's shouts of fury, but that did little to console

Fendrel. His body felt like it was on fire. Fendrel couldn't tell if his tears were more so from the pain or from the false promise he had made to the others.

He could not find Mist, and now he had to tell Fog that she put her faith in a failure.

Fendrel became dizzy and he could feel himself growing colder.

The bolt must have hit an artery, Fendrel thought as his eyelids grew heavy. He blinked in and out of consciousness.

The sky was brighter each time his eyes fluttered open. Venom must have felt the warmth leaving Fendrel's body, because he sank his fangs into Fendrel's back and released a bit of his healing elixir. Fendrel barely flinched from the prick, and he found himself becoming more aware as the golden liquid coursed through him. But his injuries persisted, and so did the pain.

Venom landed in the oasis and laid Fendrel down as gentle as he could. Free from the confusion that clouded Fendrel before, he now saw just how haggard the black dragon was. It was often difficult to tell when a dragon had been crying, but the whites of Venom's eyes were plagued with pink veins.

"Do not fall asleep, Fendrel." Venom's gaze traveled the length of Fendrel's body, stopping on the bolt that stuck from his thigh. "Tell me what happened."

Fendrel willed a new wave of tears to subside. "She wasn't there," he croaked.

"What else?" Venom started to turn Fendrel over but stopped when Fendrel gasped in pain. Venom inserted his fangs into Fendrel's side, dulling the ache of Sadon's kicks.

"Sadon moved her somewhere else." Fendrel felt his anger from the vault returning. "He made a report saying she died, just like Charles claimed he would, but I know he was lying."

"Where is she?" came Fog's meek voice.

Fendrel tilted his head back against the cool sand to see her standing a few paces off. Cassius and Thea were beside her, staring at the blood on Fendrel's clothes and the holes in Venom's wings.

This time, Fendrel could not choke down the tears. He managed a weak, "I'm sorry," before resting his head flat again.

"We will have this discussion later. Right now you need healing." Venom looked to Fog and asked, "Do you have Fendrel's bag?"

"Yes," Fog said hurriedly as she finally took in Fendrel's injuries.

She left and returned in a matter of seconds, handing the bag off to Fendrel.

"What do you need this for?" Fendrel accepted the bag from Fog's paws and held it against his chest.

"My healing has limitations." Venom's ears flicked back at the disheartened look on Fendrel's face. "With an injury this severe, there is a risk you will not heal properly. My elixir speeds up the body's natural means of fixing itself, but if muscles or tissue grow in wrong, there will be nothing I can do to reverse it."

"Thea? What about you?" Fendrel asked.

Thea shook her head with her mouth agape. She said, "There's a similar risk with my magic, especially since I used a lot of my energy making that fire wall illusion. My spell might not even activate if I don't have enough power, or it could do the same thing to you as Venom's elixir."

"And Fog, you can only heal surface wounds," Fendrel said.

Fog nodded. "That is right."

"I will remove the bolts and heal you enough to where you can still travel, but I cannot in good conscience do more for you." Venom's wings sank. "I could leave you with a leg that will never regain its full mobility."

"How bad is the risk?" Fendrel clutched his bag tighter. "If it's small enough, I'd like for you to heal me fully. You helped Charles, and the bones in his arm were completely shattered. Why is this different?"

"We had no other choice with Charles. The alternative would have been to amputate his arm." The black dragon gave a heavy sigh, then softened his gaze toward Fendrel. "I am not sure if you have noticed, Fendrel, but Charles has avoided using that arm. I know it is painful for him. I know he will never make a full recovery, but we had no choice. I do not want you to live like that."

Fendrel stared at Venom for what felt like an impossibly long minute. "All right . . . let's get it over with. We don't know if Sadon has sent hunters after us, but I don't want to stick around and find out."

Venom gave a somber nod. "Open your bag and take out anything you think will be useful to help us."

As Fendrel rifled through his bag for supplies, his mind whirled.

What use am I if I can't even find a single dragon? Venom and Fog would be better off searching for Mist without me. All I've done is steer us toward trouble, and because of me Venom is hurt, and Fog might never see her sister again, Fendrel thought. He choked down another sob. *I'm no good. I don't deserve forgiveness, especially not after this.*

Fendrel finished digging out his supplies and put them on top of his bag. Clean rags, a steel canister of water, and a dwindling roll of bandage wrap.

Thea placed a small vial in Fendrel's hand when he was done.

"What is this?" Fendrel tilted the vial and watched the berries inside roll around.

"Pain suppressors. Squeeze them over the wound before you start." Thea began to back away, swaying slightly on her feet with a sick look on her face. "I'll only inhibit the process, so I'm going to—" Thea pointed off into the oasis, then walked off.

Cassius followed her lead. His horrified eyes were enough of a sign that he was too squeamish to watch.

Fendrel rolled onto his belly so Venom could get a clear look at the wound. The black dragon used a single claw to slice the blood-soaked fabric around the bolt, leaving most of the pantleg intact. Fendrel opened the vial and handed it to Venom. He heard his steel canister being screwed open and cool water poured around the protruding bolt. Then the squelch of the berries before their juice dripped onto the wound.

"Can you feel this?" Venom asked as he brushed the bolt's fletching with a claw. Fendrel tensed, clenching his teeth, and nodded.

"It's not as bad now," Fendrel acknowledged. "But it still hurts."

Venom nodded. "We have prepared all we can. Try to lay still." He pinched the bolt between two claws and started to tug.

"Wait!" Fendrel could not help the reflex to pull his leg away. "Wait, wait. It won't come back out through the entry."

The Dusk dragon shared a mortified look with Fendrel. The bolt would have to be pushed through. Venom gave another wordless nod, helped Fendrel roll to his side, and put as much pressure down on Fendrel as he could without hurting him. Venom asked, "Fog, can you hold his other leg still?"

Fendrel shut his eyes as he heard Fog remove her metal claws. When her paws pressed his good leg firmly into the sand, Fendrel grabbed the closest thing his hands could find. His fingers were met with cool, glossy scales that were so tightly overlapped Fendrel could not dig his fingernails between them.

Venom wound his tail around Fendrel's ankle and anchored it to the ground. Then, he cut off the fletching and started to push the bolt through.

An unrestrained cry of pain tore through Fendrel. No matter how much he tried to move, the dragons had him pinned. The bolt head split through his thigh, tearing every layer of muscle, tissue, and blood vessel it came across.

"Please!" Fendrel gasped. His fingers struggled for purchase on the black dragon's scales. "Please, please!" He could not tell if he was begging for Venom to stop or to get it over with. He just wanted it to end.

"It is almost out," Venom reassured. His voice was almost too soft to be heard over Fendrel's screams. When the bolt finally pierced through the skin of the front of Fendrel's thigh, Venom ripped it out.

Fendrel's throat was raw. He could barely manage a whimper at the bolt's exit. He lay underneath the two dragons, shivering and clenching his teeth with his eyes shut like they would never open again. Sweat and tears mingled on his skin until he could not tell them apart. He wanted it to be over, but he knew it was not.

The feel of rags being stuffed into his wound was the strangest sensation Fendrel had ever experienced. He bit down on his own wrist. He groaned as Venom stuffed in more and more abrasive cloth, keeping pressure all the while. When the bolt's path had been filled, Venom wrapped what little was left of the bandage roll Fendrel had provided around his thigh.

Venom eased off of Fendrel, only holding his bandaged leg in place while he injected his golden elixir next to the bloody site. The warm, tingling liquid found its way to the injury. The pain kept on strong, but it was dulled slightly.

"There." Venom released a heavy, burdened sigh, and helped Fendrel lay on his back. "I will give you a little more healing each day to speed up the process, but it will still take a while for you to recover."

Fendrel's chest heaved. He managed a small nod. Though they were shaded by the oasis' palms, the desert sun had begun to heat up everything it touched.

"I will get you some water," Fog said quietly.

Dazed, Fendrel could not quite tell if he was falling asleep or not. Everything was blurry and his eyelids kept fluttering closed. He must have dozed, because when he came to his head had been propped up under Venom's tail. The bolt in his heel had been removed as well, and after rolling his ankle Fendrel found no pain. Fendrel's eyes finally focused. Looking down, he realized the dragon leather chest armor had been taken off him.

Thank the stars I don't have to wear that anymore, he thought. His mouth cover had also been removed, and Fendrel reasoned it must have happened during the flight back from the Stronghold. He did not remember losing it, but it must have fallen off while he was dizzy.

Fog returned with Fendrel's steel canister clutched in her wing claw. She unscrewed the cap and handed it to Fendrel.

"Thank you," Fendrel croaked. He took the canister into his hands and drank. When he had his fill, he also accepted the cap and closed it.

The Vapor dragon breathed a puff of mist over Fendrel's forehead to cool him down. She mumbled, "It is the least I can do."

Venom lay in a crescent shape, almost encircling Fendrel. His chest rose and fell with slumber, but his ears remained perked as though Venom was ready to rise at the slightest alarm.

"Venom stayed awake all night waiting for you to come back." Fog lay down opposite Venom's head, on Fendrel's other side. "He went to fly around Stronghold and wait for you. He said he had a bad feeling. It looks like he was right."

Fendrel nodded. "Everything was going fine, but I got carried away. I took too long, and Sadon found me. He must have gotten paranoid and set up an ambush before confronting me."

"What happened, Fendrel?" Fog inched closer. "Why was Mist not there?"

"She used to be . . ." Fendrel dug in his pocket and pulled out the fragments of fur that had been laying beneath the shackles. "It must have been recent because they didn't clean this up. She's still alive, but Sadon claims she's hidden somewhere we'll never find her."

Fog scooped Mist's fur into her paws and cradled them as if trying to hold water. "Charles said the only places she could be were Stronghold and the city of Sharpdagger, so she must be there. Right?"

"She must be," Fendrel echoed. "It's a big city. I don't know where they might have hidden her."

Unless Sadon moved her again after Charles left. If he did, Mist could be anywhere in the Freelands right now.

"We will find out soon," Fog whispered so quietly Fendrel was not sure if she had said it to him or to herself.

Venom shifted in his sleep, stretching out a wing before returning it to his side. The membranes of his wings had been sealed and his pierced ear looked to be healing fine.

Fog followed his gaze. "Thankfully those parts of dragon wings are only made of skin, so I was able to help him. His paw will give him a bit of trouble for a day or two, though."

Fendrel shuddered at the memory of Venom being pelted by the bolts. He was sure Venom was going to walk away beaten and bloody if he even could walk away, but the crossbows did not leave a single scratch on his scales. Fendrel scowled.

"What is wrong?" Fog asked, drawing him out of his thoughts.

"Sadon keeps all his best weaponry in the Stronghold, the ones made from dragon claws and teeth that can pierce any hide." Fendrel switched his attention back to Fog. "But he didn't use those bolts on Venom. It's not like Sadon to use something inferior, unless he's saving his better weapons for something big. I'm worried about what that could be."

Fog's ears flicked back at his comment. She looked down at Mist's fur, still clumped in her cupped paws. "I am sure we will find out what that is soon, too."

The Vapor dragon's voice gave off the impression that she was being reassuring, but Fendrel found no comfort in it.

I just hope when we do find out that it won't be too late for us to stop it, Fendrel thought. *Could it have something to do with Zoricus? Why was he at the Stronghold?*

"Do you know if Cassius is busy?" Fendrel asked. He propped himself up, so his shoulders rested against Venom's tail. "I need to ask him a few questions, and I think you should hear it, too. Everyone should."

"I will go find him and Thea." Fog handed Mist's fur back to Fendrel. "Could you keep this safe for me, please?"

"Of course." Before Fendrel could ask Fog where they had put his bag, she was already hurrying away. After a quick visual search, he saw it tucked behind one of Venom's paws. He lifted his injured leg, scooched closer to Venom's claws, and pulled his bag to his chest. Fendrel settled back down with a grunt, feeling his packed wound flare up with an aching throb. He gave a disgruntled sigh. "I hope that doesn't happen every time I move."

It took Fendrel a moment to find a small pouch that was empty. Once he had sequestered the fur within, he set his bag to his side.

Fog returned with Cassius and Thea. The prince seemed to be looking everywhere but at Fendrel. Thea was wringing her hands with a sympathetic look on her face.

"How is it?" Thea asked.

"Bad," Fendrel answered honestly. "Do you have any more of those pain suppressor berries? Or can you make more?"

Thea took a small vial out of one of her skirt pockets. "I have this, but it's only good for a few hours. After that, I'm out. I'm sorry."

Fendrel nodded in acceptance. He reached out and let Thea place the vial in his hand.

I'll have to save them for when I truly need them, Fendrel thought.

"Venom?" Fendrel reached as far as he could without moving from his spot. His fingertips grazed the black dragon's nose. "We need to talk."

Venom's nose wrinkled as if he were being tickled. He opened his eyes and lifted his head. "You should be resting."

"Not yet, I want you all to hear something." Fendrel gathered his thoughts, then turned his gaze to Cassius. "Your cousin was there."

Cassius met his eyes for the first time since that morning. "What?"

Fendrel continued, "Your theories were a little true. Zoricus has actually been the one poisoning you and your father, but I never found out why. I think Zoricus must have advocated for it, because Sadon wanted you and your father dead, but he wanted it done sooner."

"Wh—" Cassius' eyes started to brim with tears. He blinked them away as soon as they showed themselves. "Why does Sadon care?"

"I can only guess it's because of the law." Fendrel shrugged. "It's unlawful to do what Sadon has been doing, but if it becomes legal, he won't have to make shady deals anymore. He can involve the public, and by extension he can recruit more members without having to rely on blackmail or manipulation. Sadon must want your father dead so a ruler who aligns with his beliefs can come to power."

Cassius appeared to take a moment to digest Fendrel's words. "But why is he poisoning me too?"

"Well, Zoricus already wanted you dead." Fendrel tilted his head as he thought. "He may have convinced Sadon to work it into the plan. Or perhaps Sadon assumed you would hold fast to the law, like your father."

"But Sadie respects the law just as much as I do." Cassius shook his head. "No, even more so! Why is she not one of Sadon's targets?"

"I'm sure she is," Fendrel said. He felt a pang of empathy at the horrified look on Cassius' face. "Sadie is the only thing keeping Zoricus on a leash. As long as Sadon keeps her alive, Zoricus will do whatever he wants, but as soon as Sadon doesn't need Zoricus anymore . . ."

This time a few tears escaped the prince's eyes. He quickly wiped them away. "What is their plan, anyway?"

Fendrel took in a shaky, anxious breath. "I have no idea, but there's something I need to ask you."

"What is it?" Cassius mumbled.

"Zoricus knows about Mist. I'm not sure if Sadon told Zoricus as a means of making him feel *important*—" Fendrel made air quotes "—or if Zoricus helped capture Mist, but he knows about her. He knows she's hidden somewhere, and from what Charles told us we know that somewhere is in the city of Sharpdagger. Do you have *any* idea where she could be?"

Cassius made a noise halfway between a scoff and a confounded laugh. "The dungeons, Zoricus' old estate before he moved into the palace, the catacombs underneath the city, any vacant building . . . Mist could be anywhere."

Fendrel rifled through his bag, hoping to find something to write with. He sighed in relief when his fingers found purchase on paper and a stick of writing charcoal. He handed them to the prince. "Can you make a list?"

"I can." Cassius took the handouts, crouched in the sand, and used his thigh as a writing surface. After a few scribbles he looked up at Fendrel. "They did not hint at where she might be, did they?"

"No." Frustration at his lack of clues bubbled inside Fendrel. "All they said was she was hidden somewhere no one would ever think to look."

Cassius rolled his eyes, exasperated. "How am I supposed to make a list of places she could be if she is hidden somewhere we will never think of? That is ridiculous." He kept writing despite his complaints. Then, his gaze moved to Fendrel's again. "What if she is not really hidden? What if she is in a location that is so mundane it slips the mind?"

"She could be, I suppose." Fendrel shrugged.

"How can that be?" Thea crossed her arms. "She's a grown dragon. Wouldn't it be difficult keeping her out of public view if she is somewhere so 'mundane?'"

"Perhaps Zoricus knows exactly where she is and has access to her?" Fendrel's brow furrowed as he thought. "That could be why Sadon let him in on Mist's existence, so Zoricus could keep an eye on her for Sadon."

Venom's pupils expanded like a cat on the prowl. "If that is true Mist must be somewhere Zoricus has access to, but still away from the public eye. It must also be somewhere the royal family does not go, at least not often."

"The other knights could be in on it, too." Cassius' hands worked tirelessly as he wrote down a growing list of locations. "Zoricus is a loudmouth, especially if he has something to brag about." The prince's head shot up with a wide-eyed look. "I told you about that, did I not? I told you Zoricus gloated to his comrades about owning a Vapor dragon. He *has* to be in possession of her!"

Fendrel thought back a moment, then nodded. "You also said he was drunk when he claimed that."

"It is still a possibility," Cassius said, ignoring Fendrel's retort. He returned to making his list. "All right! I have written down every place I can think of. What is the plan?"

"We'll start at the locations with the least amount of attention." Fendrel felt hope starting to build within him.

Perhaps this mission isn't as doomed as I thought. Perhaps we'll have Mist with us by tomorrow. Perhaps I haven't failed just yet.

"After clearing those, we'll work our way up until we find her." Fendrel drummed his fingers on his bag, trying to disperse his excitement lest it overwhelm him. "I'll interrogate every single knight if I have to."

"You cannot," Venom said in tone as firm as stone.

Fendrel shook his head. "I have to."

"Fendrel," Fog pleaded. "Your leg . . ."

"I'll manage! If Thea, Cassius, and I all search, we might be done in a matter of days," Fendrel retorted.

"You *do* have wanted posters all through the city." Thea took a step closer to Venom. "I agree with Fog and Venom. If you get recognized, you can't exactly run away."

"You gave me those pain suppressing berries. I'll use them for the search."

Fog's tail curled and uncurled in what looked to be a nervous habit. She said, "But you will still be in pain, even if it is lessened."

"I don't matter here!" Fendrel shouted, exasperated. He took in the group's shocked faces. When his eyes met Venom's, Fendrel looked down. "Sadon said he was going to kill Mist soon. Now that he knows I've been looking for her, that 'soon' could turn into tomorrow or tonight. We don't have time to waste. Fog—" Fendrel looked to the Vapor dragon "—you asked for my help. *I will finish this.* It's what I'm good at."

It's what I'm meant for.

The Vapor dragon's mouth opened and closed. She gathered the tip of her tail in his paws, fiddling with her feathers. "I just do not want to lose a friend, even if I would be getting my sister back. I want both of you to be safe. You matter to *us*, Fendrel."

A concoction of confusion and shame mixed in Fendrel's chest. He rolled his shoulders to ease the feeling, but glancing at the group's faces brought it back stronger.

"Even so, I refuse to sit this out." Fendrel tried to force a reassuring smile on his face. "Have a little faith in me. I promise this won't be like the Stronghold."

Silence followed his words. Then, Venom cleared his throat.

"It is your decision . . . I understand that. But you in turn must understand we will not accept you throwing your life away." Venom's yellow eyes bore into Fendrel. "I know Mist would not accept that, either. I support you going inside the city to search but, you must promise to use every second between now and then to rest. No planning, no staying awake wondering where Mist is. You will sleep or by the stars I will use knock-out powder on you to make you sleep."

Fendrel sat still as if the slightest movement would make Venom change his mind. "Yes, sir."

"Good." Venom lowered his head a bit. "We should all rest for a few hours. None of us slept well last night, if at all. I will stay alert enough in case we need to move."

Sighs of relief passed around the others.

Fendrel eased himself down, so his head rested on Venom's tail. He waited for the throbbing in his leg to subside before he shut his eyes. Drowsiness took him faster than he anticipated, but he welcomed it, knowing when he awoke, he would be closer to fulfilling his mission.

I will not fail, he told himself. *And my friends won't either.*

CHAPTER 33: FENDREL

THE THROB IN FENDREL'S LEG grew too intense for him to stay asleep. He held his eyes shut, trying to will himself back into the embrace of slumber, but to no avail. It was only after accepting his fate of remaining awake that Fendrel opened his eyes.

A clear blue sky reigned above, but the palms blocked Fendrel from seeing the sun's position. It could have been morning or afternoon. Fendrel hoped it was not any later than that.

After a moment of waiting, the pain in Fendrel's leg dulled to a more bearable ache. *I must have moved it in my sleep*, he reasoned.

For a brief moment, something shifted in the corner of Fendrel's vision. He turned his head. Fog was curled into as tight a ball as she could manage, shielding her legs and face from the outside world with her wings. Her shoulders shuddered for a moment, and Fendrel realized she was crying.

"Fog?" Fendrel whispered, trying not to wake the others.

The Vapor dragon stilled. She lifted one wing enough to see through her feathers. She sniffled and said in a hoarse voice, "I am sorry. I did not mean to wake you."

"You didn't wake me." Fendrel shook his head. "Are you all right?"

"As much as I can be, I suppose." She forced out an unconvincing, breathy laugh. "I think I have cried most nights since she went missing. I just try to do it when everyone else is asleep. Ever since we went to Stone Edge, I keep seeing her blood in the grass when I close my eyes."

Fendrel stayed quiet. He gave her a slight nod, urging her to continue.

"They did awful things to her, Fendrel." Fog choked back a whimper. Through the slit between her wing and tail, Fendrel could see Fog burying her face in her paws. "They hurt her, chased her from her home, locked her up in that giant castle . . . I cannot even begin to imagine what she must be feeling right now. I do not know if she has any hope of being saved. She might have given up on us, and that makes me feel worse."

"If there's one thing that's been constant with the dragons I've rescued, it's that they never stop hoping," Fendrel said in a calm, soothing voice. "No matter how dire their situation, they don't give up. They can't. The moment you give up is the moment you lose any chance of survival. But Mist is still alive. She hasn't given up yet."

Fog continued to stifle her sobs. She at first made no move to indicate she heard him, but then she opened her wing just an inch.

"I want to thank you for helping us so far," Fog said. "Even if we fail—"

"We won't," Fendrel cut her off. "We'll bring her home. I know I said that yesterday, but I mean it."

I have to free Mist. If I can't save her, then what good am I? Fendrel looked at Fog as though she would have an explanation for his unasked question.

"Please just do not get yourself captured like her," Fog whispered. "You are the truest friend I have had in a long time. I do not want to lose you so soon after meeting you."

"Don't worry, this won't be my last mission." Fendrel gave the Vapor dragon a reassuring smile as he said, "I'm not anywhere close to finished fighting the hunters."

Fog's whimpers ebbed away. She went quiet for long enough that Fendrel began to wonder if she had fallen asleep. But then, she asked, "Why did you start fighting them? Were you not scared?"

Fendrel let out a small laugh. "Of course I'm scared, but if I don't fight them, who will? The dragons I've talked to about this say they want to stay out of the matter in case the hunters retaliate, and the humans don't care." He shrugged out of resignation. "I'm the only one who knows how the hunters operate. I'm the only one who knows where their bases are. I can speak the language of humans and of dragons. If I don't use my knowledge for good, then I'm just as bad as the rest of humanity."

"I do not believe that," Fog said. "What you are doing is so consuming. It is dangerous, especially to do it alone. Has anyone from your clan ever offered to help you?"

"They have," Fendrel confirmed with a nod. "I won't let them, though. The hunters have hurt enough dragons, and I don't want any of my clan added to that list. They told me they would let me do this by myself unless something happened to me. Until then, I'll keep fighting the hunters alone."

"But, Fendrel, something *did* happen to you." Fog pointed at his bandaged leg. "If you were looking for Mist without our help, you would not be alive right now."

Fendrel opened his mouth to argue, but the words evaporated on his tongue. He said, in a voice so quiet he could scarcely hear himself, "It would worry them too much if they knew about this. The last time I let anyone worry about me, my adoptive parents died. I can't let that happen to anyone else."

Fog drew her wings away so Fendrel could see the look of disbelief on her face. He half-expected the Vapor dragon to reprimand him for going back on the promise he made to his clan. Instead, her eyes traveled to the pendant that hung around Fendrel's neck. "Why do you show your pendant to the dragons you rescue?"

Relieved to have moved on from the subject of his safety, Fendrel relaxed against Venom. He let his mind wander into the past as he recalled his reasoning. "When I saved a dragon for the first time, I wanted him to know that I was on his side. He was an Ice dragon, and I figured if he was from one of the Frost Lake clans, like I was, he might recognize the craftsmanship. I also—"

Fendrel's mouth shut as if an unseen force was keeping him from speaking. He knew his fears were the source of the impediment, and it took him a few beats before he could keep on. Even as Fendrel pushed out his words, his memory flashed with unwanted images of his last day as a dragon hunter recruit.

"I killed a rogue Ice dragon for my initiation test. I know it was a rogue and I shouldn't have felt guilty about it, but . . . even today I still get disgusted with what I did." Fendrel lowered his eyes, not wanting to see Fog's reaction until he had finished. "I suppose as I was saving this other Ice dragon, I wanted to apologize to him as if he were a stand in for the rogue. I wanted him to know I was sorry for everything he had been put through, but I couldn't find the words. So, I showed him my pendant and hoped he would understand. It worked, surprisingly, so I kept doing it with my other missions. Eventually it became something I was known for."

"I see," Fog said. She emerged a bit more from her self-made cocoon of feathers. "Why does your pendant have antlers on it?"

Fendrel flipped the pendant in his hand and looked down at it. The center of the bone-carved pendant had been shaped into antlers. "Every Ice clan relies on caribou for survival, especially those living around Frost Lake. Their flesh feeds us, their fur keeps our dens warm, and our parents use their bones to make coming-of-age pendants for their children. Every member of the Inviers gets one when they turn fifteen-years-old with some part of our culture carved in the center."

As Fendrel rubbed his thumb over the pendant, he almost lost himself in his memories. "My parents carved antlers into mine because male caribou are symbols of resilience and strength. Frederick and I were so sick when our parents found us that they weren't sure we would survive, but we did anyway. It impressed them, so they nicknamed me 'Stag' while I was growing up."

"That is sweet," Fog said with a smile.

"Frederick had one, too, but . . . now I have it. A flame is carved into his because he was the first human with red hair anyone from our clan had ever seen before." Fendrel placed a hand on his tattered bag, where Frederick's pendant lay inside. "I wasn't able to save my brother from the hunters, but I *will* save your sister. You can hold me to that or tell Cloud to lock me in a dungeon if I fail."

"That is a little extreme." Fog giggled. "Could you tell me more about the pendants? I love hearing about other tribes."

Fendrel smiled, happy to share something from his past that was not tainted by the dragon hunters. "They're a symbol for us taking our first steps into adulthood. On our birthdays, starting the year after we get our pendants, our parents clip on a wood-carved charm to mark another year as a full-fledged Invier."

Fog eyed the necklace. "But, yours does not have any charms."

"No." Fendrel shook his head. "Frederick and I were training at the Stronghold year-round starting when we were fifteen and ending when we were eighteen. That's the same year my parents passed away, so they never added any charms."

"None of the other Inviers could?" Fog asked, looking perplexed.

"They could have, but I didn't want anyone to," Fendrel admitted. "I didn't want anyone to take my parents' place, if that makes sense."

"It does, to me at least," Fog confirmed. "Your family sounds lovely . . . I know it is not my place to tell you what to do, but I think you should rely on them more, for help with the hunters or for anything else."

"I know." Fendrel sighed. "I just think they're too quick to forgive me for everything that happened. I can't tell if they forgave me just because I'm family or if they truly, honestly forgave me."

"Well, I do not see why they had to forgive you in the first place." Fog averted her gaze solemnly. "From what you told Venom, it sounds like you were tricked into joining the hunters, and you could not leave sooner than you did because it would have gotten your friend killed. That does not sound to me like something that needs to be forgiven."

Then why do I still feel like I need to make up for all of it? Fendrel wondered. *Is there something I've forgotten that I need to atone for? Have I been wrong in blaming myself all this time?*

". . . I think we should get some sleep before we have to leave," Fendrel said, shutting down the conversation. "We need all the rest we can get for our search."

Fog gave a tired nod, then withdrew her head into her wings and tightened herself into a ball. Soon enough, her breathing deepened.

Fendrel found himself growing tired once more, but the bright sky above made it impossible for him to shut his eyes peacefully. He gathered his strength, dragged himself closer to Venom's side, and laid under the black dragon's wing. Though he used his bandaged leg as little as possible, the ache intensified. Fendrel lay awake for a few minutes waiting for it to subside.

Hidden from the sun, drowsiness returned to claim Fendrel. He shut his eyes and hoped he would get to sleep a few more hours before they would have to leave the oasis.

CHAPTER 34: FENDREL

THE FLIGHT TOWARD THE CITY of Sharpdagger was arduous. Venom's back was broad enough that Fendrel could rest his punctured leg semi-flat, but every time Venom's wings caught air, his body shifted to ride the wind currents. Fendrel grit his teeth with each of Venom's wing strokes, but he was glad to be on Venom's back as opposed to his shoulders, where he usually sat. There was not enough room up there for him to stretch his leg out, and far too much jostling for him to manage.

Countless times Fendrel's hand hovered over his bag to dig out the pain-numbing berries Thea had given him, but each time he resisted. He needed those for when he was putting actual weight on his leg. Eating them now would be a waste. They could not afford that, especially with Mist's life in more danger now than it had been before.

Venom had sunk his fangs into Fendrel's wound for a small bit of healing before their departure. "I will administer to you at the start and end of each day," Venom had said. "This way we will wholly avoid any abnormalities in the healing process."

They did not have enough material to completely redress the wound, but Venom's abilities would be enough to keep Fendrel's blood vessels sealed and destroy any possible infection.

Cassius and Thea sat farther up, with Cassius being the closest to Venom's long, serpentine neck. It seemed as though, while they were boarding, the two were debating on who would be forced to sit up front. Even though Venom's shoulders were broad, they were constantly moving with every arc of his wings, and before them, save for Venom's neck, was the vast open sky. Leaning forward too far would send you plummeting to your death.

I can't blame him, Fendrel thought as he watched Cassius leaning back as far as possible. *He didn't grow up alongside dragons. This is completely new territory for him.*

Fog was much less of a steady flier than Venom. She had the luxury of tipping and weaving through the air without needing to worry about losing passengers. Her feathers sliced through the sky effortlessly. Remembering her stealth during their night in the oasis, Fendrel listened for Fog's wingbeats, but no such sound came from her. She was as quiet as the vapor that laced through the trees of the Hazy Woods.

She must have felt Fendrel staring. She glanced at him a moment, then returned her gaze ahead. "We are getting close," she said softly.

Fendrel followed her gaze. She was right.

A grove of trees shaped like a crescent lay not an hour's flight before them. Cradled in the center was the city of Sharpdagger, encompassed by its massive stone wall. On the opposite side of where they faced was the city's main entrance, set between the two points of the crescent.

Venom and Fog began to fly lower to avoid raising any humans' suspicion. Fendrel focused on his breathing during their descent. He found that if he devoted enough of his mind to a certain thought or repetitive action, he could distract himself from a modicum of pain.

Once we land, I can eat one of those berries. If it doesn't help much, I'll have a few more, Fendrel planned. He wanted to ration out what little he had just in case their search took them all day.

Fendrel's anticipation and nerves grew the closer they approached. He felt his anxiety mount when Venom touched down just before the tree line. The grove was too thick to fly through and looked as though the branches and roots of every tree were melded with its neighbors'. It was the perfect cover.

A chill from the dense shade passed over Fendrel when Venom and Fog stepped inside. After a few minutes of snaking between trunks and over knotting roots, Venom stopped in an area that was a bit more open.

Venom knelt down in the grass. He waited for Cassius and Thea to dismount, then he stretched his wing out straight for Fendrel to support himself on as he slid down. The pressure of his weight on the wound sent a jolt of pain through Fendrel, but he managed to stay standing.

Fendrel fished through his bag and pulled out the berries. He shook two out of the glass vial and ate them.

From the sun's position, Fendrel could tell it was midday. Before their departure, he, Cassius, and Thea agreed to search until nightfall.

I gave six berries to ration over eight hours, Fendrel thought as he counted what was left in the vial. *I hope they last that long.*

"You're still wanting to search the outskirts of the city?" Fendrel inquired of Thea before anyone could ask him if he was all right. "It's a lot bigger than what Cassius and I will be looking through."

"Yes!" Thea nodded. "I know the outskirts like the back of my hand. Anything out of place I'll pick up on right away."

"Our search might take just as long, if not longer." Cassius said in a voice full of nerves. "The inner city is not as big as the outskirts, but there is more to look out for, and more people to avoid."

The prince was still dressed in commoner's clothes, but his face was a dead giveaway to anyone who had worked with the royal family. Fendrel knew spending the whole day in Sharpdagger was bound to get one of them discovered but between his wanted posters and Cassius' status he wondered who would be recognized first. Either way, they would be traveling together. It was a last-minute condition Venom had forced Fendrel to agree to.

Fendrel cautiously put more weight on his bandaged leg. The numbing had kicked in, and Fendrel was pleased to feel only an uncomfortable ache rather than the usual sharp pain. "Let's get started, then," he said before turning to Venom and Fog. "We'll be back after dusk."

The dragons nodded solemnly. Fog attempted to hide her worry with a smile, but Venom made no such move to conceal how he felt.

"Do not come back worse for wear . . . please," said Venom.

"I'll be more careful," Fendrel promised. "Sharpdagger isn't as dangerous as the Stronghold, but I'll stay alert."

Venom stared at Fendrel for a long moment. Then, he bent his head toward him. "I will give you a small boost of healing to aid in your search, but nothing more until you return."

Fendrel allowed himself a grateful smile. "Thank you."

The Dusk dragon's fangs did not bother Fendrel as much as they used to, and he did not flinch or look away as Venom bit him. Fendrel hoped he would feel relief, but no such sensation arose. The berries were working.

"I know a secret way inside the city." Cassius jabbed his thumb over his shoulder. "This way."

Thea and Cassius went farther into the grove. As Fendrel followed behind he gave one quick look at the dragons and hoped he would find

The Dragon Liberator: Escapade

Mist once and for all. Not just for the sake of completing his mission, but for Mist herself and the dragons who loved her.

When Fendrel caught up with the other two humans, he found them standing before a flat, earthy, square-shaped object. Cassius reached down and brushed some dirt away, revealing a handle. With a heave, the trapdoor rose on its own and revealed a set of stone stairs.

"This is one of the escape routes we use if the palace ever undergoes a siege, but that has not happened for generations," Cassius explained. "No one uses them anymore, so we will be hidden for as long as we travel through them."

"How are we going to see?" Fendrel squinted into the dark. "It's pitch black down there."

Thea turned to him with her arms crossed. "Didn't I give you an enchanted lantern for your birthday?"

Fendrel avoided her gaze, remembering how the lantern had shattered during his rogue encounter at the Cliff Base. "It . . . broke."

"*It* broke or *you* broke it?" Thea accused.

"Technically a rogue broke it."

"Right," Thea said with a hint of skepticism. "I was going to try to save as much of my magic as I could, but I guess we're going to need some extra help." Thea took two river stones out of a pocket. She held her fists to her chest, closed her eyes, and started to mouth something inaudible. If Fendrel did not know any better, he might have thought she was praying.

Perhaps she is, Fendrel thought. *Perhaps mages cast spells by asking the stars for their power.*

When Thea emerged from her self-induced trance, she motioned for Fendrel to open his hand. She slid one of the stones into his palm. "It will light up when we're in the passage, but only once the door has shut."

"All right." Fendrel started toward the stairs.

"One more thing." Thea pulled a gathering of pine needles out of the same pocket, repeated the enchanting process, and handed them to Fendrel. "Keep this on you until you can get better clothes. No one is going to think you're an average citizen looking like that."

Fendrel hid the pine needles up his sleeve and looked down at his attire. Before his eyes all the rips and blood stains he could never quite wash out vanished. His bandage also blinked from his vision, but he could still feel it. Fendrel knew it was all an illusion, and if he brushed

268

his hand over any of the imperfections in his clothes, he would still be able to detect them.

"Could you do something to make me look different?" Fendrel asked.

Thea smirked. "I just did. I couldn't change your face too much or I wouldn't have enough magic later on, so don't let anyone look at you too long or they'll realize it's a façade."

Thea, Fendrel, and Cassius stepped into the passage, and once inside the prince shut the trap door. For a split second, they were plunged into total darkness. Then, the stones sprang to life with a calm, bluish light that illuminated their surroundings by a few feet.

"They won't go out very far," Thea explained. "I only put a little magic in them in case I need to make more spells later, and they'll only last for today."

Fendrel held the stone out in front of him and started down the path. The stairs leveled out to a flat surface that slowly descended. Soon the dirt and roots that were present at the top of the passage melded into hard, cold rock. The chill seemed to make Fendrel's wound ache even through the pain suppressants, but he did his best to hide it.

Cassius walked between Fendrel and Thea. He kept his eyes forward as if watching out for something despite their visibility being heavily limited. Their journey was full of cold air, Cassius choosing different branching paths, and the sounds of pebbles skittering from their echoing footfalls.

After they had traveled for a few minutes, they met another fork in the road. "This is a shortcut to the outskirts," Cassius said as he pointed to the right. "Just keep choosing the right-side paths and you will reach the surface."

Thea's fingers clasped tighter around her stone as she made an uncertain face. "You give me your word?"

"Absolutely." Cassius nodded in affirmation. "The end of the path spits you out into an abandoned building. You will have to move a small bookcase out of the way, but it is not heavy."

"Here." Fendrel pulled a small dagger out of his bag and handed it to Thea. "Just in case."

The mage took the blade into her other hand but made no move to put it away. She sneered at it and said, "I don't know how to use this."

"Let's hope you won't need to." Fendrel grinned. "Trust me, just showing that you have a weapon is enough to deter some attackers."

"You had better be telling the truth, Fendrel." Thea gave him and Cassius a sarcastic curtsey as she said, "Farewell, gentlemen," and started down the right-side tunnel. Even when her light dwindled away, Fendrel could still hear her footsteps.

"It will not take us long to reach the inner city," Cassius said as he led the way down the left side and waited for Fendrel to join him.

Just minutes later Fendrel noticed Cassius fidgeting with his fingers, picking the kin around his nails.

"Nervous?" Fendrel asked.

At first Cassius stuck his hands at his sides as though he were trying to act casually. Then, he sighed in resignation. "Yes. I chose this route because it leads to a corner of the royal gardens where none of the knights patrol around. It is so small I think they forgot it existed, but my fiancée frequents it around this time of day. I would have chosen another path, but it is too risky that we would be seen. All the areas the other tunnels lead to are either inside the palace, to the dungeons, or somewhere the guards like to spend time."

Fendrel was about to nod in understanding, but he stopped short. "Are you afraid of running into your fiancée because you think she'll tell someone where we are? Or is it because of the spell?"

"It is both, but more so the latter," Cassius confessed. "Even if Thea was right about Adila being innocent, that does not change how the spell works. I will still lose control of myself."

"Then we'll avoid her," Fendrel said. "Although, if we do get caught, it's best we talk about what to do now so we're not scrambling for an exit later."

"Good idea," Cassius agreed.

"I won't be able to run away if I'm spotted, so we need hiding spots." Fendrel lowered his voice after hearing it echo down the hall. He did not think anyone else was in the escape tunnels, but it was better to be safe than sorry.

"I know the best places." Cassius smiled confidently. "I have been sneaking around the city by myself for years and have not been confronted before. But if we are found out, I will vouch for you."

Fendrel made a noise of understanding, but he did not fully believe the prince.

Cassius is a stranger, Fendrel thought. *Only time will tell if he's honest or not, but I don't really have any other choice than to take him at his word.*

"Vouch for me how?" Fendrel asked.

Kassidy J. Ridenour

"Well, if my father knows you are connected to me, he will likely want to speak to you, and I will be there to defend you." Cassius' fidgeting ceased as the conversation moved away from Adila. "We once had an incident where a servant was found wearing one of my sister's bracelets. My father put *everything* on hold until the issue was sorted, and it turned out Sadie had simply gifted the bracelet to her. There have been a few other times, too when my father saw to whatever was bothering us, even ahead of more pressing matters."

"Except for when you told him about what Zoricus has been doing to you," Fendrel said. He studied the prince's face with skepticism, trying to catch any inaccuracies in Cassius' previous statements.

"Yes." Cassius frowned. His chin dipped a little. "Except for then. That was different, I think. My father always favored Zoricus over me, so of course he defended him then. I did not have any proof either."

"I thought you said the High Mage is able to make people tell the truth during trials?" Fendrel asked, feeling his animosity for Zoricus flourish.

"We did not have a trial," Cassius said meekly. "Father did not want to make it a public issue, because it was a family matter. He did not say it out loud, but he made it clear I was forbidden from bringing it up again." The prince kept walking, but he looked as though his mind had gone somewhere else.

Fendrel did not press any further.

He reminds me of you when you were around his age. He's scared, confused, doesn't have anyone he can trust, Charles had said of Cassius when they were in the Sanctuary. Fendrel wanted to roll his eyes, but something in him made him pause.

Before Fendrel could reel himself in, he blurted, "Some people don't deserve to be considered family just because of blood."

Cassius gave Fendrel a curious look. He asked, just above a whisper, "You have experience with this?"

"Unfortunately."

The prince stood a little straighter at Fendrel's admission. "Who was it, if you don't mind me asking?"

"My blood father, and my aunt." Fendrel shrugged, trying to mask his upset. Even with his discomfort, Fendrel was surprised by how willing he felt sharing this with the younger man. "The people of my home village weren't so welcoming either. They hated my mother, and because I'm a bastard they hated me, too. Sometimes you have to make

271

your own family when the one you're born in fails you."

"Surely not everyone you are related to treated you like an outsider." Cassius shrank back when Fendrel did not respond. "Right?"

"Not everyone. My brother and my mother were kind." Fendrel kept his eyes on the darkness ahead. "They're both dead now."

Cassius' brow furrowed with sympathy. "I am sorry," he mumbled.

Fendrel pretended not to hear him.

The ground rose beneath their feet, leading to the surface. It continued upward on and on until Fendrel began to wonder if they would ever reach the top. Eventually the light stone Fendrel held illuminated a cobblestone wall mere feet in front of them. On the left side was a lever.

"We are here." Cassius pulled the lever. There was a soft click and Fendrel felt a draft emanate from between the stones in the wall. Cassius pushed against it until it slid outward. Muffled machinations whirred, just barely above a whisper, as the wall Cassius pushed slid to the side. Near-blinding light filtered in through the revealed doorway.

Fendrel squinted and held an arm in front of his face. When his vision adjusted to the brightness, he saw a lattice above them that filtered the sunlight through hanging stained glass decorations. The lattice stretched on for a bit, with leafy vines that grew through it acting as a sunshade. Beyond the lattice lay a sprawling garden in full bloom. Between neatly-trimmed hedges and mosaic-laden walls were ornate pots holding flowers so beautiful Fendrel at first thought they must be fake.

Every shoulder-high hedge, flowerpot, and mosaic wall served as the perfect cover. The only obstacle Fendrel saw was the palace itself and the numerous windows that looked down on the garden. Thanks to the lattice, he and Cassius were currently shielded from sight.

Before he walked out of the tunnel, Fendrel dug a tattered brown scarf out of his bag. He grimaced at its torn, frayed appearance, but put it on regardless. The enchantment Thea placed on his clothes must have extended to the scarf, because when Fendrel looked down at it, the holes and imperfections were gone. He took a deep breath to prepare himself for the search and followed Cassius out of the tunnel.

Cassius pushed the displaced piece of wall, and it shifted back into place, leaving no trace it had ever moved.

"All right, where to?" Fendrel asked.

The prince took the lead down the shaded path and Fendrel

followed. Gravel crunched beneath their shoes, but Cassius appeared not to notice. When they reached the end, the prince stuck his head out and checked their surroundings.

"This way." Cassius snaked out from the shade.

Fendrel kept close behind Cassius down winding paths, tight corners, and close calls with patrolling guards. The royal gardens seemed as complex and branching as the escape tunnels, albeit much more beautiful and basked in the sun's warmth.

Some stretches were longer than others and the two had to speed up their pace so they could find cover before a knight or servant rounded a corner. The change of pace from walking to rushed sneaking, to crouching, to walking again was putting more stress on Fendrel's leg than he wanted to admit. Still, he could not ignore the pain in his thigh. He ate one of the numbing berries, found it did little to alleviate his discomfort, and took another.

Four left for the rest of the day, and we haven't even started looking yet, Fendrel thought with disdain.

Fendrel could not tell how long they had been winding through the gardens, or how close to getting out they were, but that ceased to matter the moment Cassius stumbled backward into Fendrel after peeking around a corner.

"Your Highness?" called a voice from where Cassius had been looking. Boots stomped over gravel, growing closer to their position.

Cassius cursed under his breath and turned to face Fendrel. He pointed toward an offshoot they passed. "Go down that way and keep straight until you reach a gazebo. I will catch up with you soon."

Fendrel retreated to the path Cassius had directed him to. He pressed himself against the mosaic wall and kept low, inching onward.

Repressing the urge to sigh in frustration, Fendrel stayed in a crouch. His leg screamed in pain. The wall rose high enough for him to stand up, but still bent over. With his heart pounding with adrenaline, Fendrel followed Cassius' directions until he met a four-way path. Ahead sat a ring-shaped hedge around ten feet tall with a slit small enough for a person to walk through. The left and right paths were clear for the moment, but footsteps were sounding on either side. Fendrel hurried into the hedge ring and pressed his back against the leafy wall once he was inside.

In the center of the secluded ring was a gazebo. Fendrel let himself sink to a sit with relief. He gingerly pressed his fingers to where his bandage should be and felt the softness of it despite Thea's spell hiding the wrapping from view. Fendrel tried to see if he could notice any stiffness caused by dried blood. He had not bled since Venom first injected him, but Fendrel worried the stress he put on his leg had reopened a few weak veins. Thankfully, he could feel no dampness nor any sign that his wound had gotten worse.

It was only after bringing his eyes up that Fendrel realized he was not alone. Someone sat on the smooth stone bench inside the gazebo. A young woman with stormy gray eyes and black hair. She stared at him with a mix of shock and confusion. Her arms were crossed in front of her midsection as though she were trying to keep warm. Fendrel had only ever seen Cassius and his sister a handful of times from far away before actually meeting the prince, but even from those fleeting sights Fendrel knew this could not be the princess. This must be Adila.

The engagement ring on her finger was proof of Fendrel's assumption.

Fendrel braced himself for the pain of standing up. He greeted, "You must be the prince's fiancée. I'm an acquaintance of his."

Adila stayed silent as she fiddled with the ring. The longer she stared the more her expression shifted to one full of fear. "What is your name? The prince has never mentioned you before."

"Fendrel." The name slipped out before he could think of a different one.

"I have seen your face on the wanted posters." Adila moved to the edge of her seat as though she were ready to flee.

Fendrel reached toward his face. His scarf had slipped under his chin while he was hurrying from the guards.

The spell must have worn off when Adila started staring at me, Fendrel realized.

"So, you *do* get out of the palace?" Fendrel smiled to cover his nerves.

Adila looked away a moment as her cheeks started to flush. "I-I tried to leave once."

"Why would you want to leave?" Fendrel approached her slowly.

"I do not belong here." Adila's voice became solemn, and tears started to spring in her eyes. "Something happened to me here. I no longer feel like myself."

Could she be under the same spell as Cassius? Fendrel wondered. *He claimed he didn't feel like himself while he was in Adila's presence. Perhaps Adila*

274

has the same enchantment placed on her.

As Fendrel neared, he tried to decipher any unspoken signs in her body language. She had a look in her eyes Fendrel had seen hundreds of times. It was the same look prevalent in every dragon before their cages were unlocked. He had seen it at the abandoned Cliff Base, in Sour while he was strapped to the dragon hunters' cart, and in Fog when they first met.

Adila truly was trapped.

Fendrel found himself feeling more sympathy for Adila than he had felt for another human in a while. He said softly, "You're a long way from home, aren't you?"

With a shaky nod, Adila chocked out, "Yes." She reached for a pendant on her necklace Fendrel had not noticed before and twisted it between her fingers. As she did so, a sense of overwhelming dread seized hold of Fendrel's heart, making him shudder.

The spell . . . it's on the necklace.

A headache came on suddenly, forcing Fendrel to squeeze his eyes shut in pain. Even with his eyes closed, he could see swirling shapes and colors at the edges of his vision that threatened to distract him from the situation at hand. Fendrel hesitantly opened his eyes, which had become blurred with the stain, and asked, "Where are you from?"

Adila opened her mouth to speak, but nothing came out. She tried again. Still nothing.

"It's all right, you can tell me." Fendrel walked closer to Adila only to find the headache growing more painful. He flinched. It hurt to keep his gaze on her, but Fendrel refused to shut his eyes again. "I'll keep it a secret. I promise."

"I really cannot say it." Adila placed a hand over her throat, as though she were trying to dig her words out.

Every bit of Fendrel was screaming for him to collapse, to make the stain end, but he fought it. He staggered backward until the headache lessened enough for him to stand up straight.

I can't leave her here like this . . .

Something was terribly wrong, more wrong than Fendrel originally thought. There was a sinking sensation in his chest that he could not place right away. Fendrel looked at Adila again, at the way she curled her fingers around her neck like claws, and how her eyes drifted about like prey searching for an escape.

You've hidden her somewhere no one would ever think to look, Zoricus' voice echoed in Fendrel's memory.

Fendrel felt around his own neck for the necklace which held the pendant he showed every dragon he rescued. He pulled it from his collar, and in Drake-tongue, Fendrel asked, "Can you understand me?"

Adila's breath caught. She cupped her hands over her mouth and let out a sob that sounded like it had been fighting to get out.

Fendrel's throat went dry. He dug in his bag for the fur he had recovered from Sadon's vault, pulled it out, and held it up for Adila to see. "This is yours, isn't it?"

CHAPTER 35: FENDREL

FENDREL'S HEAD WAS SPINNING, BUT he could not tell if it was from euphoria or disgust. Mist stood before him in a prison he had never seen before. He had found her, but her current state shocked Fendrel so deeply he could feel a pang of distress in his bones.

She looked unharmed, but she was far from safe.

This isn't over until she's back home, Fendrel thought.

His chest filled with a sense of purpose. He let the necklace fall below his collarbone and returned the blue-gray fur to his bag.

Mist was still crying on the gazebo bench with her face hidden in her hands. Her sobs were growing louder, and Fendrel began to worry that someone might hear her.

Fendrel shut his eyes and crept toward the gazebo in hopes the stain would not affect him as much if Mist's necklace was out of sight. Just as before, the shapes still swirled, but the headache had lessened. He felt his foot knock against one of the steps of the gazebo, then he used the railing to guide himself up. Once his shoes settled on the flat wooden planks, Fendrel asked with his eyes still shut, "How do we reverse this?"

The feeling of Mist's fingers on his hand made Fendrel flinch, but he settled when he realized she was bringing his hands up to feel the enchanted pendant. There was what felt like a keyhole on the backside.

"Is that the only way to get the necklace off?" Fendrel realized Mist might not be able to answer that question, so he went with a different one. "Who has the key?"

Mist traced a "Z" on the back of his hand.

"Zoricus," Fendrel said.

A pat of affirmation let Fendrel know his guess was correct.

"That isn't good . . . he isn't here." Fendrel sighed with deep annoyance. "Do you think I'd be able to cut the necklace off of you? The chain looks dainty enough."

"I do not think that will work." Mist dropped Fendrel's hand. "I have already tried. Nothing can break it, and it is too tight to lift over my head. And you are wrong about Zoricus. He is here. He arrived this morning."

Fendrel nodded. "I will get that key. Do you know where he is?"

"Yes. He—"

Before she could finish, someone shouted from the entrance of the hedge ring. "Intruder! State your business or we will cut you down where you stand."

Fendrel froze. He pushed the scarf back over his nose and turned slowly with his hands half-raised. Now that he was facing away from the necklace, he opened his eyes.

There were four guards standing at the entrance with their swords unsheathed. One of them stepped before the others but kept his gaze trained on Fendrel.

"Don't waste your breath," said the guard closest to him. "The captain will see to interrogating you. He'll make sure you don't spout any lies. Come away from the lady at this instant."

Where is Cassius? Fendrel wondered. *Is he still talking to that guard who caught him? Is he in the palace? Does he know Zoricus is here?*

Fendrel questioned if mentioning Cassius would get the prince into trouble. *Well, he said he would vouch for me,* Fendrel reasoned.

"The prince knows I'm here. I was meant to meet with him but got lost. I saw his fiancée and thought she might be able to direct me to him." Fendrel put on the sincerest face he could muster, hoping the scarf and Thea's magic would be enough to keep the guards from recognizing him. He moved away from Mist to alleviate some of the tension.

"What business would you have with the prince?" spat the closest guard. His eyes moved up and down Fendrel's clothes with contempt.

"I am an apothecary," Fendrel lied. "His Royal Highness sought out my services to solve what has gone wrong with the king's health."

"How does he know about that?" muttered one of the guards farther back. He was silenced with a glare from his comrades.

"I truly do need to see the prince." Fendrel approached the guards with his hands still raised. "He sounded very worried. I do not want to upset him with my tardiness, especially with a matter this urgent."

The guard who had first spoken to Fendrel turned his gaze to Mist. He asked, "Has he been honest, Lady Adila? He has not hurt you?"

Mist shook her head with fervor. "N-no. He only asked for directions."

"Hm," grumbled the guard. He sheathed his sword. "Very well. We will escort you to His Royal Highness ourselves. But if we catch a whiff of dishonesty from you, you will pay the consequences."

Fendrel's mouth dried. "As is your duty," he said with a small nod. He waited for the four guards to take their places around him with two in the front and two behind. They kept their weapons sheathed, but their hands still rested on the pommels of their swords. As the guards marched Fendrel through the gardens, Fendrel did his best to hide his limp.

One of the soldiers appeared to notice. He cast a sidelong glance at Fendrel who smiled and explained, "Bad leg."

The suspicious guard's gaze traveled about Fendrel's state of dress. He said, "Surely an apothecary worthy of catching the prince's eye would be wealthy enough to own a more suitable bag."

Fendrel placed a hand on the bag, worn and tattered and scorched. "I find it important to use something until it is no longer functional. Better not to waste anything, even if it's old."

The only response he got was a "Hmph."

It was not a far walk to the palace's nearest entrance. Fendrel tried to keep track of the turns they made through the halls, but with his thoughts swirling about Mist, he found it hard to make sense of where they were headed. The two leading guards stopped before an ornate door, taller and more decorated than the others they had walked through. Fendrel's breath caught when the door was opened, and he saw who was inside.

They entered the throne room, a massive space made to fit hundreds of people, but only a few were there. At the back sat a throne, proud and shiny in the center of a wide pedestal. Before the throne stood who Fendrel assumed was the king. Despite the exhaustion on his face the king made an effort to stand upright. He was embracing Cassius, who looked surprised. No doubt the look of shock and fear on the prince's face was aimed at Zoricus who stood on the king's other side.

Zoricus was one of the tallest men Fendrel had ever encountered in his life with a muscular build and tan skin. The knight's black hair was always kept long enough to cover his forehead, and never an inch longer. His blue eyes were full of pure irritation as he glared back at his cousin and dark circles marked the skin under his eyes.

He must have ridden all night to get here before us, Fendrel realized.

The king's stance, how he leaned against Cassius and how thin he was reminded Fendrel of Cassius' own sickliness. The poison was obviously taking a greater toll on the older man. Still, he had made an effort to dress in heavy, luxurious clothes. He was not quite as old as Fendrel had assumed, but nonetheless the man's face was marred with wrinkles and a graying beard.

Surrounding the royal family were armed knights, each one standing still and disciplined. A duo of ants with their heads bent sequestered themselves before a nearby doorway.

Fendrel and the guards corralling him drew near to the gathered palace denizens. The sound of marching boots must have drawn attention, because Zoricus looked over to nod at his comrades. He did a double take at Fendrel and stared hard for a moment.

"You," came Zoricus' murderous voice once his eyes widened with recognition. "Finally agreed to turn yourself in, have you?"

One of Fendrel's guards drew his sword. "You deceiver!" The other guards followed his lead, each one aiming the tips of their blades at Fendrel.

"Wait!" Cassius let go of his father and stepped between Zoricus and the others. "He is no intruder, I brought him here."

"Get out of the way." Zoricus pushed Cassius aside. "This is a wanted man."

"Zoricus, what is the meaning of this?" The king's voice was more commanding than Fendrel had anticipated. "Why would you push your cousin, your prince, aside? Explain yourself."

Stricken, Zoricus took a few steps back and gave the king a short bow. "Apologies, Your Majesty. This man—" Zoricus glared at Fendrel "—is a wanted criminal I have been hunting for years. I was simply getting Cassius out of harm's way."

Cassius rolled his eyes in response.

"Is this true?" The king turned to his son.

"Not to my knowledge, Father." Cassius feigned a shocked expression. Fendrel wondered if the prince's poor acting was a lack of skill or a deliberate choice to annoy Zoricus. "I brought this man here because I believe we need his aid."

Zoricus opened his mouth to interject, but Cassius beat him to it. "There is something you must know about Zoricus."

Zoricus scoffed. "I have only done my duty."

Cassius approached his father and placed a hand on his shoulder. "Father, we have a traitor among us, and this man can help us weed him out."

The king studied Fendrel with his haggard, hazel eyes which perfectly matched Cassius' own.

"I would—" Cassius stumbled over his words as he spoke, as if he were afraid of his proposition "—I would like to call for a trial."

"For this criminal." Zoricus gestured at Fendrel. He narrowed his eyes at Cassius. "Correct, my prince?"

"To a lesser extent," Cassius mumbled. "But also for you."

Zoricus' face grew red with rage.

The tension between Zoricus and Cassius broke as the king hunched over with a nasty cough. The king waved away the ants that rushed to his side. He composed himself, cleared his throat, and then looked between his son and nephew.

To Fendrel's surprise both Cassius and Zoricus looked troubled by the king's sudden coughing fit. Even from several paces away Fendrel swore he saw sweat start to bead on Cassius' forehead. Zoricus turned his face away with his cheeks still red. Fendrel could not tell if his flush was a result of shame or if the head of the guard was still angered by Cassius' proposal.

"As you wish, son, if that will entertain you," said the king. He took a few shaky steps toward his throne and sat down.

"You do not need to entertain me to keep me around, Father. I left for other reasons, which I will enlighten you on later." Cassius waved for Fendrel to step forward. "But first, the trial. I am sure you will get more enjoyment out of it than I."

The king nodded as a look of intrigue overtook his face. "Bring out the High Mage."

One of the ants bowed before she ducked out of the room.

"Kneel before the throne," commanded the king. "You will be interrogated one at a time."

Fendrel approached the pedestal with little prodding from his guards. Zoricus, more reluctant, dragged his feet to stand next to Fendrel. The king gave Zoricus a look as if to say, "Just play along for now."

He isn't taking any of this seriously. He's only doing this to appease Cassius. Will he even listen to what we have to say? Fendrel wondered as he looked to Cassius for an answer but saw a contention of worry and anger bubbling in the prince's visage.

What if the king denies everything Cassius and I have to tell him? Will he believe Zoricus no matter what? Am I going to be imprisoned? Fendrel's stomach sank. *Mist will be stuck here until Sadon decides to kill her. I have to get through this, even if it means playing nice with these people.*

One of Fendrel's guards held out a hand, palm-up. "Your bag."

Fendrel clutched his bag tight. His heart started to thunder in his chest. *Just play along,* he told himself. Fendrel mustered up the will power to hand his bag over to the guard, who marched it toward the throne and set it on the pedestal.

The door the ant disappeared through reopened, and the same ant emerged through it. Behind her, walking at a leisurely pace was who Fendrel assumed to be the High Mage.

It was not the man's enigmatic appearance that led Fendrel to that conclusion, but the stain that affected Fendrel as soon as he laid eyes on the mage. The corners of his vision grew crowded with a sea of swirling shapes and colors that threatened to block out Fendrel's vision. An ache unlike anything he had ever felt before split his head open. The pain combined with the throb in his thigh, which his kneeling forced pressure on, brought Fendrel to tears.

Is this the mage Thea warned might be behind Adila's, er Mist's transformation? The same one who seemed to be stalking Thea and who knew exactly how to find me? Fendrel worried.

He shut his eyes and forced his head low to avoid all contact with the High Mage. Fendrel thought he could feel the man's magenta eyes roaming over him, searching for any weakness. He told himself he was just being paranoid, but when he gathered the courage to look up, the High Mage's gaze was indeed fixed on him.

A long, hooded maroon robe concealed most of the mage's body and cast his face in an uncanny shadow. Fendrel thought it must have been the hood's shade at first, but upon further inspection he realized the mage's skin was charcoal gray. Covering his mouth and nose was a black cloth so similar in color to his skin that it almost appeared as though the mage had no mouth at all. Fendrel shivered, and the mage's eyes crinkled in amusement.

Just past the mage stood Cassius. The prince's eyes were averted,

Kassidy J. Ridenour

and he appeared to be putting on a brave face, but his clenched fists gave him away. Fendrel shifted his attention to Zoricus. The knight looked just as uncomfortable as Fendrel, and he kept squinting as though his vision was also being affected.

The realization almost made Fendrel forget about his current affliction. *I feel the stain because I've been exposed to magic before—Thea's magic. Cassius has the stain because he's had a spell cast on him by Mist's necklace. Mist said Zoricus had the key to her necklace, which means he had to touch it in order to lock it, so he also has the stain.*

If Zoricus is the one who put the necklace on Mist, he must be working with Raaldin, too. Fendrel squirmed at the implication. *Will Raaldin cooperate, or will he refuse to use his magic for the trial?*

Sitting on his throne the king was unaffected by the mage's presence. The ants and the knights also showed no sign of being under the stain's effects.

In one smooth motion, the mage stopped before the king and bowed. Then, he moved aside.

Cassius rolled his shoulders once the mage had left his line of sight. He gestured at Fendrel. "Please, reveal yourself."

Is he sure about this? Fendrel raised an eyebrow at Cassius. After a prompt wave from the prince, Fendrel pulled down the scarf. It took the guards beside Fendrel a moment to recognize him, but soon they each tightened their fingers around the grips of their swords.

"It is my understanding that people refer to you as the Liberator, correct?" Cassius addressed Fendrel.

"Yes." Fendrel kept his tone flat.

"But your real name, for sake of brevity, is Fendrel, correct?" Cassius asked.

Fendrel narrowed his eyes. "It is."

"Liberation is often seen as a good thing, so why would people call you the Liberator while simultaneously calling you a criminal?" Cassius made an expression of exaggerated confusion. "And how did you earn that title?"

Fendrel was about to roll his eyes, but he stopped himself. *He's putting on a show to get the king invested. Just go along with it so you can bring Mist home.*

"I think they use it to mock me, more than anything. I free dragons, even if they're someone's 'pet,' and I take them back to their homes," Fendrel answered honestly. "I don't know why the humans started

The Dragon Liberator: Escapade

calling me 'Liberator.' It's usually just the dragons who use that term."

"So dragons can talk?" Cassius crossed his arms. "What else do they say?" A few hushed laughs sounded from the knights and ants. This time, Fendrel did nothing to suppress his eye roll.

The king held up a hand to silence the snickers. "I have never heard of you before. Not from my advisors, my guard, nor my servants. What laws have you broken?"

"You've never heard of me?" Fendrel blinked in surprise.

Does he never leave the palace grounds? How could he miss all the wanted posters? Fendrel wondered.

When the king shook his head, perplexion still clear on his face, Fendrel answered, "I've been in quite a few scuffles, in various towns, trying to free dragons from their human captors."

"But it is illegal to participate in dragon trading. Why are you handling this instead of my guard?" The king leaned forward as he spoke. His attention was focused on Fendrel alone.

"Your Majesty . . ." Fendrel forced himself to address the king by title. The last time he had considered himself a part of the humans' kingdom was when he was a child, not yet taken in by the Invier clan. Referring to Cassius' father with such respect made Fendrel feel like an imposter masquerading as a human.

The humans are not my people, Fendrel remembered saying to Cassius. He believed it with his entire soul, but Fendrel pushed himself to keep up the façade of a Sharpdagger citizen.

"I regret to inform you, Your Majesty, but your royal guard is less law-abiding than I." Fendrel cast a disdainful glance at Zoricus. "Many of the fights I found myself in were with members of the guard."

One of the knights at Fendrel's side flicked his blade closer to Fendrel's neck. A subtle warning. Fendrel hoped Cassius caught on to the message, but the prince was watching his father with eagerness.

"You are being truthful with me?" the king asked.

"Yes." Fendrel gave him a single, clear nod. "Unfortunately, I am."

Zoricus shook his head. Even on his knees, he still had to look down to see Fendrel. "You are a deceitful man with no evidence to back your claims."

"Actually, we *can* prove it." Cassius gestured at Raaldin without looking at him. "Do you mind aiding us?"

Fendrel watched in horror as Raaldin walked over to him. Out the corner of his eye, muddled by the stain, Fendrel thought he could see a

Kassidy J. Ridenour

look of betrayal on Zoricus' face.

So, they are working together . . . but for what reason?

There was no time for Fendrel to speculate. Raaldin held his shoulders back to stand taller as though gloating to Fendrel about his power. The High Mage took an iron chain with a charm out of his pocket. The charm had a silver frame with tiny pieces of stained glass held together in its center. Embossed on both sides, laid over the glass, was a strange eye symbol.

As soon as the charm fell into Fendrel's vision, the stain came back with full force, just as it had assailed him when he found Mist. Fendrel tried to back away, but his guards latched onto his shoulders and held him firm.

Cassius peered at Fendrel from behind Raaldin. The prince gave Fendrel a look of reassurance. "This is the only way to bring out the truth," he said.

Before Fendrel could prepare himself, Raaldin pressed the charm to Fendrel's forehead and began to whisper something. The stain's vibrant, too-bright colors warred with each other in response to the magic. They intensified until Fendrel could only see white. He was so taken by the spell's effects that he could not tell if he was reacting or frozen in place. The throne room melted away from his gaze, as did the people surrounding him. Even the feel of the guards' iron grip fell away as Fendrel was consumed by whatever spell Raaldin had cast on the charm. Among a blank world of white and nothingness, the only thing Fendrel could hear was Raaldin whispering in a tongue he had never heard before.

As sudden as the world disappeared, it came flooding back. Fendrel felt himself falling and his hands slammed down on the cool, polished floor. Sweat had moistened his brow, his neck, and his back. Fendrel's lungs heaved with panicked breath. He lifted his gaze and saw Raaldin holding the unadorned end of the chain high above his head.

A window Fendrel had not noticed before shone light on the charm and cast its glittering, stained-glass projection on the floor in front of the throne.

"What do you wish to be revealed, Your Majesty?" Raaldin asked the king.

The king tapped his fingers on the arm of his throne for a moment. Then, he turned his attention to Cassius. "You called this trial. What is your decision?"

"Thank you, Father," Cassius said with a nod. His face brightened somewhat, like a child receiving a gift they were not expecting. "Reveal a time when Fendrel saw Zoricus buying, abusing, or fighting over a dragon. Perhaps all three, if such an instance exists."

Raaldin flicked the charm. It spun faster and faster until the shapes and colors projected on the floor showed a full picture. He whispered once more, and the image began to move. The crowd of guards, ants, as well as Cassius and his father leaned in to watch the stirring picture. A muffled sound came from it, as if voices were rising from within the floor. Raaldin snapped his fingers until the sounds could be made out clear as day.

Mesmerized, Fendrel stared at the scene unfolding before him. It was one of his memories, laid out for everyone to watch, but it was not through his eyes. The past played as if from the view of someone following behind Fendrel, even though no one was truly there.

Fendrel was in a human village up north. It was biting cold and every surface was frost-laden. Fires burned in controlled pits, on torches, and lanterns spread all throughout the village. Most of the denizens were inside to avoid the elements, but Fendrel in his layered caribou fur coat was out and about.

He noticed something on the dirt in front of him. He crouched to pick it up and twirled it between his fingers. A tuft of white fur. It was silky, soft yet sturdy. "Dragon fur." His breath came out as a puff of white.

The road ahead of him was littered with small bits of fur, almost indistinguishable from the snow and ice.

"Another abduction." Fendrel sighed. Hatchlings going missing was starting to become more common, and for reasons Fendrel was not quite sure of Air dragons were the main target. At the moment, the why did not matter. Fendrel followed the trail, staying clear of carts pulled by moody cattle and stamping draft horses.

Peeking out from behind a cart piled high with hay, Fendrel gasped when he saw Zoricus in an alley. He was talking in hushed whispers to a man. The stranger gripped a rope in his hand, the other end of which disappeared from sight behind a house.

Zoricus dropped a loaded bag of coins in the man's hand and received the rope from his trade. The knight tugged on the rope. The other end became visible, tied around the waist of a white-furred Air dragon hatchling.

The hatchling seemed to be just days old, only as big as a cat. She would not yet learn how to speak for a few weeks, possibly longer now that she had been removed from her parents. She squeaked and tripped over her overly large wings.

The knight did not wait for the dragon to get up before he started walking, dragging the hatchling through the frosty mud.

Pitifully, the dragon tried to scratch at the ropes, but her claws were dull, and her wings kept getting in the way. She resorted to squealing madly and thrashing. Her tail lashed out and whipped a nearby horse's leg. Spooked, the horse whinnied and reared up, about to smash its hooves down on the hatchling.

Zoricus yanked the rope toward himself, causing the hatchling to crash into him. He must have lost his balance on the ice, because the collision sent them both to the ground.

Fendrel dashed out from behind the hay cart. He scooped up the hatchling before Zoricus could regain his hold on the rope.

Terrified, the hatchling flung her wings open, slapping Fendrel's face, but he did not stop running. He pinned the dragon's wings to her sides.

"Get back here!" Zoricus' enraged shouts followed the Liberator.

Fendrel wound through side streets and between houses until he was sure he had lost the knight. He stopped and pressed his back against the side of a house, his breathing labored. The baby dragon squirmed and whimpered. Fendrel held her against his chest and gathered up the rope so its trail would not give them away. As the hatchling continued to cry, Fendrel started whispering to her in Drake-tongue, "You're all right. You're safe, just try to be quiet for a little while."

The hatchling was stunned into silence.

"You must have been around dragons before, if you recognize that language," Fendrel reasoned out loud. He smiled, glad that she had not hatched among her abductors.

Shivering from the cold and from fear, the hatchling latched onto Fendrel's shirt through his coat. She chirped as Fendrel pulled his cloak around her.

Zoricus trudged out on a road, mere feet from Fendrel's hiding place. The knight clenched his fists and spat curses in rage, then stormed back to the village. "Ready my horse!" he shouted.

The sound of rumbling wheels approached. A cattle-drawn cart covered by a tarp pulled out of the village. An easy escape. Fendrel ran up to the back of the cart and pulled himself inside with the hatchling still clutched in his other arm. He hoped the rattling wheels would drown out the hatchling's cries if she became fussy.

Fendrel blinked. The scene that showed his memory became nothing more than swirling colored light that disappeared as Raaldin covered the eye symbol on his enchanted chain.

The throne room was silent.

Fendrel chanced a glance at Zoricus. The knight's face was grim, and he kept his eyes lowered.

"You have disobeyed me," the king said as contempt filled his gaze. His voice, though quiet, seemed to carry through the entire room. "What do you have to say for yourself?"

"Nothing, Your Majesty," Zoricus mumbled almost too quiet to hear.

The king pinched the bridge of his nose. He drew in a deep breath, then looked to Fendrel. "And you. What language did you speak to that dragon?"

Fendrel bowed his head. "That's Drake-tongue, it's their native language."

"You are fluent in it?" The king took his hand from his face. He seemed intrigued, yet still angered by his nephew.

"Yes, sir. Sometimes I feel I know it better than my birth tongue." Fendrel could not help the small twinge of pride in his voice.

"Incredible," the king said, his voice returning to calm. He asked, "How?"

Fendrel wished he had his bag beside him so he could scratch at it to release his nerves. Instead, he tapped a few fingers on the cool, polished floor. "My birth mother and my adoptive parents taught me."

"And how did they know?" Cassius' father leaned forward.

"My birth mother was close friends with a dragon, so she learned through him, and my adoptive parents were dragons." Fendrel smiled, knowing it would sound ridiculous to them.

They've already laughed at me. What more can they do?

"Raised by dragons. It is no wonder you strive to keep them safe." The king tilted his head as he pondered. "Can you bring me one? Er, introduce me to one."

Fendrel raised his eyebrows. "Excuse me?"

"I want you to bring a dragon here and introduce it to us, if you can get one to come here."

What if I brought Mist in and had Zoricus free her? It would solve all of this right here. Fendrel's eyes landed on Cassius, and he realized what a horrible mistake that would be. *Zoricus or Raaldin could do something to hurt her, and Cassius would be under that spell again. He wouldn't be himself, so he wouldn't be able to help me get out of here. I can't be rash.*

Fendrel cleared his throat. "I-I don't think that's safe, Your Majesty."

"Are you afraid the dragon will try to hurt someone?" the king asked as a troubled expression crossed his face.

"I'm afraid the dragon is the one who will get hurt. You see, there's one other thing I need to tell you about Zoricus," Fendrel said. He could feel the knight's glare intensify on him.

"What now?" The king cast another scowl at his nephew.

Cassius stepped forward. "Father, I think it would be best if you dismissed the guards and ants for a moment."

The king gazed at his son. His mouth opened and by his expression Fendrel could tell the king was about to refuse Cassius' suggestion, but then he paused. "Very well, if that is what it takes to bring out the truth." The king waved his hand.

At the dismissal, each guard hesitated where they stood. Then, they left the throne room with the two servants in tow. Once the door closed behind them, Fendrel blurted, "Zoricus has been working with the dragon hunters, and we're afraid your other guards are as well."

Zoricus pointed an accusatory finger at Fendrel. "How dare you insinuate such an outlandish—"

Fendrel cut him off, "And I have proof that Zoricus has been threatening to kill you and your son." He stared up at Zoricus as he said, "I found your horse in those stables last night."

All at once the anger in the knight's face was replaced by terror. "What do you . . . I-I have no idea what you're talking about."

"I would advise against creating such horrendous lies about my family," said the king. His stony face was centered on Fendrel. "Zoricus is my nephew. He would never do such a thing to us."

Cassius reached for the king's arm. "Please hear him out."

The king shook Cassius off in a dismissive manner. "And allow your cousin to be accused of attempted murder?"

"*Please,*" Cassius said with more sincerity.

Something in the air shifted in that moment. The king took a long, suspenseful breath, and then looked to Raaldin. "You know what to do."

Raaldin's eyes twinkled with mischief, making Zoricus go pale.

Are they not working together? Why does Raaldin seem so eager to expose Zoricus' misdeeds? Is it so he can cover his own? Fendrel wondered as he studied the robed man. He wanted to warn Cassius about Mist. He wanted to tell the king how Raaldin was involved with her capture, but it was taking all Fendrel had just to keep focused under the stain's effects.

Just as Raaldin had drawn the truth out of Fendrel's mind earlier, he did so again. This time, Fendrel leaned in. He was eager to show the king how corrupt his nephew truly was. Now that Fendrel knew what it was like to be enchanted by the High Mage's charm, he was able to brace himself. When he reopened his eyes after the blinding light and Raaldin's chanting, he saw the halls of the Stronghold. It was a memory of the previous night.

Fendrel flicked his eyes between Cassius, the king, and Zoricus, then back again. Over and over until the memory ended. He saw Zoricus' empty stare, the king's growing distrust, and Cassius' mix of fear and vindication. When the projection ended, the room was silent once more.

"Young man . . ." the king began. "Am I correct in assuming the only crimes you have committed were in the defense of dragons you were trying to save?"

"Yes, Your Majesty," Fendrel said with his voice full of conviction. "You can search my memories for proof."

"There will be no need for that," responded the king. "You may stand now. Your questioning is over."

"Why are you taking his side?" Zoricus pointed at Fendrel incredulously. "You do not know him."

The king rose from his throne. "I am not sure I know who *you* are anymore. The Liberator's trial is *over*, seeing as he has been more upfront with me than you have. Now it is your turn." He walked to the edge of the pedestal. "How many of my guards are loyal to me and not to you or your outlaw allies?"

When Zoricus dropped his head without a response, the king continued, "Are you going to speak, or will I have to force the truth out of you?"

"I cannot say for certain how many obey you alone, Sire," Zoricus said with his head still lowered.

"Do not call me 'Sire' when you do not mean it!" The king shouted. "You threatened the lives of myself and my son, your future king, and you still expect me to see you as part of my family? I brought you in when you had nothing because your aunt, your queen, saw promise in your abilities." He shook his head in disgust as his lips curled into a

Kassidy J. Ridenour

snarl. "You have sorely disappointed her."

Zoricus' breath caught. His eyes darted to Raaldin, but the High Mage made no move to act on his behalf. "Do something," Zoricus pleaded.

Raaldin tilted his head like a bird of prey studying an injured, cowering rabbit. He shook his head, slow and unapproving. "My allegiance is to the throne."

"You're a snake," Zoricus spat.

"Enough! I will not have you slander my staff as well." The king gestured at the door the knights had disappeared through, and ordered "Cassius, tell the guards to apprehend him."

"Uncle, please." There was a look in Zoricus' eyes that made the hair on the back of Fendrel's neck stand on end. His voice lost all warmth it may have held as he said, "Don't make me do this."

The king scowled. "Adding more threats will only make your sentence heavier."

"You aren't giving me much of a choice." Zoricus rose to his full height. "It's true, I . . . I have been poisoning you, but I was only doing it to make this easier."

"Make what easier?" Cassius' face had drained of all color.

"That doesn't matter anymore. If I don't kill you, he will." Zoricus unsheathed his sword. "I just thought you deserved a more sympathetic executioner."

Fendrel went to slide his hand into his bag, then remembered it was no longer at his side. It was close enough where it rested on the pedestal. If he was standing and in good health he could reach it without a problem, but in his current state it would take him too long to brace himself on his injured leg and grab his bag, let alone dig through it for a dagger. Cassius or the king would have to toss it over, but their eyes were trained on Zoricus' blade.

"Cassius, I ordered you to call for the other knights," the king said.

Zoricus shook his head. "They're with me. Don't make this longer than it needs to be."

A stifling feeling filled the air. Fendrel stayed still, trying to formulate a plan. His thoughts were cut short when Zoricus spoke again.

"Cassius, if you had just stayed where you belong, we wouldn't be in this mess right now. If you hadn't gotten him—" Zoricus flicked the tip of his sword at Fendrel "—involved, your death would have been a lot more peaceful. You could have just succumbed to the poison in your sleep. Now it has to be violent, and you've doomed your father to the same fate."

The king looked at the High Mage. "I command you to stop him."

Raaldin ducked his head. "I apologize, my liege, but my magic does not work like that." Before anything else could be said, Raaldin was consumed by gray sand that seemed to explode out from his hood. The sand cocooned him in a whirlwind and within a second, the sand and Raaldin had vanished.

As Zoricus, the king, and Cassius gawked at where Raaldin once stood, Fendrel realized the opportunity that had presented itself. He inched toward his bag.

Zoricus turned his head toward Fendrel. He raised his sword and readied to strike. "This is even more your fault than Cassius'."

Fendrel lunged for his bag and brought it to his chest. He heard the clang of Zoricus' sword striking the ground behind him. When Fendrel rolled out of the way and got to his feet, he saw Zoricus about to attack once more. Daggers were much better suited for Fendrel's infiltrations of the dragon hunters' bases, and thus it had been years since he picked up a sword. He did not even have one stuffed away in his bag.

"Cassius, get Adila! Tell her I need her help." Fendrel shouted as he dodged another swing from Zoricus.

"No! Are you insane?" Cassius locked his arm around his father's and backed away from the swinging steel.

"Just trust me," Fendrel pleaded. The tone of his voice must have convinced Cassius to look for the enchanted woman. Cassius hurried his father out of the room through a different door.

Fendrel shoved his hand in his bag and pulled out one of his knives. In this light he could still see a faint bluish trace of the knock-out liquid on the blade.

If Zoricus is right about the other guards being more loyal to him, then this is our only chance at escape, he thought.

He wished he had more time to take the last two pain killing berries, but Zoricus was advancing once again. Fendrel tossed his bag to the side and widened his stance as best he could. His wound pulsed with pain, but Fendrel tried to ignore it. He had fought other members of the royal guard before, but this would be his first time facing off against their commander. Fendrel hoped the stars would be in his favor.

CHAPTER 36: FENDREL

IT WAS NOT JUST ZORICUS' sword and Fendrel's leg injury that he was worried about. Zoricus was taller than any man Fendrel had ever faced, with Fendrel himself being about two heads shorter than the knight.

Fendrel barely had time to make sure Cassius was gone before Zoricus rushed forward and kicked him onto his back. "You are *not* getting away from me this time!"

The impact made Fendrel gasp for breath. He was lucky not to have landed on the pedestal step, but the ground was still hard and unforgiving. Fendrel managed to suck in a breath, but it was forced out of him when Zoricus slammed his knee down on his chest.

Zoricus ripped Fendrel's knock-out blade from his grip and tossed it away. He pinned both of Fendrel's hands above his head with just one of his own. Zoricus then raised his sword in his free hand, ready to plunge it into Fendrel's chest.

Fendrel gathered his strength and wrenched his wrists free. He punched Zoricus in the jaw and twisted out from under his knee while the taller man reeled. Fendrel pushed himself to his feet and darted for his dagger. His hand closed around the hilt.

If I can cut him just once, it'll be over, Fendrel told himself.

Whirling toward Zoricus with his dagger at the ready, Fendrel saw the knight advancing once more. Just as Zoricus flourished his blade, a woman's voice called out, "Zoricus? What are you doing?"

Only when Zoricus stopped his pursuit did Fendrel allow himself to glance at the lady. She was a young blonde who looked to be Cassius' age wearing a regal, fluffy gown.

This must be the princess, Fendrel thought. He stared at Zoricus in anticipation. *Is he going to try and kill me with her as a witness?*

Zoricus' mouth gaped. He straightened up. "Sadie."

The princess stood at the edge of the throne room with her hand braced apprehensively against the doorframe. She said with a voice full of nerves, "I was told Cassius came back home." She looked between Fendrel and Zoricus. "What is happening? Where are Father and Cassius?"

"This man snuck in to assassinate them!" Zoricus pointed his sword at Fendrel.

"He's lying!" Fendrel shouted in surprise. He turned his gaze toward Sadie. "I'm a friend of your brother's."

Sadie glared at Fendrel. She bunched the skirt of her dress with her fists and took a few purposeful steps toward Fendrel. "Cassius has never mentioned you before. What have you done with him? Where is he?"

"Wait," Mist called out. Still trapped in her prison of a human body, she emerged behind Sadie. Cassius was at her side, covering his eyes with his hands.

Blocking your vision seems to do the trick against Raaldin's magic, Fendrel realized. *I hope he doesn't find a way to work around that.*

Mist gently grasped Sadie's arm as she said, "He *is* Cassius' friend. I can attest to that."

"Adila, Sadie, it isn't safe for you here." Zoricus narrowed his eyes at Mist, as though he were talking solely to her. He commanded in a harsh tone, "You need to go, *now.*"

I need to stop him while he's distracted! Fendrel urged himself to move.

The only places Fendrel would be able to slip his blade were between the joints in Zoricus' armor. He could try to cut near Zoricus' neck, but Fendrel did not want to risk a near-out-of-reach target, especially on such a vulnerable body part. He needed to be precise and swift, or he would never get another chance.

Fendrel tightened his grip on the dagger. As Zoricus continued to demand that Sadie and Mist leave, Fendrel struck at the space between Zoricus' chest plate and shoulder guards. He felt the blade's resistance as it sliced into flesh, and the knight staggered back with a yelp.

Zoricus grasped his injury with a wild look in his eyes. "You filthy criminal. I'll have your head for that!"

Sadie gasped. "Stop that! Both of you, stop, please. You're acting insane!"

Mist held onto Sadie's arm to tried and keep her from intervening, despite the princess' attempts to get away.

Fendrel kept his eyes on Zoricus. He watched the knight start to sway a little.

"What did you do to me?" Zoricus stared at Fendrel's dagger. "Did you just poison me?"

"Nothing you won't sleep off," Fendrel answered. He could tell by the look on Zoricus' face that the taller man did not believe him. As Zoricus tried and failed to lift his sword for one final strike, Fendrel charged and threw his shoulder against Zoricus' chest plate. Pain flared where he made contact with the metal, but Fendrel barely felt it through his growing elation.

Zoricus crashed to the ground. His sword clattered out of reach as his eyes shut. Sadie screamed and ripped free from Mist. She rushed to Zoricus' side, stooping down to get a better look at his face. Fendrel paid her no mind as a small metallic object flew from a pouch around the knight's waist.

Fendrel limped toward the metal piece and bent down to pick it up. It was a key, much smaller than any Fendrel had ever seen before. When his fingers pinched it to pry it from the ground, the stain reemerged.

This is it, Fendrel thought as he squinted through his headache. He tossed the key to Mist, who caught it between her two hands.

Sadie watched Mist cradle the key in her palms. The princess asked, "Adila, what is that?" Then, her gaze switched to Cassius. There were tears rolling down her cheeks, and she clutched her dress skirt for comfort. "And why aren't you doing or saying anything? What is happening? Where is Father?"

Mist fumbled with the tiny key as she twisted it into her pendant. There was a resounding click, and a sudden burst of the pendant's magic assailed Fendrel with the stain once more. It was intense. Not as all-consuming as when Raaldin himself pressed the eye symbol to Fendrel's forehead, but more blinding and head-pounding than when Fendrel met Mist in the garden. Then, it was gone.

With elated tears bubbling into her eyes, Mist smiled. Her necklace dissolved into a string of vapor that grew until it was thick and large enough to enshroud her imprisoned body. Even as it enveloped her, it kept growing taller and darker.

Fendrel watched the morphing silvery shape in awe. As the cloud dissipated, Adila was nowhere to be found. In her place stood a tall, sinewy Vapor dragon with blue-gray fur that coiled down her form like wispy tendrils.

Cassius hesitantly took his hands away from his face and opened his eyes. Upon seeing Mist, his breathing began to quicken with fear. The prince reached for Fendrel, but he was too far and his hand grasped at empty air. "I think I am hallucinating!"

Fendrel shook his head. He explained, "You're not. I tried to tell you about her earlier, but I got escorted here before I could find you."

"I—" Sadie rose from her place beside Zoricus and staggered backward. She had gone pale. Cassius made his way to his sister to keep her from falling, but his eyes were on Mist the whole while. His hands on Sadie's shoulders were the other things keeping her from collapsing. Sadie muttered, "I don't understand . . ."

"Neither do I." Cassius looked to Fendrel with a bewildered, quizzical expression.

"Zoricus said they hid her where no one would think to look." Fendrel gestured at the thin dragon. "This is Mist."

"Cassius, you must tell me everything that's going on," Sadie demanded, still crying, and visibly trembling.

"And I will . . . I just—" Cassius shook his head. He glanced at Fendrel again. "You are telling me this whole time my fiancée was a dragon? And Zoricus was going to force me to *marry* her?"

Sadie turned to face her brother. "Cassius, please . . ."

The prince held her hand reassuringly. He gave one final look to Mist and Fendrel, then pointed through the doors the knights had used earlier. "Go down the hall and to the left. There is going to be another false wall, like in the garden. Keep on straight through the tunnel and you will get to the grove."

Fendrel nodded. "Thank you. Keep your wits about you, and make sure he gets locked up," he said as he jutted his chin at Zoricus.

Cassius gave Fendrel a brief smile. "Most definitely."

In a gentle tone, Fendrel gestured for Mist to follow him, as he said, "Come on. Let's get you home."

It took Fendrel a few seconds to locate the light stone among the clutter in his bag. Once it was in his palm, it sparked to life. Cassius' instructions were true, and Fendrel began to lead Mist through the dark, cold, stony passages that ran underneath the city.

"How did you find me?" Mist asked, shakily. Her voice was a bit deeper than Fog's, but still held the lilting tone of what Fendrel recognized as a northern Drake-tongue accent. He had developed the same accent growing up with the Inviers, though his seemed to fade in and out depending on who he was interacting with. Fendrel made sure not to cover it as he spoke to Mist.

"It wasn't easy," Fendrel said. He looked up at her with a grin.

Mist was also taller than Fog. Her legs were a bit longer and she held her neck straighter, whereas Fog's neck always seemed to be arched like a swan's.

Fendrel continued, "It took us the better part of a week, and from what I understand you went missing several days before your sister told me about you."

"Oh, Fog." Mist smiled to herself. "How did she manage to find you?"

"Well . . . she got captured," Fendrel answered. "Not on purpose. She was looking for you by herself when dragon hunters caught her."

The fur on Mist's nape raised as her eyes widened. "Was she hurt?"

"She was, but a friend of mine was able to heal her right after," Fendrel said. "I found Fog the same day she had been taken, so she wasn't in trouble long."

"Thank the stars." Mist breathed a heavy, burdened sigh. "I do not think I would be able to forgive myself if she had gotten hurt on my account."

"She's very brave," Fendrel responded with a nod. For a moment, he pondered how much he should divulge of the danger they ran into during their travels. He did not want to get Fog in trouble due to his words. "She faced down dragon hunters and rogues just to make sure you were safe."

"Did she?" Mist asked, with a laugh halfway between astonishment and worry. "Did she come to the city with you?"

"Not inside." Fendrel shook his head. "She's in the grove around the city, waiting with Venom."

"And . . . Cloud?" the older Vapor dragon's voice was hesitant as if she were afraid of the answer.

Fendrel had not thought much of the dragon king since he left the Hazy Woods. He tried to recall how Cloud looked the last time he saw him. Fendrel said, "He wanted to search for you, too, but the nobility convinced him that he was needed at home."

Mist nodded, accepting Fendrel's answer. "He did not sound angry with me, did he?"

"Not angry," Fendrel reassured with a slight shake of his head. "Just worried that he had scared you off with the responsibilities you were about to take on."

The blue-gray dragon groaned. "All this was so ill-timed."

"It's over now." Fendrel smiled at her once more.

Just ahead at the edge of the enchanted stone's light was the staircase that bridged the space between the surface and the tunnels. It was shut, just as they had left it. Fendrel pocketed the stone and braced both hands against the trap door. He pushed as hard as he could and sent the door swinging upward.

"Venom, Fog, I'm back," Fendrel called as he led Mist up the stairs. He kept it ajar, so Thea would not have to push it open when she finished her search.

Fendrel guided Mist through the dense grove, thankful that the shade hid the blinding light of the setting sun from his eyes.

"You are back early," Venom remarked, though Fendrel could not see him yet.

"Did your pain medicine wear off too soon?" Fog asked, equally hidden behind the trees.

"Almost, but that's not why I'm back." Fendrel could not help the grin that infectiously spreading from the corners of his lips. When he pushed past another layer of foliage and overhanging branches, he saw Venom and Fog. Fendrel stepped aside and let Mist enter before him.

Both dragons' faces contorted in confusion. Fog stood immediately, but her legs locked before she could take a single step. The younger dragon's wings dropped like weights, and she forced out a single word, "Mist?"

"It *is* you—" Before Mist could finish, Fog was barreling toward her. Mist caught her sister in her wings with a burst of laughter. "Be careful with those claws, little dove! You almost cut me."

Fog could not speak. She buried her face in Mist's neck and sobbed, her wings awkwardly overlapping the older dragon's.

Fendrel felt a weight being lifted from his chest. He sighed with relief and leaned his shoulder against a tree to keep the pressure off his injury.

Venom nearly enveloped both Vapor dragons in his vast, black wings as he said a hushed, "It is good to see you again, and safe."

Then, Venom took to Fendrel's side. He watched Fendrel fish the last of the pain-killing berries out of his bag to eat them. "You will get another treatment tonight," Venom promised. "And again in the morning."

With a nod of understanding, Fendrel once again felt the pain in his leg ebb away to an ache.

"Where are Thea and Cassius?" the Dusk dragon asked.

"I wanted to get Mist out as fast as possible, so Thea doesn't know Mist is here. She's still looking for her." Fendrel adjusted his footing. "Zoricus gave Cassius and I some trouble, which got him arrested. Cassius is probably debriefing his family on everything right now."

"Then once Thea returns, we will make our way back to the Hazy Woods." Venom laid down. "Charles and Oliver will be fine with my tribe until Mist is home, then we will retrieve them."

"Oh, Mist, you are going to love them. They are *humans*." Fog squealed. "Can you believe it? I made human friends!"

"Yes, I can see that, dove." Mist let Fog out of her embrace so she could look her over. "How many?"

"Well, you already met Fendrel." Fog gestured at Fendrel with her wing. "He also has a mage friend, Thea, who helped us while we were looking for you. And in Black Brick Ruins we have two more friends who also wanted to help. One of them was a little scary at first, but he has proven to be a worthy companion. The other one is a child."

"You will get to meet them soon, but for tonight we must rest and prepare for the journey home," Venom said.

Fog and Mist laid down across from each other. The younger sister talked with more excitement than Fendrel had ever seen from her. She caught Mist, who smiled as she listened, up to speed on the past several days.

Fendrel sunk down with his back against the tree. He stretched his leg flat and kept an ear out for Thea's return.

We did it, Fendrel thought with a small smile. *We saved her . . . I suppose I'm not a failure after all.*

CHAPTER 37: FENDREL

THEA WAS MORE THAN A bit miffed when she emerged from the tunnels to find Fendrel had returned well before her. The mage's disappointment, however, evaporated when she saw the new dragon in their midst.

Once night fell, soon after her return, Fendrel found it difficult to sleep, more so from his excitement that the mission was over than from his pain. His leg had been treated once more, and again in the early hours of the morning when Venom awoke the group.

Flying back to the Hazy Woods was shorter than Fendrel remembered it being. The last leg of their adventure was filled to the brim with conversations between the Vapor dragon sisters. As the sea of pine trees and endless, dense mist fast approached, Fendrel prepared himself for the weather inside. It looked as if a giant, invisible shield was keeping the rain from the Hazy Woods out of the plains beyond. When they crossed the tree line, Fendrel welcomed the tickle of cool raindrops on his skin and in his hair. He pulled his cloak out from his bag, happy to have an excuse to wear it.

The tall silhouettes of the pillared cliffs stood out from the vapor as the group flew nearer to the Meeting Cliff. Venom flew as straight and as gentle as he could manage, but the jolt of pain in Fendrel's leg was unavoidable when the Dusk dragon landed on the outstretched platform. Venom rushed under the shelter of the hypaethral palace with Fog and Mist following suit.

The humans dismounted in the threshold. Though it was not yet midday, the gloom outside made the hallway dark as evening. Cloud's voice carried a greeting to them from the main chamber, where he sat behind the circular table. When the group made their way through the hall, Cloud's wings lifted with a hopeful look on his face. He took in Fendrel's limp, and the tired expressions each of them carried.

"Welcome back," he said, though he sounded a little crushed.

Venom was the first to enter the main chamber. He bowed with his wings spreading out at his sides. "Your Majesty, we found her."

From behind Venom, Mist crept into view. She froze once Cloud's gaze landed on her.

"Mist," Cloud said in a faltering voice. He broke away from the table and began to unfurl his wings. Before he could get far, Mist was already running into his embrace. The two almost fell backward as Mist buried her face in Cloud's shoulder and their wings overlapped.

Fendrel felt Fog's wing brush against him as she danced on her toes. By the giddy look on her face, Fendrel assumed her tears were those of pure joy.

Cloud cupped Mist's face with his paws. His ears pinned back with concern as he asked, "Where were you? Why did you go?"

Mist placed her own paws over his. She was crying, but her voice was clear as day as she spoke. "I just wanted some space before the ceremony . . . then I was chased away by hunters. They speared my wing so I could not fly."

The dragon king stretched out her wings with his own, only to find no injury.

"I ran so far, almost all the way to the Black Brick Ruins," Mist continued. She closed her wings. "They kept herding me away from anywhere I could hide, anywhere I could look for help. Then they caught up to me. They healed my wing and trapped me in a spell."

Cloud glared once Mist had finished. "What were dragon hunters doing in the Hazy Woods? They never come here. Fog—" Cloud looked to the younger Vapor dragon "—have you ever seen hunters here, even on the outskirts of the forest?"

Fog shook her head. "Not here. I have only seen them on the borders of our domain."

Venom made a thoughtful noise. His eyes narrowed in suspicion. "That is odd," he remarked.

Fendrel's lips pressed into a thin line as he pondered. "They must have planned this. Perhaps they didn't intend on capturing Mist, but just any female Vapor dragon to masquerade as a human."

Cloud stretched his neck higher to peer at Fendrel. He asked, "What did you just say?"

"We don't know why, but the dragon hunters kidnapped Mist and placed her under a spell that turned her into a human," Fendrel said. He rubbed a thumb over a scratch in his bag to help him focus. "The spell limited her speech as well. It seemed like she couldn't say a word about where she was from, who she truly was, or the fact that she was even under an enchantment."

"It is true." Mist nodded solemnly.

Fendrel approached the still-embracing dragons. "The hunters were working with some of the royal guard, and they took her to the palace to be married to their prince."

Cloud looked at Mist again. "You did not—"

"No," Mist assured Cloud as she leaned against him. "The prince ran off before the ceremony could take place."

"What reason would he have for doing such a thing?" Cloud asked.

"He was looking for me." Fendrel sighed tiredly. "It's a long story, but I remember hearing him say he didn't want to get married. Especially since he could tell something was off with Mist. The same spell that affected her was forcing him to behave completely different."

Cloud made a thoughtful, humming noise. "It seems your search was much more eventful than the other group's was. They covered their end with a day to spare and arrived here last night."

Fendrel suppressed a frown of disgust as he thought, *Even if we hadn't found Mist, they didn't know that. They were comfortable returning early with nothing to show for it?*

"Well, come join us." Cloud waved the group over with his wing. He walked beside Mist, entwining his tail with hers. As they settled at the head of the meeting table, Fendrel realized the size difference between them. Cloud, being royalty, was naturally larger than any other dragon of his tribe should be, with Mist being around half his size.

The Inviers said that whoever marries the monarch grows gradually with each shed, Fendrel remembered. *I wonder how long it will take for Mist to grow as big as Cloud.*

As Venom took his spot at the table, he gestured for Fendrel to sit beside him. Thea and Fog huddled around the other side, with Fog being the closest to her sister.

Cloud slid a disk of wood in front of himself and poised his claw above to write. He said, "I have already gathered notes from other nobles. Now, tell me what happened to you all."

"I do not know where to start," Venom said. He seemed to hesitate a moment, then continued, "We searched every dragon-hunter base we crossed just in case they had Mist. We did not find her at any of them.

We also asked Fragrance, but he did not know where she was either."

Are we going to tell them about our incident at Everspring Grove? Fendrel wondered. *Cloud is going to find out about it sooner or later.*

Venom's eyes shifted to Fendrel for just a moment, as if to tell him that they would discuss that later. Then, he returned his attention to Cloud. "There has been a decrease in the amount of dragons captured recently."

Cloud nodded. "That is a relief."

Fendrel made an unconvinced noise.

"Yes?" Cloud raised his head.

Fendrel shook his head as he answered, "I have a bad feeling about that. The hunters have never paused their activity before."

"Well, we will go into more depth later." Cloud stuck his claw into the bark. "Venom?"

"The hunters are also abandoning some of their bases."

Cloud continued to write.

"Fragrance—" Venom cleared his throat. "We may need to choose a new Flora noble."

The king arched his neck. "Is he ill?"

"It is difficult to explain, but we need to have a discussion with him about his position." Venom's wings shifted as though he was uncomfortable.

Cloud pushed the circular bark aside and stared at Venom with concern. "Did something happen with him?"

Venom looked down at Fendrel. "Do you want to tell them?"

Fog and Thea dropped their gazes while Mist's and Cloud's drew to Fendrel.

"I'd rather not say yet. Although if it's all right with you, I'd like to be there when you have the meeting with Fragrance, to explain what happened." Fendrel scratched the imperfection in his bag's leather with more ferocity.

With a troubled expression, Cloud said, "That is fine. You may join us then. I do not know when we will hold the meeting, however. We have been a bit behind schedule due to recent events." He sighed and recentered the disk of bark. "Venom, please continue."

Venom nodded. "A rogue spoke with us."

"Is that a joke?" Mist asked. Her eyes flicked between Venom and the others.

The Dusk dragon shook his head. "Write it down. And some of the human knights are in collaboration with the dragon hunters. Specifically, the captain of the royal guard."

Even if Zoricus has been removed from power, we need to keep an eye on him, Fendrel thought.

"I believe those are the main points," Venom finished.

Cloud released a heavy sigh through his nose and brought Mist in closer with his wing. "It is all over. We are safe again."

And I can go back to chasing the hunters soon. Fendrel tried to hide his longing smile.

"Ah, Liberator, I shall now complete my promise to you," the dragon king said.

"Promise?" Fendrel's brow furrowed.

"Do you not remember?" Cloud's voice was amused. "I promised that once the mission was complete, I would reward you for putting your personal work aside to help us. I suppose I should reward you, as well." Cloud smiled at Thea.

I was hoping he'd forget. Everything I did was my responsibility. I don't need a prize for that. Fendrel thought he would feel different after saving Mist. He thought he would feel more accomplished, but he realized he did not. Some piece of him felt missing. *Is it because the hunters are still out there? Why do I still feel like this isn't over?*

"Reward?" Thea's head perked up.

"Can I think about it a little longer?" Fendrel gave the dragon king a sheepish grin.

"You may, but you are not leaving the Hazy Woods without your reward." Cloud steeled his gaze.

Fendrel bowed his head. "Thank you."

"And now you, miss mage." Cloud looked at Thea once more. "What is it you would like?"

Thea tilted her head as she pondered, then her eyes brightened as an idea seemed to strike her. "Would it be all right if I set up my shop in the Hazy Woods? Or at least nearby? I have a feeling dragons make nicer customers than most of the people I've been dealing with."

Cloud nodded. "I do not see why you would not be able to, as long as your business is fair."

"Thank you, sir." Thea clasped her hands together tightly.

"Of course. And thank you, *all* of you, so much." Cloud hugged Mist with his wing again. "Now, if you will excuse us, we are going to notify the other nobles. You can stay sheltered here from the rain as long as you like."

Mist bowed her head, repeated an endearing, "Thank you," and joined Cloud. As they left, they spoke in gleeful whispers.

Fog made a squeal of delight as she collected Fendrel and Thea in a hug. She opened her wings and looked at Venom. "You come here, too!"

Venom smiled and crouched to try and fit under her wing.

"Your knee is in my ribs," Fendrel protested, giving Thea a sideways glance.

"Oh well." Thea shrugged smugly. "You'll stay like this for as long as Fog wants to hug."

The Vapor dragon let them all go. "Oh, sorry. I am just so excited!"

Venom nodded at her. "Go ahead and let out your steam. I will take everyone to the guest caves."

Without another word, Fog shot out of the meeting room and through the long hall. Even from this distance and with the rain pouring outside, Fendrel thought he could hear her laugh of delight as she leapt off the platform.

When the Dusk dragon crouched, Fendrel pulled himself onto his shoulders using his wing as a foothold. Thea joined just behind him.

Fendrel tried to keep smiling, but something felt off. His expression faltered as he found he could not shake his troubles. He wondered, *Why do I still feel like I haven't done enough? I just completed the most important mission I will probably ever go on, but it felt like any other. Haven't I redeemed myself yet? Or was Fog right? Do I even need forgiveness for my time with the hunters?*

CHAPTER 38: FENDREL

A LIGHT BREEZE SHIFTED THE flowery vines that served as the room's door. Rock-carved shelves housed glazed pots and lanterns, offering a warm, calming light to the cozy space. Wolf fur blankets were neatly piled at the back of the room, waiting to be used.

As soon as Fendrel had been brought to his room, Venom proclaimed he would retrieve Charles and Oliver. Unburdened by the weight of human passengers, and unhindered by Fog's slower flying speed, he returned with the other two humans faster than Fendrel could have ever imagined. It was only early evening four days later by the time Venom was back, and Fendrel wondered if the black dragon had slept at all during his journey.

Oliver had been brought to Thea, who was no doubt telling the boy Fendrel's explanation of how he found Mist. He seemed much happier than he had days prior, when Fendrel took him from Sadon's grasp.

Fendrel had not moved much while he waited for Venom's return. He did not want to put stress on his leg when the Dusk dragon was not there to heal him, but staying in the room was not torturous.

He liked being alone, when he could choose it. What little time he spent outside was used to wash and dry his clothes while he wore a new pair. Sat in the stone-walled room, feeling the breeze on his skin, Fendrel held his dry clothes in his lap. They were riddled with rips and bloodstains, but not just from his encounter with Sadon at the Stronghold. He knew from experience it would be difficult to lift those stains from the fabric, but the holes he could fix.

Charles sat beside him in the stone-walled room with an alert look in his eyes. He was silent, and as long as Charles did not speak Fendrel was content to keep his own mouth shut.

Fendrel poked a needle through his pantleg where the crossbow bolt had torn through him. The Inviers taught him to sew when he was young. They relied on the practice to craft dragon-sized blankets from caribou fur, and their teachings had served Fendrel very well in sewing his own clothing and cloaks when old ones were too damaged to wear.

An almost inaudible sound came from Charles. Fendrel looked up to see the older man's tense expression. After pointing at the vine door, Fendrel asked, "Why are you staring at it?"

"Sadon." Charles kept his gaze ahead. "He never entered while I was in my room, but I always thought he might, just to keep me on my toes. Even now it feels like he'll break his way in."

"Hm," Fendrel hummed in acknowledgment as he continued to work the needle. "The royal guard barged in on me at a few inns. I had to jump out the windows. That's when I always opt for sleeping outside."

Charles continued to stare at the vines while Fendrel finished his stitching. After a few moments, the older man stood and retrieved one of the wolf furs for himself. He said, "I'm surprised you agreed to share a room with me after you've gotten used to living alone."

Fendrel shrugged. "I forgot what it was like having company. The only roommate I've ever had was Frederick."

Charles grimaced. "Was he as messy in your living spaces as he was in public?"

"Even more so," Fendrel said with a chuckle. "I used to joke around with him that I'd get married quick just so I could move out and never be forced to put up with his mess again."

A burst of laughter erupted from Charles. "I believe it."

Fendrel opened his mouth then closed it. He cleared his throat before he spoke. "You told me Frederick escaped, but you never *really* told me what happened to him."

Charles dipped his head. "I know, I'm sorry. I didn't want to upset you further."

"What do you mean?" Fendrel tugged at the new stitches in his clothes nervously.

The former dragon hunter sighed. "I never heard from him after he got out. He could never keep his mouth shut, and I was *always* stuck at Sadon's side. If Sadon heard about Frederick's whereabouts, I would have heard, too, but no news ever came. It's like he dropped off the edge of the world."

Fendrel slouched back against the stone wall. "So you think he's truly gone."

The Dragon Liberator: Escapade

Charles kept his voice at a whisper as he said, "Yes."

Of course he is, Fendrel told himself. *You know that. You've always known that.*

"How did he escape without a plan when it was risky enough just to get me out?" Fendrel asked.

"I had to run into a few walls and cut myself to make it look like he attacked me." Charles removed one of his gloves and pointed at a long, raised, white line on his hand leading up his forearm. "I went a bit too deep here. At first, I thought Sadon could see right through me, but he figured if you were good at pretending to be loyal then Frederick must have been good at pretending to be a horrible fighter."

Fendrel let out a hollow laugh. "He was pretty bad . . ." A silence grew between them. For a moment, Fendrel's attention turned back to the flowery vines and glimpses of serene forest that lay beyond them. He asked, "What are you going to do now that you're free?"

Charles shrugged. "I have no idea. I used to think I'd go out and look for Raquel and Josephine, but not anymore. Even if they miraculously forgave me, I'm not the same man they knew. I'm sure they're different, too."

"Why wouldn't they forgive you?" Fendrel's brow knit with confusion. "They don't know any of the things you did as a dragon hunter, do they?"

"I doubt it. But I'm sure they saw the wanted postings." Charles gave him a somber smile, as though a bittersweet memory came into his mind. "You know, I wanted to be a knight back then. I was in the training program. I'd already been given armor and a sword. On one of my training days, while I was walking to the guardhouse I saw some black-market dealers in an alleyway. I was young and foolish and thought if I stopped them or brought them to justice that I would get some recognition from my peers. Instead, I got blackmailed by Sadon."

Fendrel felt heavy, like if the floor were softer, he would sink right through it. "I had no idea."

"Sadon had his men follow me to training and then back home. I led them right to my doorstep and didn't even realize it." Charles cleared his throat. "So, no, I don't think they'd ever forgive me because I'm the one who put their lives in danger in the first place."

"I get it." Fendrel nodded. "You could always stick with me if you wanted."

"Thank you, but no thank you." Charles shook his head with a

308

scowl. "I don't want to go near a dragon-hunter base ever again. I'd like to never smell dragon blood for the rest of my life."

"Noted." Fendrel smiled. He turned his attention to the door as something appeared on the other side of it.

"May I come in?" Fog's voice came from outside the vines.

"Sure," Fendrel called back.

Fog poked her head through. "Oh, you two are staying in the front room?"

"The what?" Fendrel leaned forward, confusion lacing his voice.

"There's another room?" Charles asked.

"Oh, I am so sorry, we forgot to tell you." Fog entered the cave and pulled the pile of wolf furs aside, revealing a large wooden trapdoor. "There should be at least two personal rooms down there." She pulled the trapdoor open and sat before Fendrel. "May I speak with you for a moment?"

Charles gave Fendrel a slight wave goodbye as he made his way below.

Fendrel nodded. "Is everything all right?"

"Yes." Fog wore a sheepish grin. "Did you truly mean it when you said I could join you against the hunters once we found Mist?"

"Of course!" Fendrel sat up straighter. "And you're still dead set on joining me? Cloud and Mist will be able to find a new noble?"

Fog nodded, her seashell earring swaying. It was so small that Fendrel had completely forgotten she was even wearing it. "The royal family does not actually need a noble from their own tribe as long as there are two monarchs. So once they marry, I will not have to stay here."

"And you do realize that it's *a lot* of traveling and going without sleep," Fendrel told her.

"I know." Nodding, Fog smiled. "Oh! I should let Thea and Oliver know about their trapdoor just in case they have not found it yet. I will see you later."

Fendrel waved at her as she hurried out of the room. Through the swaying vines, he could see the evening setting in. After stuffing his repaired clothes in his bag, Fendrel retreated down below.

Fendrel jolted awake, finding himself curled up in a ball even though his

The Dragon Liberator: Escapade

caribou blankets were more than warm enough. He must have kicked himself out of slumber, because his leg pulsed with pain. It had not done so in a couple days, but now the throbbing was all he could focus on. Fendrel shut his eyes and willed himself to sleep, but that only seemed to make him more aware of his injury.

I don't have any more pain suppressors. I took the last ones after washing my clothes, Fendrel remembered. *Perhaps Venom will be able to do something . . . No, isn't he sleeping in one of the caves near the Meeting Cliff? I would have to climb all those stairs.*

Resolving that he would need to wait until Venom was in reach, Fendrel tossed and turned.

Perhaps I just need to stretch it out. He wondered for a moment if that would make the pain worse. Then he reasoned, *I might as well try, just in case it helps.*

Fendrel rose with the blanket still wrapped around him. He dragged his feet forward in a limp, out of his room and along the forked hallway beneath the trapdoor.

As Fendrel ventured up the ladder and lifted the trapdoor, he noticed how dark it had become. The only sufficient light in the front room shone from a few lanterns. Faint moonbeams filtered through the flowery vine door. Charles sat at the room's entrance, pulling the vines aside to peek through them.

Tugging the fur tighter around himself, Fendrel pulled himself up and shuffled to Charles. "Have you slept at all?" Fendrel asked.

Without looking Fendrel's way, Charles shrugged. "I tried."

"I haven't had much luck either." Fendrel sat opposite him and leaned against the cave mouth. The look on Charles' face told him the older man had been thinking about something troubling. "Is it about—"

His family? The dragon hunters?

"Them?" Fendrel asked, resolving Charles would talk about whatever he was most comfortable divulging.

Charles' eyes flickered as if he were thinking about his response. "A bit of both, I suppose."

"Hm," Fendrel acknowledged, too tired to press.

"Do you . . ." Charles started. He shook his head, as if dismissing whatever he was about to say. Then, he continued. "Is there anything I've done to you that I should apologize for?"

Fendrel sat up, surprised. "Why would you think that?"

"Well, if it weren't for me, you never would have been recruited.

Kassidy J. Ridenour

You would still have your brother, and I'm sure your life would be a hell of a lot more peaceful than it is." Charles looked at Fendrel with an eagerness in his eyes.

"I wouldn't go that far, especially about Frederick." Fendrel sighed, defeated. "The last time we spoke, we had a fight. I'm sure no matter if we had met the hunters or not, it would have played out the same way. It was only a matter of time."

We finally found somewhere we both fit in, and now you want to throw it away, Frederick had said.

"No matter what humans we ended up falling in line with, we still would have fought." Fendrel reached for his bag to drum his fingers on, then realized he had left it in his room. "He felt more at home with humans, and I felt more at home with dragons, but neither of us wanted to compromise."

"I see," Charles said with a frown. "Perhaps you always would have fallen out, but perhaps you wouldn't have."

"Do you think, if Frederick were here, he would have forgiven me for keeping Sadon's motives a secret for so long?" Fendrel asked, hoping Charles' answer matched his own beliefs.

Charles sighed. "I think you're too hard on yourself. You were protecting him, as best you could, and you were both young. Well, you're *still* young. You can't beat yourself up about it forever."

Fendrel gave him a small smile. "If that's the case, you don't need to apologize to me either, especially after everything you've done to help me over the years."

Charles let out a short, breathy laugh. "Well, that's one person I can cross off the list."

"Who else is on the list?" Fendrel inquired.

"Raquel and Josephine, if I ever find them again. I would say the families of all the dragons who died to the hunters, but that's far too many." Charles rested his head against the cave mouth. "If I turn myself in to the royal guard, I know I won't be punished like I should. Especially since they've been working with dragon hunters."

"I don't see it that way." Fendrel pulled a few vines aside to stare out at the forest Charles had been observing. "You were a prisoner already. I think you deserve to live freely now."

The older man gave Fendrel a contemplative look before saying, "That makes two of us."

Fendrel scowled. "What do you mean?"

"Like I said, you're too hard on yourself. It's almost like you're a self-made slave to fighting the hunters. It's endless and exhausting, and you're doing it all on your own." Charles shrugged. "Would it kill you to take a break every now and then?"

"I can't," Fendrel protested. "It's my responsibility."

"No, it isn't." Charles chuckled incredulously. "It's not your fault Sadon decided to kill as many dragons as he could. It's not your fault he manipulated you into joining. You have nothing to apologize for."

"I . . . I do." Fendrel hugged the caribou fur tighter around himself until it felt as attached to him as his skin. "When I returned home without Frederick, and I told my parents that he wasn't coming back, they shut down. They wouldn't eat anything I brought them. They barely spoke to me anymore. All they wanted to do was sleep, and one morning they didn't wake up."

"That wasn't—" Charles started.

"I should have tried harder to bring Frederick home. I should have knocked him out and dragged him with me if I had to," Fendrel interrupted before Charles could let him off easy. "If I had brought him home, he and our parents would still be alive."

Charles leaned forward. He said, with an intense edge to his voice, "You are not responsible for other's actions. You let your brother have his free will, and he did with it what he pleased. You need to give yourself some grace."

In the wake of Charles' words, Fendrel's mind returned to his brother's stinging accusations. It had been four years, but Frederick's sentiments cut just as deep as they had when he said them. *"Why are you sabotaging yourself?"*

Fendrel froze. He felt his entire body tense, but his heart was beating as if it were not tethered to his chest. Something felt different about that question now. It somehow hurt more, and at the same time it made more sense.

Why am I sabotaging myself? Fog said she couldn't see why I would need forgiveness in the first place. Charles thinks I'm too hard on myself. Why am I sabotaging myself? Fendrel bunched the blanket up in one of his fists. *I . . . I've never forgiven myself for failing, have I?*

A lump formed in Fendrel's throat, too big to ignore. It almost brought him to tears, but he pushed them down.

"Did someone tell you that it was your fault?" Charles asked as he scooted closer to Fendrel.

"No . . . It was me," Fendrel realized. "I've never forgiven myself for leaving without him. I thought, if I told my clan everything that happened, they would treat me like how I believed I should be treated for abandoning him. I thought they would disown me, but they didn't. It made me feel more guilty, like I had somehow deceived them into thinking I could do no wrong."

Charles blinked in astonishment. "So you started punishing yourself because they wouldn't?"

Fendrel wanted to refute, but when he took a moment to let Charles' question sink in, he realized the former dragon hunter was right. He *had* been sabotaging himself.

"Even after they welcomed me back, I promised I would make *real* amends for what I did." Fendrel lowered his gaze. "Or at least, what I thought I did. But, no matter how many dragons I saved, I still felt like a failure. I thought I would be redeemed after I found Mist, but I still felt like it wasn't enough."

"Do you feel different now?"

"I feel like an idiot," Fendrel admitted. When Charles grasped his shoulder, Fendrel raised his head just a bit. "Why couldn't I see it? All these years I assumed I needed to gain everyone's trust back."

Charles shrugged. "Just goes to show that we all need people in our lives to steer us right. I'm free now, so if you need any more advice, you know who to talk to."

Fendrel paused for a moment, then he nodded. "Thank you. I'm sorry about how all this came out."

"No need to get twisted up about it." Charles leaned back to give Fendrel some space. "You know better now."

The two sat in silence, each one looking out the cave mouth at the forest beyond. A sudden chill sent Fendrel wrapping himself tighter in the fur. "We should probably try again to get more sleep. Oh, and in a few days, everyone will be here. It's mandatory for every dragon in the Freelands to a monarch's wedding."

That means Sear will be here, too, Fendrel thought. He rose and walked back to his room, satisfied to have found his leg had stopped pulsing. But when he laid down, the ex-rogue popped back into his mind. As he drifted off to sleep, his last thought was of the Fire dragon.

I wonder if he feels as guilty as I did. Perhaps I should ask him . . . perhaps I shouldn't be afraid of him anymore.

CHAPTER 39: FENDREL

FENDREL SAT ON A FALLEN log, looking out at the forest before him. It was a relatively quiet afternoon, save for the sounds of celebration deeper in the woods. A great number of dragons from all the tribes had glanced at him during the marriage ceremony, and Fendrel realized just how out-of-place he looked. He did not want his presence to take attention away from Mist and Cloud, so he stayed just long enough to watch until the end. Once it had concluded, he made his way down the stone-carved staircase that wound around the cliff's sides until he reached the forest floor.

Trekking down the stairs was not as burdensome as it would have been a few days previous. Venom was slowly increasing the amount of elixir he gave Fendrel. From the Dusk dragon's words, it sounded to him like there was less risk of his leg healing improperly now that he was on his way to recovery.

Not much time passed before Fendrel felt as though someone was looking at him. He turned his head, and saw Fog drifting between the trees, getting nearer with each second.

"Hey!" Fog greeted him cheerfully. She landed, her paws kicking up loose dirt and pine needles. "What are you doing out here? The celebration is in the *center* of the forest." She flicked her tail toward the Meeting Cliff. "Well, Thea and Oliver are in Sharpdagger to bring back the rest of Thea's stock for her shop, but they should be returning today! Besides that, why are you here alone?"

With a shrug, Fendrel twisted on the log, so he was facing her. "I didn't want to draw attention away from the ceremony. It must have been weird for most of the dragons to see a human in ance. How did it go, by the way? I saw most of it, but it was too far for me to make out."

"It was beautiful! I do not know how better to describe it and how *gorgeous* Mist looked." Fog's wings lifted with glee. Free from the stresses

314

of the past week, she seemed to hold her head higher, and her movements were more animated than before. "You should come back. I do not think you will be noticed much now that everyone is spread throughout the Hazy Woods."

Fendrel gripped the strap of his bag. "You're sure? I just . . . I'm not very good with talking in large crowds."

Fog nodded. "Definitely. If you stick with me, you will be all right. Hardly anyone talks to me at gatherings."

"Oh." Fendrel frowned as he stood. "Why not?"

"Well, my mother had a big personality and a reputation for caring more about humans than dragons." Fog gave him an awkward smile. "That reputation is stuck on me now, especially after the last several days."

Fendrel's mouth pressed into a thin line, knowing how hard it was to get rid of a reputation that had been forced on you. He nodded and said, "I understand."

"Come on." Fog dropped one wing out of the way. "I will fly you there. I promise you will have fun."

"If you insist," Fendrel said, though his brow knit with skepticism. He climbed onto her back.

The Vapor dragon spread her wings and crouched. She warned, "Keep your head ducked or you might hit a branch."

Fendrel pressed himself as flat as he could and wrapped his arms around the base of her neck. "Good to know."

Fog braced herself and jumped into the air. She climbed higher in the sky until they rose above the trees, then she leveled out her flight. Fendrel grit his teeth preemptively, expecting to feel pain in his leg, but after the treatment Venom had given him that morning, he found his ache to be much more manageable. He sat up and let the wind catch his hair.

"I am sorry I have not visited you much in the last few days," Fog said, tilting her head so she could see Fendrel. "I have just been so busy helping Mist get ready."

"Oh, no, it's all right." Fendrel grinned. "By the way, do you know where Charles went? I saw him in the morning, but he watched the ceremony from a different cliff than I did."

Even if he's not with the hunters anymore, his clothes might still smell like dragon blood, Fendrel thought. *I don't blame him for wanting to separate himself.*

"I saw him just before I came to search for you. He looked a bit sheepish, but I told him to go find Venom on the Meeting Cliff." Fog slowed her flight just a bit so she could talk without exerting herself. "I think it will be good for him to spend time around dragons in a friendly manner."

"He wants to learn Drake-tongue, eventually, so that will help," Fendrel said with a nod. As they flew, a realization popped into his head. He asked, "So, Mist is the queen now. Does that make you a princess?"

Fog almost stalled her flight at his words. She looked back him, then forward again. "I suppose it does," she answered mirthfully. "I never thought of that before."

"I should have bowed to you when you came to find me," Fendrel joked. "I guess I'll have to once we land."

"Do *not*!" Fog shouted back him, though her voice was jovial.

"All right, I won't." Fendrel chuckled. "Whatever you wish, Your Highness."

Fog shot him one last amused glance before she picked up her pace. The two drew nearer to the pillared cliffs in the heart of the Hazy Woods. Fendrel did not need to look up to know this was the clearest day he had experienced in the Vapor tribe's domain. The sun was shining, and with a smaller amount of mist than usual, Fendrel could make out just how many cliffs were spread throughout the forest. There were the larger, thicker, and taller ones that could be seen even in rainy weather, but there were also innumerable smaller pillars that looked to be used more for traveling along bridges than for housing. Every single cliff, small or towering, was covered in dragons.

Fendrel's breath caught. In awe, he said, "I never thought I'd see all the tribes in the same place."

"The last time we were united like this was during the War Across the Sea," Fog remarked. "At least is what I have been told. I was too young to remember."

As they continued, Fog let an updraft carry her higher. She glided past all the dragon-covered pillars, until she landed on the platform that extended from the Meeting Cliff.

Charles, as well as all the nobles, were there, resting just in front of the palace.

Fendrel got down from Fog's back and tried to ignore the stares he received from the nobility who had not been introduced to him. He bowed his head at them in greeting. "Hello."

"Hello, Fendrel!" Ember, the noble of the Fire tribe, approached him. Her amber earrings swayed as she walked. "Where have you been?"

"Not far. I didn't want to intrude on anything." Fendrel gave a slight smile to each of the nobles, but his grin dropped when his eyes landed on Fragrance.

Is he going to bring up what happened in Fresh Grove? Fendrel wondered. *If he does, he'll have to admit to stealing from the dead.*

"I see you are also friendly with the humans, Ember," Fragrance spat disdainfully. The Flora noble still had scratches and missing scales from his fight with Venom, but it appeared Fragrance had also doubled up on his jewelry in an attempt to distract any wandering eyes. Beside him were the nobility who Fendrel had not yet met, each one appeared antsy that Fendrel and Charles were in their midst, shifting their gazes between the two as if they expected an attack.

Ember frowned with annoyance. She did not bother looking at the lemon mimic as she said to Fendrel, "Don't worry about him, he's just jealous you've been invited to more Fire tribe festivals than he has."

"At least I don't fraternize with murderers," Fragrance mumbled.

Fendrel rolled his eyes. "Ember, don't—"

Not heeding Fendrel's warning, Ember whipped her head around. "Fendrel hasn't killed any dragons!" She looked at her friend. "Right?"

"Only rogues," Fendrel answered quietly.

"He's only killed rogues!" Ember made a triumphant face at Fragrance.

Charles nodded. He added, "In self-defense."

Fragrance scoffed and looked at Venom. "Rogues are quite difficult to deal with, I imagine, but is it not your responsibility to kill any *before* they reach humans? If so, how was he in contact with one? Are you that incapable of fulfilling your duties?"

"Oh dear," Fog said so quietly that Fendrel thought only he could hear her. The Vapor dragon was sinking lower and lower with each new input.

Venom glared at the Flora noble. "At least I care when my subjects go missing."

"Venom—" Fendrel walked over and placed a hand on his foreleg "He's just trying to get you to lose your temper."

With a sharp inhale, Venom seemed to absorb Fendrel's words. He nodded and said nothing further.

"I find it strange how you are able to trust humans so *easily*," Fragrance continued as he glanced down at Fendrel. "After everything they have done. They killed His Majesty's parents. They killed the rulers of the Fauna Wilds. They killed Fog's mother, who I thought you cared for oh so deeply. Surely, you are not so callous that you have pushed Wisp's murder out of your mind just to sympathize with humans."

Fog's quiet demeanor changed to one of anger. She joined Fendrel's side as she defended, "These humans had nothing to do with the War Across the Sea."

"Silence, Fog!" Fragrance snapped at the gray dragon. "You were a hatchling. You did not know your mother like we did." He arched his neck, trying to appear more poised than he was. "The humans captured, tortured, and murdered *thousands* of us. They think we are just animals. It is a disgrace that they are here in the first place."

Venom stepped in Fragrance's way as the Flora noble began to pace toward Fendrel.

The yellow dragon peered down at him. "I see my dear friend Fog has healed the scratch I gave you. Aw, but you must have thought it was a gash, due to your small size." He swiveled his head around Venom's leg, so he was face to face with Fendrel. "That is all I gave you, little rodent. Just a scratch."

"Step *away*," Venom growled through clenched teeth.

Fragrance cocked his head to the side. A malicious grin stretched across his face, revealing a row of sharp teeth. "You are too protective of him, Venom. He is an adult, yes? Is it not your tribe's custom for parents to send their children to spar so they may earn their place within the ranks of your tribe? If you consider him to be your son, then let him prove himself."

"What does he mean?" Fendrel looked up at Venom.

Even as Fragrance rose to his full height, he was still dwarfed by Venom. He kneaded his polished, glistening claws against the ground. A few drops of acid spilled from his claws onto the rocky surface. "Let us see, what are the rules, again? Ah, yes! The young one must fight a dragon twice his age, and it cannot be a relative."

There was a defeated look in Venom's eyes as he stared at the acid.

"How old is—um—what is its name?" Fragrance gestured at Fendrel.

Venom sighed. "Fendrel is twenty-two."

Fragrance's eyes lit up. "Oh, perfect! I am just about twice his age."

Fog stormed up to the yellow dragon. Her snarling snout was inches from his. "No! Fendrel does not have to fight you."

Fragrance flicked his ears back in disgust. "I see you have grown up to be just like your mother."

"Fog is right," Venom intervened as he placed his wing over hers to console her. "Fendrel does not have to do this. He is a member of one of the Ice clans. This trial you speak of does not apply to him." Venom crouched for Fendrel to get on. "Come, we are leaving."

Fendrel leaned and put all his weight on his injured leg. To his delight, he noticed only an ache. He still felt far from normal, but any stress he put on himself could be fixed almost immediately.

A petty thought popped into Fendrel's head. He asked, "May I fight him?"

"What?" Venom stood up in shock. "Do you not remember what he did—"

"He caught me off guard last time," Fendrel cut off the Dusk dragon, knowing if he let Venom continue it would spiral into a lecture. "I can beat him now. I've fought worse before."

"You think wrong." Fragrance's tail swished with anticipation. "But I would love to see you try to best me."

Venom looked between Fendrel and Fragrance, then back to Fendrel. "Your leg—"

"Is healing fine, great even." Fendrel tried to make his voice sound as reassuring as possible. "Do you trust me?"

For a long moment Venom stared at Fendrel. There was doubt written all over his face, but with a blink of resignation, Venom gave in. "Fine, but we are not doing this on a cliff. The sparring match will take place on the ground."

"I'll accept," Fendrel addressed Fragrance. "But this isn't a rite of passage. I already have a tribe. This is just a little competition."

Fragrance scoffed. "Nevertheless, we keep the same rules."

"Which are?" Fendrel asked.

"No attacks that will deal serious injury, though I apologize in advance if I fail to restrain my strength," Fragrance gloated. "The match will be over once one of us is able to pin the other for five seconds."

Fendrel nodded in agreement. He climbed onto Venom's shoulders and Charles followed him up, saying, "I've missed too much already. I am *not* missing this."

Once the humans were seated, Venom flew down to the moss-covered forest floor. Just behind him were Fragrance and the other nobility. After all the dragons had landed, the nobles formed a ring around Venom and Fragrance.

Before Venom could crouch, Fendrel slid down from the dragon's shoulders. When his feet planted on the ground, there was a slight jolt of pain, but it subsided within seconds. He gave the Dusk dragon a look as he said, "See? I'm fine."

"I still do not like this." Venom crouched to let Charles down. Then, he lowered his voice to a whisper. "I will never legally be allowed to spar with Fragrance, so break his spirit for me."

That dragon took my mother's headstone and tried to make me feel guilty for finding out about it. He did nothing when two of his children were taken by dragon hunters, and he never showed up to help look for Mist, Fendrel thought. *He deserves what's coming to him.*

With a grin, Fendrel replied, "I was already planning on it."

Fragrance ventured to the center of the ring. He threw his wings open, so they caught the sunlight. "Before we begin, drop that—" Fragrance commanded, pointing at Fendrel's bag. "You can only use your environment or your natural weapons, which, unfortunately you have none."

"Fine by me." Fendrel took off his bag and his coat, handing them to Charles. He kept his attention on Fragrance while Venom's and Charles' footfalls retreated to the ring.

It was chilly and crisp where they had settled. Overhead stretching branches blocked most of the sun while mist crawled across the ground.

Fragrance gave Fendrel a sly smile. "You are quivering. Are you afraid of me?"

"Afraid of someone named Fragrance?" Fendrel shook his head. "Don't flatter yourself. It's just a bit cold."

The lemon mimic scowled. "You should watch your tongue when speaking to a noble."

"Act like a noble and perhaps I'll start treating you like one." Fendrel rolled his shoulders in anticipation.

With a snarl, Fragrance whipped his tail toward Fendrel.

Fendrel jumped back, then sidestepped as Fragrance's teeth snapped inches from his face. Out of reflex, he punched the yellow dragon in the eye, splitting open his knuckles on the dragon's scales. In one fluid motion, Fragrance recoiled with a sneer then reared up and plunged his claws down.

With only a second to react, Fendrel rolled out of the way and stayed in a crouch, picking up a rock barely hidden by pine needles. He flung it, which struck one of Fragrance's horns, breaking the tip off.

"You impudent little—" Fragrance charged at Fendrel, knocking him on his back. While Fendrel struggled to catch his breath, Fragrance pinned him to the ground, his claws digging into Fendrel's shoulders. Fendrel cried out in pain as the acid within the lemon mimic's claws pumped into him. He gathered his strength into his legs and kicked the Flora noble's throat with both feet. Fragrance gasped and backed off, grasping at his neck.

Fendrel raced for a fallen branch as big as a sword and brandished it. The acid had started to burn in his veins, through his shoulders, his arms, and his chest. Fendrel grit his teeth. The burning was nothing compared to what he had been dealing with in his leg. As he stalked toward Fragrance, Fendrel could not help but wonder if the Flora noble had fought before.

He's quick, and he doesn't like any hits landing on him, even if the pain is temporary. That punch shouldn't have affected him as much as it did, Fendrel realized. *I can use that.*

Fragrance continued to cough as Fendrel approached. Fendrel gave him enough time to recover before he swung the branch at Fragrance's head. Not allowing himself to be struck, Fragrance bit down on the middle of the branch.

Running off of pure adrenaline, Fendrel found his body reacting almost on its own. It had been a long time since he had truly fought a dragon, and Fendrel realized he was acting purely off of muscle memory. He twisted and jumped onto Fragrance's shoulders, then grasped each end of the branch in his hands. Locking his legs around Fragrance's neck, Fendrel pulled back as hard as he could.

With his wings flaring out, Fragrance reared up and tried to toss Fendrel off. He roared against the wood caught in his teeth.

The pressure Fendrel put on his own leg was starting to hurt more than the acid, which was quickly wearing off. Angling the branch, Fendrel caused Fragrance to lose his balance and crash onto his side. Before the dragon could get up, Fendrel wrapped his arms around Fragrance's snout and held it shut. The Flora dragon tried to wriggle away, flapping his frantic wings and kicking, but his polished claws were slipping on the moss. Fendrel held him there, and right when he felt himself losing his grip—

"That is enough!" Venom stomped his tail against the ground.

Fragrance finally ripped his head free and spit out the branch.

The Dragon Liberator: Escapade

Venom walked toward the two. He said with a toothy smile, "The match is over."

Lashing his tail, Fragrance marched up to Venom and stuck his nose in the Dusk dragon's face. "This is not possible. He must have cheated!"

"How?" Fendrel shrugged. "I used the environment, like you said." As Fragrance sputtered, Fendrel accepted his bag and coat back from Charles who shared a victorious smile with him.

"This is a disgrace," Fragrance complained.

"What is?" Ember shouted teasingly from the ring. "You losing at all or you losing to a human?"

Without answering her, Fragrance retreated to a few nobles who looked displeased at the sparring match's outcome. Ember followed, poking fun at Fragrance's performance all the while.

"He is a human!" Fragrance protested. "He should not have won. He should not have been allowed to accept my challenge."

Hypocrite, Fendrel thought. His annoyance vanished when Fog gave him a congratulatory cheer.

"Where did you pick that up from?" Charles asked, astonished. He placed a hand on his chest. "*I* didn't teach you that."

Fendrel shook his head. "It's from sparring with my cousins. Ice dragons like playing rough."

While Fendrel was speaking, Venom lowered his head and sank the tip of his fangs into one of Fendrel's shoulders. Used to the prick, Fendrel did not flinch. He stayed still until the burning ceased. An itching sensation on his knuckles let Fendrel know his broken skin had healed as well.

"Are we done here?" Ember asked, seemingly satisfied with her amount of gloating. "I want to get back to talking with you. This *is* a celebration after all!"

Still high off the rush of the fight, Fendrel was content to pick their conversation back up, but out of the corner of his eye, he saw a flash of bright red. Fendrel turned his head, and his gaze locked with Sear's piercing white eyes. The Fire dragon stood a few paces away from where the nobles had been sitting. He was corralled between two massive Dusk dragons, either one strong enough to dispatch Sear in a heartbeat.

Fendrel glanced at Venom and asked, "Could you wait here a moment?"

The Dusk noble lifted his head and noticed the Fire dragon. "As you wish."

Before Fendrel could convince himself to turn around, he was walking up to Sear. He stopped a safe distance away. Sear appeared to take notice of Fendrel's hesitation, and he retreated one step.

"My family has a legend that all rogues were normal dragons once," Fendrel started. "Apparently the Dusk tribe also believes it. Is this true?"

Sear's balanced shifted, clearly uncomfortable with the question. "I used to be in control, I think. I had been in that state for so long I could not remember if I was ever free. My memories only started coming back to me when your friend—" Sear jutted his chin at Venom "—cured me. Even today, I do not recall much."

"So you don't know how you got sick?" Fendrel asked, knowing the answer before Sear could confirm.

"I do not." Sear shook his head. Even though Fendrel had suspected as much, he still felt disappointed.

Fendrel nodded slightly. "If you do remember, later on, could you tell me?"

The Fire dragon gave Fendrel a look of pure sincerity as he said, "Of course."

"Thank you." Fendrel glanced away, not knowing what else to say. He took a step back and nodded farewell. "I'll speak to you later, then."

Fendrel rejoined Venom and climbed on top of the Dusk dragon's shoulders. "Let's go," he said as his heart started beating faster with anticipation. "I have to introduce Ember to Charles, if she hasn't talked his ear off already."

CHAPTER 40: CASSIUS

CASSIUS LAY AWAKE IN BED, unable to quiet his racing mind. With Zoricus and his closest confidants in custody, Cassius had been sleeping well for the first time in months. However, he doubted all of Zoricus' allies were apprehended. That thought had been plaguing him all day.

One thing that always seemed to ease his recent anxieties was how his father's health had been improving with Zoricus unable to poison their food. Cassius was over the moon with how he no longer grew sick during his meals, and even more excited that he could walk the palace corridors without fear of running into Adila—or at least, the woman he had been told was called Adila.

The prince's mind reeled from the memory of what she truly was, and disgust bubbled in his belly when he realized he would have been forced to marry her if there had been no intervention. Still, Adila's lack of presence was an issue of its own. The king had asked where she went and why no one saw her go, but Cassius did not have the right words to offer an explanation. Afterall, he himself did not understand why Zoricus brought Adila to them in the first place. Until Cassius found out, he would keep his mouth shut about the situation. They all needed to recover, some more so than others.

Sadie never looked so drained. On several occasions she seemed to catch herself before mentioning how much she missed their cousin and Adila. It tugged on Cassius' heart to see her torn between her closest family members, but still, Cassius was glad to have sought help.

He rolled on his side, annoyed that no matter how many times he tossed or turned he could not find comfort in his bed. Zoricus' full trial was to be held the next afternoon. Cassius could not help but feel that even after Zoricus showed his true colors, the king would forgive him.

Footsteps sounded down the hall.

Have I been awake so long that the guards are already changing shifts?

Cassius wondered.

He turned again, facing away from the bedroom door, but then he heard it creak open. Four pairs of feet marched away from his door but were not replaced by more sets.

The prince reached under his pillow for the knife he had pocketed at dinner. He had previously felt foolish about keeping it for protection with Zoricus locked up, but now his nerves were shot, and he was thankful to have it. Afterall, Zoricus still had friends roaming free.

Someone walked to Cassius' bedside and stood at his back. The sound of a sword being pulled from a sheath rang in the prince's ears.

Cassius whipped his arm toward the intruder, but the knife bounced off a metal chest plate. He tried to jump out of bed. His constant tossing had tangled his legs in the sheets, and he fell, hitting his head on the floor.

While Cassius tried to free his feet from the coiled blankets, the intruder walked around the foot of his bed. His silhouette was framed by the torchlit doorway.

In desperation, Cassius cut the sheets with the knife, slicing his ankle in his haste. He crawled backward against a wall. "Who are you?" he asked in a frantic voice.

The swordsman pointed the tip of his blade at Cassius' throat. "Don't speak unless spoken to, or I'll cut your chords."

Zoricus, Cassius realized with horror.

"Where is Sadie?" Zoricus kept his blade still.

She is not in her room? That is not like her.

Cassius sat up. "Why would I tell you?"

Zoricus scoffed. "I'm not here to kill *her*."

"Then why do you—"

The ex-knight grabbed Cassius' neck and placed the edge of his sword over his hand. "*Tell me* where she is."

"I really do not know," Cassius answered in a cracking voice. "I thought she went to bed."

The sound of gentle footfalls approaching the door made Zoricus turn his head. His eyes went wide. "Sadie?"

"I didn't want to believe it." The princess' voice quaked. "Why are you trying to hurt us?"

"I would never harm you, Sadie." Zoricus took his hand off Cassius' throat and reached out to her. "I want to keep you safe, so I need you to come with me."

Sadie shook her head. She clasped her shaking hands to her chest. "No."

"There isn't much time left. We need to leave now," Zoricus said as he lowered his sword.

Cassius braced his foot against the wall and rammed his shoulder into his cousin. The knight fell to his back with a grunt. Cassius jumped over him, ignoring his stinging ankle and throbbing shoulder. He grabbed Sadie's hand, and they raced down the dim hallways.

"Someone, help!" Sadie called as she tripped on the hem of her dress.

"Shh!" Cassius stopped her in her tracks and cut at the bottom of her dress, more careful with her than when he had freed himself. "We do not know who we can trust."

"What are you talking about?" Sadie's voice was filled with more fear than Cassius had ever heard before.

"Most of the guards are more loyal to Zoricus than to Father." Cassius helped his sister stand and continued to run, her hand in his. "We have to get to the stables. From there, we can escape."

"Where are we going?" Sadie grabbed her tattered skirt to keep the uneven strands out of her way.

"We are going to find help." Cassius squeezed her hand in an effort to reassure her. "Wait, we need to get Father."

Sadie paused again. "No, I was going to your room to tell you—"

Cassius halted and looked back at her. "Tell me what?" Now he could see she had been crying a while, not just in the past few moments.

"He's gone, Cassius." Sadie's sniffles made her words almost unintelligible. "There was blood everywhere, and I went to tell you, to warn you, but then Zoricus was there—"

Father is . . . Father is dead? What does she mean blood? Did Zoricus kill him? Cassius caught himself with his hand on the wall before he could fall. His breaths came out in shivers of fear and rage. *I have to get Sadie out of here, but I cannot just abandon the kingdom. With Father gone I need to accept the crown. But . . .*

His eyes trailed down the hall they had been running through. It was dim and quiet. Even still, Zoricus could not be far behind. *Zoricus is free and so are his friends*, Cassius reminded himself. *It is not safe here. We need help.*

No, I cannot leave! Cassius told himself. *This crown, this kingdom is my parents' legacy. How could I run away instead of fighting back?*

He clenched the dinner knife in his fist. It felt so small and weak in his grip, completely useless in a real fight.

"We have to go," Cassius said, finally making up his mind. He grabbed Sadie's hand again and began to walk away. "We need the Liberator."

"What could he do?" Sadie matched his pace. Her nails dug into Cassius' hand. "He has no political power. Even if he did, how long will it take to find him?"

"I do not know." Cassius shook his head, checking every hallway they passed for guards. "But he is the closest thing we have to an ally right now."

Our deal is not finished yet, not until Zoricus is dead, Cassius thought. *I hope Fendrel does not go back on his word.*

CHAPTER 41: THEA

THEA OPENED ONE OF THE tattered curtains in her house just a sliver and peered out. Every part of the city was dark at this time of night, but the outskirts, where no lanterns hung, were even darker. Thea squinted to try and separate shapes from shadows to no avail.

Oliver ran up to the window excitedly. He lifted the bottom of the curtain and asked, "What are you looking for?"

The mage was quiet for a moment, her eyes searched the darkness. Then, she answered, "I'm playing a game called 'spot the stranger.'"

"Oh." Oliver smiled up at Thea. "How do you play?"

"You look for that pink-eyed man from Wing's Caress, and then you play 'keep away' with him." Thea closed the curtains and frowned at the holes that moths had eaten through them.

Oliver backed away from the window. In a meek voice, he said, "You sound angry."

Thea calmed herself with a deep breath. "No, Oliver, I'm all right. I just want to make sure he isn't here, and he isn't. That's a very good thing."

"Are you scared of him?" Oliver's voice was barely above a whisper.

Yes, but I don't want him to worry, Thea thought.

Oliver seemed to cower at her lack of an answer. "Should I be scared of him?"

"I just want you to be safe." Thea turned to the boy and crouched before him. She cupped his face in her hands as she explained, "Some mages choose to create spells that are dangerous. Raaldin is one of them, and even though he knows his magic hurts people, he still uses it." She moved her hands to his shoulders. "I want you to stay safe. I want to keep him away from you."

Kassidy J. Ridenour

The boy's lip quivered with fear. "But what if my magic hurts people like his does?"

Thea shook her head with a smile. "As long as you follow the rules, everything will be all right."

"There's rules?" Oliver's shoulders slumped.

Laughing, Thea stood. "Everything has rules, Oliver, and don't worry. For now, we only have one rule." She held up her finger. "Until you're experienced enough to do magic on your own, you must never *ever* create a spell without my help."

Oliver nodded with exuberance. "Does that mean I'm your apple-tense?"

Thea blinked in confusion. "My apprentice, you mean?"

"Mm-hmm!" Oliver nodded again.

"It does." Thea smiled warmly. She moved to her desk, where only a few glass vials were left. She stuffed them into her dress pockets and took a final look at her now barren house. Once she was certain the house had been cleared of anything important, Thea grabbed Oliver's hand and walked to the door. "I bet, with a few years of practice, you'll be a better mage than me."

"Really?" Oliver's eyes lit up.

Thea opened the door and let it shut by itself, the wood creaking as it swung. "Definitely. I didn't start learning as early as you, so you'll have a lot of time to improve."

Just outside the house, tied to a post, was a draft horse latched to a tarp-covered cart. Thea had rented them earlier in the day. In the cart sat her belongings and the rest of her spells.

"Thea! What a surprise!"

Raaldin, Thea thought with a shudder, wishing she had stayed by her window just a bit longer to see the man approach. She grit her teeth as a headache assaulted her. The stain combined with the darkness of night made it difficult to see, but Thea urged herself not to panic. Her eyes would adjust soon, and then she could leave.

Beside her, Oliver also had a pained look on his face.

"You must travel a lot nowadays. I feel like every time I see you, you're on the move. Business must be good for you this year." Raaldin stepped out from a shadow in Thea's peripheral. He tilted his head a bit when their eyes met. "Would you like to enlighten an old friend on where you are heading next?"

Thea gave him an unconvincing laugh. "You know how I like my private life to stay private. We should be going now." She squeezed Oliver's hand and helped him into the seat at the head of the cart. Then she seated herself next to him. Thea took the reins and urged the horse forward.

Raaldin matched the horse's calm pace. His eyes surveyed the two.

Dread and unease made the hairs on the back of Thea's neck stand on end. She kept herself from rolling her shoulders to ease her discomfort lest Raaldin see how his presence affected her. *All right*, Thea thought pettily to herself. *I can make him uncomfortable, too.*

"I *have* been busy," Thea agreed. "It seems you have been, too, what with your dealings with the dragon hunters."

"Well, it was an untapped market." Raaldin shrugged. "You know dragon parts lend more magical potential than other resources do."

"But what did Mist have to do with that?" Thea turned her head, so her gaze bored into Raaldin. She hoped the look on her face was as stoic as she was trying to portray. "Or should I say 'Adila?'"

Raaldin clucked his tongue in response. "I am afraid that is a private matter, my dear. Client confidentiality and all that."

"Right." Thea returned her gaze ahead, disappointed to have not drawn a more concrete response out of the older mage. As her mind struggled to come up with a new question to interrogate him with, Raaldin looked behind at the wide cobblestone street.

"Oh my," Raaldin said in a flat tone. "Something must have happened at the palace."

What? Thea's brow scrunched with confusion. She turned in her seat as horses' hooves clopped on the stones where Raaldin had been looking. It took a few tense seconds for Thea to make out the faces of those approaching, but when they neared, she realized it was Cassius and who must have been his siter.

The prince's eyes lit up with hope. "Mage!"

"Uh—" Thea studied the riders.

"Are you leaving the city?" Cassius asked hurriedly. He looked around as if he expected someone to be listening in on them.

"Yes, why?" Thea sat straight once again when the prince's horse was alongside her.

Cassius lowered his head. He whispered, "Can we hide in your cart? Zoricus—" he eyed Oliver "—did something . . . awful."

Although Thea had not been anywhere near the palace at the time of Fendrel's trial, he had filled her in on all that happened.

What did Zoricus do that would make both Cassius, and his sister leave so suddenly? Thea wondered.

She sucked air in between her teeth, realizing the gravity of the situation. "Get in. We were just on our way to the Hazy Woods."

Cassius dismounted his horse and helped his sister down. "Is Fendrel there?"

Thea nodded. "Yes. Everyone is. You're welcome to ride with us. Just tie your horse to the back of the wagon."

Once Cassius and his sister boarded the wagon, Thea urged the draft horse to pick up its pace. Looking over her shoulder, she realized she had not seen nor heard Raaldin's departure, but the mage was gone as if he had never been there.

CHAPTER 42: FENDREL

IT HAD BEEN DARK FOR a while, but Fendrel still stood with his back against a tree trunk. He leaned his head against the bark and closed his eyes for a moment, enjoying the stillness of the forest. It was a moonless night, and if it were not for the scales on Venom's chest, Fendrel doubted he would be able to see any of their surroundings. He grinned and said, "Thank you for bringing me here."

"Of course." Venom smiled widely. "You did a lot better than I expected you to."

Nodding, Fendrel thought back to his sparring match with the noble of the Flora tribe. "Do you think Fragrance will use what happened today as ammunition for our meeting with him and Cloud?"

"He might," Venom answered curtly.

"What happens if he refuses to give up his title? Doesn't the tribe technically belong to him?" Fendrel asked.

The Dusk dragon shook his head. "The tribes used to belong to their individual nobles before the first monarch united us all under one rule, but now the citizens serve the royal family first and their tribal nobility second. At least, they are supposed to."

Fendrel nodded in understanding. The quiet of the woods was broken by the sound of clomping horse hooves and the rumble of wagon wheels. Fendrel stiffened and peered through the trees.

Is that a merchant? Fendrel wondered. *What are they doing so deep inside the Hazy Woods, and why are they moving so fast?*

Venom lifted his head and sniffed the air.

Is that—?

"Thea?" Fendrel ran to try to catch the mage's attention, waving his arms over his head. Oliver, sat next to Thea, waved back while the mage pulled on the horse's reins to halt it.

"You two were in a hurry." Fendrel walked closer to them.

The tarp over the cart rustled and Cassius stumbled out. Behind him, the princess pulled back the tarp so she could sit up.

Fendrel frowned as a sinking feeling took hold of his heart. "What are you doing here?"

Cassius limped toward Fendrel. Dried blood caked his ankle. "Zoricus just killed my father and tried to kill me, too!"

Thea clapped her hands over Oliver's ears.

Fendrel caught Cassius by the arm just as the prince was about to fall. He said, "Hold on, I thought Zoricus was brought to the dungeons. How did he get to you?"

"His friends must have freed him. The guards posted outside my room were in on it. They let him in." Cassius held his injured foot off the ground. "And he was trying to take Sadie somewhere."

The princess stayed in the cart. Her eyes looked distant, glazed over, and she was not moving. If she had not been sitting upright Fendrel might have believed she was dead.

"Cassius, calm down." Fendrel grabbed the prince's shoulders and forced him to still. "Start over."

Cassius took a deep breath. "My father was killed, and I think Zoricus was trying to get rid of me so he could take the crown for himself. I do not know who is on his side or if *I* even have people on *my* side, so we came here looking for you, and I do not know if you can help, but I just really, really need somewhere safe right now." He took another gasping breath. "He kept trying to convince Sadie to leave with him, like it was not safe for her to be in the palace."

Fendrel felt cold all over. He loosened his grip on Cassius' shoulders.

Zoricus was working for Sadon, and they were planning something that involved killing Cassius. Was Sadon trying to get Zoricus to be king?

Venom growled. His spines bristled and he bared his teeth. He was looking somewhere off into the forest.

"What is it?" Fendrel turned to the Dusk dragon.

"I smell fire." Venom flicked his ears back. He crouched. "It does not smell large, but we should still check on it."

Fendrel pulled himself onto Venom's shoulders. He looked at Thea and asked, "Can you take Cassius and Sadie to the others?"

Thea nodded. She removed her hands from Oliver's ears and waited for Cassius to board before moving the horse into a trot.

The Dragon Liberator: Escapade

Venom flew low until he found a break in the tree canopy large enough to fly through. Fendrel looked down as Venom neared the tree line. A group of horsemen with torches were riding away from the Hazy Woods. The Dusk dragon growled again. He swooped a bit lower.

Fendrel squinted. From the torchlight he noticed each horseman had dragon teeth sewn to their gray leather shoulder guards. "Dragon hunters," Fendrel said as he gripped the spines on Venom's neck.

The Dusk noble stopped his pursuit so that he and Fendrel would not be seen should one of the horsemen look back. He turned and flew in the direction of the cliffs. "We should send someone to follow them."

By how aggressive the wind rushed by, Fendrel guessed this was the fastest Venom had ever flown with him on his back. They reached the Meeting Cliff's platform quicker than Fendrel ever had with Fog. As they landed, Fendrel saw Charles and the nobles by the palace's opening.

With Fendrel still perched on his shoulders, Venom approached the others. He nodded slightly at the nobles of Spark and Air, who approached with attentiveness. Venom kept his voice low. "I will compensate you with whatever you wish if the two of you follow the horsemen riding away from the Hazy Woods and observe them for a while."

The Air noble bowed his head. "I do not need compensation. Your faith in my abilities is enough payment."

Following the Air dragon's lead, the Spark noble nodded. "We will do our best."

Venom returned the gesture, grimly. "Thank you, both of you. Please report to me when you are finished. I do not want to worry His Majesty if nothing turns out to be amiss." With a wave of his wing, the other two nobles took off.

Fendrel watched them leave. He asked, "What do we do about Cassius and his sister?"

The Dusk dragon peered over the Meeting Cliff's edge. "We need to learn what happened to them, after the prince calms down."

Nodding, Fendrel offered, "We'll take them to my room."

"What is going on?" Charles came up beside the two.

"Cassius is here." Fendrel tried to keep his face calm. "Something happened at the palace."

Charles raised his eyebrows in interest. "May I join you?"

"Yes, but we must hurry." Venom took off once Charles was seated. Upon arriving at the ground-level room Fendrel and Charles

334

shared, Venom left to retrieve Thea.

"I assume this isn't a good thing that Cassius is here?" Charles pushed the vine door aside and walked in the cave.

"Not at all." Fendrel followed him inside. "He was talking pretty fast, but from what I gathered, he was attacked by Zoricus. His sister is here too."

Charles sighed. "*Fantastic*," he said sarcastically.

Fendrel went to the threshold and held the vines open, peering out at the woods from his room. He stayed waiting until Venom and the horse-drawn cart came into view. Venom kept his distance from the horse so as not to frighten it, moving a bit behind the others.

Oliver's mouth looked like it was moving a million miles a minute, but he was too far away for Fendrel to hear. Thea appeared exhausted and weary. Once they were near, Thea stopped the cart and hugged Oliver against her.

Cassius emerged from the back and helped his sister out once more. The siblings trudged through the opening Fendrel made.

"Here." Charles brought wolf furs to the newcomers and gestured for them to sit against the back wall.

When Venom made his way inside, Fendrel dropped the vines. Cassius had wrapped himself in the wolfskin and was already seated. Sadie was beside him with a blank look in her eyes. Fendrel, Charles, and Venom crammed on the other side of the room.

"You said—" Fendrel cleared his throat "—Zoricus tried to kill you?"

Cassius nodded and took a shaky breath. He answered, slower, "He killed my father, and he tried to get me while I was sleeping, but we managed to escape."

"And he was trying to take Sadie away?" Fendrel felt weird talking about her as if she were not there, but the princess made no acknowledgement of his words.

"I do not know why." Cassius pulled the fur tighter around himself. "It was like he did not want her to be in the palace, but he wanted to stay with her. It is probably foolish of me to ask, but do you think you might know Zoricus' plan?"

Fendrel tapped his fingers on his bag. "As far as I know, his plan is the same as Sadon's. Back at the Stronghold, Sadon promised he wouldn't hurt Sadie as long as Zoricus followed orders. Perhaps Zoricus didn't trust him, or perhaps getting her out of the palace was part of keeping her safe."

Cassius paled. "What could he be doing that she would need to leave?"

"I still don't understand Sadon's plot, but I can guess he has Zoricus under his thumb so he can hunt dragons without hiding from the law," Fendrel said. He glanced at Charles, who made a thoughtful noise.

"Sadon was probably afraid you would reinforce your father's laws, so he wanted someone in power who agreed with him." Charles leaned forward a bit. "Right?"

"Perhaps." He rubbed his face with his palms. "This is horrible."

"Oh, was that why they needed Mist?" Charles elbowed Fendrel. "Sadon probably wanted to use a distraction—Cassius' wedding—so he could take over while the king's loyal guards were busy guarding the ceremony. That's why he's working with Zoricus! So he could infiltrate from the inside while everyone was distracted."

Venom cocked his head to the side. He looked unconvinced. "But why would they take Mist? She is a dragon."

Charles shrugged. "Sadon, for all his faults, doesn't like involving innocents if he can help it. Perhaps he thought using a dragon—a lesser being in his eyes—would make it so he didn't have to force a human girl to marry Cassius. The Hazy Woods is close to Sharpdagger, and Vapor dragons are smaller than other dragons, so Sadon must have assumed she was easy prey. He probably sought her out for those reasons alone."

The Dusk dragon snorted. "Well, Mist did not make it easy for them."

Cassius looked at the three who sat across from him. "What do you all mean?"

Fendrel leaned toward Cassius, ignoring his question. "But besides that, do you have a plan?"

"Do I—" Cassius stared at Fendrel for a few moments with a frustrated look on his face. "Do I *look* like I have a plan? I cannot fight. Zoricus has the public wrapped around his finger. *How* could this work out for me in *any* way?"

"You're right. I'm sorry." Fendrel held his hands up defensively. "But remember those servants who witnessed the trial? Won't they stand up to Zoricus?"

Cassius scoffed. "Not if they want to stay out of the dungeons and keep their livelihoods."

Venom stood, although he was hunched over to avoid hitting his head on the low ceiling. He made his way out the vine-door. "I need to check in with a few dragons."

Fendrel followed Venom out and kept his voice low as he asked, "Do you think those horsemen have something to do with what happened tonight?"

The Dusk dragon sighed. "I do. Stay here. Do not be reckless." He spread his wings and took off.

CHAPTER 43: FENDREL

FENDREL JOLTED AWAKE TO SEE yellow eyes peering at him. Venom's frantic voice came from the darkness. "Wake up, we need you."

"Wha-what?" Fendrel groggily got to his feet. The night air chilled him once he no longer had his blanket's cover. "What happened?"

"We are having a meeting, and we need you for a second opinion," Venom said. He guided Fendrel out of his room and toward the vine door's threshold. Then the black dragon retreated to gather Cassius and Charles.

While Fendrel shook his head to try and wake up, Venom returned with the other two humans. He flew them to the palace within the Meeting Cliff and directed them to sit at his side. All the nobles were present. Some nodded with respect to the newcomers, while others refused to acknowledge their arrival. Fendrel noticed the colder ones were those who had seemed to take Fragrance's side earlier. Cloud sat in his usual place with Mist beside him. Despite the different demeanors, everyone looked worried.

"Zoricus did not accept the crown," Venom started as he looked down at the three humans. "Instead, he gave it to Sadon."

Fendrel stared blankly at the Dusk dragon. "You're lying, he can't do that."

"It is real," growled Venom. He turned his gaze to the table they sat around. "Sadon has the crown, and it looks as if Zoricus is keeping his former position as the head of the royal guard."

Charles' breath caught. He mumbled, "I shouldn't have left them when I did. Perhaps I could have stopped this."

Cassius looked sick, but he stayed seated regardless.

Sadon? Sadon is the king now?

Fendrel felt his body grow heavy with dread. "This doesn't make any sense. Sadon was never power hungry. Why would he become king instead of allowing Zoricus to be coronated?"

"Because now, instead of breaking the law and having Zoricus scrub his record clean, he can change the law." Charles' voice rose in anger as he said, "He has the royal treasury to fund his operations, too, and he can force any knights under his rule into being dragon hunters."

"I fail to see how the affairs of humans have any bearing on us," Fragrance spat as he took a moment to inspect his claws.

Mist's ears flattened against her head with a scowl. "The leader of the dragon hunters is in control of the human kingdom, and you do not see how that could affect us?"

"Whether you like it or not, this *is* a dragons' issue," Venom said, allowing the contempt in his voice to carry across the table.

Cloud nodded curtly. "We cannot deal with this threat unless we are fully aware of what the dragon hunters are capable of. Can any of you give us an idea of how big a threat this is?" he asked as his gaze drifted from Cassius, to Charles, and then to Fendrel.

Fendrel shook his head. "I-I didn't even know he had the resources to take the throne in a single night. I didn't know he had the *intention* of taking over the kingdom."

"Neither did I." Charles had both fists clenched. "He was very secretive. For all we know, what he's done tonight could be just a small piece of his overall plan."

Cassius shuddered. He hugged his same blanket from earlier tighter around himself. "And now he has full authority over the High Mage."

A chill went down Fendrel's spine.

If I had just made up my mind about Cloud's gift and left the Hazy Woods sooner, I could have been able to stop Sadon, Fendrel thought. *Charles and Fog were wrong. I'm a failure, and now Cassius' family and all the dragons are going to pay for it.*

"I don't see why we can't just attack the humans' city right now and get rid of the dragon hunters for good," Fragrance said as he glared at the Fendrel.

"No!" Cassius stood, slamming his hands on the table. "There are good, innocent people there. You cannot attack. You may hurt them!"

Fragrance directed his vitriolic look at the prince, who sat back down. "We know where their leader is. We can catch him by surprise."

"I agree with Fragrance," the noble of the Ice tribe declared.

Venom's spines bristled in agitation. "Killing innocent humans without a care would make you just as bad as the humans who kill our kind for profit."

"Believe me, I want him dead just as much as you do—" Charles pointed at the Flora and Ice nobles "—perhaps even more so, but most of the humans in Sharpdagger have never even touched a dragon. If you want him dead so badly, why don't one of you fly me to the palace and let me kill Sadon myself."

Charles' arm will never be the same after it got crushed by the Earth rogue, Fendrel thought, recalling how tenderly Charles moved whenever pulling himself onto Venom's back.

Fendrel shook his head. "That better be a joke. With your injury, you're suggesting a suicide mission!"

"Who's to say you won't just betray us and warn him that we are aware of his whereabouts," accused a noble whose voice Fendrel had never heard before.

"Charles is trustworthy," Venom asserted.

Fog nodded in agreement. "He saved my life, and if it were not for him, we would not have found out where the hunters were keeping Mist."

Smoke curled from Ember's nostrils as she said, "I thought we were going to *avoid* wars, not start them. We all agreed to that after the War Across the Sea ended."

"We will not have to start a war if we cut off the head before the snake bites." Fragrance, clearly frustrated, failed to keep his poised position.

"Sadon's followers are too loyal to disperse if he dies." Fendrel raised his voice to match the others. "He's probably already chosen a second-in-command to take over if he dies early."

Cloud raised his wings, and everyone fell silent. The dragon king looked to Cassius. "I am sorry for the loss of your father, and I appreciate you for gifting us with your input." His eyes swept over all those gathered. "I will follow my parents' lead and avoid war if possible. If we cannot, we will carefully strategize how to destroy the dragon hunters without many casualties for both humans and dragons."

There was a moment of silence.

"What do you wish for us to do?" Venom asked.

The dragon king took a deep breath, then let it out slowly. "Until we are able to return the human prince to his kingdom, we may want to seek aid and council from our allies."

Allies? The dragons of the Fauna Wilds?

Fog's wings sank hopelessly. "But they could not win their own war against humans. How could they help us now?"

"Numbers or resources," Venom answered. "Although, I doubt they will be quick to give those up. They may need whatever they have just to survive."

Ember nodded. "Even if they could help us, we lost contact with them at the end of the War Across the Sea."

"Then we will just have to find them and ask for their help in person." Cloud's eyes met Venom's. His expression seemed pleading, as though he was searching for wisdom within Venom's visage. "Leaving the Freelands for a short while to recruit them is our only chance."

"Say we do send some of our own to reconnect with the Wilds' dragons," Ember started. "What happens if the hunters destroy the rest of us before we are able to receive aid? Are we supposed to sit and wait?"

"Not if we all go to the Fauna Wilds. They cannot destroy us if we are not here." Cloud looked about the group. His voice was still, but his eyes were full of uncertainty and a look Fendrel knew all too well. Fear that his peers would not trust him.

Many of the nobles mumbled unsurely.

"Leave the Freelands behind?" Cassius hugged his knees to his chest.

"There are a number of injured dragons back at Black Brick Ruins who can barely stand as they are. What do you suggest we do with them?" Venom glanced out of the palace's doorway.

Cloud followed his gaze. "How many?"

"Approximately a dozen," Venom spoke as if delivering a report.

"I am sure we can create slings or hammocks to carry them—" Cloud tilted his head in thought "—and any other dragons unable to fly. We can take turns carrying them, so the burden does not hinder our travel."

"Then you *are* being serious?" Fragrance straightened his posture.

"Yes," Cloud said in a more assertive tone. "Even if our allies are unable to help us, it is safer to strategize away from the conflict than it is to stay here. We are not running away. We are simply allowing ourselves more time to take action."

Fragrance scoffed. "You would have us abandon our home because you refuse to take the lives of those who threaten ours?"

Venom gave him a warning glare. "This is a complicated issue."

The Dragon Liberator: Escapade

"I agree, and one too complicated for our young king to handle." Fragrance left his seat, stomping out of the meeting room with his head held high.

Cloud had a mortified look on his face. Mist entwined her tail with his to give him comfort. In the silence that followed, the nobles of Water, Earth, Air, and Stone took their leave without a word.

Fendrel watched them go, disappearing into the dark of night.

They have no idea what they're getting themselves into.

"I hope they don't intend on storming Sharpdagger." Charles' words cut through the air.

"They will not." Venom's voice sounded like a dam holding back a raging sea. "They have always relied on the Dusk and Ice tribes to fight for them. They are not used to taking matters into their own paws."

"I hope you're right." Fendrel's voice came out quieter than he had meant it to.

"Your Majesty?" Fog gave Cloud an apprehensive glance. "I just want you to know . . . I do not think you did anything wrong."

Cloud's only response was a noncommittal nod. "I believe there is no going back now. We must set forth with our plan."

Venom sighed through his nose. "We can leave through the southern shore. It is the closest part of our home to the Fauna Wilds."

Across from him, the Spark noble gave an uneasy glance toward the hallway. "I and my subjects will follow wherever you see fit, Your Majesty, but I must warn you that sea storms are commonplace this time of year."

"Hmm. I thank you." Cloud still had a sullen look about him. "Would you and your tribe act as our guides and shields during our travel?"

"To draw the lightning away from the rest of you? Of course." The Spark noble thrust his wings back with pride. "It would invigorate us to do so."

Fendrel imagined how the sea must look during a storm, roiling and thrashing. He asked, "How long will it take to reach the Fauna Wilds?"

"It may take us an entire day, sunup to sundown." Venom tilted his head in thought. "Perhaps longer if we do encounter storms."

"And you can all fly for that long?" Fendrel asked, anxious to hear their answer.

"We must." Mist steeled her voice as well as her face. "For our survival, we must endure."

"Let us not waste any more time," said the Ice noble as she gave Cloud a nod of encouragement. "We will each take the time to explain to our tribes what is transpiring. From there, we will meet at the southern shore."

"I second that." Venom shared the Ice dragon's expression. "Focus on telling the Vapor tribe. Let us deal with the rest."

Cloud attempted a smile, but it faltered. "Thank you, friends. In times like these, a team effort is what we need. I can only hope the Fauna Wilds' dragons will aid us in our cause."

With that, the dragons rose from their seats and exchanged goodbyes. Fendrel's ears were filled with a muffled silence, as if his head was underwater.

This can't be real, Fendrel told himself. *This cannot be real!*

After a full day and a half of traveling, Fendrel sat in the sand. His head hung low, more from shock than exhaustion. After hearing a gasp from Fog, his head snapped up.

"I see them!" Fog pointed at the approaching Spark tribe, the last of the escaping party to arrive at the southern shore.

While the others had been waiting for the Spark tribe's arrival, they wove hammocks for the injured dragons and hatchlings to be carried in. A surprising amount of rope from broken and abandoned ships offshore lent themselves nicely.

The tribes still loyal to Cloud and Mist were all gathered, resting their wings in preparation for the trek ahead of them. As the Spark dragons touched down, Cloud moved to meet their noble. "You are sure you do not need to rest before we depart?" the dragon king asked with concern scrawled all over his face.

With an adamant shake of his head, the Spark noble said, "We are in perfect condition to make the journey."

Cloud nodded. He turned to the rest of the dragons spread across the sand. With a loud voice, he directed them to take the hammocks into their paws.

Fendrel climbed on Venom's shoulders. The group had agreed that it would be best for each human, save for Oliver, who rode with Thea, to be on different dragons so as not to hinder Venom's flight. Fendrel noticed that those who stepped up to aid them were all Dusk dragons.

The Dragon Liberator: Escapade

His stomach churned when his thoughts returned to the reason for their need to escape.

It looks like my deal with Cassius isn't over after all.

With the ascent of the monarchs and the nobles, Fendrel watched the dragons of the Freelands lift off in one huge swarm.

EPILOGUE: ZORICUS

ZORICUS PEEKED AROUND A CORNER into the throne room. He felt like a coward the way he had been avoiding Sadon all day. Still, he could not bring himself to speak with the man he begrudgingly pledged his allegiance to. If Sadie had just trusted him, Zoricus would not feel as shameful as he did, but the girl made her choice. She wanted to stay with her brother, weak and unfit to rule as he was.

She'll see that I can protect her better than Cassius can, Zoricus had been telling himself since Sadie ran off. *I just have to find a way to convince Sadon she won't cause any trouble when she comes back to me.*

Pacing in front of the throne was Sadon, who had set the crown to rest on the throne's cushioned seat. The older man's stride stopped when the High Mage waltzed up to him from a door on the other side of the room. In complete contrast to Sadon, the mage looked unbothered and unhurried.

"Good morning, Your Sadism," the hooded man said as he gave an exaggerated bow.

Sadon groaned. "What do you want, beast?"

Zoricus cringed at the sight of the mage, trying to keep his eyes open through his headache. After the mage had refused to help Zoricus during the trial, the knight knew better than to make himself an enemy of someone so powerful.

If Sadon keeps talking to him like that, the mage won't lend him any more aid. Then, we'll be completely out of our depth and with another enemy to watch out for, Zoricus worried. He did not know what exactly the enigmatic man was doing to help Sadon, other than crafting that shapeshifting spell that had been used for Adila. *Perhaps Sadon needs magic of some sort to fulfill his plans. But what is the mage getting out of all this?*

"I just have a small task I need done before you continue your murderous exploits." The mage leaned against the throne casually, keeping his eyes on Sadon.

"Yes, and—?" Sadon gestured for the hooded man to continue.

"There's one dragon I won't allow you to kill, at least for now," the mage started. "He's yellow with branches growing from his back, wears emerald jewelry. It's very hard to miss him. I've already made a deal with him that I don't plan on breaking any time soon."

Sadon clenched a fist in agitation.

The mage's eyes crinkled, seemingly amused. "You can kill him once I'm done with him."

"Fine. Where is he?" Sadon relaxed his hand, but his fingers kept twitching.

"He should be arriving in the forest west of here right about now. All you have to do is follow the streams until you reach him." Just as Sadon turned to leave, the mage called out. "Oh, one more thing. Keep him healthy and unharmed, or *our* deal is off."

Zoricus swallowed. He had never seen Sadon and the mage interact in person before, but Zoricus had always assumed Sadon was the one steering this operation. *Perhaps he is as afraid of the mage as he should be, but still . . . what could Sadon be offering that the High Mage wants so bad?*

As Sadon wordlessly stormed out of the throne room, Zoricus caught a glimpse of the dragon hunter's furious face.

The mage chuckled. His magenta eyes landed on Zoricus as the knight peeked farther around the corner. "Don't be sad to be left out. I'm sure you and your cousin will be of use to me soon."

Shuddering, Zoricus backed away.

I need to find Sadie. I need to protect her from whatever that man has in store for us.

The story continues in Book Two

DRAGON TRIBES

~DUSK TRIBE~

Description: Dusk dragons have black hides with green, purple, or gold markings, making them expert hunters in the dark. Sheathed within their jaws are fangs which can fold against the roofs of their mouths. They carry themselves on powerful legs ending in serrated claws. Depending on whether these dragons have feathers, fur, or scales, their wings may look like those of a bird or a bat. Their larger size as well as their thick necks and tails make attacking them difficult.

Abilities: Aerial and terrestrial agility. Night vision. A keen sense of smell, hearing, and taste. Good climbers. Poison- or antivenom-producing fangs.

Dominion: Black Brick Ruins

~SPARK TRIBE~

Description: Spark dragons have dark gray scales with markings in every vibrant color, as striking as the lightning they fly through. Their bat-like wings are large in proportion to their bodies and can be used as an additional pair of legs. They have rather short legs which they do not use often. The tails of Spark dragons are lengthy and whip-thin, just as useful in combat as they are for high-speed flight. Small, pyramid-shaped spikes adorn Spark dragons' chins and the backs of their jaws.

Abilities: Aerial agility. Night vision. A keen sense of smell and sight. Can harvest lightning for energy and transfer it to other dragons. Electricity emissions from spikes, teeth, and claws.

Dominion: Storm Peaks

~Air Tribe~

Description: Air dragons have hides in brown, red, orange, blue, white, and gray which allow them to hide against the sandstone ravines and wide-open skies they call home. Their wiry legs are not used as often as their massive wings which appear like those of a bat or a bird depending on whether the dragon is feathered or furred. Their long, slender necks and tails make Air dragons the longest of all the tribes.

Abilities: Aerial agility. Keen sense of hearing and sight. Good climbers.

Dominion: Gust Ravine

~Vapor Tribe~

Description: Vapor dragons seamlessly blend into their mist-shrouded home with their gray, silver, and pale blue hides. Their wings, bat- or bird-like in appearance, allow them silent flight. They are smaller than most other dragons with many only growing as tall as horses. Their sharp claws are perfect for scaling tall trees and cliffsides and their prehensile tails aid them in keeping their balance on narrow branches.

Abilities: Aerial, terrestrial, and marine agility. A keen sense of hearing. Good climbers. Can see through vapor. Can emit vapor through breath. Prehensile tails. Waterproof hides.

Dominion: Hazy Woods

~*Water Tribe*~

Description: Water dragons live the majority of their lives deep underwater where their blue, green, purple, and coral orange hides reflect the reefs of their home. Like most other tribes, Water dragons can have feathers, but theirs are penguin-like and aid in streamlined swimming. However, all Water dragons have bat-like wings. Their hindlegs are much shorter than their forelegs and are better suited for swimming than for walking. Their tails are long and paddle-shaped, and their paws are webbed between the talons.

Abilities: Marine agility. Night vision. A keen sense of taste, smell, hearing, and vibrations. Can breathe underwater.

Dominion: Sunken Grotto and Ash-Loom Beach

~*Ice Tribe*~

Description: Tall and stocky, Ice dragons are perfectly suited to survive their harsh snowy lands. Their layered coats of fur and feathers are typically white and light gray, but many are pale blue, green, or purple. They have tall shoulders with forelegs that are a bit longer than their hind legs. Each claw and tooth is serrated, and they have pronounced canines twice the size of their other teeth. With blizzards being a common occurrence, Ice dragons have sturdy wings for flight control, padded paws for snow trekking, and double-lidded eyes to protect them from harm.

Abilities: Terrestrial and marine agility. A keen sense of hearing, smell, taste, and eyesight. Can survive in extreme cold and without food for several weeks. Can spit globs or shards of icy saliva.

Dominion: Frost Lake

~*FIRE TRIBE*~

Description: Fire dragons reside in the desert and have abrasive feathers, fur, or scales in a variety of reds, oranges, yellows, browns, and white. Able to breathe fire, their teeth are fire-proof but may blacken after years of accumulating damage. They are quite small compared with other tribes but are still larger than Vapor and Spark dragons. Similar to Ice dragons, Fire dragons have padded paws for sand trekking and double-lidded eyes to protect from sandstorms.

Abilities: Aerial and terrestrial agility. A keen sense of sight and hearing. Can survive in extreme heat and without water for several days. Can breathe fire.

Dominion: Twin Oases

~*Flora Tribe*~

Description: Flora dragons physically mimic whatever plant their egg was bathed in, so they come in a wide range of shapes, sizes, and colors. No matter their differences, they all have four legs and two wings, which may be bird- or bat-like, depending on if they have feathers, fur, or scales. Each dragon, depending on its mimicry, also has special abilities pertaining to the plant it mimics.

Abilities: Abilities depend on mimicry.

Dominion: Everspring Grove

~Earth Tribe~

Description: Earth dragons have brown, rusty, or reddish-brown scales or fur that reflect the sandy caves they live in. Lacking legs of any kind, Earth dragons resemble monstrous snakes that walk using their large, bat-like wings. They have frills that can flare out or fold against their necks and their faces are armored with blunt nasal and chin horns.

Abilities: Aerial and marine agility. Night vision. A keen sense of taste, smell, hearing and vibrations. Jaws can split into four individually moving parts.

Dominion: Sand Caves

~STONE TRIBE~

Description: Rivaled only by Flora dragons in versatility, Stone dragons are the most diverse in colors and features of any of the tribes. A Stone dragon's body mimics the type of stone, mineral, precious metal, or crystal its egg is surrounded by. The clubs at the end of their tails as well as their horns appear to be made of that same, pure substance that their colors mimic. Apart from their specialized markings, Stone dragons have gray scales which are reflective under direct sunlight. Their sharp claws are great for climbing and they have padded paws to protect them from rough terrain. While Stone dragons have wings, they are much smaller than those of other tribes and they have trouble flying for extended periods.

Abilities: Night vision. A keen sense of hearing, smell, and vibrations. Good climbers.

Dominion: Geode Caverns

About the Author

Kassidy J. Ridenour uses her passion for fantasy and all things dragon to write the kind of stories she would love to read. She was raised and lives in Southern California, surrounded by supportive friends and family. This is her first novel.

Visit Kassidy on Instagram **@kassjr.books** to learn more about her future stories!